Blood Sea Tales
Book Five

Blood Walker

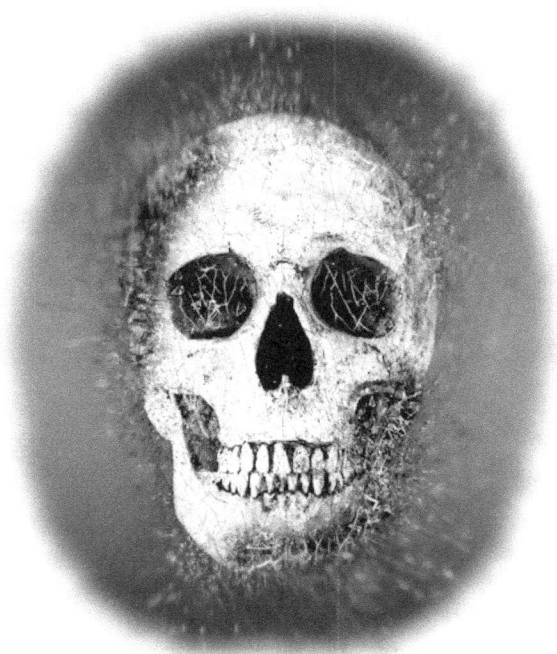

Chris A. Jackson

Copyright © 2022 by Chris A. Jackson

Edited by Gabrielle Harbowy

Published April 2022 by Jaxbooks Publishing

Cover design by Fiona Jayde

Interior art from Wikimedia used under creative commons licensing

Title page art from Pixibay by Amir Boucenna

ISBN 978-1-939837-31-8 (paperback)
ISBN 978-1- 939837-33-2 (ePub)
ISBN 978-1- 939837-32-5 (Mobi)

jaxbooks.com

Dedication

This novel is dedicated to the men and women who spend their lives on the sea. She is a harsh mistress, but she is in our blood.

Acknowledgements

As always, thanks to my wife, Anne, for her help, patience, and passion for the world we have created together.

Special thanks to Gabrielle Harbowy, my editor, for her willingness to take on this project, her patience, honesty, and professionalism

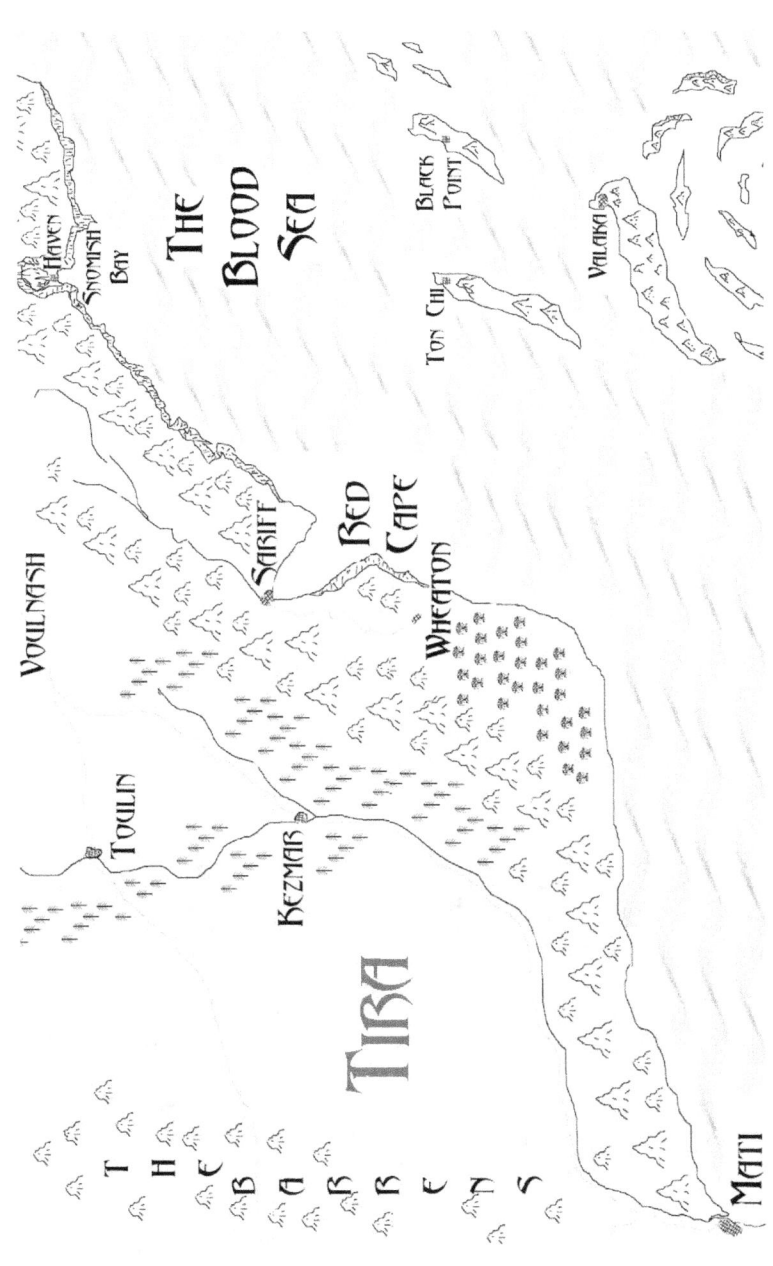

Chapter One
A Most Unwelcome Welcome

From the journal of Hashi Severn —

Whatever happened to being left the hell alone? In this instance, I'm the victim of my own insatiable curiosity. I have the history of two millennia at my fingertips, and not some historian's account, but first-hand. The question is, can I tolerate Tori Blackbriar's presence without murdering him?

He's going to kill you, you know.

I ignored Saraknyal and continued shuffling through my wardrobe.

He's only pretending an interest in you. Tori Blackbriar is a high elf, and high elves hate necromancers.

Black silk, black cotton, black leather. My monochromatic attire had served me for years, feeding the rumors of my grim persona, so why did it now strike me as more monotonous than practical?

That fancy elf blade of his can slice through my defenses like...well, like I slice through things.

Frustrated, I pulled out an airy skirt of brushed silk, deep purple with a random pattern of black. I added a black silk shirt with a high neck and blousy sleeves, not dressy, but comfortable.

HASHI!

"Oh quit it!" I tossed the clothing onto my bed and whirled to glare at the obsidian dagger on the dresser. *He's not going to murder me! You're being paranoid.*

It's not paranoia if people are genuinely bent on your destruction, Hashi. It's called caution.

Granted, but Tori isn't going to kill me.

How do you know that?

1

Because he's got a vested interest in keeping me alive. If he killed me, the Council would—

Are you delusional? He's been lying about what he is to everyone for years! High elves are masters of illusion and mind-bending magic! He could have the entire Council wrapped around his finger!

Which only proves my point. He's in Haven for a reason, Saraknyal, and I want to know what that reason is. Why would a high elf come to Haven, the cesspool of the Blood Sea? Besides, he might be able to beguile some with magic, but not me, and certainly not Nahli Twince.

*Well, he didn't come for the *scenery*, that's certain,* he quipped.

Exactly. Now let me concentrate! I'm nervous enough!

Good! You should be nervous! He'd deadly.

That's not why I'm nervous.

Then why?

Because I've never had a guest in Ash Keep before, I admitted. *I have no idea what to do.*

Oh, just be your usual gregarious, social, entertaining self! I'm sure you'll have him eating out of your hand in no time.

"Sarcastic ass," I growled. I was none of those things, and he knew it. Sighing, I dropped my bath robe and picked out a clean chemise and scanties. *Do you understand just what talking to Tori means to me? Hundreds—no, thousands—of years of history witnessed firsthand.*

You're obsessed with history!

"If I weren't, you'd still be boxed up in your sarcophagus." That shut him up long enough for me to finish dressing. I slipped on a pair of flat sandals and, last, picked up Soul Drinker and strapped the sheath to my forearm under the blousy sleeve, the perfect accessory for the well-dressed necromancer.

I strode from my bedroom to my sitting room/office, closed the door behind me, and resisted the urge to pour myself a brandy; Tori had said he'd bring wine. With nothing else to do until he arrived, I paced, mentally cursing my impulse to invite him into my home.

I'd decided to meet with Tori in here because it was the only private room in the keep suited for casual conversation. It was also comfortable, familiar, and had one additional advantage, one I hadn't mentioned to Saraknyal because I knew he wouldn't like it. The only other real option was my library, and I didn't want Tori to see my books. You can tell a lot about a person from their bookshelf, and I'd be sharing enough with him already. The thought of sharing personal details grated on my nerves.

Stop pacing! I understand you're nervous, Hashi—so am I—but you mustn't show it.

"I know, and you're not helping."

You're not going to let me talk you out of this, are you?

"No. There's too much to gain, and from the sound of it, he already knows everything about us that matters." I sighed and flopped down into an overstuffed chair.

You don't honestly think he'll give you any deep dark secrets about himself, do you?

"He's already revealed he's a high elf. What darker secret could there be?"

Maybe he's a closet devil-worshiper.

I snorted a laugh and got up to pace some more.

Finally, the hour came.

Joss knocked at my door and peered in. "Your guest is here, mistress." He looked to be suppressing a smile. In fact, my entire staff—at least the living ones—had been shocked and amused that I was entertaining one of the Council in my private sitting room. I gritted my teeth at the rumors that were undoubtedly spreading. Maybe I should have met with Tori in the dining room.

"I'll come down." I followed him down to the entry hall, and found Tori inspecting one of my Toki statues.

He had no escort and dressed casually, a loosely laced shirt of light green cotton worked with intricate patterns along the hems and cuffs. Riding pants and soft kidskin boots told me he'd not come in a coach. He carried a leather satchel over one shoulder, and, of course, wore his elf blade.

Have him leave that blade here, Saraknyal insisted.

Outside my door, I think.

"Lord Blackbriar, Lady Severn." Joss bowed and stepped aside.

"Hashi!" He turned and grinned that blazing smile I'd come to expect, but I knew now it was only an affectation. In fact, everything about him was probably a disguise. He bowed and eyed me from head to foot. "You look—"

"No flattery tonight, please, Tori." I gave him a tight smile. "Welcome to Ash Keep."

"Very well, and thank you." He nodded politely and hefted his satchel. "I brought wine, as promised."

"Wonderful." Truth be told, I longed for a drink. I don't know why I was so nervous. This wasn't exactly a social meeting. "I thought we'd relax in my office, if that's all right." I gestured to the stairs.

His smile blazed. "Perfect."

"Anything else, mistress?" Joss asked as we started up.

"Not right now. I'll ring if we want something."

"Very well."

"Your décor is intriguing." Tori eyed another piece of statuary as we rounded the corner to the second flight, a pair of entwined merfolk. "You deal in antiquities, yes?"

"Yes. That's from a temple ruin in Valaka. Pre-war, about tenth century. The artist's name was LeRoch. Let me know if you see anything you like. I'll cut you a deal."

"I like *this* very much." He gave me an amused look. "You know they're having sex, don't you?"

I gaped at him for a moment. "No, I didn't." I also didn't like the look he was giving me. I squared my shoulders and faced him. "Let me be clear, Tori: I have no interest in a dalliance with you or anyone else. If you persist, I'll—"

"Truce!" He raised his hands disarmingly. "Old habits. I apologize. It won't happen again."

"See that it doesn't." I whirled back and we climbed to the tower in silence.

Two shades stood at my door, armed, but not armored. I stopped there, and turned to my guest. "Tori, if you'd please leave your sword here?"

"Of course." He unclipped the blade and leaned it against the wall. "I'd suggest you instruct your...guards not to touch it. The magic will—"

"I'm well aware of how elf blades interact with necromantic magic, Tori." I pointed to the blade and told my guards, "No one touches that sword."

"Yes, mistress," they both growled.

I opened the door and stepped inside, gesturing Tori through. He paused and looked around as I closed the door behind us.

I can hardly believe he trusts you so much, Saraknyal said. *Can we kill him, now?*

No. I strode past Tori to my desk. "As a gesture of good faith, I'll put Soul Drinker away for our chat." I lifted the lid to the lead-lined lockbox and unsheathed the dagger from my arm.

*You'll *what?* Hashi! Don't be a fool! You need me to—"

Hush, old man. I'll be fine. I lay him atop a book of dwarvish poetry and closed the lid, then turned back to my guest. "There. We're alone, Lord Blackbriar. Saraknyal can't see or hear us."

He looked a little stunned. I took some pleasure from that.

"I...appreciate that, Hashi."

"Please make yourself comfortable." I gestured to the chairs and the low table between them, determined to show him that I wasn't afraid or intimidated. I strode to the sideboard and picked two cut crystal wineglasses and a corkscrew. "I'm sorry I can't welcome you with the same elegance that you did me, but I rarely entertain." Never would have been more accurate.

"I didn't come here for silver and porcelain, Hashi." He sat and delved the satchel. "I came here to talk to you. I'd like to *know* you, the *real* you, not this...dreadful persona you've cultivated."

I barked a laugh and sat down. "If my outward appearance is an affectation, what's yours?"

"An illusion, actually." He withdrew several bottles from the bag. "I brought a variety. Some of my favorites. Red, white, port, icewine? Whatever you prefer."

I didn't recognize any of the bottles. "Port, please."

"Absolutely." He took up the corkscrew and peeled away the wax seal. I watched his hands—strong and callused, but dexterous, sporting numerous dueling scars—wondering how much was illusion.

"Would you mind if I asked you a question?"

"Not at all, if you return the courtesy? I'm quite curious about you, Hashi." He pulled the cork free, wiped the neck with a napkin from his satchel, and poured. The wine matched the hue of my skirt almost perfectly.

"Very well, a question for a question." I accepted a glass from him, and touched his with mine. The crystal chimed. "Why are you in Haven, and why the disguise?"

"Ah, that's technically *two* questions." He grinned and we sipped. The port was very good.

"All right. Why Haven? What interest does a high elf of the House of Tree and Star have here, of all places?"

"Very well." He leaned back, crossed an ankle over his knee, and sighed. "I'm here because the Blood Sea is a...nexus of interest."

"Well, *that's* as clear as mud," I scoffed.

"Sorry. It's rather difficult to explain to...anyone not elvish." He sipped and pursed his lips. "Suffice to say that true elves have a better understanding of the world, of how everything interacts, than any mortal does. Magic, energy, politics, racial tensions, and the world itself, are all perceived by us on a scale you couldn't possibly comprehend. The Blood Sea's currently acting like a fulcrum, an area of importance. Forces are coming together here. We feel it. The Death Stone or the Serpent's Eye might be part of it. Jhavika's scourge might also be. *You* might be. I was sent to...investigate."

"Sent?" My brow furrowed. "By whom?"

"Ah, one question for one question, yes?" He smiled and sipped his port.

"Fine. Ask." I leaned back, crossed my legs, and sipped, girding my nervousness.

"How old are you?"

I nearly spat wine, but recovered and cleared my throat. "Haven't you ever learned that asking a lady her age is impolite?"

"Oh, were we asking only *polite* questions, then?" He grinned devilishly.

"Fine. I'm about seventy." I watched him for a response, but he only nodded.

"As I thought. The necromancer's magic sustains you."

"Yes, and it came as quite a shock to me at first. It gave me an entirely different perspective on things. Saraknyal calls it playing the *long game.*"

"Interesting that." He finished his glass and poured another, offering to top mine up. I accepted. "Elves have difficulty seeing the *short* view of things. Years pass us like the beat of a hummingbird's wings, the lives of mortals barely a summer's day." He sighed rather sadly and raised his glass to me. "Remind me to thank Saraknyal for sustaining your youth. I'm not flattering you, Hashi, but you're a stunning woman."

I took the complement for what it was, and smiled. "Thank you. You're not a torture to look upon, yourself."

He laughed and raised his glass to me, for he'd described himself with those very words. "Well played, and your turn."

I nodded. "Who sent you to investigate Haven?"

"You're a scholar of history, Hashi? Can you not guess?"

I found that slightly annoying, like I was a school girl being tested, but I decided on a more politic counter than telling him to bugger himself. "Oh, I can *guess*, but why should I? I have the very *font* of history sitting right here in front of me." I sipped and smiled.

"Point taken." He pursed his lips again and shrugged. "It's no real secret that there's a council of elders among the high elves. It functions not unlike Haven's Council, and they bicker almost as much. They sent me."

"And you're one of the council?"

He laughed out loud. "That's technically another question, but no, I'm not. I'm...merely one of their trusted investigators. I go where I'm needed."

"Hmm, and you're needed here, of all places. I'm still having difficulty believing that."

He shrugged. "Nevertheless, it's the truth. Now, if you don't mind, I'd like to ask a more...difficult question."

"Were we only asking *simple* questions, then?" I smiled at him and sipped my port.

"Fair touch. I'd like to ask about your *soul*, Hashi."

I suppressed a shiver. *Damned to hell...or not?*

He sipped and I watched his throat convulse as he swallowed. "I...felt, when we first touched, that your soul's been damaged. If you remember, you'd just finished your suicidal foray into the Tinworthy mines, so at the time I thought you might have been damaged by the

Void essence. I later found out that Soul Drinker is actually a soulblade. I assumed that the soul was that of a necromancer, and that it was...consuming you, shaping you, carving you like a piece of sculpture into its liking. *You* told me you gave Saraknyal *consent* to consume a part of you for your own survival. I'd like you to tell me how that happened."

I thought for a moment and fidgeted, uncomfortable telling anyone stories about myself. I decided to give him the bare facts. "I lived in Mati, working for a dealer of antiquities. He taught me his trade, and I acquired things from various ancient ruins for him to sell. I found Soul Drinker and discovered what it was. Gunyan, my mentor, thought we might sell it as a curiosity to one of the princes of Mati. Several are collectors of...dangerous artifacts."

"Because owning them makes them feel *powerful*," he said with no small bit of scorn.

"Yes, well, they *are* powerful. When I told them about the dagger, they accused me of necromancy, and had me arrested." I drained my glass, willing my nerves to quiescence. The memory of that helplessness still plagued my nightmares. "They tied me to a pyre in the city square and lit it beneath my feet."

"They tried to burn you alive?" His eyebrows arched. "And you *allowed* them to? You didn't use the dagger?"

"I didn't know at the time what Saraknyal was capable of. I knew he wanted me to...feed him souls. He promised me power, but I knew it was a trap. I didn't want to...damn my soul." I took up the bottle and filled my glass, offering it to Tori. He accepted, and I forged on. "When I was burning, my...priorities shifted. I couldn't take the agony. I asked him to consume me completely. I begged him to. I...couldn't die like that."

Tori said nothing, his face set in attentive stone.

"Then Saraknyal told me he could save me if I gave him a *part* of my soul, a part of my choosing, something I didn't want. I told him to take my loneliness, my need for companionship and love, and he did. He quenched the flames and helped me escape."

I wasn't going to tell him about Gunyan.

His face remained grave. "That's hardly *consent* while you're on fire!"

I shrugged. "I had a choice and I made it. End of story."

He nodded. "Very well. Your turn."

I thought for a moment. "Okay, why the disguise?"

"Ah, yes, well, humans find high elves uncanny." His form shifted before me in the blink of an eye. The tall, pale, rainbow-eyed elf I'd seen before, facial features harder, elongated, edgy, his ears so long they topped the crown of his head. He still looked like Tori Blackbriar underneath, just very different. "Don't you?"

"All right, yes. So you needed to blend in." He seemed more alien even than Nahli Twince, and I wondered why. His hands, though longer fingered, bore the same scars I'd seen before.

"Correct." In an instant he took on another form, that of the woman I'd met at his home, Bea Galt, right down to her revealing gown and distracting cleavage. "I can take on another form if you wish," he said in her voice, smiling sweetly.

"No, thank you. It's an illusion. How do I know you're really an elf, not some other kind of magical creature?"

"You don't, but I swear to you on my honor, I'm telling you the truth." Instantly, he resumed the appearance I knew best and smiled. "I couldn't very easily investigate anything if I drew too much attention. The persona of a suave, debonair, self-assured, handsome...um...what am I missing?"

"Egotistical," I said flatly.

Tori smiled and nodded. "Yes, well, I'm not the *only* one in this room putting on an act, am I?"

"Is that your next question?"

"No." He drained his glass and reached for the bottle. "If I may ask, where exactly did you find Soul Drinker? I don't know the name Saraknyal, though he was obviously an accomplished necromancer."

I chuckled and smiled at him. The wine was easing my nerves. "So, the two-thousand-year-old elf admits to not knowing *everything*? Hmmm."

He smiled back and offered me the bottle, which I declined. "Well, not *everything*!"

I snorted a derisive laugh. "Okay, I found it in a ruin in the Roo Lands. A castle in the mountains called Twakh Keep. I didn't know it had been the home of a necromancer until I explored it."

His eyebrows arched. "And the roo allowed you to dig through the ruins?"

"We had an understanding. I took only things they allowed me to take and followed their rules. They're reasonable people once you get to know them."

"Reasonable people don't commit *genocide*, Hashi." His voice had hardened, and I wondered about his anger.

"Depends on your point of view, I suppose. The roo did what they did because they considered what the necromancer-governed empire was doing to the land an evil act." I sipped my wine. "Tell me, high elf: would the elves not eradicate every last orc or goblin if given the chance?"

"You weren't there, Hashi," he said, his eyes sharp on me. "The roo didn't just kill necromancers. They slaughtered every man, woman, and child in Tinaros."

"I know. I've walked through the ruins, seen the skeletons." I sighed and finished my wine. "I also found four disposal pits in Twakh Keep with the bones of *thousands* in them. I'm not saying that the acts of either side were *justified* or *moral*."

"All right, I'll accede that point." He reached for a bottle and offered it. This time I accepted. "Twakh Keep. I was sent to Tinaros when the empire was at its height. The Elvin Council was interested in the only known stable society in the world that allowed necromancy."

"You mean besides Haven, right?"

"Well, Haven's not what they would consider a 'stable society.'" He tilted his glass to me. "I think I remember that keep. Rather...oddly constructed, haphazard almost, isn't it?" He swirled his port and sipped.

"Yes, and it's one of the few structures still standing in the entire empire." I let my glass sit on the table for now. "The roo don't like the mountains, and Saraknyal had already put his soul into the dagger before they arrived. You've seen the keep?"

"Yes, a very long time ago, before the roo waged war." He sighed and sipped his wine. "Tinaros was a very orderly nation, albeit brutal in its enforcement of laws."

"So Saraknyal's told me."

"Yes, I imagine he has." He shrugged. "I never introduced myself to the keep's lord. I didn't think it...prudent."

"Wise." I gave up and picked up my glass.

"So, if I may, why keep the dagger?" He tipped his glass toward the box on my desk. "Why spread the rumor that you're a necromancer?"

"Rumor?" I shrugged. "Consider this: I have no magical talent, but Saraknyal does. He has no means to exert that talent except through me. Without one another, we're both impotent, but together we actually *are* a necromancer."

"Well, I suppose that's accurate, but..." He frowned. "Why not throw it away? Surely you realized it's evil."

"*He's* evil," I corrected. "Saraknyal's a person, Tori."

"Granted. Why keep a dagger filled with a malevolent soul, Hashi?"

I smiled and nodded. I'd known this question was coming, and didn't have a solid answer. "It's complicated, but the easy answer is that he keeps me safe, and I don't want Soul Drinker in anyone else's hand. Think what someone like Jhavika Keshmir would have done with it."

"Good point." He tipped his glass to me again. "But why the dreadful persona?"

"That's a harder question to answer." I sighed and sipped more of the lovely port. "Mainly, for peace and quiet, and to keep people at a distance. I've...never had any luck with people. The closer they get to me, the more likely they are to die, or worse. If they fear me, they're safer." I wasn't going to tell him about Miras.

"But your retainers, they know you're not *really* a necromancer, don't they?"

"No, and as I said, together, Saraknyal and I *are* a necromancer."

"Then... Pardon me, but why do they *stay* with you? It must be hard to get good people to live alongside wraiths and shades."

"I keep them safe, and they know I'm not a maniac. They *also* know what it means to betray me." I gestured to the door. "The results of that kind of betrayal stands right outside that door."

"A formidable deterrent," he admitted.

"Exactly." I considered my next question for a while, enjoying the port and the silence. Finally I asked, "Two thousand years... Were you alive when the stars fell?"

"No. I'm not *that* old! Not by about four thousand years."

"The Lost Ages..."

"Yes. Humans have few records of that time, and even fewer *accurate* ones. I was born when the world was still recovering from the cataclysm. The Bitter Sea had accumulated in the impact crater that all but destroyed the Dwarven Kingdoms, and the Serpent's Eye had fully formed, drawing most of the dragons from the rest of the world." His eyes took on a far-off look. "I witnessed the elves and humans of the Northlands banish evil from their lands and build Fengotherond. I watched the crystalline dome take shape over the city, helped usher in an age of peace, art, music, and science."

"*Peace?*" I knew history better than that. "How's that going for you?"

He leveled a knowing smile at me. "Comparatively? Not as poorly as you might think." He waved a hand at my balcony. "There's still pain and war and evil in the world, but less now than before by far. There's balance now. For millennia, we were on the brink of oblivion."

I shook my head. "I can't *imagine* more conflict than the last thousand years has seen."

"You don't *want* to imagine it." He sighed and shrugged. "Demons walked the land, and dragon lords and godlings fought them. *Millions* perished in flames that devastated entire regions. Forests older than the oldest high elf burned, and mountains greater than any still standing crumbled. The forces unleashed..." He shivered and shook his head. "It was a near thing, Hashi."

I swallowed and nodded. "Ignorance is bliss, I suppose."

"Sometimes, yes, it is." He sipped and smiled at me. "Would you mind if I asked you a personal question?"

I chuckled. "I thought you already had."

"Well, I mean *deeply* personal."

I thought for a moment, then shrugged. "Go ahead, but I may refuse to answer."

"Your choice, of course." Again, he pursed his lips, then asked, "Why, of all the portions of your soul, did you sacrifice your need for human companionship and love?"

I scowled and a rueful smile flicked across my lips with the memories of my childhood. I considered refusing to answer, then reconsidered. If anyone could understand loss, a two-thousand-year-old elf who had witnessed the near ending of the world probably could.

"Because I never had it and always wanted it." I drained my glass and reached for the bottle, but it was empty.

Tori promptly reached for the bottle of red and the corkscrew. "Please. Continue."

I shrugged. "My mother resented my very existence. My stepfather saw the face of another man in mine. I saw how other children were loved, and it tortured me. I left home before things...escalated."

"Escalated?" His eyebrows arched.

My temper flared. "Before my stepfather decided to take me to his bed, to get back at the woman he loved for taking another man into hers."

"Ah, I see." The cork popped from the bottle, and he offered it.

"You don't, but it doesn't matter." I allowed him to pour, then stood and strode to my balcony doors, opening them to look out at the cesspool of Haven. "I obsessed every night about having a loving family, but I never risked it because I'd watched first-hand what could happen if things went wrong. I gave that part of me to Saraknyal because it only ever caused me anguish."

"And if you could heal that portion of your soul, would you?"

I turned to look at Tori, still seated, wineglass trembling in his hand. I wondered if the question was actually moot, or if a high elf might actually be able to heal a human soul. Then I realized the answer.

"No. I'm better off without it." I sipped my wine and a bouquet of summer flavors exploded on my palate. I let it sit on my tongue for a while, then swallowed and enjoyed the varied afterglow. "Now, it's my turn to ask a personal question."

"Fair enough," he acceded.

"Why do you seduce women?"

He looked mildly surprised, then barked a laugh. "Seriously?"

"Seriously. Why the parade of broken hearts? Why the long string of lovers?"

"Well, it's never been my *intent* to break anyone's heart, but humans are inherently jealous when it comes to relationships." He sighed and shrugged. "In answer, two reasons: First, I very much enjoy intimacy with humans, and not only women. Most elves do. We find humans...intense in that regard. Their rapture is...transcendental. Why do *you* think there are so many part-elves in the world?"

"All right, I suppose I can understand that." I honestly couldn't, having never experienced it myself, but I wasn't going to tell him that. "The other reason?"

"Well, I must admit that here in Haven, I use my relationships to extend my network of informants." He shrugged with a mischievous smile. "My vaunted spy network, if you will."

"Do you enchant them?" I asked, mildly horrified by his admission.

"No, or not with anything other than my charm and dashing good looks." He chuckled and grinned.

I snorted a derisive laugh and shook my head. "All right, I can accept that. Your turn."

He looked at me with an expression that could have been thoughtful, or appraising, neither of which made me comfortable. "Nothing comes to mind. I think I'd much rather just chat."

"Okay." I turned back to the view, the night sea breeze ruffling my skirt against my legs. "What are your plans now that Haven's reasonably stable?"

"Assuming things *are* stable, and someone doesn't show up with Jhavika's scourge and ten-thousand enchanted slaves, you mean?"

A chill raced up my spine at the thought. "Um...yes, *assuming* that."

"Well..." The chair creaked and I looked back to see him approaching with the wine bottle in one hand, his glass in the other. His gait seemed unimpaired, though my head was buzzing more than a little. The port had been strong. "Survive, seduce more women, drink good wine, and continue my mission, I suppose." He held out the bottle, and I let him top up my glass. "You?"

"I'm working on a project, but I'm still worried about Haven." I wasn't going to tell him about my plan to contain the Death Stone. "Like you said, the Blood Sea's near a tipping point. I'm afraid Jhavika might have done more damage than we know. If Longbright returns with that fucking scourge in his hand, we've got a problem. If he doesn't return at all, we'll need a new admiral."

"Captain Tan, perhaps, if she returns."

I blinked at him. "You said she was Malchi's tool."

"No, I said she had a dalliance with young Maurice. It was no secret, and might have only been a harmless fling. Reginald did, however, push for her being given a ship by the Council. That might well have been her own ambition. Maurice also had an affair with Lady Roque, remember? His father wields him like a sword."

I nodded and smiled coldly. "I probably shouldn't tell you this, but I thought about taking him to bed and returning him to his father a wraith."

His jaw dropped. "You *wouldn't.*"

I laughed at the look on his face, and wondered if it was genuine. "No, I wouldn't, but I *thought* about it."

"Well, I can't blame you for being tempted. He *is* attractive." Tori topped up his glass and leaned against the door jam, looking out at Haven. "Mind if I share an...observation I've recently had?"

I looked him over, suspecting some subtle seduction. "No, unless it's about me."

"No, not about you, but about Saraknyal."

"Saraknyal?" I glanced at the box on my desk. "What about him?"

"He's...not what I expected at all. This afternoon, when I put a hand on your shoulder, he felt...different."

"Different?" That caught my attention, for I'd been thinking the same thing since our descent into the Tinworthy mine. "Different than what?"

"Different than any other necromancer I've known. He's...damaged somehow."

"*Damaged?*" Another cold chill raced up my spine. "What do you mean?"

He turned to face me and cocked a leg to place a boot against the door jam. "Hashi, please don't take this the wrong way, but his soul is very like yours. Something's missing. I don't know what it is, or rather *was*, but there's a...void. A part of him has been destroyed somehow."

Destroyed... I thought about our adventure in the Tinworthy mine, and wondered if he could have been damaged by the Void essence. Or, he could have lied about using excess energy from the potion Tori gave me to recover. Perhaps he got the energy somewhere else.

"Do you know if there's any way a necromancer could...consume a portion of their *own* soul?"

"Not that I know of, Hashi—at least not a *conventional* necromancer—but there's something else. He's not as cold as I expected him to be. He *cares*." Tori tilted his glass to me. "I think he cares for *you*."

"Well, of course he *cares* for me. We're soul bonded."

His eyebrows shot up. "Soul bonded?"

"Yes. I'm sure you know about soulblades bonding to their masters."

"Of course, but Soul Drinker wasn't designed that way. It was only made to be the receptacle for Saraknyal's soul."

"Well, we *are* bonded."

"How do you know that?"

"Because a woman tried to stab me with him once." I drained my glass and wobbled a bit. "It didn't work out so well for her. The blade can't hurt me."

Tori's eyes widened. "Well, I'll be *damned!*"

I barked a laugh and reached for the bottle. "Keep hanging around with me, Tori Blackbriar, and you just well *might* be!"

He laughed and helped me pour. I was a little drunk, and didn't need more wine, but it felt good to laugh.

"I think you're having a positive effect on Saraknyal, Hashi. If he cares for you, I mean *really* cares for you, there's hope for him."

"Hope?" I sipped my wine and scowled at him. "You mean for his soul?"

"Well, since that's all that's left of him, yes. I never thought anyone could redeem a necromancer, but you well might be halfway there, Hashi Severn."

"Or halfway to Hell, you mean." I shook my head.

"You're *not* doomed, Hashi. I've *felt* your soul."

"Felt my soul..." I eyed him narrowly. "And can all elves do that?"

"It comes with experience, and I have a lot of experience." He pursed his lips and swirled his wine. "Whether you believe it or not, you're a *good* person."

"And you're still an insufferable ass, Tori, but I think I might be starting to like you."

"See? I told you. Only *good* people like me." He grinned at me. "It's part of my undeniable charm!"

I tried not to laugh, but failed.

"So, you wanted to ask me *historical* questions, didn't you?"

"I do." I sighed and indulged myself. "Gods, where to begin?"

Chapter Two
Home Again, Home Again

From the diary of Kevril Longbright —

They say home is where your heart is. If that's true, my home lies wherever Preel is. Every moment she's in danger is a knife at my throat, and piracy isn't a safe profession. I can't help thinking that we'd both have been better off if she'd stayed with Shepherd, but I don't know how I could have survived the loss.

Preel woke with a start, jerking upright in bed, eyes flashing wide to dart around the cabin like those of a caged animal. Of course, she *had* been caged for a time, and this cabin had been that cage, complete with bars and chains. Both were now gone.

"It's all right, love. You're safe." I put my book down and lurched up from the navigation table. We were on a broad reach in open sea, and a high swell was putting *Scourge* through a torturous corkscrew motion. "Are you all right?"

"I..." She put a hand on her mouth and looked around again, thought and memories returning behind her eyes. Memories of hating me, no doubt. Memories of Jhavika, and the monster she'd become. "I need to use the head." She struggled out our bed and made a zig-zag path to the quarter gallery.

I resisted the urge to help her. Preel was still having problems, though much of our mutual trauma had begun to heal. Even after three days together since our reunion at Valaka, she sometimes jerked away when I touched her casually. "I'll have Hemp bring breakfast."

"Thank you." She smiled over her shoulder before she closed the door.

I wove my way to the cabin door and opened it. "Hemp!"

"Aye, sir!" He poked his head out of the galley, crumbs on his chin.

"Preel's awake."

"Breakfast in two shakes, sir!" He vanished back into the galley, and I heard Bert snapping orders.

I tidied up and lay Preel's favorite robe on the bunk. I heard splashing, and remembered the first time I'd heard her singing to herself in the quarter gallery. That seemed a lifetime ago now, before she was free, before we fell in love, or perhaps while we were falling in love. At the time, I'd wondered how she could ever sing having gone through the torments of slavery. Now, there was no singing, and I wondered if she'd ever sing again.

I sat and picked up my book, quashing again the urge to ask if she was okay. The first couple of days out of Valaka had been difficult for both of us. I was too solicitous, and she was torn between clinging to me like a barnacle, and flinching away. Our lovemaking had been awkward at first, but intense in a way neither of us expected. I'd barely left the cabin for watches, and Preel hadn't at all. After many long hours of quiet conversation, pouring our souls out to one another, we finally reached an equilibrium. She loved me and knew that I loved her. That was enough.

We'd also discussed what might be happening in Haven, and the obvious question arose: Who knew of Preel's truthsayer talent? If Jhavika's people, released from their enchantment-enforced silence, had spread word far and wide that Captain Longbright's wife was a truthsayer, we might be better off sailing away than returning to Haven. The night before, four days since her last question, when she said it was safe to invoke her talent, we'd asked how many in Haven knew.

The answer was eight, startlingly few, which gave me hope. As we always had in the past, we'd discussed how her answer would affect our plans, and the small number confirmed our course back to Haven.

The quarter gallery door opened, and Preel ventured out, clutching the door jam. She looked adorable in her sleeping shift, her short hair sticking up at all angles. The new look made her seem younger, her face rounder despite the weight she'd lost during her ordeal.

I smiled at her. "Breakfast in two shakes."

"Thanks." She made her way to the bunk and struggled into her robe, the morning light from the stern-gallery windows catching her just so. She noticed me staring and blushed. "Sorry I look like a dandelion. This *stupid* hair..." She tried to pat it down and it sprang back up.

"I think it's adorable." I moved from the navigation table to the dinner table. "Come take a seat before this damned roll has its way with you."

"Sure." She looked out the stern windows and blanched at the swells looming above the horizon. "I hate a following sea."

Hate... The word grated on my nerves. I wondered if we'd ever be as we once were.

"Probably a hurricane beyond the islands. It'd be worse if we were beating against it." I peered out the windows at a high white-capped swell and cringed. "Hold fast!" I braced my legs and held out a hand to her. She grasped it as the swell slammed into the starboard quarter.

Curses rang out from the corridor, then a knock on our door.

"Come!" I grinned at Preel, who looked a little pale but smiled back, and released her hand.

The door opened, admitting a scullery lad cradling an armful of fiddles to keep our breakfast on the table. Hemp followed, balancing a platter laden with covered dishes, pots, cups, and silver, all now in disarray from the lurch. That he hadn't dumped the whole thing attested to his seaworthiness. "Right bitch of a sea, sir. Sorry about the mess."

"Can't blame you for the weather, Hemp." I helped the lad fix the clamps on the fiddles until a lattice of fitted teak rails crisscrossed the table. "There! All secure!"

"Thank you, sir." Hemp placed the covered dishes and a wide-bottomed pot of blackbrew on the table. Two cups, a pot of preserves, and silverware were placed with military precision, though another roll threatened to send the eating utensils skidding.

"All secure on deck, Hemp?"

"Far as I know, sir. Kivan and Rauley are havin' a grand ol' time."

I'd rated Kivan fit for duty, but worried for her. She still had about two hundred stitches in her back where Jhavika had peeled the skin away. "Send a pot of blackbrew up for them, Hemp. Lifelines for the waisters, if they're not already rigged."

"Aye, sir!" He pressed a knuckle to his forehead and grinned. "Good to see you up and about, Lady Preel."

"If this keeps up, I may go back to bed!" She looked at the covered dishes dubiously.

"Just give a call if you need anything!" Hemp grinned and ducked out.

"He's full of himself this morning." I uncovered the dishes; plump omelets, oat cakes, sausage, and another of toasted soft tack. "And Bert's obviously trying to fatten us up."

"They're both worth their weight in gold." Preel cut a corner from her omelet as I poured her half a cup of blackbrew and added a touch of goat's milk. Her eyes rolled as she chewed. "Make that worth their weight in diamonds."

I chuckled, imagining a pile of diamonds the weight of my rotund cook. "That's a lot of diamonds."

"Mmmm." She chased another bite with a sip of blackbrew.

We ate in silence for a while, simply enjoying the food and each other's company. Our feet found each other's under the table and she ran a toe across the top of my foot. Every time I looked at her, I had difficulty believing that this was real, that we'd won free of Jhavika's enchantment.

"So," Preel said finally, pouring more blackbrew for us both, "eight."

"Yes, eight," I agreed.

"That's not many." She added milk and sipped her cup, eying me. "I wonder why so few."

"No way to know, but I think it's safe to assume they're Jhavika's people."

Her brow furrowed and she assumed a far-off look. "I can think of a dozen, at least, who *must* have known what I am. Guards, mostly. At least six were there when Jhavika spoke to me about my talent. Nala and Binch, of course. Jhavika's sage, probably. Ty-lee, certainly, but he's dead. A few servants."

"Then something must have happened." I didn't venture a guess. "Maybe the guards were aboard *Crimson Hawk*. Who knows what happened after we got out?"

"What's done is done, love." Preel gripped my arm. "The past is past. Let's look at the future, shall we?"

"Yes, ma'am." I grinned and put my hand on hers. "So, if only eight people in Haven know you're a truthsayer, they aren't spreading the news far and wide."

"True. I wonder why not."

"Well, there's no enchantment holding them back anymore." I shrugged. "Loyalty, or fear?"

"Do you think it's safe to go back?"

"Well, as safe as Haven ever was, but I think it would be a good question to find out who these people are."

"We'll be there before we use my talent again, won't we?"

"With this blow, yes. Probably two more days."

"Two days..." Preel stared into her cup as if looking to the future.

"Cheer up, love. We've got a tight ship, a loyal crew, and each other." I grinned and snagged a piece of toast that wanted to escape the plate with another roll.

"How are the crew doing, by the way?" she asked. "I've been...well...a little self-absorbed, I guess."

"They're hurting, but healing, just like you are. I appointed Doria as purser, against her protests. Rauley's settling down, and Boxley's positively ebullient. The whole crew's treating her like she's first officer." Boxley had earned the crew's adoration by killing Jhavika Keshmir, thus saving everyone's lives, including mine.

"Good. She deserves it." She pursed her lips. "And Wix?"

"Wix is tough as old shoe leather. Bert stitched him up, and he's walking fine, but he's not climbing the rigging yet." I'd slashed his legs deeply after Jhavika lashed him with the scourge and ordered him to murder me. "And before you ask, Kivan's doing well. She's...dealing with it."

"I can't imagine..."

"She's obviously a lot tougher than she looks." Kivan had refused to tell Jhavika where we'd gone despite the torture.

She fixed me with a solid stare. "She idolizes you, Kevril."

"Idolizes?" I snorted a laugh. "I don't know about *that*, but she's certainly shown an unwavering loyalty, even if it nearly got her killed. Spike saved her life with his ploy. He's a wily one."

"We're so lucky, Kevril." Preel gripped my arm hard. "Sometimes I feel like I don't deserve it."

"You deserve it, love." I squeezed her hand. "We've all been through hell. We deserve everything we have. We fought for it every inch of the way."

"Yes, we did." She sighed and smiled, but it was strained.

"Now, about this *plan* of yours..." I said.

"Plan?" She looked puzzled.

"Yes, going back to bed for the rest of the day." I gestured out the stern gallery windows. "It's certainly too rough for you to do your exercises, and a turn on deck's out of the question."

"I'm stiff from bed already." She twisted her back and rolled her shoulders.

"I'm sure we can think of *something* to give you some exercise." I grinned at her and raised an eyebrow.

Preel looked me square in the eye, licked her lips, and shouted, "Hemp!"

He was through the door in a heartbeat. "Yes, lady?"

"Clear the dishes, please." Her eyes never left mine, two dark pools that I longed to drown in.

"Straightaway!" Hemp moved with a will, stacking everything on the tray, expertly balancing it in one hand, and headed for the door.

"And Hemp," Preel said, still staring at me, "lock the door on your way out."

"Aye, lady!" Hemp grinned and worked the latch with one hand, happy as a lark.

"Why, Lady Longbright, why *ever* would you want to lock the door?" I tried for a bewildered look but couldn't help smiling.

Preel glanced down, then back up at my eyes. "You've got egg on your shirt. You should probably take that off before the stain sets."

"Oh?" I looked down at my spotless shirt. "I don't—"

"Take it *off*, Captain Longbright. Right...*now*."

"Yes, ma'am." I stood and pulled my shirt over my head. Before I could finish, Preel's hands were on my belt, working the buckle frantically. She wrenched it through the loops and flung it aside. I dropped my shirt, but she gripped my codpiece and jerked hard enough to send buttons flying. Her cheeks were flushed and her eyes looked fevered. "Preel! What's gotten into you!"

"Nothing yet!" She pulled my pants down over my hips. "But I'm sure I can find *something*."

That, of course, was the perfect moment for a violent lee lurch. With my pants around my knees, I couldn't catch myself. I hit the floor hard, but laughing, and Preel was on top of me in a flash.

"So much for the bed," I said.

"This is better!" She flung her robe aside and wrenched her nightshirt up over her head. "We can't fall off the deck!"

"The bed would be more comfortable." I ran my hands up her dusky torso.

"Later!" She leaned down and kissed me hard, urgently, her dark eyes wide, delving my soul. We broke, gasping for breath. "I love you, Kevril Longbright!"

"That's all I want to hear for the rest of my life!"

Tears pooled in her eyes. "Then *show* me!"

And I did.

We sailed into Snomish Bay in the predawn hours, the tips of the mountains painted pink by the sun. I'd taken the morning watch, but virtually everyone aboard was on deck. As Haven harbor opened up beyond the headland I called aloft.

"Lookout! How many ships in port?"

"Ten, sir! Two junks, four galleons, and four smaller brigs. One under sail headin' in."

"Heading *in*?" I raised my own glass, but couldn't see anything from deck. "What ship under sail?"

"One of them brigs sir! Flyin' every stitch!"

"That's interesting," Miko said beside me. "We didn't spot them at sea. A sentry?"

"Maybe just coincidence, but they certainly would have spotted us before we saw them." I closed my spyglass and looked over my shoulder at the eastern horizon. "My complements, Lieutenant Kivan. Your timing's perfect." I'd instructed her to plan our arrival for sunrise and adjust our speed accordingly.

"Thank you, Captain."

"At least the seas have settled down," Miko said.

"Aye to that." I scanned the shore as the bay opened up further. "And the city's not on *fire*, anyway."

My comment drew a chuckle, and Boxley reached up to scratch a stay for luck. We watched in silence.

"Lady on deck!" Wix bellowed, and we all turned to the stairs leading to the main deck.

Hemp ushered Preel up the steps. She was garbed in a Marathian cloak and veil, her eyes lined with kohl and her tattoo covered with makeup. I caught her gaze, and the corners of her eyes crinkled with a hidden smile. I stepped aside and motioned for her to take a spot near the mizzen.

"Spyglass, love?" I held it out for her but she shook her head. She'd asked if she could come up to watch as we sailed into port, and I'd relented. Half of Haven had already seen her with me on numerous occasions. Of course, only eight people in Haven knew she was a truthsayer.

"Galleon making sail, Captain!" the lookout called, then added. "That brig sailed right up to her before she set sails!"

"Well, *that's* not coincidence." I raised my glass and caught a flicker of white amongst the shoreside clutter. The ship was still hull down from our lower vantage.

"Coming out to meet us?" Miko surmised.

"Or sink us," Boxley muttered.

"Well, I did attack a council member in the middle of a formal ball." We'd worried long how the Council of Lords might respond to that, but the fact that she controlled people had also come to light at the party, so I'd imagined I wasn't top of their lists of enemies.

"Battle stations, Captain?" Miko asked.

"Better safe than sorry. Pass out weapons, but let's not look like we're spoiling for a fight. No archers aloft."

"Aye, sir!" She relayed the orders to Wix.

"Kivan, take the foredeck and direct archers from there if things go awry." I mentally damned Jhavika for taking our ballistae. They would have come in handy if we faced a hostile reception.

"Aye, sir!" She hurried forward, still moving stiffly.

A hand settled on my arm, and I turned to find Preel with a note. "Do you think they'll attack us?"

"They might not be happy to see us, but they'll also want to know what happened." I didn't add that they could as well ask questions after I'd been clapped in irons as not. "So do I, for that matter, and I'd rather find out at sea than on shore. I think they're being careful, but there's no sense in not being ready."

She nodded.

We watched the galleon make more sail and begin beating out of the harbor toward us.

"Intercept course, sir," Miko said.

"Maybe." I looked aloft. We were flying our own pennant. "We'll see, I guess. Steady on course, helmsman."

Bosun's mates began handing out cutlasses and boarding axes, and Kivan arranged her foredeck crew armed with crossbows. All in all, I gauged them unready for a serious fight. Many were still recovering from injuries, but we had no choice.

Hemp returned to the quarterdeck with my best cutlass, a dress jacket, and a brace of daggers. I clipped the cutlass to my belt and took one of the daggers. The other, he handed hilt first to Preel. She took it and tucked it away. I thought about sending her below, then reconsidered. I needed her by my side.

Rauley came up from below, having been asleep. "Reporting for duty, sir. Bert asked if you wanted a nibble."

"No thanks, and if you're game, why don't you take the helm, Rauley." He had an uncanny hand when it came to conning my ship.

"Happy to, sir!" He shouted for word to be sent below to Bert, then took the wheel.

We waited.

I watched the galleon come hull up, and thought she looked

familiar. A moment later, the foretop lookout confirmed my suspicion.

"She's *Tiger Lily*, sir!"

"Fa-Chen's, isn't she?" Miko said.

"Yes, and Tan told me Jhavika commandeered her." I gritted my teeth.

"Well, she's not exactly cracking on, but she looks well handled."

"She's flying Fa-Chen's colors!" the lookout called down.

I grunted, "Better than Keshmir's."

Another tug at my sleeve, and Preel presented a note. "Didn't you burn one of his ships last year?"

"Yes, but that was on Jhavika's orders." I watched the approaching ship. Her braces were drawn tight, trisails flat as boards. Someone knew how to trim sails—though we could still outmaneuver any galleon on the sea. But *something* wasn't right. "They don't sail like a merchant, do they, Miko?"

"No, sir."

"White flag on the mizzen!" The lookout bellowed. "Parlay!"

I shifted my view aft, and spotted the white square below Fa-Chen's house crest. Curiously, another flag flew higher, one I'd never seen before, a silver crescent and crossed swords on a red field. Something new was afoot.

"Who the hell's commanding her?" I wondered aloud.

"Should we heave to and fly a parlay flag, sir?" Miko asked.

"Fly the flag, but hold course. They can come about and sail in company."

"Aye, sir!" Miko relayed the order, and Boxley opened the deck locker for the proper flag.

It rose on the mizzen halyard a minute later, and almost instantly, the foretop lookout shouted down.

"They're coming about!"

"Now we'll see what's what?" I raised my glass and watched as they came around and shifted from close hauled to downwind sail configuration.

Again, it was done smartly. I could barely make out the quarter deck and a big man in a blue jacket looking back at us with a spyglass. He had a dark beard and skin. I wracked my brain to think who it could be. The sails were luffed just enough to slow them so we could catch up easily.

"Deck's crowded, sir," Boxley said. "And they're armed."

I scanned the rigging, but spied no archers aloft. "Just the deck crew. I don't think they're intent on mayhem."

"Sir!" Kivan shouted from forward. "That's Captain Patak from *Crimson Hawk*!"

"Well, I'll be a..." I centered my spyglass on the quarterdeck and recognized him. "I thought he was dead! How the hell did he get to Haven?"

"Maybe Jhavika took him prisoner and sent him back with the *Lily*?" Miko surmised.

"Like she did to us?" Rauley added.

Preel tapped my shoulder and held out a note. "Jhavika wouldn't waste a potential ally. She'd hold him until she could lash him with the scourge."

I'd read it aloud and Miko nodded. It made sense. "That may just be, love. But why is he commanding one of Fa-Chen's galleons?"

Preel shrugged, then scribbled a note. "Ask him!"

I grinned. "Good suggestion." I opened the deck locker and pulled out a hailing trumpet. I strode to the port side and hopped up to the rail, gripping the ratlines in one hand and waving the trumpet with the other as they came closer. I raised it to my mouth and bellowed. "Bikka Patak, you hoary old bastard! Good to see you alive!"

"Kevril Longbright! You're a sight for sore eyes, you old sea-fox!" He grinned and barked orders to his crew. They altered sail and closed to fifty yards off our beam, matching our sedate pace easily. "Welcome back to Haven!"

That was a good sign. "Thanks! What the hells are you doing here?"

"That festering bilge cunt, Keshmir, clapped me and my crew in irons!" I could hear the venom in his tone. "The Council said they needed captains, so I signed up. Harbor duty, but it's a ship!"

"The Council survived?" I asked.

"Oh, aye, and they're chompin' at the bit to talk to you!"

Also good news. I glanced to Preel and she nodded. I raised the trumpet and bellowed, "I'll talk to them, but I've got bad news, Bikka. *Crimson Hawk* was lost!"

His grin fell, but he nodded and raised his trumpet. "Just tell me that motherless bitch Keshmir's dead, Kevril!"

"She's dead!"

An undeniably genuine cheer went up from the deck of *Tiger Lily*, and Patak shot me a smart salute, which I returned. When the roar died down, he raised his trumpet again.

"And that scourge of hers?"

That took me aback. If Patak knew about Jhavika's scourge, then Council certainly did, and likely all of Haven. I bellowed back, "Destroyed!"

"Bloody fine! I'll send word to the Council! They'll want to see you this afternoon, I'm sure."

"Very well!" I glanced back at Preel, and she nodded again. We'd spoken about this and formulated a plan that would best ensure our safety. "Tell them Fancy's Folly at four bells, and I'll be bringing an escort!"

"I'll tell them! You won't have any trouble, Kevril. They want to hear the tale!"

"And I want to tell it!" I had one more question before we parted company. "But what of the Council? Who survived?"

His face went grim. "Balshi, Fa-Chen, Hatsu, and Tinworthy were murdered at the party you escaped! Temuso had his bodyguard kill him before Jhavika could take over his house. Roque, Matesh, and Brilla Balshi have come back, as well as some of Jhavika's people that were under her spell. Fa-Chen's, Hatsu's, and Tinworthy's heirs were rescued. Jhavika had them captive."

I swallowed hard at the mention of Temuso, but nodded. Tan had told me he'd died, but that was second hand from Jhavika. Regardless, the news scored a line of pain through me; he'd saved my life. "And what of Jhavika's people?"

Patak grinned. "Seems the Council assaulted her keep! Some necromancer witch all but waded through her people like a scythe through grass!"

"A *necromancer*?" Miko said.

I remembered the woman in the bone dress at the party with her pale companion on a leash and nodded. "Lady Severn. She's...a scary one." I waved to the other ship. "I'll talk to you later, Patak! Buy you a rum!"

"Aye, but the rum's on me, Kevril!" He waved, and another roar went up from their deck. He shouted orders, and *Tiger Lily* bore off slightly to give us sailing room.

"Well, *that* was interesting!" Miko stuck her thumbs in her belt and laughed. "A gods-damned necromancer! Jhavika bit off more than she could chew on *that* one!"

"Yes, she did. I'd heard Severn was a necromancer, but always doubted it." I looked to Preel. "And it explains what happened to Jhavika's people."

Preel nodded and handed me another note. "You don't think the Council meeting's a trap, do you?"

"I don't think so, but there's no point in being careless." I brushed her cheek above the veil and grinned. "You're starting to think like a pirate, love."

She poked me hard in the stomach, her eyes smiling.

"Orders sir?" Miko asked.

"Straight on for the harbor, and don't spare the canvas!" I squinted at *Tiger Lily* and chuckled. "There are two ships on the sea, Miko! You know what they say!"

"Aye, sir! Two ships means a *race*!" She strode for the forward rail and bellowed. "Stand down battle stations and make all sail she'll bear! Let's show this slug of a galleon what *Scourge* can do!"

My crew roared and Wix bellowed orders.

I took Preel's hand in mine and we strode to the leeward quarter of the quarterdeck, out of the way. She squeezed my hand hard and drew my eye. The worry in her gaze told me all I needed to know.

Haven...and eight people in this city knew of Preel's gift.

Chapter Three
The Pirate's Return

From the journal of Hashi Severn —

Just when I thought everything would settle down to the new normal, that gods-damned pirate throws a wrench into the machinery again. At least this time he didn't cut off anyone's hand. What people do in the name of love baffles me. I'm grateful that I'm immune to that particular form of mental illness.

I don't see why we have to be here, Saraknyal whined. *It's a waste of time!*

It's not a waste. I want to know what happened to the scourge.

I strode up to the gaudy awning of Fancy's Folly in a mood. I was sick to death of inscribing runes. When I got word of Longbright's arrival and the pending interview by the Council, I jumped at the chance for a break, but the gods-damned necromancer in my head wouldn't shut up.

Nahli already confirmed it's not on Longbright's ship. Who cares what happened to it?

I do! Now live with it and shut up!

"Lady Severn, I presume." The massive woman at the door to the club looked me over like I might taste good. Two blunt tusks jutted from her lower jaw, indicating her part-ogre heritage, and two huge men wearing scimitars flanked the portal, their bare chests sheened with oil in the Fornician custom.

A Fornician motif? Really? Saraknyal grumbled.

"I am," I admitted. Her eyes flicked over my escort of four well-dressed but grim shades. I'd brought Jhavika's former sage, Lewin, with me, too, at his request. Since he knew more about Jhavika and

Longbright's relationship than any other living person, I'd agreed. "Is there a problem?"

"None whatsoever. I'm always willing to accommodate the needs of council members. I'm Gurt; welcome to my club." She stepped aside and gestured us through.

Her club? I thought you said this club belonged to Roque.* Saraknyal said.

Roque owns it. This small mountain must run it for her. I nodded politely to the mountain as I passed through the door. "Has Captain Longbright arrived yet?"

"Not yet."

I paused inside to take the place in as I handed my hooded weather cloak to an attendant. The Folly had a cavernous interior arranged in concentric circular terraces that descended to a star-shaped stage in the center. I wondered why Longbright had chosen this particular club for this meeting. It seemed too large a venue. The dining floor had been cleared, and a large banquet table arranged with chairs and plenty of space around. Staff in Fornician attire hovered, and most of the council members were already there. Malchi sat at the head of the table, of course.

He's certainly positioning himself as our fearless leader, isn't he? Saraknyal seethed.

Whatever polishes his fragile ego, I thought.

I surveyed the rest of the table as I approached, nodding to the other members. I was surprised to find Brilla Balshi seated there. She hadn't seemed capable of attending a meeting when I'd seen her three days ago. She still looked half dead, but then, so did Ursula Roque and Tambris Matesh. Tori stood as I approached, his ever-present grin in place.

"Hashi. Good to see you. That's a new look for you!" His eyes crinkled in amusement. "It suits you."

"Thank you." I wore a snug brocade waistcoat of crimson and black with a high frilled neck, a blousy black silk shirt beneath, snug black trousers, and my calf-high boots. I fingered the waistcoat. "A gift from Mah Hatsu for the rescue."

"Well, she's got exquisite taste, then."

I never would have bought the garment myself, but I'd taken a lesson from Jhavika Keshmir and had my armorer, Hipshill, fashion stays of spring steel sewn into the lining. It wasn't as restrictive as a corset, and the steel might stop an enchanted blade. Saraknyal had suggested it, and in this I couldn't naysay his caution. There were three blades in this room that would cut through my necromantic defenses like a sheet of paper. Besides, I looked damned good in it.

On impulse, I nodded to Tori and said, "You're as dapper as ever."

"Why, thank you!" He blinked at my compliment, clearly taken aback.

"Have you seen our pirate yet?"

"Only from afar. He seems in good health, though his ship looks to have suffered slightly."

"And how did Nahli search it?" The fate of Jhavika's enchanted scourge concerned me as much as Jhavika's.

He nodded to the door. "Why don't you ask her."

Nahli arrived, accompanied by her usual escort, and I gave her a nod. As she took her seat, I opened my mouth to ask, but Mah Hatsu entered in the company of a komei in full armor. That surprised me, for I hadn't known any had survived. I eyed the warrior warily—yet another blade Saraknyal couldn't foil—as I smiled and nodded to Mah, fingering the lapel of my waistcoat. She beamed to see me wearing her gift.

"Nahli," I said as I took a seat beside Tori. "How did you search *Scourge?*"

"Quite simply. Ships all have cats to reduce the rodent population."

I remembered the form I'd taken under her magic and nodded. "And you found no scourge."

"No. Which begs the question of what happened to it, yes?"

"Yes, it does." I exchanged a glance with Tori, but he just shrugged.

The Tinworthy entourage arrived, and Vinchi gave me a nod and a smile as he took his seat. With his arrival, all the council members were present.

"So, everyone's here but our esteemed captain." Malchi pulled a pocket watch from his waistcoat pocket and looked at it.

"Apparently, he—"

Movement and voices from the entrance to the club drew everyone's attention.

In strode Captain Longbright and a contingent of six grim-faced pirates, all armed. They were well dressed, at least, though the massive half-ogre hovering at his shoulder bore more scars than a pit fighter. Longbright wore a blue brocade dress jacket and an elaborate cutlass with a guard fashioned into the likeness of a dragon. A dark-skinned woman with a shaved pate also wearing an officer's jacket separated from the group as they descended to the table. An elvish woman I hadn't noticed before met her with a warm embrace and a kiss.

What's that about, I wonder? Saraknyal said.

My eyes were elsewhere, for Ursula Roque rose from the table and met Captain Longbright. They clasped hands, then embraced.

Well, that explains why he wanted to meet here. He knows Roque, and she owns the Folly.

Longbright's no fool, that's certain.

"Welcome, Captain Longbright." Malchi gestured to the table. "Good of you to come."

Roque glared at him. "Allow us one moment, Lord Malchi! I will thank Captain Longbright *properly* for saving my life!"

"Of course. I—"

But Roque ignored him and turned back to Longbright, still clasping his hands in white knuckled ferocity. "Anything you need, Kevril. Anything at all. I'd...like to speak to you about Temuso. He..."

"I know, Ursula." A sad smile flicked across his face. "We can talk later."

"Yes, I... I'd like that." Roque released his hands and took her seat.

Longbright nodded to his escort, and they took up positions at the edge of the open space while he claimed the only remaining chair at the opposite end of the table from Malchi.

Look at Brilla, Saraknyal said, and I did.

Lady Balshi glared at Longbright, tight lipped, the muscles of her jaw clenched. *She hates him.*

She was in love with Jhavika, even though it was probably an enchantment.

I thanked the gods once again that I didn't suffer from that curse. *I wonder if she still thinks she is.*

*I imagine she hates you, too. You *did* turn her father into a shade, remember.*

I glanced back at my escort to find the former Lord Balshi standing among them. *Shit! I shouldn't have brought that one.*

Oh, I disagree. It sends just the right message.

If she even notices. Brilla's attention remained fixed upon Longbright.

"Captain Longbright," Malchi began, "I want to make it perfectly clear that this is not an indictment of your actions, but simply an inquiry. We're all indebted to you for—"

"*Indebted?*" Brilla screeched, her face blanching bone white. "He tried to *murder* a guest in my home!"

Everyone stared at her outburst.

Then Tori Blackbriar burst out laughing. "Are you completely *delusional*, Brilla?"

Brilla stood, fists pressed to the table. "You will address me as *Lady* Balshi, Lord Blackbriar, or I will reduce your house to ashes!"

"You're only head of your house because you murdered your brother in cold blood, *Lady* Balshi." Tori gave her a cool smile. "*Congratulations* on your ascension."

I gaped at Tori in surprise. He usually mediated disputes between other council members, rather than instigating them himself.

"I'll not stand here and be insulted! I can't be held responsible for my brother's death!" Her voice wavered near hysteria.

Tell her to sit the hell down, Hashi.

I opened my mouth, but Malchi beat me to it.

"Lady Balshi, *please!*" Malchi stood. "We're not holding you responsible for anything. You can't seriously blame Captain Longbright for trying to kill Jhavika! She tried to murder the entire Council and held his wife hostage! You were ensorcelled by her yourself!"

"I didn't... I was only..." Brilla stammered.

"Jhavika nearly destroyed Haven," Malchi reiterated. "Now, please sit down. We want to know what happened." He turned to Kevril. "You told Captain Patak that Jhavika's dead."

"Yes, she is," Longbright said flatly.

"And that her enchanted scourge was destroyed." Nahli added, her pupiless eyes impassive.

"Yes. We intended only that. Jhavika's death was...incidental."

"And how, *exactly*, did you manage to destroy such a weapon, Captain?" I gestured to Lewin, whose eyes were now fixed on Longbright. "I have it on good authority from Jhavika's former sage that the scourge was all but impervious to harm."

"That's a long story." Longbright waved a waiter over. "Whiskey, please."

"A story that we will *hear*, Captain Longbright," Malchi insisted.

The captain sipped and cleared his throat. "I'll tell you right now that there are details I won't share because doing so would violate the trust of people who aided me in this endeavor. I *will* tell you, however, that I learned that the scourge would be destroyed if it was cast into the center of the Serpent's Eye. With the aid of a dragonlord from the Isle of Valaka, we did that very thing."

Everyone at the table stared in slack-jawed silence.

"That's *preposterous!*" Brilla snapped.

"How did you sail into the Eye without the magic effecting you, Captain?" Tori asked.

"Again, all I can tell you is that I had the aid of a Dragonlord." Longbright took another sip of whisky, and shook his head as if trying to banish a memory. "Their magic offered us protection from the effects of the Eye. Jhavika had no such protection, but sailed in after us regardless. By the time we reached the center of the Eye, her entire ship and crew were...transformed."

"*Transformed?*" Malchi looked skeptical. "Into what?"

"Into a single monstrous creature, Lord Malchi. Jhavika tore herself free from it when I threw the scourge into the Eye, and dove in after it." He frowned. "When she emerged, she wasn't even *vaguely* human. She tried to take our ship, and was killed."

"If I may ask, Captain, where did you learn that casting the scourge into the maelstrom would destroy it?" Tori asked.

"And again, all I can say is that I had the aid of a Dragonlord. I won't tell you who or where they are. They value their privacy, and I won't betray their trust in me."

He's being evasive as hell, Saraknyal said.

"I don't believe the details are pertinent." Malchi waved a dismissive hand. "I'm satisfied that both Jhavika and the scourge are gone. Captain Longbright *did* assault a member of the Council, and had her home invaded, but only to rescue his wife. In my opinion, we can't thank him enough for revealing Jhavika's machinations. I hereby move that we absolve him of all responsibility for his actions in doing so."

"Seconded!" half a dozen council members said in unison.

"I *object* to this!" Brilla seethed. "He tried to murder a guest in my home! Regardless of his *intentions* or the outcome, that violated the sanctity of Balshi Keep!"

"A motion has been put forth!" Malchi said. "All in favor of absolving Kevril Longbright of all responsibility and reinstating him as our privateer and naval consultant, raise your hands."

Everyone but Brilla did so.

"I'd move that we *officially* advance Captain Longbright to Admiral of our privateer forces, and task him with recruiting additional captains!" Roque added. "Jhavika may have been a *maniac*, but the idea of a naval force is still a good one, and Kevril knows what needs to be done."

"Seconded," Ingrid Brickhammer said.

"All in favor?" Malchi raised his hand, and we all, save Brilla, followed suit.

Longbright looked stunned.

"If I may, Admiral," Malchi said in a more conversational tone, "do you know the whereabouts of Captain Tan, and *Golden Harlot*?"

"I believe she's anchored in Mati Harbor awaiting word." Longbright downed his whisky and waved away a refill. "We met at Valaka Isle, and she filled me in on some events. She had no choice but to follow Jhavika's orders, but knew something was *very* wrong. I told her about the enchantment, and she sailed to Mati to wait out the storm. She's willing to return, but didn't know if there would *be* a Haven to come back to."

"Well, there nearly wasn't, but that's another story." Tori caught my eye and grinned.

"You should send a message to her quickly. If Jhavika had survived and got the scourge back, Tan intended to inform the Mati government of the threat."

"Well, we certainly don't want *that!*" Malchi said.

"I'll send a fast ship immediately," Que-Chen said.

"I'm afraid there's even *worse* news," Longbright said. "Jhavika ensorcelled the Mati ambassador to Toki. I don't know what his orders were, but with the destruction of the scourge, he's likely already informed the God-Emperor what happened. Tan knows this, too, and will inform Mati if we don't get to her in time."

"Gods and devils!" Malchi blanched, and many other council members muttered under their breath.

I looked to Lewin, "Did you know this?"

He shrugged helplessly. "No, mistress. She had many plots that I knew nothing of."

*Toki will *not* take kindly to having a spy in their midst, and Mati won't like having their ambassador compromised by Haven.*

I agreed with Saraknyal, and repeated his concerns to the Council, adding, "Even if we tell them this was all Jhavika, not the Council, they won't believe us."

"An alliance between Toki and Mati spells trouble for the entire Blood Sea." Tori's usual light-hearted tone had gone dire. "They've suffered for decades from piracy, and this might push them to unify their efforts."

"They could subjugate the entire region, island by island, city state by city state!" Ingrid agreed.

"Which is why we need a navy as quickly as possible!" I reiterated.

Longbright nodded. "Yes, and to inform the other city-states of the situation. We intended to form a...protectorate of sorts eventually, but this just tipped over the apple cart. They have resources we need, and we'll have the means to defend them. As soon as we have a privateer fleet, that is."

"Admiral, I'm afraid we must ask you to be our ambassador, of sorts. You'll be out recruiting pirates to our cause anyway, so..."

"I'm not a diplomat," Longbright stated flatly. "I can find and talk to pirates, but..."

"Well, I'm afraid we're quite short of diplomats *and* ships, admiral," Tori quipped. "We're not exactly pillars of the international community ourselves, after all."

"And none of *us* can leave Haven," Malchi put in.

"And we can't risk merchantmen," Que-Chen added. "We need to reestablish *trade!*"

"And you know the Blood Sea," Malchi reiterated. "You know the rulers, how they govern, and the sociopolitical situation, not to mention the *economic* one. You know how best to apply the carrot *and* the stick, so to say."

"The *islands*, yes, but I have a death warrant on my head in Sariff." Longbright waved a waiter over to refill his glass.

"As do I." I shook my head and chuckled, wondering if anyone else at the table did. "Perhaps we could send Captain Tan there with our offer."

"A good idea," Longbright agreed. "Tan's a wise woman and has a level head."

"Except when it comes to Maurice Malchi," Tori whispered to me.

I glared at him. "And there's Hyko to consider. They're closest to the Toki Empire. We should at least warn them."

"Yes, we should," Nahli agreed. "They've been friendly with the fae for decades, harboring refugees from Toki incursions into the jungle."

"Agreed," Malchi nodded. "We won't be telling you how to do your job, Admiral, but we must clearly prioritize our approach."

Longbright looked grim, but nodded. "And time is short."

The conversation diverged into sea defenses, the new shipyard, and the arming of merchantmen. Longbright agreed that Patak would make a good privateer if they found him a better ship, but warned that he was short-sighted and hot-headed. He also offered designs for ship-mounted ballistae that he'd put to practical use aboard *Scourge*. The Council agreed to fund the rearming of *Scourge*, as well as whatever repairs were necessary.

As we were settling down to the strategies of conscripting pirates and approaching city states, a disturbance at the door drew everyone's attention. Longbright's pirates faced the door, hands on weapons. Several burly bouncers stood facing down six armed figures dressed in black.

Tori glanced at me. "This meeting could become very interesting very quickly."

They're nokitu, Hashi.

What the hell are they doing here? I slipped a hand to the hilt of Soul Drinker, and felt the entire room tense as well.

Then Lewin stood without a word, striding toward the stalemate at the door.

"Lewin?" I stood, and my shades immediately closed in behind me.

The sage paused and looked back, clearly anxious. "Lady Severn, esteemed council members, these are Jhavika's former retainers. I know them. Master Busashi and his people were enchanted by Jhavika. They were in command of one of the ships she commandeered. Let me see what they want, please."

"The ones who vanished so thoroughly," Tori said, and I remembered the name.

That makes sense, but why would they come here?

"Jhavika's *retainers?*" Longbright looked uneasy.

"This is a *council* meeting, not a public forum!" Malchi complained.

"And this is *my* establishment, Lord Malchi," Roque countered, her eyes flinty. "And I'm curious to know why six of Jhavika's former *assassins* are here. *Perhaps* they have some information we might need to know!"

"I'm curious as well," Longbright put in. "If those are Jhavika's nokitu, they're the ones who abducted my wife from this very club!"

Roque's eyes widened, then snapped to the Folly's vast manager. "We have more than enough security to quell *any* nonsense. Gurt, have your people let them speak to Lewin."

"Thank you, Lady Roque." Lewin worked his way through the wall of pirates and bouncers, and nodded politely to Busashi. The nokitu returned the nod, and they began speaking in low tones.

"If I can ask a question, Captain Patak told me the Council took

Jhavika's keep." Longbright's eyes settled on me for a moment before shifting to Malchi. "I'd like to know how, and *why* you did that."

"Yes, well, interesting tale, that," Tori began before Malchi could open his mouth. "The night of your hasty departure, Jhavika abducted the heirs of Fa-Chen, Hatsu, and Tinworthy houses." He gestured to each of the heirs in turn. "We agreed that their rescue would tip the balance of power in our favor. Lady Severn was kind enough to recover them for us, but I'm afraid Jhavika's entire force of soldiers was...um..." He waved a hand at my shades.

Longbright stared at me wide-eyed. "Gods and devils!"

I ignored him and turned back to our uninvited guests. "Lewin! What's this about?"

"Lady Severn, forgive me, but Master Busashi tells me he and his cadre *must* speak to Captain Longbright. It's a matter of some urgency."

*Those are *nokitu*, Hashi. Have a care.*

He didn't know the half of it. Saraknyal might be old, but he wasn't the obsessive history addict that I was. Toki history fascinated me, and nokitu were even more dangerous in some respects than komei. Masters of martial arts with and without weapons, preternaturally agile and quick, they posed a true threat to me, for while I could transform their weapons to dust, I couldn't do the same to fists and feet that could strike with deadly force. Here, however, among the bodyguards of every member of the Council, and Gurt's burly bouncers, they weren't likely to start a fight.

They're not going to attack anyone here, old man. "The council meeting will be finished shortly. Can this wait?"

Busashi took a step forward and raised his voice. "We have...an offer for Admiral Longbright, and a suggestion for the Council." Busashi bowed to the entire table. "A suggestion that would benefit *all* of Haven."

"This is preposterous!" Malchi glowered. "We have *business* to conduct!"

"Color me curious," Tori interjected. "And if they *do* have something that we need to address, doing so now would preclude *another* meeting." He glanced at me and then the rest, his persuasive smile on full. "Not that I don't *live* for these gatherings, but..."

*Gods and devils save us from yet *another* meeting!*

I gave Tori a nod. "I'll agree to anything that'll save time. I've got work to do."

"I say we let 'em speak!" Ingrid called for a vote.

Only Malchi and Brilla dissented.

"Admiral, it's honestly up to you," Tori told Longbright.

He still looked startled by all this, but nodded. "I'll speak to them." He stood and tugged his jacket straight.

Meaningful glances flashed between Longbright and his piratical escort. They split and fanned out to flank the approaching group. I sat down and waved my shades back.

"Admiral Longbright," Busashi bowed deeply, "We offer our thanks and congratulations."

Longbright opened his mouth, but before he could speak the six nokitu took a knee, drawing and proffering their weapons to him on open palms. The entire room drew a shocked breath, hands moving toward weapons.

"We offer you our lives, our service, and our most humble apologies for our actions." Busashi bowed low, his bared sword flat on his hands. "By freeing us from Jhavika's enchantment, you've restored our honor. Our lives are yours."

"You..." Longbright took a step forward, his eyes narrowing and his hand clenching the hilt of his cutlass. "You're the ones who kidnapped Preel."

Preel? Who's Preel?

His wife, I assume. Longbright's escort looked ready to pounce, but the nokitu didn't move. Lewin stood aside, looking from one to the other nervously.

"Yes, Admiral, from this very spot," Busashi said. "We also aided Lady Keshmir in enslaving your steward. Our lives are yours."

"Hemp..." Trembling, Longbright drew his cutlass. All of the council members stood, their bodyguards shifting, but nobody said a word. The blade lowered to the back of the nokitu spokesman's neck. "Your name's Busashi?"

"Yes, Admiral." Still the man didn't move, even when the edge of the pirate's sword rested on his exposed neck. "Our service, or our lives, are yours. Our honor is restored."

"Yes, you *said* that." Longbright looked to his people. "Miko?"

The dark-skinned woman with the bald pate shrugged, her hand flexing on the katana thrust through the sash at her waist. "Gift horse, sir."

That's a komei sword she's wearing, Hashi, Saraknyal said.

That makes three in the room: hers, Mah's komei's, and Que-Chen's. Plus, Tori's elf blade and Ursula's rapier. I fingered Soul Drinker under my sleeve. *Talk about a threat-rich environment...*

*Tori *did* say the meeting could be interesting.*

"Well, we *are* short-handed." Longbright sighed and sheathed his cutlass. The tension in the room eased. "Stand up, Busashi, and sheathe your weapons."

"Yes, my lord Admiral!" The nokitu stood, bowed, and sheathed their blades.

Lewin sighed and color returned to his wizened features.

"Miko, my first mate, will show you your duties." Longbright's eyes shifted to Lewin. "Now, Lewin, is it? You were also one of Jhavika's retainers? Her sage?"

"Yes, Admiral." He bowed and then turned to me. "I'm currently working for Lady Severn, but we've all found places elsewhere. We didn't know you'd survived. We all owe you our lives. I'd like to speak to you after the meeting, with milady's permission."

"Of course," I told him, wondering what he had to say to Longbright.

"Very well," Longbright looked back to Busashi. "And what's this *suggestion* of yours to the Council?"

Busashi faced the table and bowed politely. "The Council has rightfully confiscated Lady Keshmir's keep, her material possessions, and her personal effects. We know how important Admiral Longbright's work will be to the stability of Haven, and also how...*fragile* his situation is."

"Fragile?" Malchi scowled at the man. "What do you mean?"

"Consider, if you will, lords and ladies, that Jhavika was able to apply pressure to Admiral Longbright through the one thing he cherishes most, his wife." He turned again to Longbright. "I trust she's well, Admiral?"

Longbright's jaw clenched. "She's *quite* well, thank you."

"I'm most grateful to hear, milord." Busashi turned back to the Council. "Yet his efficacy as your admiral hinges on the continued safety of those he loves. A pirate ship is not a safe place, but neither is Haven...unless the admiral had a secure place to leave her in the care of loyal retainers. A fortified keep, for instance."

His point clicked into my mind. "You're suggesting the Council give Jhavika's keep to him?"

"Precisely, Lady Severn." Busashi bowed again to the entire table. "It's *certainly* secure and defensible."

"Not defensible from a necromancer." Tori flashed me a grin.

"With all due respect to Lady Severn, her attack on Keshmir Keep would not have been successful if *we* had been in residence." There was no hubris in Busashi's claim, and I didn't doubt him for a moment.

"This is *outrageous!*" Brilla lurched to her feet, her hands clenched into fists. "You want to reward this pirate for *murder!*"

"Oh, *do* shut up, Brilla." Tori shot her a glare.

"Please!" Lewin interjected. "Master Busashi is quite right. This *entire* situation came about because Jhavika abducted the admiral's wife with the sole intent of using her to pressure him." He turned to Longbright and bowed respectfully. "Admiral Longbright remains *critical* to Haven's efforts. A keep is a far safer place for his loved ones to reside while he conducts his duties elsewhere. It's in the Council's best interest to accommodate his needs, and ensure his family's safety."

"Well, I..." Malchi muttered.

"I don't have the means to support a keep." Longbright shrugged helplessly. "And I have no retainers other than *Scourge*'s crew, and they'll be sailing with me."

"On the contrary, Admiral. Many of Jhavika's former retainers would be willing to serve you." Lewin flashed him a smile. "*Trust* me; if you accept us into your service, you *won't* regret it."

Lewin just jumped ship, Hashi, Saraknyal said.

Well, it's not like he owed me anything, but I find it curious that he's so eager to serve Longbright. I fingered Soul Drinker's hilt. *I wonder why.*

"As for funds to support the keep and retainers," Lewin looked to the Council again, "surely you'll be *paying* him something, considering you've removed his sole means of income."

Longbright barked a laugh. "Well, I certainly won't be *pirating* much, that's true."

"He's got a point," Tori said. "Seeing to the admiral's needs will benefit our efforts, and it's not like we have another use for Jhavika's keep." He stood. "I move we bequeath Keshmir's keep to Admiral Longbright and negotiate a suitable stipend for his support."

"Seconded," I said.

"All in favor!" Tori raised a hand, and everyone but Brilla followed suit.

I think Brilla's going to explode, Saraknyal warned. *And she's got an army...*

She does bear watching, and she's certainly holding a grudge against Longbright.

Longbright stared at the Council, then Lewin, in utter shock. "Well, I...suppose I accept." He looked sheepish and chuckled. "Though, I should probably ask my wife."

"A wise man, indeed!" Tori crowed, eliciting a round of laughter.

We fell to discussing the details and negotiating Longbright's stipend. He assured us he would sail as soon as he repaired and re-armed his ship and settled his new land-side residence. When the meeting finally broke up, Lewin approached me with a sheepish look.

"I'm sorry, Lady Severn, but I'm afraid I need to leave your service."

"I don't keep my retainers prisoner, but I'd like to know why?" We moved toward the exit, not far behind Longbright's people.

"I feel I owe the admiral an even greater debt than I do you, milady." Lewin shrugged. "And Busashi's suggestion rather hit me like a falling star. Longbright needs security for his family; it'll make him a thousand times more effective. That's vital now with the news of the Mati ambassador."

Why didn't he know about that, I wonder? Saraknyal pondered.

So did I, so I asked.

"Oh, well, Jhavika had *hundreds* of plots in motion. I knew she had agents abroad, but not who they all were." He shrugged again and looked to where Longbright stood speaking with the nokitu. "I'd like to speak with the admiral, milady. Arrangements must be made. I'll collect my few personal items from Ash Keep later, if that's all right."

"Perfectly all right."

"Thank you, Lady Severn!" He bowed and hurried off.

That was odd, Saraknyal said as I start off toward home.

It was, I agreed, lengthening my stride. *But we've got bigger issues to deal with right now, don't we?*

I do remember something about a Death Stone, yes.

Snarky bastard, I thought silently.

Chapter Four
Matters of Trust

From the journal of Preel Longbright —

Secrets, like cancer, grow, metastasize, and eventually kill you. Trusting someone, anyone, with the truth of my nature gives me nightmares. My freedom balances on a razor's edge. Kevril, of course, wants to keep me safe, even if that means going against my wishes. Our disagreement has brought nearly as much strife to our relationship as Jhavika did.

The entire ship buzzed with worry at Kevril's delayed return. I'd taken a page from his repertoire to pace the quarterdeck instead of our cabin. The confinement wore on me. I loved our home, but it had also been my prison, and I'd done all the yamshi I could take. The air stank of the city, but the weather wasn't threatening, so I paced and fretted.

"Don't worry, Lady Preel." I looked up to find Hemp with a tray of tea and biscuits. "I'm sure we'd know if something went amiss."

I strode over and tapped my veil insistently. I wore the enchanted gag beneath out of necessity, but there were currently few people on the quarterdeck and no other ships anchored close enough to see.

"Oh, right." Hemp reached behind the hood of my cloak and untied the gag, handing it to me. "Now, have a spot of tea and some of Bert's tartberry jam on a biscuit."

"I'm not hungry. How would we know if something went wrong?" I hated to be put off, told not to worry, assured that everything would be fine, and generally treated like a child.

"Well, the foretop lookout can see the Folly. If things went bad,

I imagine the place'd be in flames."

"That's *not* very reassuring." I handed back the gag and lifted my veil for him to put it back in place. "Please."

He tied it behind my neck without a word, and left the tea and biscuits sitting there. I paced and watched as the shadow of the mountains crept across the city and bay. Finally, as the mountains' shadow reached the deck beneath my feet, the lookout cried out.

"Deck there! Captain's on the quay!"

"About damned time!" Kivan muttered.

I ran to the rail and raised my spyglass, but found it hard to pick out Kevril among the people on the quay. I spotted two in blue, one shorter, probably Miko. The other had to be Kevril, but there seemed to be too many others. They boarded the launch, and a number of figures in black strode away to board one of the lifts along the line of warehouses. As the launch struck out across the bay, I put the spyglass away and hurried down to the middeck to wait.

I stayed out of the way as the crew rigged a boarding ladder. Kevril climbed up first and spotted me. His face split into a grin, but I could see trepidation in his eyes. Something had gone wrong. At least he wasn't bleeding.

"Welcome back, Captain." Kivan snapped a salute. "We were beginning to worry."

"There were...developments that took some time to resolve." He strode toward me. "Sorry, love."

I clutched him in my arms.

"Not the least of which was his appointment as Admiral of Haven's privateer fleet!" Miko announced loud enough for the entire deck to hear.

The crew burst out in ragged cheers. I thrust Kevril to arm's length, my mouth gaping open in shock. There had been plans to make him admiral, but that was before he tried to murder Jhavika. Kevril winced, but he must have seen the surprise in my eyes.

"Come aft with me, love, and I'll tell you everything."

I nodded, and we hurried aft to the cabin. The door closed and I pulled my veil off to tap the silk gag.

"Sorry to worry you, love, but..." Kevril untied the knot with a smile, "the Council wanted to—"

The instant the gag was off, I grabbed him by the hair and kissed him. "*Admiral*, huh." I grinned and kissed him again. "Do I have to salute you now?"

He chuckled, but his smile was strained. "No, and you don't know the half of it." He stepped around me to his locker and reached for a bottle. "I need a drink to get all this into my head. Join me?"

"Sure." Glass clinked, and he handed me a tumbler. "What more is there than your well-deserved promotion?" I took a seat at the navigation table. Something was bothering Kevril, but I couldn't force the facts out of him.

"Well, I don't know how many of them believed me when I told them about the Serpent's Eye, but they didn't call me a liar." He sipped his whisky and sat down to pull off his boots. "Well, most of them didn't. Brilla Balshi wanted my head on a pike, but the others talked her out of it."

"Why would *she* want you dead? It was Jhavika who—"

He held up a forestalling hand. "She's...still dealing with what happened to her. Ursula Roque and Tambris Matesh were also recovering but Brilla seems to be...unhinged. Matesh was badly injured in a battle with a pirate ship, and Ursula's...a mess. She offered to help us any way she could, but she doesn't seem quite stable yet."

I nodded, having experienced slavery under Jhavika, but this still wasn't what was really bothering him. "And what else?"

"Well, the Council wants me to do more than just recruit pirates." He sighed and rubbed his eyes. "With the God Emperor likely readying for war, they want to spread the word to all the city states as soon as possible, especially to Hyko."

"And they're sending you?" Hyko worried me, so close to Toki that imperial warships often visited.

"Yes, which ups the ante somewhat."

It did, but I could still see that there was something he wasn't saying. "Okay, and what else?"

"So, no easy way to say this, so..." He took a deep breath and held it, his lips pressed tight, then said, "We have a keep."

"A what?" The word caught me so flat-footed it didn't register.

"A keep. You know, walls, towers, rooms, dungeons." He sipped his drink, but I just stared at him. "It's Jhavika's keep. The Council gave it to us outright, and several of Jhavika's former retainers offered to...um...work for us."

"What the ever-loving *fuck*?" My mind whirled. "Why in all the Nine *Hells* would we want a keep, least of all *her* keep?"

"I know, but—"

"No, you *don't* know, Kevril!" I lurched up and started to pace, my drink forgotten, my hands clenched so hard my knuckles cracked. "I was a *prisoner* there! And we've got *Scourge*. What the hell do we need a keep for? We've got work to do out on the sea!"

"Preel, listen to me for a second, please." He stood and put his tumbler aside, stepping into my path with his hands up. "Some of Jhavika's retainers crashed the council meeting, six of the nokitu who kidnapped you from the Folly."

"The..." My knees almost gave way. "They *know*, Kevril! They must know what I am!"

"Yes, they do, but it didn't come out." He took a deep breath. "They...apologized for what they'd done under Jhavika's control, then knelt and pledged their *lives* to us, to *me*. Then her sage, this Lewin fellow, backed them up. He offered to work for us, too. After the meeting broke up, he insisted we talk privately. He knows more of Jhavika's secrets than anyone else still alive."

"*What?*" I felt dizzy, and staggered back a step. "You mean..."

"Yes, love. He knows you're a truthsayer, too." Kevril stepped up and gripped my shoulders gently. "He was there when you were...delivered to Jhavika."

My stomach clenched and my mind did the math; six nokitu, one sage...who else? "Did he tell you who else knows?"

"Yes. Jhavika's physician, Doctor Yiv." He squeezed my shoulders, steadying me. "They've *all* pledged their silence. The guards, your attendants, and everyone else who knew are dead. Our secret's safe."

"Nala and Binsh..." I closed my eyes, recalling their kindness. Even if they were compelled by Jhavika, I'd grown to care for them. I shivered at the thought of how they might have died.

"So, you see, things aren't *that* bad." Kevril enfolded me in his arms. "The keep was stripped by the Council, and Jhavika's people scrubbed it clean. It barely looks like the same place."

"You went there?" I looked up at him. "You seriously want to *live* there?"

"Well, when I'm not at sea, I thought so, yes." He put his hands on my shoulders again and looked down into my eyes. "Lewin brought up some very valid points to the Council in support of gifting us the keep. I want you to hear this through before you make a decision."

"Before *I* make a decision?" I shrugged out of his grasp and went back to the navigation table. I hadn't needed a drink when we came in, but I certainly did now. "It sounds to me like you've already made the decision for the both of us." I knocked back a third of the spiced rum and tried to breathe.

"Preel, please, just hear me through. I *didn't* make the decision, but it makes sense. The final decision is yours. I told the Council exactly that." He strode back to his locker and retrieved his tumbler, then took a seat on the bed.

I didn't feel like sitting, but leaned back against the table. "Okay, then explain."

"This whole situation escalated because Jhavika kidnapped you. She wanted her own truthsayer, yes, but she also used you like a lever against me, to keep me quiet about her scourge and to force me to do her bidding."

"So? She's dead! Problem solved!"

"Yes, but that doesn't prevent it from happening again, and sailing around recruiting pirates to join the Haven Navy is going to be dangerous work. Sailing into Hyko to deliver the news of pending war will be even more dangerous. Hyko's near Toki, and if the emperor has truthseekers anywhere, they'll be there. If you're aboard *Scourge*, I'll only be able to think about your safety."

It hit me like a thunderbolt: he intended to leave me alone, locked up in Jhavika's keep while he risked his life on the sea. "That's bullshit, Kevril! You're *safer* with me along! I'm a gods-damned truthsayer, for fucksake!"

"You're right, our mission *would* be easier with you along, but my thoughts would always be on your safety, not our work. Sailing into *Hyko* with you aboard..." He sipped his rum and sighed. "One slip, and we've got the entire Toki empire after you. Jhavika's keep's a fortress. You'd be safe, and I'd be able to focus on my work."

"How *dare* you suggest that you're better off without me!" I trembled so violently that rum splashed over the rim of my glass.

"Preel, I'm not suggesting that. I'm *dead* inside without you! When Jhavika held you captive, I... I died every day. All I could think of was what was happening to you, what she was doing to you, making you do, think, believe. I can't lose you again."

"So your solution is to lock me up and sail away? That's *ridiculous!*" I downed the rest of my drink and slammed the tumbler down on the chart table, whirling away in rage.

"I knew you wouldn't like the idea, but I want you to think it through. We've got a few days, at least, before *Scourge*'s ready to sail." I heard him move, but didn't turn. "Just come see the place, meet Jhavika's people, talk to Lewin and Busashi."

"How do you even know *they're* trustworthy?" I refused to even look at him for fear I might throw something at him.

"They haven't spread the word yet, and even though I thought they intend to blackmail me with what they know, they haven't." Another sigh. "That would be a good question for your talent, in fact. Busashi's assured me that they'll protect your secret to the death. It's a point of honor for them."

"I won't trust *anyone* until we confirm it with my talent."

"Agreed, and even if they are sincere, I'll leave the decision up to you whether you stay or come with us, but consider it. The keep's a blank canvas. With Jhavika's money—"

"*Jhavika's* money?" I finally turned back, glaring at him accusatively. "You're leaving out some details, Kevril!"

"Oh, sorry; I got sidetracked." He sighed and rubbed his eyes. "Lewin doesn't just know about you, he knows a lot of Jhavika's secrets, including where she kept her secret stashes. He didn't tell the Council about them. He's truly a sly fellow. The instant the enchantment was broken, he started making contingencies. The avarice and paranoia of a dragon came home to roost there, Preel. She hoarded treasure in secret troves, bricked it up behind walls all around the city. Some of it was pillaged by her people, but most is hidden right there in her keep, buried behind stonework. Lewin wants me to have it. Us, that is."

"How much?" I barely whispered the question, too stunned to think.

"More than enough to make that keep ours, *yours*. Hire whoever you want, decorate however you like, and make it utterly safe and comfortable. Busashi and his cadre assured me that they'd make *sure* of our privacy and safety." He tried to smile, but failed. "There's enough to make it our *home*, Preel."

I remembered walking in the gardens with Jhavika, the expansive bed in my prison, silver and porcelain, silk and satin, water at the turn of a tap in the washroom. I looked around the cabin; cramped, prone to damp, cluttered, the frames of the transom windows still scarred where iron bars had been fitted. This cabin had also been a prison.

Home... I thought. Then I looked to my husband, the man who had freed me from a life of slavery, and my heart broke.

"*You're* my home, Kevril Longbright!" I saw the pain those words scored across his heart, but I didn't care. "You thought this through without me! You've already made up your mind! You want to *leave* me!"

"I *have* thought it through, love, but I don't *want* to leave you. I'd love nothing more than to spend every moment of my life with you until I die, but I've got a *job* to do." He strode back to the locker and pulled down the bottle of rum.

"So to *hell* with your job! Gods and devils, Kevril, let's just sail away!"

"Don't think I haven't considered that, but where would we go?" He poured and shrugged. "We'd have to carve out a whole new life somewhere. Or we stay and make Haven our home. To do that, I need to do my job. If I don't do that job, the Toki Navy's going to station a dozen warships in Snomish Bay and starve this city to death. If Haven isn't safe, we have no home port, and *you're* not safe. I can do my job better if you're here surrounded by loyal retainers." He held the bottle over my glass and hesitated, his eyebrows a question.

I nodded to the tumbler and he poured. "How can you know *they'll* be loyal?"

"We use your talent to make sure those who know you're a truthsayer are utterly loyal, then trust them to make damn sure the others are. We've got a day before we can ask." He sat back down on the bed. "Will you at least come look at the keep once we confirm their loyalty, meet Lewin and the nokitu?"

I picked up my glass and held it under my nose, breathing in the heady scent of spices and sweet liquor. His logic made sense, but my heart still wanted only to be with him. I nodded. "I'll look the place over."

"Good. Thank you."

"But we have to be *careful* about this!" I glared at him, still angry, but now able to think straight. "We make sure about the nokitu, Lewin, and Yiv, and until we are, we have to keep eyes on them."

"Okay, I agree. I'll put someone on Yiv, and we can sequester the rest in the keep, surround them with pirates, until we ask the question."

I nodded. "And you have to *promise* me, Kevril, that you'll keep your word. The decision is *mine* whether I stay or go with you. I *am* a free woman, after all!" I had no intention of staying in Jhavika's keep while he sailed away.

"I promise." He lifted his glass to me and I mirrored the gesture. We both sipped. "I won't be sailing around the sea forever, Preel. Regardless of your decision, it'd be nice to have a home to come back to."

I thought about that for a moment, then nodded. "Yes, it would."

Two days after our tumultuous argument, the morning after confirming the loyalty of the nokitu, Lewin, and Dr. Yiv using my talent, I ventured to inspect Jhavika's keep, now ours, the one place on the planet I least wanted to ever see again.

Kevril, of course, was busy seeing to his new duties as admiral, repairing *Scourge*, and transforming the other ships assigned to our nascent fleet into warships. We were speaking, at least, but I was still angry, though I didn't know if I was angry with him or that having a keep was a good idea. If nothing else, we would have a home here. I took Boxley and half a dozen pirates as escort, as well as half of the nokitu. The others were watching over the keep. I realized as we approached that I'd only seen the outside of the keep once, and that at night from the back of a wagon as I was being rescued. I peered out the carriage window at the lofty walls capped with crenelations, the stone ramp flanked by bartizans, the thick iron portcullis and gates. It was certainly a substantial structure.

We rode up the ramp and into the courtyard, and two more nokitu bowed as we passed. They made me nervous, so grim and dangerous. We pulled to a stop, but before I could even touch the door latch, one of my escorting nokitu opened it for me and bowed. I stepped down and took in the courtyard; it was utterly blank, spotless, cold, and featureless. I shivered despite the building morning heat. Boxley and the others dismounted from their hired mounts to join me, but a greeting from the main doors drew my attention.

"Lady Longbright!" I recognized Lewin as he approached with one more nokitu at his side. They both bowed. I was already tired of that. "Master Lewin, scribe and sage, at your service. You may remember me from your previous stay here. This is Master Busashi, commander of your nokitu."

My nokitu. I wondered if they would assassinate someone for me. I nodded to them both, then tapped Boxley on the shoulder.

"Yes, lady." She faced them, looking far more serious than any fourteen year old girl should. "I'm Midshipman Boxley, senior officer here." Her hard tone stated clearly that her statement included both of them as well as the pirates. "You know of Lady Preel's...talent, but you may not know this: her talent is dangerous for her, taxing her severely. She'll be taking off her enchanted gag to speak with you all. If you ask her a question that she doesn't know the answer to, she'll fall unconscious and likely die, since she recently used her magic to make sure you were trustworthy. So no questions. Do you understand?"

"We understand perfectly, Midshipman," Lewin assured her,

nodding to me. "We're familiar with Lady Preel's talent."

I nodded, and tapped Boxley again, then my veil.

"Yes, lady." She untied the enchanted gag, and handed it to me.

I dropped my veil. "Thank you, Boxley. Please have your detail secure the gate while I look around."

"Aye, Lady Preel." She snapped a salute and motioned to her detail.

"My people will help you," Busashi said with another bow, and the two nokitu stationed at the gate dashed forward.

"Very well." I looked Lewin and Busashi over, and the irony of the situation almost made me smile. I'd been a prisoner here. Now, I was their lady. "Master Lewin, show me the keep."

"Delighted, milady." He gestured, and we strode through the lofty doors into the entry hall.

This, too, I'd never seen before, but even so, I stopped dead and stared around. The hall was utterly empty, the walls blank stone, no adornments, no statuary, no sign of habitation at all.

"If you have any questions, please ask," Lewin said.

"It's so...*blank*."

"Yes, well, it was utterly scoured by the Council, and after the battle it needed a good scrubbing."

I imagined the stairs flowing with blood and shook my head to banish the macabre image. "How...big is it?"

"Fifty seven rooms, including nine suites, six sitting rooms, three dining rooms, a library—empty, I'm afraid—kitchens, store rooms, wine cellar, and...um...a dungeon. That doesn't include the stables and smithy."

"Bloody hells and high water," I muttered. "And they're all this blank?"

"Most, yes, though there are some stores in the cellars, and some rooms retain bookshelves and lighting. The masters' suite is quite extensive, but unfurnished."

I looked around again, trying to see this place and imagine it a home. "A blank canvas..."

"*Quite*, milady." He bowed once again.

"Stop that, please. It makes me nervous."

"I...um...of course." He looked uncomfortable.

I closed my eyes and took a deep breath, imagining the vast entry hall around me as a welcoming room, something that we could come home to and feel comforted. "Blue."

"Milady?"

I opened my eyes. "You're a scribe, Lewin, please take notes. I'm thinking blue and gold here. Nothing overpowering. A runner up the stairs, and a banner with the Longbright coat of arms. I'll want to hire a decorator, someone with taste."

"Coat of arms?" He blinked at me as he pulled a small notebook and pencil from under his jacket.

"Our flag," I said. "I'm sure you've seen it."

"I have." He scratched notes.

"Good. I'll want that in the courtyard, too, but not a banner, bass relief over the doors, maybe blue and gold pennants to either side. And I'll want to hire an artist for a painting," I pointed to the first landing. "Right there, I want a painting of *Scourge* on the high seas. Get someone with *talent*, and I want it as soon as can be arranged."

"Yes, milady."

"Good. Now the dining rooms..." Kevril had given me free rein, and I intended to make this place our home, someplace that would never, *ever*, remind me of Jhavika Keshmir. "Show me everything."

"This way, if you please, milady."

A blank canvas, and Jhavika's money was my paint and brushes. *More irony...* A vindictive smile of determination curved the corners of my mouth. *So be it...*

Chapter Five
Longbright Keep

From the diary of Kevril Longbright —

I never wanted more than my own ship and the open sea. Now, I find myself with a wife, a household, a ship and crew, and the responsibilities of an admiral. I keep having to remind myself that this is all for the good. The only way to keep Preel safe is to keep Haven safe.

"You're cutting holes in my ship!" The young lord's face flushed the color of a ripe plum as he strode across the gangway onto *Tiger Lily*'s deck.

"Indeed we are, milord, but not to worry." I wove my way through the maze of timber, shavings, sawdust, and busy carpenters to bow to Lord Que-Chen. "Nothing's been done that can't be undone once the Council's procured a more fitting vessel for Captain Patak."

"But she looks like a wedge of highlander *cheese!*" the young lord squawked.

"True, but she'll be able to fire a broadside of a dozen incendiary ballista bolts when we're through. She's currently the most formidable defense we have afloat, milord. You should be proud of your people, as I am."

Kivan—gods bless and curse her—had been busier than a satyr in a brothel refitting both *Scourge* and *Tiger Lily* with armament, and Rauley had restepped the merchantman's masts and reworked her rig. The crews of both ships had been as busy as bees for four days, and the shipyard—still a work in progress itself—had hired about fifty workers.

"I *am* proud, Admiral, but she's also *my* ship!" Que-Chen growled. "I *lent* her to the Council for the defense of Haven, I didn't bequeath her outright! I expect to get her back in exactly the condition she was in before when this crisis is over!"

"You'll get her back in significantly *better* condition, milord," I assured him.

"Unless she burns to the waterline under my feet first." Captain Patak strode up with a scowl and a respectful nod to the young lord. "Longbright, you gotta have a talk with that young lass of yours. She's brought aboard ten barrels of distilled naphtha!"

"Incendiary ammunition for the ballistae, Captain. Better than tar-soaked rags. Make sure they're stowed where no sailors will be smoking." I wasn't pleased with the volatile liquid either, but the tactics of war were different than piracy, and burning enemy warships before they could grapple and board played significantly into my evolving strategy.

Que-Chen went from scarlet to pale. "*Admiral*, I really must—"

"We're being *careful*, milord, I assure you." Our biggest concern was catching the ship on fire before they could inflict any damage on an enemy. Gnomish alchemists were devising a way to thicken the liquid into the consistency of jelly. "All of the firing ports are being lined with tin to resist fire. We've brought it aboard *Scourge* as well and are also using it for the shore batteries."

"I see." The young lord swallowed and nodded, somewhat mollified. "I'm...unfamiliar with the arts of warfare, Admiral. We're trusting you a great deal."

"I appreciate that, milord. Rest assured, once we have a proper ship for Captain Patak, you'll get *Tiger Lily* back." I spotted a coach bearing the dragon skull and crossed scourges of my flag on the door rolling up the quay, and thanked the Gods of Light. "I must be off. I have duties to attend to. If you have more concerns, milord, please speak to one of my officers."

"Very well, Admiral." Que-Chen turned to Patak, who shot a glare at me.

I strode off the ship without pause. If I even hesitated long enough to bid Miko farewell, I'd have been smothered in a dozen more concerns. The driver nodded to me, and the four armed guards riding fore and aft snapped salutes. The soldiers we'd hired from those who'd served aboard Jhavika's ships seemed loyal and skilled. Busashi had explained to them that they owed their freedom to me, and betrayal meant death.

Freedom... I climbed aboard and slammed the door. I'd fought my whole life to be free and beholden to none; now I had more duties and obligations than ever before. *All to the good, Kevril,* I told myself. Still, I felt like I was driving a runaway coach.

I sifted through the myriad details as I rode: Our messenger ship would arrive in Mati soon with Captain Tan's orders. While she sailed to Sariff to pitch our proposition to the Jaguar King, the captain of the messenger ship would look for suitable ships to purchase. I'd personally instructed her what to look for. We had four more days to finish our refit; four more days and two more questions to ask Preel. One tonight.

Preel... She'd not yet made her decision or forgiven me fully. We were talking, at least, and she had agreed to take on the task of refurbishing Longbright Keep. Keeping busy helped, and learning to run a household, procuring new furnishings and decorations, filling the library and wine cellar, and vetting every single soldier, servant, and worker who stepped through the door, did that. She even seemed to be enjoying it.

My driver bellowed our arrival to the gate guards, and we clattered through the fortified entry into the courtyard. I took some comfort in the grim faces of the soldiers as they snapped to attention. A question to Preel had ensured the loyalty of all who knew of her talent, but we'd hired on dozens of soldiers in recent days. Busashi had evaluated each and every one.

Trust came hard.

I stepped down from the carriage and started up the foyer steps, under the scaffolding of the stoneworkers fitting our new crest above the portal. *A pirate flag for a crest...what was she thinking?* I strode between two more guards into the entry hall, completely redone in royal blue tapestries and carpets with gold accents and a nautical motif. Preel had a flair for bold colors. I barely recognized the place. Most of the keep was still bare, but she'd made amazing progress. Money and enthusiastic retainers helped a great deal.

"Welcome home, Admiral." Our butler, an amiable man named Brindal who used to work under Jhavika's butler, Ty-lee, held out a hand for my jacket and sword belt. He balanced a silver tray with a glass of iced lime water with a sprig of mint in the other. "All's well, I trust?"

"Well enough." I unclipped my sword belt and shrugged out of my stifling jacket. My shirt stuck to my skin beneath from the sweltering heat and humidity. "Where's the lady of the house?" I took the glass from the tray as I handed over my things and drank greedily.

"In the gardens, I believe, sir."

I put the empty glass back on the tray with a sigh. "Thank you, Brin, that hit the spot. You're spoiling me."

"I endeavor to make your steward aboard *Scourge* apoplectic with jealousy, sir." He smiled slyly and gave me a nod. He'd met Hemp, and the two despised one another.

"Just don't let it come to blows, Brin." I strode to the stairs and shot over my shoulder, "The last person who trespassed on Hemp's duties met with an untimely end." Not exactly true, but it made a good story.

"I stand forewarned, sir." Brindal strolled off, seemingly unconcerned.

I made my way through the keep, still only sparsely decorated, to the room that had once been Jhavika's business office. Its glass doors opened onto the patio and gardens beyond, and had been redecorated as a day room, with paintings of ships, nautical knickknacks, and a vast bookshelf, still mostly empty. Cushioned divans, polished teak tables, and rugs of Fornician silk gave the room a warm, exotic feel.

All this in two days... Amazing... Preel must have scoured half the antique shops in Haven.

I stepped onto the small patio and up to the granite balustrade. The gardens hadn't been changed, and upon the central lawn I beheld my wife and her honor guard of six nokitu performing Yamshi in perfect unison.

I leaned on the balustrade and watched, mesmerized by the precision and grace of their movements. They progressed from pose to pose in utter silence, like a dance troupe performing to music only they could hear. The nokitu wore black, as always, but their weapons had been set aside for the exercise. Preel wore one of her old outfits, blousy pantaloons and wrap-around halter of matching silk, her feet bare, but her face and hair covered in the Marathian fashion. Her arms and abdomen shimmered with sweat as she moved.

I watched until they finished, bringing their hands together and bowing to the lowering sun, then trundled down the steps to the lawn.

"Enjoying the gardens, I see."

The nokitu bowed to me in unison. "Lord Admiral!"

Preel's eyes crinkled with a smile as she nodded. Many of Jhavika's former retainers had seen Preel speaking to Jhavika, so knew she wasn't mute as we continued to pretend for the general public. That brought a host of new worries about rumors spreading, but Busashi told us flat out that everyone had been warned. Even so, Preel wore the enchanted gag for safety. She tapped her veil and I untied the gag without removing her concealing drape.

"You look like you've just trekked over a mountain." Preel lowered her veil and gave me a kiss. She smelled of fresh sweat and tasted salty.

"I've been in the shipyard all day." I nodded to Busashi as he and his nokitu recovered their weapons. Four of them hurried off, but two took up station nearby, our discreet escort. "It's mesmerizing to watch you do yamshi with them. You're like a troupe of dancers."

"It's nice to have the company, and they know even more routines than I do." Preel slipped on a pair of sandals. "They're teaching me some other disciplines, too."

"Oh?" We climbed the steps to the patio and into the keep, our escort following silently. Busashi and his nokitu had become very protective of Preel, and I approved heartily. "Like what?"

"Some unarmed martial disciplines that mesh well with the Yamshi." She shrugged. "It's fun, like learning a new language that I've been hearing my whole life without understanding."

"You'll have to show me some of it."

"Sure." She handed me the enchanted gag, and I put it on her, always warry of bumping into a maid or footman.

We climbed two flights to our suite, once Jhavika's. Neither of us had ever seen it, so we had no compunctions about making it our own, newly refurbished in yet another nautical motif. The walls of the sitting room had been paneled in ship-lap teak oiled and gleaming. The rugs, furniture, and even the balcony balustrade looked like they'd come right out of a ship. A maid was just leaving the washroom, and gave us a curtsy and a smile. She bustled out and closed the door, our nokitu escort stationed outside.

As soon as the door closed, I removed the gag.

"So, how goes the work?" Preel cast her headscarf and veil aside and headed for the washroom.

"Well enough." I poured myself a drink and sat to take off my boots. My feet ached. "Another few days at least, to get all three ships outfitted. Kivan and Rauley are happy as pigs in shit, but nobody else is."

"Three?" She stopped at the washroom door and looked back to me. "Another besides *Scourge* and *Tiger Lily?*"

"Oh, yeah, the Council bought one of the smaller brigs, *Daisy*, from Que-Chen and gave it to Niland. Patak threatened to cut his...um... Well, he convinced Niland to take the posting, and he's training the poor lad hard."

"A warship named *Daisy?*" Preel laughed and unwound her halter. "That's hilarious."

"Can't rename a ship. It's bad luck." I watched her as she removed the sweaty garment.

"Of course." She wadded up the halter and stared at me. "So, you going to sit there and *drink*, or will you join me?"

"I thought you'd never ask." I downed my drink and followed her into the lavish washroom.

This was one room of the keep that Preel hadn't changed. There was no need. Neither of us had ever seen such luxury, and after using the tiny quarter gallery aboard *Scourge* for years, I wondered if I'd ever be able to go back. Tile-lined and airy, with high windows on two walls, the washroom had direct plumbing from cisterns built into the top of the tower above the suite. It had a built-in tub, a commode that flushed with the pull of a lever, and something I'd never seen before: a stand-up bathing chamber.

The pull of a chain sent a shower of cool water cascading down from copper nozzles above, and a drain in the floor took it away. Preel and I had fallen in love with it and reveled in the luxury. We washed each other's backs, and simply embraced under the cool rain, letting it patter over our shoulders and leech away the heat and fatigue. After toweling dry, we donned robes and emerged into the sitting room refreshed and invigorated.

"So," Preel poured herself a glass of wine and refilled my tumbler, "did you talk to Hemp today?"

"Yes." I accepted my drink and touched her glass with mine. "He's not happy about it, but if you decide to stay here, he'll stay on *Scourge*."

"Good."

Hemp had wanted to stay with Preel, but also felt he owed me his devotion. He'd begged me to let her sail with us, but I'd told him it was her decision. We strolled onto the balcony to lean against the balustrade. The air wasn't exactly fresh, but the view was worth it. The sun had set over the mountains, painting the sky in shades of crimson.

"Does that mean you've made a decision?"

She shot me a surly look. "Maybe."

"I think you—"

"Don't rush me, Kevril." She turned away, running a hand along the smooth balustrade.

"I'm not, love, but we should put a question to your talent tonight, and it depends on your decision." We'd discussed potential questions, of course, another sore spot between us.

"Ask something else, then." She drank some wine and stared out over the city and the bay beyond. "Ask where to find a pirate most likely to join our cause."

"I thought we decided to ask that right before we sail." I leaned on the rail beside her, facing her, watching her. "Or, we could put that one off, if you decide you're sailing with us."

She didn't answer, and I didn't press it. *Give her time*, my conscience said, but time was against us.

"I have to admit that I like it here," she said finally, sighing and sipping more wine. "It's hard not to like servants and luxury, the gardens, the view..."

"And something solid beneath your feet for a change."

"I miss the motion, actually, but it does make some things easier." She gestured to the gardens. "Yamshi, for one."

"Busashi and the nokitu would come with us, if you decide to."

"I know." She sighed again and put her glass down on the balustrade. "I feel like staying would undermine everything we suffered for, Kevril. We risked our *lives*, the lives of everyone aboard *Scourge*, so we could be together. Hell's teeth, Kivan was *tortured*, Quibly, Foist, Quiff...they *died* so we could be together, and now were talking about parting. It feels like we're betraying their sacrifices."

"We're not." I downed my drink and put the glass down.

She faced me. "*How* not?"

"We risked everything because we *love* you, Preel. Even if we couldn't be together, if you'd stayed with Shepherd, their sacrifices wouldn't have been wasted." I shook my head and tried to find a way to explain. "The entire crew of *Scourge* loves you, even though your very nature is dangerous." I raised my hands and placed them gently on her shoulders. "And I'll still love you if we're parted. I'd still love you if you'd stayed with Shepherd. I'd still love you if we all perished in the Serpent's Eye."

Tears swam in her dark eyes. "Why, Kevril?"

"*Why?*" I blinked at her. "Seriously?"

"Yes, *seriously!*" She shrugged out of my grasp and whirled away. "Gods *damn* it, Kevril Longbright you can be infuriating!"

"I'm sorry, love, it's just that...it's hard to explain, I guess."

She leaned back in the corner of the balcony, arms folded, her dark eyes fixed on me. "Try."

"Okay." I sighed and rubbed my eyes, turning to stare out at the darkening sky, the evolving colors, the beauty, and a thought came to me. "Look at that." I pointed to the cascade of pink, to red, to crimson, to purple, and finally cobalt blue. "When we first came out on the balcony, I thought it was beautiful, but it keeps getting more beautiful the longer we look at it. Right?"

She glanced at the sky. "Yes. So?"

"So that's you."

Her brows knitted. "What?"

"When we first met, I thought you were beautiful, a slave, but a valuable one. Then I saw that you'd been through hell, but...that just made you *more* beautiful to me." I shrugged. "Then, that bastard Geit... and still, you came back. You *survived*. You struggled and had the temerity to offer to help me free myself from Jhavika's enchantment, to help *me*, even after you'd been through so much already. You became more beautiful to me every day."

Tears spilled over her cheeks, and she sniffed.

"You *changed* me, Preel." I pointed to the evolving sky, the darkening colors, the first twinkling stars. "Watching you become a free woman, seeing you embrace the power of your talent instead of thinking of it as a curse... You *saved* me, Preel, and not just from Jhavika; from myself. You saved everyone aboard *Scourge*, and they know it." I swallowed hard and shook my head, looking down at my feet. "I nearly lost you, twice now. I can't risk losing you again."

"I'll stay."

"You..." I looked up to her. "You will?"

"Yes, but I want to *help*. I'm a truthsayer, Kevril. I can't just sit here like a bird in a gilded cage."

"All right, I agree." She was right, of course, and I'd been thinking on this for days. "We can communicate by messenger boat."

She nodded. "And I can tell you where to look for pirates willing to join."

"The time delay might be an issue, but you can also inform me of the situation here." I pursed my lips. "And the Council..."

"Fine, that, too." She pushed off the railing and strode across the balcony to me. "But I swear to all the gods in the heavens and devils in the hells..." She grabbed me by my hair and pulled me down to kiss me hard. "...if you don't come back to me, I'll hunt you down and *kill* you."

I laughed and held her tight. "Well, *that's* incentive!"

She looked up at me, her face tear-streaked, her lips trembling as she broke into a sultry smile. "Oh, so you want *incentive*, do you?" Her hands parted my robe and fondled me. "I can manage that."

We dined in bed that night, then made love again among the dirty dishes and crumbs. In the afterglow, sipping a spicy sweet liqueur, we discussed the question we wanted to ask.

"So, with Busashi on the job, I think isolation's a bigger issue than security." Preel sat with her back against the carved teak headboard of our bed, her legs crossed tailor fashion, a notebook in her lap.

I sprawled, watching the pulse in her neck. "And I think making sure all our new retainers are loyal would give you peace of mind."

"It would, but Busashi's...thorough."

"He's a nokitu."

"Exactly." She made a note. "I swear, Kevril, some of the things they can do..."

"There are a lot of legends about their abilities." I ran a finger down her bare leg. "Nobody outside the sect knows if they're god-gifted, arcane enchantment, or if it's some kind of mental discipline."

"Not only that. They're...so *focused* all the time. It's a little intimidating."

"Good thing they're on our side." I ran my finger down her leg again.

"Exactly, so I'm less concerned about security than I am about getting information I can trust from the Council. They're not exactly altruistic." She nudged my hand away as I started to run my finger up her leg again. "You're distracting me."

"Sorry." I stopped. "I think you can rely on Ursula."

"I'm not...so sure."

Preel didn't like Ursula much, probably because we'd been intimate that one horrific night. "Well, one question will tell us if she's trustworthy."

"Yes, but if the answer's no, we've wasted a question." Preel scratched another note. "I'll have time once you're gone to ask about the loyalty of the retainers. I think we should ask who on the Council we can trust most for information. I need a go-to council member who won't be plotting to further their own agenda."

"Then stipulate that in the question." I tapped her notebook.

"Right." She scratched another note and tapped her lips with the pencil. "Haven's a dangerous place. I'm safe enough in the keep, but dealing with those power-grasping crime lords..."

"Reginald Malchi and Brilla Balshi are your biggest concerns there," I said. "I'd steer clear of Tori Blackbriar, too."

She gave me a wry smile. "Worried he'll try to seduce me?"

"He does have that reputation, but he's also got one for manipulation and spying. He might be curious about you."

"So we word the question to eliminate anyone who might have ulterior motives without being specific."

"This is getting complicated." I rolled up and grabbed my robe.

"Doesn't it always?" She scratched a note. "So, we ask who among the Council I can trust as an intermediary for information, who won't attempt to use our interaction for their own ulterior motives."

I walked to the balcony doors and looked out. "Seems to me the answer to that is none of them."

"*Most* trustworthy, then." She scratched more notes.

"And it seems kind of ambiguous." Preel had always warned me about ambiguity in employing her talent. "I mean, we're not specifying what information or what ulterior motives."

"I disagree. We're asking for a specific person least likely to betray us for their own ends."

I turned to her and wagged a finger. "That's better wording, I think. We ask who among the Council would be least likely to betray us for their own ends, and leave it at that. That way, whatever transpires, we're picking the person most trustworthy."

She arched an eyebrow at me. "Remember, we're not looking into the future."

"True, but your talent knows every bit of information that already exists, and the current mindset of every member of the Council, all their motivations and desires." I shrugged. "Can you think of a way that could go wrong?"

She pursed her lips and shook her head. "No, but we might be missing something."

"True." I paced. "Lewin can help us vet our answer. He knows the council members better than we do." I'd already asked him for details on all of them, of course.

"That's a good idea." Preel scribbled something out on her pad, then wrote something new. "Okay, I think I have it: Who among the council members is least likely to betray us for their own ends if employed as my intermediary?"

"You might even leave off the last bit."

"I think that's important. If we don't include it, the answer's only considering what exists at this moment. Right now, none of the council members has any *way* to betray us."

"Good point." I sat back down on the bed. "And whoever the answer is, we vet through Lewin. If we think it's safe, we contact them and pitch it."

"Right. And anything I learn through my intermediary, I send you by messenger."

"And any pirates I sign up, I send back to Haven with my whereabouts and next destination."

"Perfect!" Preel finished her cordial, tossed down her notebook, and scampered for the door, leaving her robe lying. "Tidy up the bed, would you? I have to use the washroom."

"Sure." I watched her pad across the sitting room through the open door with a pang. *She'll be safer here*, I told myself, but leaving her behind felt like thrusting a knife into my own guts. "You must be insane, Kevril Longbright."

I stacked the plates on the sideboard and shook the spread over the balcony railing. Lightning flashed out to sea, eliciting another pang. I, too, missed the feel of a moving deck under my feet. By the time I had the bed straightened up, Preel returned. She donned a sleeping shift and made herself comfortable.

"Ready?"

She took a deep breath and held up a hand to me. "Kiss, please."

"Yes, milady." I complied, and she knotted her fists in my hair. We parted, and I brushed her cheek with the back of my fingers. "Requests for breakfast?"

"Surprise me." She folded her hands over her stomach and nodded. "Ask."

I read her question from her notes. "Who among the council

69

members is least likely to betray us for their own ends if employed as your intermediary?"

Her eyes rolled and her back arched as the power of her talent took hold. "Hashi Severn," she croaked in that most uncharacteristic voice.

My mouth dropped open. *Severn? The necromancer? Why in the names of all the dead gods...?*

I checked her breathing, and when it had settled, I paced.

"A gods-damned necromancer... What in the Nine Hells?" Then I remembered that Lewin had served as Severn's sage. He hadn't said much about her, other than she spared the lives of all the noncombatants enslaved by Jhavika.

It was still early, so I donned pants, shirt, and slippers and went looking for the man. If anyone in the keep knew Hashi Severn, Lewin did.

Chapter Six
The Admiral's Secret

From the journal of Hashi Severn —

First Tori Blackbriar and now this! The last thing I need in the world is friends. They're a danger, or maybe I'm the danger. I've got better things to do.

*This is stupid, Hashi. He's a *pirate*! We've got more important things to do.* Saraknyal had been surly from the moment I accepted the invitation from Admiral Longbright. *The Death Stone must be dealt with!*

"I know, but this may be more *urgent*." I reclined in my carriage drumming my fingers on the window sill. "He's leaving port in a few days, and said it was an issue of mutual importance. The Death Stone's contained for now. It won't break loose before we get the vessel finished."

You hope.

"I think after a hundred fifty years, the Tinworthys know what they're doing. Why are you being devil's advocate here?"

*Hey, devils need an advocate occasionally. Thrown out of the Heavens because they *disagreed* with the gods. *Demons*, on the other hand, are truly vile.*

"I am *so* not getting into a theological discussion with you right now. And you didn't answer my question. Why are you against me meeting with Longbright?"

What part of 'pirate' didn't you understand?

"Sell that somewhere else, old man. You're a *necromancer*, remember?"

*No, I *forgot* that part!* Soul Drinker couldn't have cut through his sarcasm, it was so thick. *I just think it's a bad idea. He's going to ask you for a favor, or some task, or worst of all, your *friendship*.*

"Longbright doesn't strike me as the type who barters favors or friendship. He wouldn't invite me to his home unless it was important. You saw his face when Tori told him what I'd done to Jhavika's soldiers." I didn't know if that had been fear or revulsion, but either way, he'd stepped past it. This had to be important.

*All the more reason not to go. He could be plotting to remove you from the Council. He *was* Keshmir's partner, you know.*

"Come on, Saraknyal. He tried to murder Keshmir himself."

Yes he did. Remember that. He paused then added, *And don't dance with him.*

I laughed out loud, which probably took Bromish for a turn. But all my people knew I talked to Soul Drinker, anyway. All things considered, if they spread rumors that I was mad, it only added to my mystique.

The coach slowed and inclined sharply, then pulled to a stop. A glance outside confirmed that we'd arrived. The outside of the keep looked exactly as I remembered.

Bromish announced us to the guards, and I caught a muffled cry of, "Open the gates!"

My mind stumbled as we rolled through the gate and into the transformed courtyard. Twin banners hung beside the main entrance, the pirate's personal flag emblazoned upon them, white on black. The same dragon skull and crossed scourges had been worked in stone above the portal, and even the soldiers he'd hired wore surcoats bearing the same grim emblem. The door itself had been painted in royal blue with gold accents.

The admiral's got an ego, Saraknyal observed.

Or he just wanted to make the place his own. My carriage stopped before the entrance and I got out before a white-coated footman could touch the handle.

"Welcome, Lady Severn." He bowed and gestured toward the now open portal. I recognized him as one of Jhavika's former people. "This way, if you please."

I turned to my escort. "Stay with the coach. Bromish, relax."

"Yes, mistress." Bromish tipped his cap to me, understanding his duties. While I met with the admiral, he'd chat up the pirate's retainers, most of whom I assumed had been Jhavika's.

I strode up the steps and through the doors.

"Welcome to Longbright Keep, Lady Severn." A butler bowed to me, a smile flicking over his familiar features. "Or, should I say welcome *back*?"

"Thank you." I doffed my weather cape and handed it to him, trying not to gape at the vastly different entry hall.

Evidently, Longbright didn't like the décor, Saraknyal quipped.

Evidently. The walls were festooned with gold and blue tapestries in a nautical flair.

He's got good taste, Saraknyal sounded amused.

All this in five days... "I see the admiral's been redecorating." I gave the butler a questioning look. "I'd have thought he'd be too busy for such details."

"Oh, he has been," the man said with a smile. "Lady Longbright, however, has gone to great lengths to lend her own bold style to their new home. She's kept a legion of workers as busy as a kicked anthill!" He gestured to the sweeping stairs that I remembered splashed with blood, now carpeted with a royal blue runner embroidered with gold in a rope pattern at the edges. "The admiral awaits you in the day room."

I followed him up. A the top, a large painting of the admiral's ship, *Scourge*, pounding through raging seas, flying all sails, stood upon the wall. I paused for a moment to admire the piece, and could still smell the wet paint.

Ego, certainly, Saraknyal said.

Or he simply loves his ship, I countered. *If it was just ego, I'd expect a life-sized painting of himself.*

Ego isn't necessarily narcissism, Hashi.

Says the necromancer who decorated his keep with the bones of thousands...

I'm a minimalist; what can I say?

I followed the butler through familiar halls, glancing through open doors. Workers spread rugs and hung more tapestries, arranged furniture, hung paintings. The place was a work in progress. He opened a door and ushered me into a fully redone room, festooned with comfortable furnishings, paintings of ships, nautical bits and bobs, and a towering bookshelf. Hints of Fornice and Marathia in the carpets and furnishings stood out in the nautical theme.

"Admiral Longbright, Lady Hashi Severn." The butler bowed, and Longbright turned from the windows.

"Lady Severn, welcome, and thank you for accepting my invitation." He bowed shortly, and I noticed he wasn't wearing a sword, though I would have bet long odds he had a blade somewhere on his person.

I certainly did.

"Thank you, Admiral." I made an expansive gesture. "I like what you've done with the place."

"Thank you. My wife's been busy, and I can't help but indulge her whims."

"She's got good taste," I said, meaning it.

And not just in décor, Saraknyal chided. *Don't think I can't tell you're eying him.*

Shut up, old man. Granted, the admiral didn't torture my eyes, in a rugged, weathered, scarred sort of way. He wore a light jacket of royal blue, a frilled ivory shirt open at the neck, and black trousers with a silk strip down the sides, bunched at the cuffs of his boots.

I wore black.

"Can I offer you something?"

"Yes, please. If I remember correctly, Jhavika's chef has a knack for iced tea with mint."

Longbright's eyebrows arched. "He does at that. Brin, two iced teas, please, and tell Preel that Lady Severn's here."

"Straightaway, Admiral."

I strolled to the sparsely filled bookshelf, taking in the diverse titles, everything from philosophy to poetry to history. I spotted a number of titles I recognized. Not what I expected from a pirate. "Your wife's?"

"Both of ours. She's a lover of history. The poetry's mine, mostly."

"She and I have something in common then." I looked over more titles, intrigued, then turned to face him. "I'm sorry, Admiral, but I'm not much for social niceties. You said this was a matter of mutual importance."

"Yes, and it is, as well as a personal one, which is why I'm approaching you alone, not the entire Council." He strode up to stand beside me, just out of arm's reach, his eyes roving over the bookshelf. "You see, I've learned that you're the one member of the Council that I can trust the most with that which I hold most dear."

"And how do you..." Realization struck and I cursed myself for being dim. "Lewin."

"Yes." He turned to face me, his eyes on a level with mine, flinty gray, his mien stony. "He's been most forthcoming, and he understands a great deal of what's necessary to make my relationship with Haven work."

I recalled Lewin's words during the council meeting and nodded. "And you're approaching me because..."

"Because I'm going to be at sea a great deal, and my wife will need someone on the Council she can correspond with to keep informed; someone we can *trust*." He paused as the door opened and the butler entered with a tray bearing two glasses. A woman in a beautiful flowing sari with matching headscarf and veil followed. Two nokitu I recognized from the council meeting trailed her, their dark eyes sweeping the room. I felt Saraknyal tense.

"Ah, Preel, thank you for coming." Longbright gestured his butler to serve, and I took a glass of tea. "This is Lady Severn." Longbright took the other glass, and I wondered why his wife didn't get one.

"Pleased to meet you," I said.

She curtsied gracefully, hands pressed together, her dark eyes cast down. She didn't speak, which seemed odd.

There's magic about her, Hashi, Saraknyal warned. *I can't tell what it is, but it's subtle.*

Her or something she's wearing? I sipped the tea, the cold mint refreshing.

I can't tell. Not without touching her.

"You're from Marathia?" Her eyes met mine, far too dark to be Marathian, and she shook her head.

"Preel's Fornician, and mute from birth. She was raised in Marathia and sold into slavery." The admiral held out a hand to her, and she took it, moving to his side, her shoulder pressed against his arm. "I found her aboard a ship and freed her."

"I see." I didn't, honestly. This exotic young woman gave me chills and tweaked my curiosity. "And then Jhavika abducted her."

"Yes, and that was the straw that broke the camel's back." He smiled to his wife, and her eyes crinkled at the corners. "I contacted you because, in my absence, Preel will need someone on the Council she can get information from. She'll be in contact with me via messenger." His eyes flicked from her to me. "We need someone incorruptible, without any aspirations to power. Lewin assured us that you're that someone. After so many years working for Jhavika, I find that...refreshing."

"I see," I said again, and I thought that I might be beginning to. There was more to the admiral's wife than met the eye, but they obviously weren't going to reveal what that was, and I honestly didn't care. They didn't need a bodyguard, but a liaison with the Council to keep them informed of goings on. "How will she be in touch with you?"

"A small messenger boat. I bought a fishing smack, the *Gull*, seaworthy and fast. Two of my sailors will crew her and deliver messages back and forth. She's small enough to evade any larger ship, and will go unnoticed for the most part. Not worth pirating." He gestured to his wife. "I'll be sending word back with every pirate I sign on, but there are things I'd rather keep confidential. Preel will keep you informed of my progress and whereabouts, and you'll inform me, through her, of developments here."

"That seems simple enough."

"Additionally," he continued, waving one of the nokitu forward, "I'd like you to meet Busashi, my head of household security and captain of my guard."

"I remember you from the meeting." I nodded to the man, and he bowed stiffly.

"His sole job is to keep Preel safe, but there are...other threats that may arise."

Here it comes, Saraknyal said.

"The council members...pose a different kind of danger. If one or more of them make a play to pressure me through Preel, I'd appreciate your...intervention." Longbright gave me a tight smile.

I mirrored his smile. "I'm not going to be your assassin."

"I don't need an assassin, Lady Severn. I need a *deterrent*." He gestured to the world outside the glass doors. "If the Council knows you're my go-to member, and that you're seeing to Preel's safety, they won't make a move like Jhavika did. It's to our mutual interest."

He's got a point, Hashi, Saraknyal said.

The captain's wife withdrew a small notebook from her sari, scratched a quick note, and held it out for me to read. She had an elegant hand. "We simply need an ally on the Council who we can trust not to betray us, Lady Severn."

"An ally..." I couldn't find any fault in their logic, and silently cursed Lewin for opening his mouth and putting me in the middle of this. "Very well, Admiral, in our *mutual* best interest, I'll be your liaison with the Council and keep your wife abreast of developments. If some threat arises, I'll deal with it, either through the Council, or personally."

"Thank you, Lady Severn." Longbright bowed to me, and his wife curtsied.

"But I want to be clear that we're allies *only*, Admiral." I fixed them both with my coldest stare. "This doesn't mean we're *friends*."

Preel's eyes widened slightly and she took a step back.

Longbright met my eyes with a tight smile. "I'm a *pirate*, Lady Severn. We don't *do* friendships, as a general rule. We do, however, make alliances."

"Then we understand one another perfectly." I finished my tea, and put the glass down on a coaster shaped like a starfish. I looked around the room. "My complements on the décor, Mrs. Longbright. It's quite an improvement over the last time I saw the place."

Oh, I don't know, I rather liked the blood-spattered aftermath look, Saraknyal quipped.

Preel curtsied again.

Longbright gestured to his butler, who stood by the door. "I'll be sailing in three days. If you hear any news from the Council, please send a messenger."

"I will."

"Thank you."

The butler opened the door and ushered me out.

That was...weird, Hashi.

The mute magical wife part, or the asking me to keep her safe part?

Both, and he's stupid in love with her, which makes him even more dangerous.

True. I wondered about her, the magic that Saraknyal had felt. *A freed slave? Why would he free a slave.*

Well, she is beautiful.

So are any thousand other slaves, and he's not a torture to the eyes, either. Why a slave?

Don't get curious, Hashi. That's just as dangerous as a pirate in love! He chuckled in my mind.

I couldn't help but smile. Saraknyal knew my obsessive impulses well. *So true...*

Chapter Seven
Sweet Sorrow

From the journal of Preel Longbright —

I don't know what to think of Hashi Severn. Necromancers don't exactly have the best of reputations, but one without aspirations for conquest is unheard of. Then there's Ursula Roque. I know I shouldn't be jealous, but I remember Kevril after that night, how shattered he was. That pain, we shared. I don't want to share it with anyone else.

The soft sod of the lawn met with my backside hard enough to rattle my teeth, even though I'd slapped the earth with my forearm and open palm to absorb some of the impact. I glared up at Ghiti, the single woman among our nokitu, who had taken on my training.

"Well done, mistress." She held out a hand to help me up. "Your timing is improving."

Not enough, I thought, though I couldn't speak through the gag. I took her hand, then, on impulse, feigned a slip and lashed out with both feet at her ankles. *Scythe cuts wheat.*

Her ankles weren't there.

Ghiti flipped over me, still gripping my hand. I pulled hard, trying to trap her arm with my legs—*Serpent climbs tree*—but her other hand slapped aside my attempt. I used her momentum to lurch up to one foot, the other lashing out as she landed. *Serpent strikes stork.*

She blocked my kick, but late, and the edge of my foot struck her in the ribs. I felt the shock of the impact up my leg, even though I'd tried to pull the blow. Then she broke my grip on her hand, twisted, and lashed out with a foot to sweep my ankle. My ass hit the turf again.

"Excellent, mistress!" Ghiti smiled and held out a hand again.

"You're improvising!"

This time I let her pull me up, and pantomimed that I was sorry for kicking her so hard.

"No matter, mistress. I'm not hurt." She flowed into a guard pose, one foot out, the other supporting her weight, hands poised in *Dragon Takes Wing*. "Your blows are strong, but need more focus. The kick should have broken my ribs. Now, assume the proper counter position."

As I assumed *Crane Meets Dragon*, a piercing whistle drew my attention to our balcony window. Kevril stood there, raising a hand to wave.

I smiled behind the gag and relaxed my posture, raising a hand to wave back.

A blur of motion, and a claw-like hand appeared at my throat, fingertips resting on my larynx.

"Never lose focus, mistress," Ghiti chided sternly. "Your attention must be on all things always. Readiness is a constant state. See far when close, and close when far. Practice this." She straightened from the strike that would have killed me, and bowed, formally ending our sparring session.

I nodded, well rebuked for my lapse, and waved to Kevril. It was time.

He'd come home early. *Scourge* would sail in the morning, and we had one last evening together. I pantomimed to Ghiti that I needed to go.

"Of course, mistress. You're progressing quickly. We'll continue tomorrow."

Tomorrow...when I'll be alone. I banished the thought and started for the keep, my ever present shadows at my heels. I hated the constant escort a little, but I'd also come to take some comfort from their presence. They were quiet, unobtrusive, and ever vigilant.

As I climbed the stairs to our suite, I remembered that Kevril had met with Ursula Roque today, and my stomach clenched. Why that woman intimidated me even more than Hashi Severn, I didn't know. I'd never even met Roque. I suppose it was jealousy, but I knew I had nothing to worry about in that regard. I wondered if I'd have been as jealous of Ghetashi Temuso if he'd survived. Probably so.

Oh, what bitter seeds you've sown in my soul, Jhavika...

I entered our suite just as Kevril emerged from the washroom, wrapped in a robe and drying his hair. He smiled, and I tapped the gag.

"Hello, love." He removed the gag and kissed me. "You took quite a tumble down there. Are you all right?"

"Fine. Bruised, but it was worth it." I brushed the grass-stain on the seat of my pantaloons. "I got a touch on Ghiti! That's a first."

"You're learning fast." He kissed me again and strode for the bedroom. "Not *too* bruised, I hope. We've got a big night tonight."

"Right. The pirate revel." That, I was looking forward to. A last chance to see the whole crew before they sailed away. "How did your talk with Roque go?"

"Oh, fine. She was mortified when I told her I was already ensorcelled when we first met." He shook his head. "She's having issues, but recovering. She was in Valaka when the scourge was destroyed, and went a little crazy. Got roaring drunk and woke up days later in the red-veil district."

"She's lucky to be alive."

"Yes, and she knows it now. She saw Temuso die at the ball, and it... She begged her people aboard *Peony* to kill her, but they wouldn't. Talking through it all helped, I think."

"Good." If there was one thing I knew well was the feeling that death was your only escape. I had scars on my wrists as a result. I kissed my husband and went to the washroom.

The cascade of cool water took my breath away, but soothed my bruises and abrasions. I enjoyed the training, the empowerment of learning to defend myself, but as I progressed to full-contact sparring, my skin had become a tapestry of contusions. Even the softest sponge felt like fire on the scrapes. I shook the water from my hair and pulled the chain to stop the flow. Reaching for a towel, I found Kevril leaning in the doorway watching me with a strange expression on his face.

"What?" I toweled my hair.

"Oh, nothing." He tried a smile, but it faltered. "Just thinking how much I'll miss you, I guess."

"Good." I swaggered up to him and threw the damp towel at his face. "Dry my back."

"Yes, ma'am." He did as he was told, his fingers lingering here and there. "You're taking a beating, love."

"Drives the lessons home." I looked back at him over my shoulder and traced the scars along the side of his face with my fingertips. "Just like your scars do." Kevril had more scars than anyone I knew save Wix. He called them flesh lessons, and now I understood that reference.

"True, though I hope your lessons don't go *that* far." He ran his fingers down my back. "I like your skin."

I evaded his grasp with a laugh. "Not *now*, you pirate. We have guests coming!"

"Yes, ma'am."

I snatched my towel from him and wrapped myself to pad across the sitting room to the bedroom.

I'd had most of my clothes brought from *Scourge*. The outfit I'd picked lay on the bed. I slipped into fresh scanties, a chemise, then the deep blue and gold sari, matching headscarf, veil, and sandals. I checked my look in the mirror, tucked a few errant tufts of hair away, and applied makeup to my truthsayer tattoo. Lastly, I added kohl to my eyes, a pair of pearl earrings, a sapphire necklace, and a dab of scent behind my ears.

"Ready," I announced as I emerged into the sitting room. "What do you think?" I did a turn for him, my sari fanning out in an arc.

"Beautiful." Kevril rose from his chair and put aside the book he'd been reading. He held out his arm to me and grinned. "Shall we, milady?"

"We shall!" I grasped his arm, handed over my enchanted gag, which he duly affixed, and we hurried down to the banquet hall.

Bert and the scullery lads had arrived early, and she engulfed me in her copious embrace. "Lady Preel, you're a sight for sore eyes!" She beamed at me with teary eyes and hugged me again. "The whole crew misses you!"

I blushed, touched by her affection.

She then bustled off to the kitchens and began arguing with our cook. The house staff weren't pleased about being banished from the event, but I'd be doffing my gag for the festivities, and couldn't risk a careless question. The scourges knew better.

As the rest arrived, Hemp greeted me with more reserve, and I took great pleasure in embarrassing him. I tapped my gag and he dutifully removed it, then I kissed him soundly on the mouth. His face flushed scarlet, and he nearly fell down.

The others roared in laughter, including Kevril.

That pretty much set the mood for the evening. We broached casks of wine, rum, and whiskey, Bert brought out four roasted pigs that had been basting all day, and enough side dishes, sweets, and pastries to feed an army. The foremast jacks and janes struck up tunes on flutes and fiddles, and the rest broke out in bawdy sea chanties.

We ate and drank and danced and sang. I capered around the floor in the arms of my husband to the clapping and discordant song of inebriated pirates. I dragged Miko out on the floor and danced with her as well, whispering in her ear that I expected her to take care of my husband, and keep him from doing anything too dangerous.

"Don't you worry, Lady Preel," she assured me. "With you to come home to, he won't be taking any chances."

I blushed and thanked her.

Boxley embarrassed me by calling for silence and reciting a poem she'd written. The verse recounted our trials in destroying the scourge, and featured me prominently, though I don't remember ever being so brave as she painted me. Half the room were in tears when she detailed our arrival back at Shepherd's Keep, my going ashore with Hemp aboard the Dragon Ship, then my headlong dash across the waves to profess my love to Kevril. Under the table, my husband clutched my hand so hard it hurt, but I didn't complain.

The crew roared their approval of her verse, and Kevril proposed a toast to her. "To our youngest and most impetuous officer, Midshipman Boxley! Poet, pirate, and swashbuckling slayer of monsters!"

We all roared and drank and laughed at Boxley's furious blush. I drank a little too much, but I didn't care. I hadn't had such fun in my life. For once, I kicked up my heels among friends without reserve.

When the revel began to wind down, several crewmembers passed out from drink, I took my husband's hand and led him upstairs to the top of the keep's highest tower. There I made love to him under the stars with lightning illuminating the sky in the distance.

Finally, utterly spent, we retired to our room and I lay down on our bed, happier than I ever remembered being in my life. But even that happiness was tempered, for I would wake up alone.

Kevril sat down beside me and ran his calloused fingers through my short hair. "I'll miss you, love."

"Just come back to me." I gripped his hand hard. "Promise me."

"I promise I'll do my very best, love."

That was all I could ask of him. I nodded, fighting back tears. This was the last I'd see of him possibly for months. "Ask me your question, you pirate!"

He nodded and cleared his throat. Much consternation and discussion had gone into this question, taking into consideration the advice of the Council. "Where in the Blood Sea, closest to the city of Hyko, am I most likely to find a pirate captain willing to join Haven's privateer navy?"

My talent took me, arching my back and plunging the world into darkness. The answer tore from my throat and cast me into oblivion. "Twin Capes Harbor."

Chapter Eight
Death Contained

From the journal of Hashi Severn —

I don't know why I'm so intrigued with this puzzle Saraknyal and I are solving. Perhaps it's self-interest, for if the Death Stone is released, my home will be destroyed. I've worked very hard for my place here, and I need to keep it safe. Perhaps, also, locking the stone away shuts a door to oblivion, forever out of my reach.

I lowered the upper half of the containment vessel onto the lower, forty pounds of iron, gold, silver, and lead. It fit perfectly, the seam between the two halves invisible. Hidden latches clicked into place.

Nothing happened, of course. Without the Death Stone to empower the inscribed spells, the thing would remain inert. Even so, the vessel was finished.

Excellent work, my dear, Saraknyal said.

"Thank you." I brushed the dull iron polyhedron with a cloth, wiping off my fingerprints. The facets were blank save for two marks on the upper and lower halves that matched to denote the proper alignment. My hands trembled slightly with fatigue, and my vision blurred, but the task was finished. "I wish we could test it."

It'll work. Trust me.

"Said every wizard the instant before something went catastrophically wrong." I touched the eleven exposed hexagonal panels in the proper sequence and the latches disengaged. Once it contained the Death Stone, even I couldn't open it. Lifting off the top section and laying it aside, I considered the next step. "I'll send a message to Vinchi Tinworthy. I hope they're willing to put this to the test in their mines."

They will. Trust me.

"That's twice you've said 'trust me' in less than a minute. You're creeping me out."

*You live in a keep full of undead, and me telling you to *trust* me creeps you out? You're a strange woman, Hashi.*

"I'm talking to a dagger. How much stranger could I get?"

I stood, stretched my back, and fetched a pen, inkwell, and paper from the shelf. Drafting a succinct yet polite note, I folded and sealed it with black wax, then took it to the door of the laboratory. Two shades stood outside, as always.

"Take this to Tinworthy Keep. Deliver it to Vinchi Tinworthy, none other. Wait for a reply."

"Yes, mistress," the shade growled, taking the note and turning to go.

You may want to delay that delivery until morning, Hashi. Saraknyal sounded amused.

"Why? What..." A glance at the clock told me it was well past midnight. "Shit! Wait!"

My minion stopped and turned.

"Deliver that note one hour after sunrise."

"Yes, mistress," it said, resuming its position beside the lab door, note in hand.

"Thanks, Saraknyal." I started for the stairs up to my chambers, stifling a yawn. "Why did you let me work so late? I'm not going to be worth a..." I stopped at the stairway as distant laughter caught my ear. "What's that?"

Oh, the retainers are celebrating something in the feasting hall. They've been at it for hours.

Celebrating? I checked the date in my head, but I hadn't missed a holy day. *Celebrating what?*

Someone's birthday, I think. I don't pay attention to those things.

More than I do, evidently. I felt strange, and didn't know why. Slighted, perhaps, that I hadn't been included, or at least told it was someone's birthday, but I'd never taken part in any of their celebrations before. I'd always encouraged them to carry on with their lives as they wished, and reiterated time and again that I preferred solitude. I hadn't wished for companionship for almost fifty years, but at that moment, I felt the void within me, not a true pang of loss or longing, but just...emptiness.

How strange...

What is?

"Nothing." I climbed the stairs, forcing my thoughts aside. "I'm just tired."

You should be excited, Hashi. The containment vessel's finished. Take pleasure in your accomplishment! He sounded worried for me, and I almost laughed.

"I am, and I do. I'm just too tired to care right now." I stopped at my door and told one of the shades stationed there to wake me when the message returned from Tinworthy Keep. I deserved to sleep late. Inside, I poured myself a nightcap and changed into a robe, taking a moment to stand on my balcony and unwind my suddenly tumultuous thoughts.

Are you all right, Hashi? Saraknyal asked.

"I'm fine." I sipped brandy and looked at the darkened city, the starry sky, the distant flashes of lightning. *Alone...just how I like it.* "Just feeling a little out of touch, I guess."

You complain when people bother you, then complain when you're not included? What's wrong with you?

"Nothing's *wrong* with me." I thought back to my meeting with Longbright and his wife, my attempt to keep them at a distance, my flat-out refusal of friendship. Then my meeting with Tori, our casual conversation, hours discussing history...how content I'd felt. The void in my soul lay there like a piece of sky without stars. I was better off without the loneliness—I *knew* I was—but something, Tori, maybe, had pointed out that absent piece of me, and now it felt like a missing tooth. Something I hadn't noticed for decades, and now couldn't stop dwelling on.

Something's troubling you, I can tell.

Saraknyal couldn't read my mind, but he got impressions. I considered putting him in the lock box, but reconsidered. He was the only person I had to talk to, even if he'd never understand what was bothering me.

"Nothing you can do anything about, old man. I'm just tired, and my mind won't stop dwelling on things I have no control over. You know how it is."

*I do, indeed. Or at least I *used* to. Now I don't have control over anything, which I've found rather freeing.* He fell into silence for a time, then asked, *Would you like me to read to you?*

A smile tugged at my mouth. "Yes, I think I'd like that. Something light."

Let's peruse the bookshelf, then.

We did, and I picked out a book of fanciful tales. I finished my drink, lay Soul Drinker atop the book on my night table, and slipped between crisp sheets. Closing my eyes, I listened to the necromancer's voice in my mind, not really paying attention to the story, and drifted off to sleep.

Hashi!

I snapped awake to late morning sun streaming into my bedroom, my mind a tumble of half-remembered dreams. "What?"

One of your shades knocked on your door. You told them to wake you when the message from Tinworthy Keep arrived.

"Oh, right." I lurched out of bed, stiff from the previous day's work and still muddle headed. Flinging on my robe, I staggered for the door. Opening it revealed a shade holding a sealed missive and one of my footmen with a tray. The aromas of eggs, ham, cheese, and tea set my mouth watering.

"The reply from Tinworthy Keep, mistress." The shade held out the note.

I took it, and waved the footman in. "Just on the desk there, thank you."

"Yes, mistress. Good morning to you." He placed the tray on my desk, poured tea, and lightened it with milk, as swiftly as I could open and scan the letter.

"Good morning." I sat down, still a little thick-headed, and read. The Tinworthys would discuss the containment of the Death Stone with me at my convenience, and gave me their compliments. I'd draft a response when I had a pot of tea in my belly.

"Anything else, mistress?"

"Um..." I looked up at the young man standing expectantly, white coat, bright eyes, hands folded. "A bath after breakfast, please, and tell Bromish to ready the carriage. I'll be visiting Tinworthy Keep this afternoon."

"Yes, mistress." He bowed and turned to go.

On impulse, I added, "Did you have a good time last night?"

He looked back at me, slightly startled. "Oh, yes, mistress. I'm sorry if we disturbed you. It was Master Joss' sixtieth. I'm afraid we got a little rowdy."

"You didn't disturb me." I smiled and nodded. "Give Joss my compliments."

"Yes, mistress." He smiled, bowed, and left me alone.

I sipped tea and started eating. "Sixty years old..." I remembered the day Joss crawled up to my door and begged to serve me in any capacity. He'd been horribly abused, gelded, and whipped within an inch of his life. I'd never asked what he'd done to be enslaved and punished, and wondered why not. "How the time flies, ay old man?"

Silence...

"Shit!" I'd left Soul Drinker on my night table. I dashed to the bedroom and snatched it up. "Sorry about that. I was half asleep."

I noticed.

I resumed my breakfast with Soul Drinker tucked through the sash of my robe. *I was just thinking how strange it is, Joss turning sixty. He was a young man when I took him on.*

You were young when you took him on.

True. I sipped my tea. *I guess it's strange that I'm old, but not old. I don't feel old, I mean.*

Physically, anyway. You've aged, Hashi, but in a good way. You're not as temperamental and angry as you used to be.

I'm not?

Not even close. You've mellowed with the years.

I remembered my headlong plunge into a mine full of void essence and chuckled ruefully. *But no less foolhardy.*

Well, there is that. Your determination hasn't changed, you just approach it with a more even temper these days.

I suppose I do. I thought again about what Tori and I had talked about, and risked bringing up a dangerous subject. *You've changed, too, you know.*

I suppose I have, he admitted, then added, *It must be the company I keep.*

I snorted a laugh and almost shot tea out of my nose. "Are you saying I have a positive influence on you, old man?"

*Well, I don't know if it's *positive*, but you certainly have an influence. You're an indomitable force, Hashi. Resisting your will is like trying to hold back the tide.*

I took a bite of toast with egg and thought, *Flatterer.*

It's the only weapon I have against you.

You and Tori Blackbriar.

Strange that he hasn't been so bothersome lately.

I think I satisfied his curiosity. We weren't what he expected.

Meaning I'm not nibbling away at your soul, and you're not champing at the bit to jump into bed with him like every other woman in Haven.

Right. I poured more tea and changed the subject. *So, do you think the Tinworthys will balk when they see the containment vessel?*

No. It's a boon for them. They get their mine back, and don't have to slave endlessly and expend resources just to keep the thing contained.

True. A knock sounded at my door. "Come in."

"Your bath, Mistress." Two maids brought in the big copper tub, and several others trooped in with steaming buckets.

"Thank you." I continued eating as they filled the tub and put out soap, oils, and towels. I couldn't help but notice how awake and alert they all looked, no bleary eyes or apparent hangovers, yet they had been up later than I. *Maybe I am getting old.*

Nonsense, Saraknyal chided. *Give it a few hundred more years before you think of yourself as old.*

I tried to think of several hundred more years of life and gave up. By the time I'd had my third cup of tea, the servants were done and gone.

I slipped into water just short of scalding, scrubbed thoroughly, then dried and dressed for my outing. Two shades carried the heavy containment vessel to the carriage on a specially fashioned miniature palanquin. We rumbled across Haven without incident, and pulled up before Tinworthy Keep.

"Lady Severn to see Lord Tinworthy!" Bromish bellowed.

The gates groaned open, and I disembarked. A squad of gnomes in full regalia stood at the entrance to the courtyard, but our carriage wouldn't fit under the arch. I recognized Quikesi Tinkertwine, the keeper of Tinworthy Keep's keys, at the fore of the group.

She curtsied, too round to bend at the waist, beaming with a cherubic smile. "Lovely to see you under so much better circumstances, Lady Severn."

"Thank you, Quikesi." Two of my shades retrieved the containment vessel from the boot of the carriage, and the angular black polyhedron drew stares from the gnomish guards. I ordered the other four to guard the carriage and gestured to the entry. "Shall we?"

"Of course." Quikesi led the way, bustling along at her usual impressive pace.

Maybe we should have put the vessel in a box. It seems to be drawing a lot of interest.

Too late now. I concentrated on not cracking my head on doorways as we wound our way through hallways and chambers to a small banquet hall or conference room. Gnomes aren't much for décor or ostentation, so it was hard to tell the room's purpose. As we entered, a dozen or so gnomes stood from their seats, among them the young Lord Vinchi.

"Lady Severn, good of you to..." Vinchi's eyes widened at the sight of the vessel. "Oh, my!"

"Well met, Lord Tinworthy." I bowed respectfully and waved my shades forward. "I believe I've achieved a solution to the Death Stone problem."

"What exactly is that...thing?" Vinchi's senior advisor, Loremaster Geoil, squinted at the black iron device.

"A containment vessel for the Death Stone." I stepped up and touched the facets in the proper order, then lifted the upper half off the lower. I wasn't worried that they'd memorize the combination. There were about forty million possible sequences. And even if they did, once it contained the stone, it wouldn't matter. "It's enchanted for just one purpose: to keep the stone safe and secure."

"How?" Another gnome stepped closer to peer into the vessel.

Tell him that's a secret, Saraknyal said.

"It's inscribed with three layers of necromantic rune magic." I tilted one of the halves so they could all see the dull luster of the rune-inscribed lead inside. "Silver, gold, and finally lead. The runes reflect and alter the Death Stone's void energy into a sphere of force that's utterly impervious. The trick will be getting the stone inside."

"Lead?" The inquisitive gnome nearest wrinkled his prodigious nose and looked up at me. "That's a problem."

"Why?" I asked.

"'Cause lead melts at a low temperature, Lady Severn." The gnome glanced around the room to his brethren. "The stone's currently kept in the middle of a coal furnace. I'm all fer gettin' the thing out of our mine, but you get that fancy box too close when we open the door, and yer rune magic's gonna run like a honeycomb in an oven."

Shit.

Why didn't we think of that? I thought to Saraknyal.

I'm claiming stupidity. I don't know about you.

I gritted my teeth. "Well, can we figure out some way to move the stone from the furnace to the vessel quickly? Once the vessel's closed it'll be impervious to anything short of dragon breath, so if a little void essence escapes during the transfer, you could neutralize it with fire."

Several gnomes broke out in a clatter of their own language. Fortunately, Saraknyal spoke Gnomish.

They're discussing building some kind of clockwork device to move the stone and clap the lid on the vessel. Sounds complicated.

More complicated than ten thousand necromantic runes etched into three layers of metal?

Probably not.

I raised a hand and cleared my throat. "Please, take your time to discuss this. The stone's currently contained, so this isn't an emergency."

"If I may, Lady Severn," Vinchi interjected, "how long will that vessel of yours keep the stone contained?"

"Indefinitely," I said with a smile of assurance. "The containment field's empowered by the Death Stone itself."

"And why, if I may ask, did you do this?" Vinchi asked, but he looked puzzled, not suspicious.

"For my *home*, Lord Tinworthy." I ran a hand over the angular edge of the open vessel. "This is a more sure means of keeping the stone contained. Haven's my home, and I'd like to keep it that way."

"And what's to keep you from using it as a weapon?" another older gnome asked skeptically.

I barked a sardonic laugh. "Well, first of all, once it contains the stone, nothing and no one can open it. Not even me." The gnome opened his mouth, but I held up my hand. "I don't expect you to trust me in that, but consider the danger of trying to use it as a weapon. If anyone managed to open the vessel, they'd be consumed instantly by void essence. I'd be more likely to destroy myself than anyone else." I smiled at the gnome without humor. "Also, please keep in mind that I don't *need* a weapon. If I wanted power, I'd have taken it already."

"If I may ask," Geoil interjected, "what will happen to the vessel once the Death Stone resides within."

I shrugged. "You mean who keeps it? I could care less."

You should keep it in Ash Keep.

Why? I thought you said it was impervious.

Oh, it is, but gnomes love to fiddle and tinker with things. They'll try to figure out how it works.

Nonsense. They know better than anyone what will happen if they manage to damage it. "You can keep it if you wish. It'll be virtually impervious to harm once the stone's inside, regardless."

Best suggest that they don't tell the Council about this. Think of Malchi's response, let alone Brilla's.

Good suggestion. I relayed that concern, and the gnomes all nodded in unison.

"It's none of their business anyway," Vinchi agreed. "It's Tinworthy business."

"Good." I sighed and gestured to the vessel. "Then all you have to decide is whether you want to keep it here afterward or not, I guess."

The gathering of gnomes muttered in their own language, and I could hear the worry in their tone.

Vinchi's reminding them what you did for the clan, Saraknyal said.

Well, that's better than discussing whether or not to light a fire under my feet.

I don't think they're stupid enough to try that.

Says the necromancer who didn't remember that lead melts, I countered.

Smart ass, he growled.

I suppressed a smile and waited patiently.

The gnomes fell suddenly silent, and about two thirds of them raised their hands.

They've voted to trust you, Hashi.

Voted? I thought Vinchi had final word.

Technically, he does, but he's young enough that his advisers can overrule him.

Interesting. As Vinchi opened his mouth to speak, I held up a hand and nodded to the table. "Thank you for your trust."

The old skeptical gnome glared at me and rattled off something in Gnomish.

He asked if you spoke their language. You should have kept that a secret.

I shrugged. "I understand enough, though I'm not fluent. I won't insult you with my horrible pronunciation." I lifted the lid of the containment vessel and fitted it into place. The latches engaged with a dull clack. "I'll leave this here until you've devised your contraption for transferring the stone. I'd like to be here when the Death Stone's placed inside."

"Why?" the same gnome asked. I didn't think he liked me.

"Because I'm more resistant to the Void essence than you are, and however sure I am that the spells to contain the stone will work, there's always a minute chance of failure."

The hell there is! It'll work!

I ignored Saraknyal. "If it fails, I'll help return the stone to your furnace." I nodded to Vinchi. "If that's all right with Lord Tinworthy."

Vinchi looked around at his elders and several shrugged.

"Perfectly all right, Lady Severn. We'll send a message when we've got this puzzle figured out."

I like that he said 'when' not 'if.'

So do I, old man. I bowed to Vinchi again and said, "I'll await your messenger."

Chapter Nine
Invitation

From the Journal of Preel Longbright —

Brilla is the last person in the world I want to deal with, but a part of my heart cries out for what she's been through. I know how the mind, the heart, memories, truth, and lies, can twist and torment the human soul.

Two days of shopping, reading, decorating, exercising, and training without Kevril in the keep, and I was already getting bored. I discovered a welcome distraction when Lewin noticed I was walking stiffly from a particularly challenging session with my nokitu trainers, and I told him I was just sore.

"One of the maids is trained in massage, mistress. That may help your aches and pains."

I remembered Nala's deft hands and nodded eagerly. The luxury would help distract me, and my muscles were taking a lot of punishment. So I asked for a massage.

They set up a padded table in our sitting room, and a tall maid named Higga, with hair the color of white gold and arms as thick as Wix's, reduced every muscle in my body to jelly. Call me a hedonist if you will, but I'd spent half my life as a slave. I knew pain, I knew anguish, I knew every violation of the utterly helpless.

I deserved this.

So I lay in a state of utter bliss as her deft fingers massaged oil scented with sandalwood into the soles of my feet, thankful for the enchanted gag that prevented moans of ecstasy from escaping my lips, when a knock sounded on the door.

Go away, I thought as Higga ground her thumb into the arch of my right foot.

"Would you like me to answer for you, milady?" Ghiti asked.

I sighed and nodded without raising my head. My nokitu were ridiculously protective, and insisted that they stand guard during my delicious torture session. I couldn't pick out Ghiti's footsteps, but heard the click of the latch and quiet voices. The latch clicked again.

"Mistress, it's a sealed missive addressed to you from House Balshi."

Balshi? I lifted my head from the cushion. Ghiti held a sealed envelope, the crest of House Balshi impressed on the wax.

"I could open it and read it to you if you wish," she said.

I shook my head and pointed to the low table between our reading chairs. I'd read it later. I put my head back down and tried to relax. But what would Brilla Balshi want with me? Kevril had told me of her vehement denouncement of his attempt on Jhavika's life. He thought her experience with the scourge's enchantment might have tipped her over the edge of sanity. But if she hated Kevril, why send a note to me?

"You're tensing up." Higga lowered my foot to the table. "I'm finished here anyway, mistress. Just let me get you a robe."

I didn't want her to be finished, but she was right. My mind wouldn't let me relax.

I levered myself up to my elbows and waited until Higga held the thick terry robe for me, looking away to give me at least the semblance of modesty. That seemed a little silly to me, since she'd already touched almost every inch of my skin, but I permitted the illusion. I sat up and nudged myself off the table into the folds of the robe, the towel that had draped my buttocks falling away. I snugged it tight and nodded my thanks.

"My pleasure, mistress." Higga handed me a towel with a smile. "I tried to work around your bruises."

I nodded to her again and wiped the oil from my hands and forearms. Truth be told, I felt better, more relaxed and languid, than I had in months. Resolving to indulge myself in Higga's expertise regularly, I slipped my feet into slippers and padded across the room to the table where the note lay waiting for me.

Curiosity vied with dread, but I knew that putting off reading it would only make my anxiety worse. While Higga cleaned up the towels and left, I cracked the seal and opened the letter to read.

> Mrs. Longbright,
>
> I would like to invite you to dinner at Balshi Keep two nights hence. I know that your husband, the admiral, is absent, and I hope to provide you with some company and distraction from what must be a tedious time for you. Additionally, I'd like to speak with you about personal matters. We share the experience of being ensorcelled by Jhavika's scourge, and are both recovering from that ordeal. I would very much appreciate your guidance in dealing with our common trials.
>
> I look forward to meeting you in person.
>
> Sincerely,
> Lady Brilla Balshi

Dinner? What the hell? This struck me as beyond suspicious. Brilla clearly hated Kevril. What possible motive could she have for inviting me to dinner?

I dropped the letter and paced the sitting room, trying to decide if I was simply being paranoid, or if my anxiety was warranted. Of course, I couldn't attend a dinner at Balshi Keep, even if I brought half of our guard to keep me safe. I couldn't risk doffing the enchanted gag, which would preclude my eating or drinking anything. But refusing might also be dangerous. How much did Brilla already know about me? Kevril had told me she'd seemed a little unhinged at the council meeting, but not much else. Could her plea for help be genuine?

I need more information, I thought. Fortunately, I had the perfect person to ask.

I took a quick shower, donned comfortable clothes, snatched up the letter, and hurried down to our library. This room was still in the midst of renovation after being stripped clean. We'd given Lewin free rein to purchase whatever books he wanted—More of Jhavika's money well spent—and I'd bought a number myself. He'd also hidden away several important documents and tomes before they could be taken, some of which revealed the locations of Jhavika's hidden stashes. At the time, his interests had been to keep Jhavika's secrets, since he'd still been ensorcelled. Then, when the scourge was destroyed, he kept them hidden on the chance that Kevril would return. We owed a great deal to his foresight.

The library had also become Lewin's office, so when I burst in with my two nokitu in tow, I found him seated comfortably behind a vast mahogany desk, bent over a thick book.

"Lady Preel!" He smiled and stood, his ancient features beaming. "You look as if you've just seen a specter! What can I do for you?"

I tapped the gag and rounded his desk, turning so he could reach the knot.

"Of course." He untied and handed me the swath of enchanted silk. "Now, what can I—"

"Brilla Balshi invited me to dinner at her keep." I handed him the letter and began pacing. "I can't go, of course, but I need to know everything you can tell me about her. Why would she want to speak with me when she hates Kevril? I'm not buying her plea for commiseration."

He read through the letter with a furrowed brow. "Hmm, yes, this *is* suspicious."

"As of twelve days ago, she didn't know of my talent. If she finds out, we're in trouble."

"Well, she may be thinking to use you against the admiral." He sat back down and dropped the letter on his desk. "She was very close to Jhavika, but wasn't privy to most of her secrets, of course. Jhavika seduced her by arranging her husband's death, then lashed her with the scourge and—"

"Captain Nightspinner?" I clenched my arms around my middle and shivered at the memory of that vile man, my fifth and final master.

Lewin looked surprised. "You know of him?"

I smiled grimly. "All too well. I used to be his *property*."

The sage's surprise transformed to shock. "*That's* where Admiral Longbright found you?"

"Yes, chained in Nightspinner's cabin." I barked a sardonic laugh. "It's ironic, really. Brilla actually *owes* Kevril for the death her husband, though Jhavika gave the order. Nightspinner had just discovered, using *my* talent, that his dear unfaithful wife was having multiple affairs with other women." I would have felt sorry for the man's situation if he hadn't taken his anger out on me.

"Well, you seem to know somewhat about Lady Balshi that I didn't, then." Lewin cleared his throat. "Brilla hated her husband and her brother for arranging the marriage when he knew she preferred female company. Jhavika commanded her to love her. I imagine having that enchantment broken has left her in a state of near breakdown, much as it did her concubines."

"But she didn't know about *me*." I tapped my lips with a finger. "*Could* she simply be trying to follow in Jhavika's footsteps? Use me as a lever to control Kevril?"

"It's definitely possible, if not murder you outright to torment him, but I think she may simply be curious about you. Perhaps even jealous. Brilla was present when Jhavika discovered you'd been rescued, right from under her nose, so to speak." He shook his head. "Jhavika's reaction was...beyond drastic, and she was cruel to Brilla."

"Cruel to her how?" I asked.

"Brilla tried to talk her out of...executing Nala and Binsh for allowing your rescue. She knew the scourge was making Jhavika into a monster, but still loved her, so..."

I'd known Nala and Binsh were dead, but not how they died. "So, Jhavika punished her for it."

Lewin's jaw clenched. "She forced Brilla to watch their deaths and take pleasure in it."

I caught my breath. "The ruthlessness of a dragon." I shook my head, for I knew the anguish of being forced to love a monster. "Gods, it's a wonder the woman's sane."

"Indeed, but my point is that Brilla may be curious why Jhavika reacted so violently to your rescue. She'd already lost her hand and her scourge, mind you, but finding you gone pushed her over the precipice." He pursed his lips and tapped the letter with a finger.

"Damn!" I resumed pacing. "I have to decline the invitation, but I don't want to tip her off that I'm suspicious or make her angry."

"Mistress?" Ghiti stepped forward and bowed stiffly. "May I make a suggestion?"

"Of course."

"Eliminate her," she said without a hint of emotion. "You have six nokitu in your service. Use us for what we were made to do."

The thought of assassinating Brilla Balshi turned my stomach, but Ghiti had a point. Nokitu were consummate assassins, but Balshi Keep would be a difficult killing field, and Brilla had an army. "I'll keep that in mind as a last resort, but there could be problems. If word got out that I had a council member killed, there'd be hell to pay."

"Yes. The operation would have to be executed cleanly," Ghiti agreed.

"Send Busashi to my sitting room later, and I'll discuss it with him. For now, we'll try a more subtle approach." I turned to Lewin. "I'll send her my regrets and explain that I'm mute, and a face to face meeting is pointless. I'll offer to correspond by letter."

"I doubt she'll be satisfied, but there *is* another option," Lewin said. "You could notify Lady Severn that Brilla's making herself a nuisance."

I tapped my lips with a finger again. "Well, this *is* a Council matter. I could just tell her that I'm suspicious of Brilla's motives, that I'm worried she might use me for leverage. That's exactly the kind of threat we told her about."

"Indeed it is, and Brilla Balshi has no love for Hashi Severn."

"Oh? Why not?"

"Well, some years ago, Brilla's father and two other council members tried to move against an upstart young necromancer. Hashi slapped them down rather emphatically."

"She did? That's..." I swallowed hard. I knew Severn had cut through Jhavika's entire house guard while rescuing the kidnapped heirs, but this seemed impossible. "She took on *three* houses alone?"

"She showed remarkable restraint, actually, and only resorted to violence with two. But she turned the elder Lord Balshi into a shade right in front of his two children." Lewin sighed. "I don't think Brilla ever recovered from that experience. She's always been a little...unstable."

"Wonderful." I rubbed my eyes. "Well, if Brilla's following in Jhavika's footsteps, maybe the Council will be able to do something without violence. Threaten to...sanction her, or something."

"Perhaps so." Lewin didn't sound convinced. "I'd advise you leave that up to Lady Severn. She's careful and powerful, and will know whether to involve the Council or simply warn Brilla off."

"I'll send a letter to Lady Severn, then. I'll want your help with the wording. I'm not much for diplomacy."

Lewin smiled. "You're learning quickly, milady."

"Thank you, but don't hesitate to tell me if I'm about to do something foolish." I held out the enchanted gag to him. "Sometimes I need to just keep my mouth shut. One misspoken word in Haven could be deadly."

"Indeed, milady. Caution is always the best strategy when dealing with powerful psychopaths. We both have experience in that practice." He smiled, took the gag, and tied it securely.

I nodded my thanks and left the library. I had letters to write. I thought about sending one to Kevril as well, but decided to wait until I had some solid information. Knowing my pirate husband, he'd throw caution to the wind, sail back to Haven, and run Brilla Balshi through with his cutlass.

Chapter Ten
Pirate Diplomacy

From the diary of Kevril Longbright —

I never thought of myself as a diplomat until I realized that a ship and crew is very like a small independent monarchy governed by her captain. One cannot be a tyrant, for therein lies revolution, revolt, mutiny, and a dance from a yardarm. So, the answer is diplomacy.

I peered through my spyglass and smiled at the sight of the corsair anchored in Twin Capes Harbor. *Right again, love.* But then again, Preel's talent had never once been wrong. My heart ached with sorrow and guilt, but four days of beating into the squalls of monsoon season had eased the pain; she was safer in Haven.

Other than that loneliness, my mood was surprisingly good. I felt at home once again; salty, unshaven, and pleased with my crew. The simple routine of standing watches, educating Boxley and my two new midshipmen—an Islander boy named Chigga, and a Toki lad Pokiri, both experienced seamen but barely literate—and letting Hemp and Bert spoil me rotten had put me back in the right frame of mind for our mission.

"She's *Blood Raven*, sir!" Boxley cried out from the main top. "Red crow on a black field!"

"Red Moll," Miko muttered, making a face. "Could be *worse*, I suppose."

"Could be much worse." I knew Red Moll. We'd even tussled with *Blood Raven* once, an argument over who had spotted a fat Sariff galleon first. We'd both left with minor damage, but no real harm, and the galleon had gotten away. "I'm sure she doesn't hold a grudge."

"She's a hard one, but no fool," Miko said, then cast me a look. "Just don't pick a fight."

"I don't need any new scars, Miko." I scanned the rest of the anchorage, but *Blood Raven* was the only corsair in port. "Chigga, hoist a parlay flag, if you please. Boxley, keep an eye on them! Rauley, take us in under reefed tops'ls and tris'ls only. Not too close to *Blood Raven*."

I watched *Blood Raven* for signs of activity, but could see little from the lower deck. The harbor bustled with activity, small cargo ships and smugglers, fishing cogs offloading to canoes, and locals diving for lobster and shellfish. Two more canoes lunched from the beach and started toward us, the usual welcoming party.

"Their captain's at their taffrail, sir!" Boxley called down.

I pointed my glass back at *Blood Raven* and spotted Moll's mop of red hair. Two other officers stood by, but the decks weren't busy, only a lookout aloft. As our best bower splashed into eight fathoms, and *Scourge* fell off the wind to ride on her mooring, a white flag ascended the corsair's mizzen.

"Well, at least she's willing to talk." I snapped my glass closed and called out, "Lieutenant Kivan, take a launch over to *Blood Raven*, and ask Captain Moll if she'd meet me ashore at a place of her choosing."

"Aye, sir!" She snapped an order to splash a launch, and sent a crewman to her cabin to retrieve her dress jacket and sword.

"And Kivan," I called as she descended to the middeck, "be polite."

"Always, sir!" She saluted and grinned. "I don't need any new scars either."

I nodded and waved her off.

"She's recovering nicely," Miko said in a voice pitched so only I could hear.

"Indeed she is." Kivan had scars that I wouldn't want to bear, and the worst weren't on her back. Being nailed to a capstan and skinned, refusing to break under Jhavika's questioning, had changed her, but hadn't broken her. "She's tougher than she looks, that's for certain."

The launch splashed, and crewmen slid down the davit ropes to secure the craft and take oars from the deck. Kivan snapped orders and followed her crew down into the boat.

"A few more years, she'll be ready for her own ship," Miko said.

"Indeed." I watched the launch strike out for *Blood Raven*, Kivan at the tiller, back straight, her dark braid flapping in the breeze. I turned to Miko and fixed her dark eyes with mine. I'd been considering how to broach this subject with her, and she'd just given me the perfect opportunity. "About that; Haven's going to need captains. If Sariff signs on, and the Council buys a few new hulls, you should take one."

Miko made a face and opened her mouth to protest, then stopped and shrugged. "Think Kivan's ready to be first officer?"

"As ready as you were when I took command of *Scourge*."

She barked a laugh and shook her head. "That's not saying much. I was pretty green."

"My point exactly. You rose to the occasion. So will Kivan. I can see it in her."

"So can I, and she idolizes you." Her eyes narrowed at me.

"I think Jhavika was more defiance than loyalty. Maybe both." I shrugged. "Now if I can only get *Hemp* to stop complaining."

She laughed. "Good luck with that."

"Kivan's talking to Moll, sir!" Boxley called down.

I raised my spyglass to watch. Kivan stood in the launch, and Moll at the rail of her quarterdeck, two grim pirates at her sides. I couldn't see Kivan's face, but Moll looked stern. Finally she nodded, checked a pocket watch, and spoke again. Kivan gave her a respectful salute, sat, and ordered the launch back.

"Well, that was quick," Miko said.

"If Red Moll's anything, she's decisive."

"Locals commin' alongside sir," Boxley called down from above and I turned to greet the two long canoes of waving islanders.

"Come on down, Boxley!" I waved to the lead canoe as a strapping man wearing a loincloth, enough jewelry to put a duchess to shame, and more tattoos than half of my crew combined, stood and waved.

"Greetings Captain! You come to trade, to sell, to enjoy yourselves?" The man grinned and waved at the canoe's crew and cargo. Half were women, as scantily clad and tattooed as their spokesman, and the craft was packed with trade goods, from iguanas, to parrots, to livestock.

"Here to parlay with *Blood Raven* and the Council of Chiefs. I bring news."

"I'll tell them. Maybe you make party before you parlay?"

I noted my crew lined up at the rail making eyes at the admittedly alluring men and women in the canoes. Islanders were famous for their uninhibited revelry. "Maybe ashore." I waved off the welcoming party—much to the dismay of my crew—and glanced back toward our approaching launch. Kivan was smiling. "Good news, I think."

"Don't count your eggs before they're in the pudding, Admiral." Miko scratched a stay for luck as the launch came alongside and Kivan clambered up the boarding ladder.

She flashed a salute and a grin as she trundled up the steps to the quarterdeck. "She's a straightforward woman, sir. She said, 'Bloody fine! The Blue Manta at sunset, and tell Longbright he's buying.'"

"Good!" I'd already decided who would go with me to negotiate with Moll. A balance of brute force and surprise seemed the best line of attack. "Wix and Boxley, you'll accompany me to the Manta. Rauley, get a launch ready. Hemp!" I'd seen him lurking on deck, and he dashed up the quarterdeck steps, grinning like a fiend. "Clothes and weapons. Nothing fancy."

His face fell. "Oh, *aye*, sir! I'll pull some rags out of one of the scullery lads' footlockers! *That'll* make a good impression!" He stomped off, muttering curses.

"And I get to sit aboard *Scourge* and worry, I suppose." Miko glared at me, but only half-heartedly.

"That's your job, Miko." I grinned evilly at her and lowered my voice. "You *sure* you don't want your own ship?"

Twin Capes City, like most Islander settlements, was a glorious, chaotic, mess. Wooden buildings with thatched rooves—most without proper walls, but grass mats that rolled up and down—

formed crooked avenues. Bustling people filled the sandy streets, buying and selling provisions and pirated goods, goats and pigs miring our boots, naked children running in squealing throngs, and Islanders painlessly fleecing every shore bound sailor for every coin in their pockets. The sailors, of course, knew they were being fleeced, and enjoyed it to the hilt.

"Hells and heavens, I miss this!" Wix caught a beautiful Islander lass as she leapt up and wrapped her arms around his bull neck.

"You take me home, big man! I good for you!" She grinned and kissed his cheek. "I like scars!"

"Maybe later, lass! And hands off!" Wix swatted her hand away from his belt pouch and tossed her away with a laugh.

"Sure, sure!" She landed gracefully and scampered away with a smile.

I had spent many of my formative years carousing in such cities. They were safer than Haven, certainly, but offered fewer amenities and just as many ways to get robbed. Boxley, I noted, knew to keep one hand on her pouch and the other free to fend off the locals. She still looked incongruous to me in her blue officer's jacket, such a narrow frame and girlish face, but she knew how to use the dagger and boarding axe at her hips.

We worked our way uphill into a more sedate neighborhood, with larger buildings, open air eateries, chandleries, markets, smoke and the scents of grilling meat filling the air. The Blue Manta was hard to miss, a towering building of rough-cut timbers with a placard the size of a longboat emblazoned with a blazing blue manta ray in the stylized Islander motif. We stepped into the shade and I removed my hat, pausing a moment to wipe the sweat from my brow and scan the massive common room.

An open stone pit fireplace dominated the space, two huge pigs roasting on spits there tended by burly men with machetes. Heat, scents, laughter, and music filled the air. Islander men and women danced and served at the same time, while trollops offered their wares, dragging inebriated sailors upstairs.

"Eyes front, Boxley," I chided, as a beautiful young man sidled up to her, his bare chest gleaming with sweat.

"Eye, sir!" She fended him off and stayed close.

"Longbright!"

The shout snapped my attention to the back corner of the huge space, and I spotted Red Moll seated at a table festooned with tankards. A lithe young man sat on her lap, feeding her from a platter of roasted pork. Three of her crew sat with her, and it looked like they'd been here a while. We worked our way to the table, and she nudged the trollop off her lap and stood.

"Good to see you, Kevril!" She held out a hand with a lopsided grin. Her grin was lopsided because an arrow had severed the nerves that controlled half the muscles of her face. "Word is you've been stirring up trouble!"

"No more than I can handle." I shook her hand firmly and nodded to the table. "Looks like you started early."

"A well-deserved respite." She gestured to the empty seats. "Have a seat and buy me a drink!" Her eyes lingered on Boxley. "Putting children on your quarterdeck now, are you?"

Boxley opened her mouth, but I silenced her with a look. "Careful, Red. Boxley's in training, but don't judge her by her size." I waved over a server. "She's quite capable, and in fact saved my life *and* Wix's not long ago."

"Oh?" Red cocked an eyebrow as the server filled tankards. "How'd she do that?"

"By killing Jhavika Keshmir." I raised my tankard to Boxley. "Jhavika was the one who started the trouble you've probably heard about. She tried to take all of Haven. I tried to stop her, and she tried to hunt me down. She lost." Bringing up magic wouldn't help the negotiations. "But not before she killed several council members and pissed off both Toki and Mati by putting a spy in the God Emperor's palace."

"Fucking hells!" Moll's eyes narrowed, her smile melting away. "And now you work for Haven's Council? I heard you worked for Keshmir!"

"It's complicated, but Jhavika stepped over the line and the Council's trying to pick up the pieces and plan for the shit-storm to come." I drank deeply and sighed. "I won't lie to you, Red. It's gonna be ugly."

She frowned and drank. "So, why tell me?"

I'd known that question was coming and had prepared. "Answer that yourself. How can the Blood Sea survive an alliance between Toki and Mati?"

Her frown deepened. "It can't."

"Not in its current state, no." I had to get her to see the answer.

"And there's no way in all Nine Hells you can unify the city states. And pirates like us...well." She gestured to the raucous room. "We're not exactly good at organizing."

"True on both counts, but what about a simple agreement to work together. I mean we all trade with one another already, and pirates prey on every city state's shipping the same. Toki can't fight piracy because they can't catch us, but if they subjugate each and every city state one at a time..."

"We'd have no place to hide, much less anywhere to sell our plunder." She drank and glare at me. "Stop pussy-footing and tell me what Haven's got up their sleeve, Kevril."

"Two things." I gestured to the room. "First, I'm recruiting pirates for a privateer fleet, a unified force is the only way to face down armadas from Toki or Mati."

"A *navy?*" Moll sneered and so did her companions. "That'll never happen."

"Not a navy in the conventional sense, but privateers. Every captain's on their own, and if they decide they don't like how things are going, they can sail away."

"But standing against the Toki navy..."

"Once again, we wouldn't be fighting a conventional war, and we know the Blood Sea better than they do." I raised my tankard to her. "But it's not all stick and no carrot. Each captain would gain two boons from joining: special treatment in Haven, and use of their brand new shipyard for repairs and maintenance at low or no cost."

Red's scowl turned introspective. "They built a *shipyard?*"

"A *repair* yard, yes, with a haul-out cradle and skilled workers." Well, they were building it, and the cradle might be ready by the time Moll arrived.

Moll looked incredulous. "Well, fuck me on a pony!"

Boxley snorted a laugh, coughing and spewing ale at the epithet. Wix chuckled and clapped her on the back.

"What's the second part?" Moll asked.

"We want to approach all of the larger city states to form a protectorate. Not any kind of unification. Everyone remains independent, but agrees to support the defense of the Blood Sea as a unified force. This, of course, would earn them favored trade status and immunity from piracy by our privateers."

"A protection racket." Moll nodded, then frowned again. "Sariff's the bugger, you know. They don't like pirates."

"True, and we're already sending one of our less piratical captains to speak to the Jaguar King." I emptied my tankard and waved for a server. "They suffer from piracy, and would gain a lot by joining. Carrot and stick, you know. They also already have a navy."

"If you want to *call* it a navy." Moll drained her tankard. "Not a single decent sailor in the lot!"

"True, but they have resources and a can build ships." I grinned at her. "And I'm sure we can teach them some proper seamanship in time."

She smiled at me. "You want me to sign on."

"Yes, I do. You're level-headed, experienced, and nobody's fool. As a show of our sincerity, each captain who joins gets their ship hauled and serviced free of charge the first time."

Red scowled at me once again. "Gotta talk it over with my crew, Kevril, but I must say I saw this comin' for years. Sooner or later, Toki, Mati, or even Sariff would try to take over the Blood Sea. It was inevitable."

"Yes, it was. I just hope we can slap them down. It all boils down to naval power, and we know the waters better than they do."

"Aye, but they've got komei and magic and fuckin' *fleets* of ships." She shrugged. "Like I said, I'll talk it over with my people and let you know tomorrow." She levered herself to her feet and stuck out a hand. "Either way, change is coming."

"Aye, whether we want it or not." I stood and shook her hand. "I'll wait for your word."

She nodded and we left the table, my thoughts trundling ahead to my other task while we were in port: approaching the chiefs who ostensibly governed the city and the island.

"Captain?" Boxley tugged my sleeve as we wove our way

through the crowd of drunken sailors and reveling islanders. "Might we get shore leave while we're here?"

I looked down at her and noted her eyes fixed on the young man who had propositioned her earlier.

"Didn't you get enough shore leave in Haven?" I asked.

She wrinkled her nose. "Too much shore leave? I don't know what that *means*, sir."

I laughed and clapped her on the back. "Maybe I'll send you out with Kivan and some of the lower deck. It wouldn't do to let Moll's crew think we're not proper pirates, after all."

"Oh, aye, sir! I promise to keep up *Scourge*'s good name!"

"Bad name, you mean," Wix added, tousling Boxley's hair.

She swatted his hand away, but only earned a chuckle from my bosun. Midshipmen earned respect from the lower deck slowly, and even though Boxley had done well, she still had far to go. I smiled, but then remembered the midshipmen before her who hadn't lived long enough to truly earn the respect they longed for.

Chapter Eleven
A Delicate Operation

From the journal of Hashi Severn —

Damn Tori Blackbriar for putting a notion in my mind that I cannot let go of: Am I damned, or am I not? Do I trust a 2000-year-old elf, or am I being manipulated? I feel like I'm painting myself into a corner.

I stepped down from my carriage once again in front of Tinworthy Keep to be greeted by Quikesi and a number of guards. The time had come to imprison the Death Stone, and I didn't know now if I had created this containment vessel to keep Haven safe, or to keep the temptation of oblivion forever out of my reach. If I *wasn't* damned, however, oblivion offered less allure.

"Are you all right, Lady Severn?" Quikesi must have noticed the lapse on my face.

See, I'm not the only one who's noticed. You're acting strangely, Hashi.

Saraknyal had been bugging me ever since we dropped off the containment vessel. Without a lot to occupy my time, I'd tried to return to my usual pastimes of reading and working on antiquities. The note from Preel Longbright took me all of two minutes to answer—an emphatic "Don't trust Brilla. She hates your husband, and will try to hurt him through you." With few distractions, my obsessive mind went on a binge of worry. I wondered about Tori's motives—was he lying or not?—Saraknyal's—overprotective or manipulating me?—and even about my own—damned or not?

"I'm fine. Just daydreaming." I tried to smile but failed, and covered it by turning to order my shade escort. "Guard the carriage. Bromish, I may be a while. You should wait inside the carriage."

Squalls had been raking through Haven off and on all day, drenching the streets without warning.

"Thank you, mistress!" He clambered down and stepped inside the carriage with a nod and a smile.

I followed Quikesi through the keep to the back courtyard where a contingent of gnomes met us. Vinchi stood among his senior advisors and beamed at my arrival.

"Lady Severn! Excellent to see you. Our endeavor is ready!" He positively bounced from one foot to another while all those around him remained stoic and somber.

"Good." I liked Vinchi for his enthusiasm and willingness. For a young man who had recently lost his father and mother, he seemed amazingly well adjusted. Maybe gnomes handled grief differently than humans. "Will you watch with me?"

"Alas, we can't risk the heir's safety, Lady Severn." Loremaster Geoil put a restraining hand on his ward's shoulder. "Our foremost engineer, Sithsle Tinworthy, designed and built the devices to aid the transfer of the stone. He'll supervise." He gestured to a gap-toothed old gnome. "There should be no mishap, but, as you stated, there's always the chance of something going wrong."

*Only if it goes wrong with *their* contraption. Our vessel will work just fine.* Saraknyal had given me hell for telling the gnomes there was a chance of failure.

"I understand completely." I gestured to the open doors of the mine and swallowed my trepidation. "Master Sithsle, shall we?"

You seem awfully eager for this, Saraknyal said.

I just want to get this over. Once contained, forever out of reach, I'd be free of the temptation to use the stone to escape my doomed afterlife. If, in fact, I was doomed. I suppressed the urge to silently curse Tori for putting that notion in my head. Saraknyal would hear it.

The mines were as I remembered them, but brighter. The gnomes lit the entire place with low-intensity glow crystals. Memories of my headlong plunge into this hole in the mountain loomed in the back of my mind like a fog of Void essence. As we neared the chamber with the flue, heat began to build. By the time we arrived, sweat had begun to bead on my brow and dampen my shirt.

I wiped my forehead and grinned to the engineer. "I should have realized it would be hot in here."

Sithsle snorted a laugh. "Your pardon, Lady Severn, but this ain't nothin'. We got braziers burnin' below to keep the Void essence in check. Might be a bit uncomfortable for ya."

Gnomes handle high temperatures better than humans. You may want to sit this one out.

I've at least got to open the vessel. I edged over to the ladder and felt the heat intensify. Looking over the edge felt like peering into an oven. "Well, if it's too hot, I'll have to climb back up, I guess."

"Very well." Sithsle and two assistants donned thick gloves and goggles. He handed me a pair of each. "To keep the heat off your eyes. And the rungs of the ladder are hot enough to scorch."

I nodded and pulled on the thick gloves. The goggles were clear glass, and fit snugly. I gestured to the ladder. "After you, Master Sithsle."

He flashed a smile and descended, followed by his two assistants. Several more gnomes would stand by in the flue chamber to assist if needed. I took a breath, grasped the ladder, and slid down.

Well, gnomes do love their gadgets! Saraknyal quipped as my feet touched the floor.

Ten coal braziers stood around the clockwork device the gnome engineers had built to transfer the Death Stone. Heat beat against me in waves, the very air wavering. The containment vessel sat upon a stand, closed, of course, the top half gripped in two large clamps mounted on an articulating arm controlled by one of the assistants. The other assistant manned several levers that controlled another smaller arm that would pluck the Death Stone from the furnace and transfer it to the vessel.

"Ingenious," I said.

"Thanke, Lady Severn. If you'd just open that magic box of yours, we'll proceed." Sithsle moved to the levers that controlled the furnace itself. "Once the lid's off, I'll open the furnace door, and we'll complete the transfer lickety-split."

Lickety-split? Really? Saraknyal chuckled in my mind.

"Right." I nodded to the engineer and moved to the vessel,

doffing one glove.

The heat was making my head swim, my skin prickling to the point of pain. Sweat rolled down my face and coursed down my ribs. I quickly touched the facets of the vessel in sequence and nodded to the engineer controlling the larger articulating arm. I backed away as he worked the levers, watching the arm lift the lid of the vessel. The interior shimmered in the ruddy glow of the coal braziers.

"Ready?" Sithsle shouted.

"Ready, sir!" the two assistants agreed.

The gnome opened the furnace door.

As before, the fathomless black Death Stone hung within a framework of white crystal tines surrounded by coal fire. Void essence and flame swirled in a torus around the stone in a perfect balance of forces.

"Proceed!" the engineer shouted.

"Yes, sir!"

The smaller articulating arm moved with the assistant's deft manipulation of the levers. Four metal tines closed on the black stone, and a chime like a struck tuning fork sang through the chamber. The Death Stone came free. As the arm swung outward, frost formed on the tines of the arm, black mists swirling out from the stone like the tentacles of some ethereal octopus, questing for something living to grasp and feed upon. The tendrils faded to nothing as they writhed outward, and I felt the heat of the room drop suddenly.

Fascinating! Saraknyal's reverent tone brought me up short.

Terrifying, you mean! I gritted my teeth as the arm moved over to the containment vessel, my eyes fixed in awe upon the deathly black stone; oblivion incarnate. Still, the temperature in the room dropped, prickling my sweaty skin. I shivered.

The articulating arm stopped between the upper and lower halves of the vessel, and the gnome gripped the lever that would open the tines. Tendrils of mist touched the rune-inscribed surface of the vessel, and light flared. A sub-sonic hum began to emanate from the layers of enchanted metal.

It's working! The spells have been activated! Tell him to drop the stone! Saraknyal's urgency brooked no argument.

"Drop it!" I screamed.

"Lever's jammed!" the assistant screeched, his eyes wide behind the glass of his goggles. He wrenched on the lever with both hands, and the entire arm jostled. "It's the cold!"

"Shit!" I stood closest to the assistant, so I stepped over, crouched down, reached around him from both sides, and gripped the lever over his clenched hands. "Pull!"

"Aye!" We pulled together, my chest pressed against the gnome's back, our four arms straining.

Chilled metal screeched in protest, and the tines opened. The Death Stone wobbled for a moment, then hung there suspended by the activated magic of the containment vessel's lower half. The assistant jerked another lever to move the arm out of the way, and Sithsle bellowed for the other gnome to close the vessel.

"Yes, sir!" He moved two levers in unison, and the lid of the vessel descended. The two halves met precisely, and a line of light flared where they joined. The latches clicked, and the light vanished.

Silence, save for the roar of the furnace, the breathing of four terrified mortals, and my own pounding heart.

*Well, *that* was fun!*

I laughed and clapped the assistant on the shoulder, grinning down at him as he looked sheepishly back at me. "Sorry for the...um..." Words failed me.

"Oh, no problem at all, milady!" He grinned. "Couldn't have budged that bloody thing without your help! Thank you!"

"Indeed!" Sithsle closed the furnace door and threw the lever that closed the damper. "I didn't ever dream them pullies would freeze up so quick." He peered at the black iron containment vessel. "Seems to be workin', ay?"

"Yes, it does." I stepped over to the vessel.

Place me against the surface, Hashi. I need to feel it.

Sure. I drew Soul Drinker and placed the haft against one iron facet. Arcane words whispered through my mind as Saraknyal cast some kind of spell. A low vibration transmitted through the dagger into my bones. *Is everything working?*

Of course it is. No residual magic at all, just a hum. Everything's perfect.

116

I sheathed Soul Drinker and related this happy news to the trio of gnomes, and they all grinned and laughed.

"Now, I think I'm ready for a cool drink!" I waved a gloved hand in front of my face and gripped the rungs of the ladder. "I'm buying!"

They cheered and laughed as I climbed up the ladder. The flue chamber that I'd thought sweltering before felt like a breath of mountain air, and my tingling skin eased from painful to merely overheated. The gnomes there had heard our cheers and met us with smiles and congratulations. We all trooped out of the mines in good humor, but as daylight loomed ahead realization struck me.

It's done, old man, I thought.

Yes, it is. I told you to trust me.

Yes, you did. I doubted that Saraknyal understood my revelation; oblivion had been forever placed out of my reach. The Death Stone was locked away, and Saraknyal wouldn't consume my soul to prevent Demia's judgment. I was damned, or not. I breathed deep of the sweet, fetid air of Haven.

"All's well, Lady Severn?" Vinchi asked, still bouncing with pent up enthusiasm.

"Everything's fine, Lord Tinworthy. The containment vessel's working perfectly." I gestured to my engineer escort. "I promised your crew a cold drink. I found your mine a little...*toasty.*"

That drew a laugh, and they immediately escorted us all to a small conference room, where cherubic gnome women were already arranging iced drinks. I took a glass of chilled mango nectar and sat, accepting the congratulations and thanks from the massed gnomes with as much grace as I could muster.

Finally, as the buzz of conversation faded, I asked, "Have you decided what you'll do with the containment vessel, Lord Tinworthy?"

"Well..." Vinchi looked to Loremaster Geoil, who nodded. "We certainly have no use for it, other than maybe a great paperweight, and we gnomes, as you may know, have an insatiable curiosity when it comes to deciphering puzzles. It's been decided that the vessel would be safer in your keeping, since you already know how it works, and the dangers of the stone itself, as well as we do."

I nodded, feeling a tingle of pleasure in my stomach that I couldn't quite define. "Very well. I'll take it back to Ash Keep and put it on my desk." I smiled and nodded to Vinchi, then recognized the feeling. "And thank you for trusting me. It means a lot."

*And thank you for trusting *me*, Hashi,* Saraknyal said. *I know you had suspicions about my motives.*

I did, I admitted.

I chatted amiably with the gnomes for a while until several workers finally entered carrying the containment vessel on the small palanquin I'd had made. "Well, thank you all again. I'll be off."

"And we thank you, Lady Severn. You've once again given Clan Tinworthy a great boon!" Vinchi stood and bowed to me. "If ever you need our aid in any regard, all you need do is ask."

I thanked them and went home.

You should put the vessel in the entry hall, Saraknyal suggested as we entered Ash Keep, insufferably pleased with himself. *Maybe on a black marble plinth.*

Your ego's showing, old man, I chided, directing my shades to lug the thing up to my chambers. I asked Joss to have a bath drawn and followed. *Not on my desk, I think, but maybe in the corner. I'll have Hipshill make a nice wrought iron stand for it. I can still feel that low hum when it's close.*

You can? Even when you're not holding me?

I think so. I ordered my shades to pause at the first landing, and stepped up close to the containment sphere. From about a foot away, the subsonic thrum began to rattle my teeth. *Yes, like a low vibration in my bones.*

Interesting.

Why. What is it?

Well, I have no bones, so can't feel anything until you place me against the sphere, but I assume it's the containment spells at work.

You're saying I'm feeling magic? I never have before.

Not magic exactly, but a harmonic of some kind. Not to worry. It's functioning properly.

It better be, or we're both doomed. I directed my shades to put the vessel on my desk for now, and went to my bedroom to get out of my clammy, sweat-soaked clothes. My silk shirt felt like sandpaper coming off. I pulled on a robe, poured myself a brandy, and stood on my balcony while my people prepared a bath. I stared out and sipped, letting my mind wander aimlessly as thunder boomed in the distance.

"All's ready, mistress."

I turned to find maids and footmen departing, everything prepared perfectly. "Thank you."

The last footman bowed to me and the door closed. I strode to my desk, the black dodecahedron thrumming there beside Saraknyal's box.

"I need some alone time, old man." I drew the blade and opened his box.

Why? What's bothering you?

"Nothing," I lied. "I just need to unwind. Here." I plucked a book from the pile he'd been reading and put it in the box. "Don't take it personally. I'm just wound up."

Fine. Saraknyal always got a little surly when I put him away.

"Thanks for understanding." I put him atop the book and closed the lid.

Silence... Solitude... Privacy.

I put a hand on the containment sphere and felt the low thrum of power, oblivion forever out of my reach. *What the hell were you thinking, Hashi.* A pall of dread loomed in the back of my mind, an eternity of torment in Hell...or not.

On impulse, I pulled a sheet of parchment from a drawer and dashed off a note to Tori Blackbriar, inviting him once again to a private chat. I knew Saraknyal would throw a fit, but it would be easier to apologize than to tell him up front. I signed and sealed the note, then took it to the shade standing at my door.

"Give this to Joss and tell him to deliver it to Lord Blackbriar."

"Yes, mistress." My shade strode away.

I closed the door, poured myself another brandy, and dropped my robe. Hot water enveloped me, pins and needles prickling my heat-sensitive skin, tingling close to pain. I wondered if I had a low-grade burn. I sipped brandy and tried to relax, but the discomfort wouldn't abate.

"Damn it!" I rose from the water with a frustrated sigh, the comparatively cool air suddenly soothing on my wet skin. I reached for a towel, then hesitated. The air felt good. A memory—swimming in the river in Tinaros, the cool water leeching the heat from my parched flesh—drew a smile from my lips.

"Simple pleasures..."

I picked up my brandy and strode to my balcony door. The sea breeze caressed my wet skin, leeching away the discomfort. I closed my eyes and soaked it in.

Thunder boomed, and lightning flashed through my eyelids. I lifted them. A white squall tore over the seaward hilltop, bearing down on Haven like the wrath of a vengeful god.

"Of course, because all I wanted was peace and quiet." I glared at the approaching wall of rain and reached to close the doors, then stopped. I looked back. The wall of rain blotted out the seaward hill already, racing toward me over the city, devouring row after row of buildings. People dashed for cover, drew awnings closed, shuttered windows.

I glared at the storm, then grinned. An impulsiveness gripped my soul that I hadn't felt since the day I'd walked away from my mother and stepfather never to look back. A scared girl on the streets, determined and alone. I'd just contained death itself, locked oblivion away forever. I had nothing to fear.

I downed my brandy, threw the empty glass into the void, and strode out on my balcony to grip the wrought iron railing. I grinned at the onrushing wall of white and laughed. "Bring it!"

The chill downdraft from the squall hit me seconds before the icy deluge, ripping the breath from my lungs. Blinding rain struck, a physical blow, so thick I couldn't see the nearest rooftops, so hard it stung, but also so cold that it numbed me. I gripped the railing and laughed, coughing and spitting water when I tried to draw breath. Lightning lit the deluge, static crackling across my drenched skin.

God this is stupid, the rational part of my mind said, but the rest of me wasn't listening.

I'd put death itself in a bottle today. I had nothing to fear in the world. After this world, maybe, but not here. I laughed into the storm and embraced it. I was done with being afraid.

Chapter Twelve
Decisions

From the journal of Preel Longbright —

What question to ask is now my greatest dilemma. Before I met Kevril, that wasn't so; I had no control how my gift was used. Now, with the reins of my power in my own hands, I wonder if I'm not my own worst enemy.

I stared out the sitting room windows at the torrential downpour, lamenting our poor gardens. The frangipanni thrashed, shedding blossoms and leaves, and the thick wall of bougainvillea roiled like a dragon's coils. Rain lashed so hard against the glass that it seeped through the cracks in the door. The grass would be soaked for days, too wet to use for my training.

I thought of Kevril at sea, battling such tumultuous weather, and clenched my hands hard. Gods, I missed him.

"Lady?" I turned to find Ghiti looking at me with concern. "May I make an observation?"

I nodded, unable to answer verbally due to the enchanted gag. I wore it constantly to avoid wasting my talent; I had important questions.

"You're obsessing. You must focus. Still your mind."

I fished my notebook and pencil from a pocket and dashed off, "How?"

"Discipline," she answered without pause or rancor. "The covered balcony is perfect for yamshi, or we can place quilted pads on the floor for sparring. You must focus your mind, vigilance, awareness."

I was already exercising three times a day, and knew it helped, but the constant vigilance seemed pointless. "But I'm safe here?

Vigilance is fine for when I'm out shopping, but here?"

"Yes, *here*, mistress. Vigilance should be constant, second nature. In time, you'll find that it stills your mind, eases your worries. You must learn to focus on your surroundings as you focus on your own body while performing yamshi. See everything. When you master this, all the things you have no control over will fade away."

It seemed impossible, but I'd witnessed the impossible. I nodded. "Yamshi then. I'll get changed."

"Yes, mistress."

I hurried to the bedroom to change. The rain hissed against the balcony windows like meat on a grille. I donned one of my old outfits, but left my feet bare. When I ventured back into our sitting room, however, I found Brindal waiting with a sealed envelope in his hand.

"Mistress, a squad of liveried soldiers delivered this." He held out the missive with a grim expression. "It's from House Balshi."

Shit! I glared at the letter.

"It may not be *bad* news, mistress." Brindal looked hopeful.

I shot him a doubtful look and took the letter. Cracking the wax seal with my thumbnail, I opened it with trembling hands.

Mrs. Longbright,

Forgive me, please. I was unaware of your inability to speak. What I have to discuss with you, however, cannot be trusted to paper and pen. The matter is deeply personal. I'm a powerful woman, and any weakness may be exploited by my enemies, of which I have many. The matter has to do with Jhavika, and that's all I can say. Both of us know what it was like, serving her indomitable will.

Please do not concern yourself that I harbor some grudge against your husband. When he addressed the council, I was still recovering from my long trials at sea. I now realize that he is no more to blame for Jhavika's death than I am to blame for my brother's. We were, all three of us, victims of the same enchantment.

I'll be happy to accommodate you with every courtesy

you require for our meeting, either at Balshi Keep, your own home, or some other place of your choosing that provides adequate privacy.

Thank you for your discretion in this delicate matter.

Sincerely,
Lady Brilla Balshi

Double shit! I cursed. Brilla wasn't taking "No" for an answer.

I tucked the letter away and retrieved my notebook. I wrote, "I must consult with Lewin about this. Yamshi later," and showed it to Ghiti, then Brindal.

"Of course, mistress." Brindal bowed politely.

Ghiti simply nodded.

I nodded my thanks and stalked through the halls of the keep to Lewin's book-filled lair.

"Mistress Preel!" The sage lurched up from his tome-strewn desk with his usual amiable if somewhat bewildered look. "How can I help you?"

A loaded question if ever there was one, I thought, approaching and tapping my gag.

"Of course." He untied it, and I turned to hand him the letter.

"I'm in trouble. Brilla's being...persuasive and unless I'm paranoid, she's tossing veiled threats." I paced as he read.

In time, he said, "She most certainly is, though she promises to be quite accommodating." He put the letter down and shrugged. "You *could* entertain her here, but it would be dangerous in the extreme."

"I don't dare." I continued to pace. "If she comes here, hospitality dictates that I offer her something. If I don't eat or drink, and keep my face covered, she'll be suspicious. If I don't offer her anything, I'm being rude and she could take offense. If I pick some neutral ground, that puts me at risk of another abduction, which I wouldn't put past her. I don't buy her sincerity, but what if I'm wrong? What if she really is simply seeking a shoulder to cry on. If I *do* befriend her, that might smooth over a lot of hard feelings, even help stabilize the Council."

Lewin frowned. "Lady Severn warned you not to trust her."

"Lady Severn could be wrong. Unfortunately, there's no way to know Brilla's true motives."

"Of course, there is." Lewin met my perplexed look with two arched gray eyebrows. "You *are* a truthsayer, you know."

"No, I'd *forgotten*," I snapped, my temper running short. "I thought to reserve my talent for Kevril. He should be at Twin Capes by now, and I wanted to find out where he should go next."

Lewin shook his head. "My apologies, mistress. I know you're concerned for Kevril, but please consider. If we ask where he should next go, and send the *Gull* to inform him of our findings, they won't reach him for at least three days, probably four, considering this spat of ill-tempered weather. Your husband is a capable seaman, and knows his task. He'll also be able to ask the locals of any other pirates nearby, and of the situation in Hyko, which the Council has encouraged him to investigate. The first few weeks of his endeavor are already planned. One question to discover Brilla's intentions won't put your husband in danger."

He was right, and I hated it. If I was with Kevril, this would all be moot. Brilla couldn't touch me, and Kevril could ask me where next to go. "Damn that pirate anyway," I cursed under my breath.

"We could ask some discreet questions about Brilla, mistress," Ghiti suggested.

"Discreet would be the key word there, I'm afraid. If Brilla gets one whiff that I'm suspicious of her, she might fly off the handle." I resumed pacing and bit my lip. "And she's got the biggest force of soldiers in Haven."

"The keep is secure, mistress," Ghiti assured me.

"And if Brilla tried to take you by force, the Council would respond," Lewin added.

"True." I thought about my options, none of them pleasant: Have Brilla killed, which would be dangerous; meet with her, which would be even more dangerous; ignore her, which would make her angry; refuse outright, which might also make her angry; or use my talent to find out her true motives. I might also goad her into doing something foolish, which would invoke a response from the Council, but that would probably end in an armed conflict.

I bit my lip until it hurt. It all boiled down to one thing: to make a good decision, I needed information, and I was nothing if not a font of information by my very nature.

"Fine, we'll employ my talent to find out her motives, but we have to be careful in crafting the question."

"Careful how, mistress?" Lewin wasn't familiar with all my limitations. I'd kept most of them from Jhavika, intentionally twisting her questions to evoke meaningless or ambiguous answers.

"Questions that ask about people's intentions often go wrong. My talent can't look into the future, and can't see variables that haven't come to someone's attention yet. So, if Brilla is merely curious about my experiences while Jhavika held me captive, or if she's subconsciously jealous, or simply distraught, the answer could be just that. Asking motivations is tricky."

"But you asked where Admiral Longbright should go to find someone willing to sign on as a privateer. How is that—"

"No questions, Lewin!" I snapped, whirling to face him. "Invoke my talent now, and we can't ask another for three days, maybe four."

"I'm sorry, mistress." He looked abashed and nodded. "How do you *think* that's different from asking Brilla's intentions?"

"We crafted the question about Kevril's destination carefully to ask only someone's current likelihood of being amenable to joining the privateer navy. If we ask Brilla's motivations, it has to be specific."

"Well, I'm sure we can work something out between us." Lewin's confidence gave me hope, for he truly was a brilliant man.

"May I make a suggestion, mistress?" Ghiti asked.

"Please."

"You shouldn't invoke your talent until this evening. That'll be four days from your previous. You need exercise to calm your mind. This will allow you to think more clearly in crafting your question. You have time. A prompt response to Brilla's letter isn't critical."

Those were all good points, and I had to admit that I felt as if I stood barefoot in a room strewn with broken glass. "All right. I'll do Yamshi, then work with you, Lewin, to craft our question. After dinner, we'll ask."

"Very good, mistress." Lewin smiled and dipped a pen from an inkwell. "I'll begin while you're doing your exercises."

I nodded, and handed Ghiti my enchanted gag. "Please, put this on me. I can't risk an incautious question now."

"Yes, mistress." She tied the swatch of cloth securely and gestured toward the door.

So, I spent the afternoon settling my state of mind. Half an hour of stretching, two hours of Yamshi, an hour of massage, then a warm bath. Languid and comfortable, I sat in the sunroom with a cup of tea, the torrential squalls having finally abated, and watched the gardeners deal with the wreckage of our poor plants while considering the question I would have Lewin ask. When I thought I had it nailed down, I sent a footman to fetch the sage and another pot of tea.

Both arrived in short order.

"Mistress Preel, you look much better!"

I waved the footman out and stood, wondering what I'd looked like before. Panicked, I supposed. I tapped the gag and Lewin removed it. I waved to a seat. "Shall we?"

"Most certainly." He sat and I poured tea for us both. "I think this should be straight forward enough if we don't ask what Brilla intends in the future."

"Intentions are sometimes difficult." I pushed my notebook over to him. "Here are some of my attempts. Please don't read them aloud."

"Oh, of course." He fumbled through pockets for a roll of parchment and handed it to me. "And here are mine."

"Thank you." We both read and sipped for a time, and Lewin nodded repeatedly. His tries were much like mine, all skirting future predictions, but while his leaned toward intentions, mine were more concerned with motivations."

"Yes, I see. This is interesting." He tapped my notebook. "Can you please tell me why you use the word motivations instead of intentions?"

"Because it should give a more in depth answer. If we ask Brilla's intentions for getting me alone, the answer might simply be to speak with me in private. That tells us nothing. If we ask her motivations for asking me to meet with her, we should get more."

"Hmm, yes, I see. Such a fickle distinction." He rubbed his chin with wrinkly fingers. "Tricky, isn't it."

"Very. I've had many masters, and some of them got so frustrated my answers that they punished me. I tried to tell them it wasn't my fault if they asked stupid questions, but that didn't help." I sighed and sipped my tea. "That was how Captain Nightspinner came to find me. My previous master was sick of me. She couldn't craft a good question to save her life, and absolutely wouldn't accept my help."

"You offered to help?" He looked puzzled.

"Of course! Out of self-preservation." I smiled grimly at his puzzled look. "A slave is only as safe as they are useful. A helpful slave is more valuable and less likely to be punished."

"Oh, I see." He shook his head. "Curious, that we were both Jhavika's slaves, but that was so different than your previous slavery. Jhavika only ever punished anyone by having them executed. She didn't need to punish."

"No, she had utter control." I sighed. "She played me like a fiddle, and I didn't even know it until the very end."

"Ah, but you played her, as well, didn't you?" Lewin smiled knowingly.

"I tried, but failed for the most part." I shook my head in dismissal. I didn't want to remember the week's I'd spent as Jhavika's pet truthsayer. "Now, I like this one best, and you have one similar." I marked one on my notebook for him, then showed him his own.

"Yes, I agree. I don't see how it can go wrong."

I chuckled. "You never know how a question can go wrong until it does. Ask Captain Nightspinner that one."

"Ah, yes." He smiled wryly. "How ironic it would be if we discovered Brilla knew that you were once Nightspinner's slave, but thought her husband simply kept you for his pleasure. Maybe she's jealous about that."

"That would be easier to deal with than the truth." I circled the question I'd indicated earlier. "Are we agreed that this is probably our best effort?"

"Yes, and now I see that you really didn't need much in the way of help." He smiled ruefully.

I matched his expression. "I didn't know what you might come up with until I asked, did I? Questions are like that. You never know the answers you're going to get, and you might not like them."

"True enough." He sighed, finished his tea, and stood. "After dinner, then?"

"Yes. I'll send a footman when I'm ready." I felt no small trepidation in this, for I'd be utterly defenseless for twelve hours and my husband was hundreds of miles away. I was putting all my trust in my nokitu to keep me safe.

"Very good, mistress." Lewin gave me a polite nod and left.

I started to pace, then stopped myself. The decision was made; worrying about it now would do no good. I watched the gardeners resurrect our battered plants, wondering how long they would last until the next squall ripped through to hammer them to the ground.

I read a nonsensical book of tales until dinner, ate—Truth be told, I missed Bert's cooking—then told the footman clearing the dishes to send for Lewin. I changed into a nightgown and robe and went to the washroom. Busashi and another nokitu, Whapo, waited in the sitting room with Lewin when I emerged. I nodded and motioned for the sage to remove the gag.

"Yes, mistress." He untied the band of silk and held it out to me.

"You keep it. You'll need to put it back on right after the question."

"Oh, yes, of course." He seemed a little uncomfortable.

"Don't worry, Lewin. I've done this hundreds of times. I'll be fine." I headed for the bedroom.

"Oh, I'm not worried for your safety, mistress, it's just that..." He stopped at the bedroom door, and looked even more uncomfortable. "I'm not used to...this." He waved at the expansive bed. "It seems I'm invading your privacy."

"You're not invading anything." I hung up my robe and climbed into bed, arranging the sheet and crossing my hands over my stomach, my long practiced posture whenever my talent was invoked. "I asked you in, and there's nothing inappropriate." I took a deep breath and let it out slowly. "Now, ask the question we agreed upon, please."

"Yes, mistress." He cleared his throat and fished a slip of paper from a pocket. "Well, then. Here we go. What is Brilla Balshi's motivation for asking you to meet with her in person?"

The question gripped me, as always, arching my back and rolling my eyes. The voice that was not my own tore from my throat in answer. "She wants to know what made me so valuable to Jhavika Keshmir."

As oblivion swept over me, a mountain of dread loomed within my fleeting mind.

Chapter Thirteen
Allies

The diary of Kevril Longbright —

There is something to be said for a proper pirate revel. There's always the fine line of enjoying one's self and maintaining a level of sobriety necessary to avoid serious injury. I wish all negotiations were so simple.

Moll's reply came early the next morning, a note sealed with red wax impressed with the likeness of a raven. I accepted it from Hemp, downed my blackbrew, and cracked the seal.

As usual, Red got right to the point.

> Kevril,
>
> We're in. Blue Manta at Noon to celebrate our partnership and discuss what's next.
>
> Red

"Bloody fine!" I snatched up a pen, scrawled a response beneath Red's signature, and handed it to Hemp. "Give this to Miko for return and tell her to take volunteers for a skeleton crew to stay aboard *Scourge*. We're attending a pirate revel, so issue cutlasses and boarding axes. I'll want one of my less-than-best jackets. One that you won't mind horribly if it gets slashed to ribbons."

He grinned and bobbed his head. "Aye, sir!"

"And sharpen my cutlass."

"Oh, aye!" He turned for the door. "Ain't been to a proper row in years! I'll tell Bert to be ready to deal with the aftermath."

"Good." I finished my breakfast and pulled down a chart. If we weren't too badly mauled from the party, I planned to set sail the next morning. There was one other thing I had to do before we sailed north. I hadn't gotten a response from shore about my request to meet with the Twin Capes chiefs. This wasn't surprising; the usual Islander response to any request was "soon come," which meant what you wanted could happen right away, or two weeks later. I didn't have time to wait, so I drafted a request for an audience that afternoon. With luck, I could cut out of the revel after a couple of hours and approach them with the idea of a protectorate.

More diplomacy... I sealed the note with a sigh and called for Hemp. He arrived before the echo died. "Clear the dishes and have Kivan deliver this letter to the chiefs. I honestly can't remember their names." The ruling families changed chiefs often enough to make memorizing who was who an exercise in futility. "Tell Kivan to find out for me."

"Aye, sir!" He tucked the letter through his belt, piled the dishes, and took my best cutlass down from my locker. "I'll have this shaving sharp in no time, then it's stitchin' and pressin' and airin' out a nice white shirt with frilled cuffs. Gotta show them *Ravens* we ain't a bunch of scrubs!"

I smiled at his muttering and changed into my work clothes, ready for my customary turn on deck. I needed to stretch my legs and work out the stiffness of four days beating into stiff head seas and squalls if I wasn't going to embarrass myself today.

I found Boxley standing watch on the quarterdeck, clearly bored out of her mind and itching to go ashore. Everything aboard had been scrubbed and polished within an inch of its life, and the crew were busy at work on their shoreside gear.

Boxley saluted with a beaming smile. "Heard the news sir! Congratulations."

"Thank you." I scanned the deck but found nothing worthy of comment, and failed. "Anything to report?"

"No, sir. Quiet as a graveyard. Everything ship-shape." She clenched her hands behind her back to keep from fidgeting and eyed me out of the corner of her eyes as I paced back and forth briskly.

I let her stew for a while, then broached the subject she

obviously wanted to discuss. "You've attended a pirate revel before, haven't you, Boxley?"

"Oh, aye, sir, but never as an officer."

"Hmm, yes, well I have to leave someone competent in command of *Scourge* while the rest of us are ashore."

"Oh, um, yes sir, a skeleton crew." She knew full well that generally meant the lowest ranking officer aboard. "But Chigga and Pokiri are—"

"Barely know fore from aft and port from starboard." I eyed her sidelong in passing. "I could wad the three of you together and barely make one decent lieutenant."

"Um...yes sir." She looked down, her lips clenched tight.

I decided to let her off the hook. "Which is why you'll accompany the shore party, and Miko will stay aboard with Chigga and Pokiri to give them some much needed instruction."

Her face split into a grin. "Yes sir! Thank you, sir!"

"You're welcome. Now, as you said, you've never attended a revel as an officer. You're free to kick up your heels, but don't embarrass me, and don't disparage *Blood Raven*. No private business, and no consorting with *Blood Raven*'s lower decks; it's unseemly."

"Of course, sir. Kivan told me how to behave. I promise, I'll make you proud."

"You'll keep your wits about you, and keep in company with at least one member of our crew at all times." I fixed her with a meaningful look. "I'd suggest you and Kivan keep each other company. This isn't Haven, or even Valaka, but you can get knocked on the head here as easily as anywhere."

"Yes, sir! We'll be careful."

"Good." I clapped her on the shoulder. "Now go get your kit ready. Spit and polish, mind you."

"Aye, sir!" She dashed off.

I watched her go with a sigh, wondering, not for the first time, what kind of an officer she'd make. I got a flash of an older Boxley in command of her own ship, standing the quarterdeck, snapping orders at recalcitrant midshipmen, and couldn't suppress a smile.

Please, Odea, let her live that long, I thought to myself as I resumed my pacing.

I strode into the Blue Manta at the head of forty pirates all bedecked in their finest and armed to the teeth. Red Moll must have sent word ahead, for the entire establishment had been transformed for the revel. Tables had been rearranged in the back to clear a space about ten strides square, the sandy floor swept clean. Locals greeted us as usual, smiling and offering tankards and cups, but we maintained our stoic façades.

Red Moll and her crew stood at the very back of the club, grim faced, armed and bedecked as we were. Glares shot back and forth across the open space.

Good thing this isn't serious, I thought, bracing myself for the formalities.

"Well, isn't this just *lovely!*" Moll took a couple of swaggering steps forward, eyeing me like she wanted to tie me to a spit and roast me over coals. "You all look far too *pretty* to be proper pirates, Captain Longbright."

I grinned at her and stepped forward. "It's *Admiral* Longbright, Captain, and don't let our beauty fool you." Granted, I had let Hemp shave me for the revel, but the comment drew some laughs. "And you can hardly call *me* too pretty when you're dressed like a high-priced doxy yourself."

A low "Oooo," rumbled through the amassed pirates at my dig.

She hadn't dressed like a doxy, of course, but certainly cut a fine figure in red leather pants and a matching corset. Her frilly black shirt accentuated her pale skin, and she'd let her hair down.

"*Admiral?*" She shot me a look like I'd just pissed on her shoes. "If you think for one minute I'm going to serve *under* you, you're barking mad." The bawdy innuendo drew laughs.

"Oh, I've been called mad before, Captain Moll, and I'm flexible as far as...positions go." I grinned and twisted my back. "As long as you agree to following orders from your superior."

"*Superior?*" She barked a laugh and drew her cutlass. "Did you just call me inferior?"

Another rumble coursed through the opposed crews, this time

sprinkled with a few lewd epithets.

"Don't get your knickers in a twist, Captain." I drew my cutlass and began to circle. "There's no shame in admitting you're outclassed."

"Ha! Oh, you've just earned an ass-kicking, Kevril." Red Moll grinned evilly and flourished her blade. "And I'm not *wearing* any knickers."

Laughter and more lewd comments fueled the fires of our faux animosity. "Feel free to try, Captain, but I think those pants might be a bit too tight to allow you to kick that high." I saluted her with my blade. "All this talk's making me thirsty! Ale for the captain!" A ready server supplied two brimming tankards and we both accepted. I raised mine to her. "Careful not to spill any, Red."

"I wouldn't waste good ale on the likes of you, Kevril." She raised her tankard and we drank, then she lunged, forcing me to parry.

We exchanged a quick rhythm of thrusts, parries, and reposts, neither of us spilling a drop of ale. The exchange ended with our swords crossed, guard against guard, our faces only inches apart above our blades.

"You're sweating, Admiral," she said, raising her tankard to sip.

"And you're panting like you're entertaining an ogre lord." I grinned and quaffed ale.

She laughed, twisted away, and lunged. I parried easily, but her repost flicked out lightning quick to snag my sleeve. I inspected the damage and cocked an eyebrow at her. "You owe me a shirt."

"And you owe me an apology."

It was a good thing we weren't trying to kill one another, for Moll was deadly quick. I had a few inches reach on her, and some strength, but that wasn't much of an advantage for this type of sparring. We alternated insults, complements, and sips of ale between clashes, enduring barbs from both crews as well as each other.

In the end, she scored a gash to my forearm that stained my already slashed sleeve red, and I bowed and sheathed my cutlass. "Well done, Captain! You've proven your worth!"

"And you've proven you're no dandy, Admiral!" She examined the blood on her blade, and wiped it on the blousy sleeve of her shirt before sheathing it. "Here's to our alliance!" She stepped up and raised her tankard to me.

"To our alliance!" I clashed my tankard to hers and we drained them amid the cheers of both crews.

The revel had begun, and bellowed challenges filled the air.

As Red and I accepted full tankards and strode off the floor toward a table, she leaned in close. "Sorry about the scratch."

"Nothing serious." I examined the cut, but it had already stopped bleeding.

"Let me make it up to you." She took a sideways step and turned into my path. "I wasn't lying about not wearing any knickers." She fingered the lacings of my shirt. "I can't think of a better way to seal a partnership."

"I'm flattered, Red, but I'm afraid I'm already spoken for." I clenched her hand and kissed her scarred knuckles.

"No!" She laughed and took a step back. "Say it isn't so!"

I shrugged and grinned. "Heart and soul, Captain Moll."

"Well strap my ass to a satyr and ride me like a rented mule!" Red laughed and leapt up to a table. "Scourges and Ravens, raise your cups and tankards and drink to Admiral Longbright, for he is no longer among the unloved! Some lucky lass has him by the balls, and has claimed his heart!"

Cheers rang out and everyone raised cups and tankards, shouting curses, lewd comments, and complements. I drank and smiled good naturedly.

Moll leapt down and stepped right up to me. "Why Kevril, I do believe you're *blushing*!"

"I'm not blushing, Captain, I—" I froze as her hand cupped the codpiece of my trousers.

She grinned mercilessly, her fingers flexing. "*Now* you're blushing, Admiral."

I gritted my teeth. "No, now I'm getting *angry*. I wasn't lying, Moll. I'm spoken for."

"No offense intended." She released her grip and whirled away to flop into a chair. She propped her boots up and leaned the chair back on two legs. "So, who's the lucky lass?"

"Her name's Preel." I sat and crossed one boot over a knee.

"She helped me out of some...difficulties with Jhavika, and one thing led to another."

"Is she with you? I'd love to meet the woman who put a lasso around *your* dick."

I grinned. "She's back in Haven. I'll give you a letter for her, and you can deliver it. She's...had a rough time, Red. She was a slave when I found her."

"A slave?" She looked dubious.

"Yes, and then Jhavika kidnapped her to pressure me." I grinned. "That didn't work out so well for her."

Moll barked a laugh and shook her head. "I can't believe Keshmir tried to stage a coup in *Haven*! Like trying to tame a pack of wolves."

"Well, there were...extenuating circumstances." At her querulous look, I shrugged. She'd hear the tale eventually. "You remember that cat-o'-nine tails Captain Kohl was so proud of?"

"Yes."

"Well, it was magical..." I gave her the short version—leaving out Preel's gift, of course—and watched her face. She didn't call me a liar, but I saw some skepticism, especially when I mentioned dragonlords and the Serpent's Eye.

"That's...incredible, Kevril." She waved over a server with a pitcher to refill our tankards.

"You'll get the details from Haven's Council, I'm sure." I accepted a refill and sipped carefully. "You should sail for Haven straightaway."

"Oh, I intend to. *Raven* could use a haul out." She drank and eyed me. "You want me to spread the word?"

"Sure, if you know any captains who might be interested, but do it carefully."

"I know a few. Where are you heading next?"

"North, island hopping to Hyko. Jhavika's death released the enchantment on all her slaves, and one was Mati's ambassador to Toki. I want to warn the governors of Hyko. The god-emperor may be planning retaliation. I also want to spread the word of Jhavika's demise, since *she's* the one who poked that particular dragon."

"But wouldn't the emperor go right after Haven?"

I shrugged. "I don't know how much the ambassador knew of Jhavika's plans, or what she instructed him to tell the god-emperor. You can bet your sweet arse he told the emperor everything he knew."

"And he's probably sent a ship to Mati." She frowned. "An alliance between Toki and Mati would be bad."

I nodded. "We had someone in Mati, and Haven's Council should find out soon if they're mobilizing their fleet." I sipped ale. "We've got to get a naval force organized before either one moves. Have you heard anything from Hyko?"

"Not a peep. There are a couple of pirates working the isles north of there. Nonny Brethwite and Terence Caul. They command a couple of small brigs, *White Lady* and *First Light*, and work together. They might be interested in joining, and would know the lay of the seas to the north."

"Good." I'd heard of them both, and had met Brethwite once, an older fellow, which meant he was a careful sort, just the type I needed. "I'll look for them." I sipped ale. "I'm also talking to the Twin Capes chiefs this afternoon. They at least need to know a storm's on the horizon."

She nodded and grinned. "Who gets the dubious task of popping the question to the Jaguar King? He's not fond of our ilk."

"The same captain who's been watching Mati for us. Her name's Tan. She commands *Golden Harlot*, a small galleon. She's not a pirate, but knows her way around the Blood Sea, and she's no fool."

"So, how many ships in this navy of ours so far?"

I shrugged. "Five fighting ships, and a few armed merchantmen so far. A few smugglers and smaller craft acting as messengers."

She cringed. "That's not much."

"We have to start somewhere, and pirates frequent Haven to sell off booty. We'll have more soon."

"And the Haven Council? It's...stable?" She gave me a clear 'Don't bullshit me' look.

"More so than it was, for certain. They're still a bunch of crime lords and exiles, but they see the bigger picture, now." I raised my tankard to her. "And they're not weak. One of them took out Jhavika's entire force of soldiers in her own keep single-handedly."

Her mouth fell open. "The *fuck* you say! Some kind of wizard?"

"Necromancer." I grinned. "But that doesn't mean she's a bad person. In fact, I kind of like her."

Red barked a laugh. "Well, *that's* good." We touched tankards and sipped.

A roar went up as Wix and the *Raven*'s bosun squared off for a bare-knuckles match. I offered Red odds on Wix, but she declined. We chatted, and I began to see that Moll also saw the big picture here. Preel's gift had pointed me in the right direction.

The five Twin Capes chiefs met me in the city's common lodge. It wasn't a government building as much as a community meeting place where they held weddings, blessed newborns, and executed criminals. A truly multifunctional structure. The three men and two women sat in a semicircle around the U-shaped stone they used to decapitate the condemned. They didn't look happy to see me.

They also didn't mince words.

"They say you speak for Haven now, Longbright," one of the chiefs said. His name was Naj, and he had so many tattoos, they joined to cover him completely, even the palms of his hands.

I wondered briefly who *they* were, but it didn't matter. "I do."

"And you talk with Moll, ask her to join you, to join Haven," another said. Her name was Fiki, and she might have had slightly fewer tattoos.

Obviously, the chiefs had eyes and ears all over the city. "Yes."

"Haven wants a navy, like Sariff has?" Naj asked.

"Not like Sariff's navy, but a fleet of privateers to patrol all of the Blood Sea. Something has happened that you need to know. It affects us all."

"What thing?" another chief, a man named Bok, asked, his face fixed in a scowl.

"One of Haven's Council, Jhavika Keshmir, tried to take control of Haven, and wanted all of the Blood Sea, through magic and intimidation. She had several other council members murdered, and took my wife to control me. I stopped her, and destroyed the magic she was using to control people."

The chiefs exchanged glances, but seemed unconcerned.

"What has this to do with navies and Twin Capes?" Fiki asked.

"Because Keshmir had a spy in the God-Emperor's palace. An ambassador from Mati." I'd already known it, but that didn't matter. "When the magic was destroyed, her spy would have revealed Keshmir's plot. This will anger both Toki and Mati."

"But Keshmir's dead, yes?" I nodded to Bok's question. "Then send messengers to Toki and Mati. Tell them this."

I shrugged. "They won't believe us. We're nothing but pirates and criminals in their eyes."

"And now you make a navy, which they will see as a threat."

"This navy will not threaten Toki or Mati, but will defend the Blood Sea against them," I explained. "The two have suffered from piracy for decades. Even without this incident to spark their anger, they would eventually decide to subjugate the Blood Sea, place warships in every port, garrisons of soldiers on every island. Haven wishes to stop this invasion, but can't do it alone. That's why I'm here. We want to form an alliance with all the islands and city states of the Blood Sea to defend against Toki and Mati."

"And if you're wrong, and they don't invade?"

"Then the alliance will negotiate with them. They trade heavily with one another. All of the resources of the Empire of Tira flow through Mati. To maintain this trade, ships must sail through the Blood Sea or far around the Serpent's Eye." I shrugged. "If they recognize the allied city states and islands of the Blood Sea, and agree to trade with us as equals, their ships will pass unmolested, paying a small tithe. If they threaten us, they'll find their trade cut off."

That instigated a few frowns, but nods from others.

"It sounds to *me* like Haven wishes to subjugate all the Blood Sea before Toki does," Fiki snapped.

I shook my head. "No. That would only pit us against one another. The Council of Haven wishes only for alliance, for we *also* live on trade. Each island and city state that chooses to join the alliance will continue to govern themselves, but we'll all share resources to face the threat from Toki or Mati. This will make trade easier among the city states by protecting our merchant ships with our privateers, and keep each other safe."

"Twin Capes has no ships. What do we gain by joining this alliance?"

Time for some carrot, I thought. "You gain by an increase in trade and protection from invasion. Our ships will frequent your port more often than pirates currently do, and they'll bring with them trade, ships, and sailors."

"We can protect ourselves, and we already have trade."

"You can't protect yourself against Toki's navy without help. None of the city states can, including Haven."

"And what of pirates like Moll? Some will choose not to join your navy."

"Those pirates will find the merchant ships they prey upon protected by our privateers." *Now for a little stick.* "At least the merchant ships of our *allies*."

"What of Sariff?" yet another chief asked. Ghoffi ruled the largest tribe on the island, but they preferred to live in the high country. He was a wiry thin man, his dark skin decorated with elaborate scars and piercings, as well as tattoos.

"We're approaching them as I speak to you. They have much to gain by joining the alliance, and much to offer."

"This is a complicated matter, Longbright." Naj glanced at his fellow chiefs. "We must discuss this."

"You're right. It *is* complicated." I nodded respectfully to them all. "I'm sailing north tomorrow to recruit more ships and captains, and to speak to the governors of Hyko, as I've spoken to you. I'll be back in ten days or so."

"We'll have your answer when you return," Naj said.

"Good. Thank you for listening to me." I nodded again. "Do you have any news from Hyko?"

They exchanged looks once again. "No. We don't share news with the governors. They make friends with the sprite people, and we find them uncanny."

I thought of the fae, Nahli Twince, and her fathomless golden eyes, and nodded. "They can be, yes, but they have also suffered from Toki's incursions into their jungle. They'll understand the threat from Toki."

They all exchanged looks and nods. "Very well, Longbright. We await your return."

"Very well." I started to turn away, then thought one last warning might be warranted. "You should be ready, Chiefs. I don't know what I'll find in Hyko, and Toki may choose to bypass the fortified city to occupy Twin Capes first."

To my surprise, the chiefs all grinned at me, some of them chuckling low. "We are *always* ready, Longbright. We're used to dealing with pirates, after all."

"Good." I nodded again and left, wondering what preparations they'd made.

Chapter Fourteen
The Essence of Souls

From the journal of Hashi Severn —

I don't know what I expect to achieve by this. If Tori lied to me, he'll continue to lie. If he told me the truth, however, it changes things. But how can I confirm if he told me the truth? If only I could know the mind of Demia without dying first.

I sat back in my carriage on the way to Blackbriar Estate, mulling over my decision to speak with Tori again. Saraknyal had gone predictably volcanic, of course. I'd tried to ignore his relentless haranguing, and finally told him to shut up or I'd put him in his box and go alone.

Go ahead! he'd countered; it was an empty threat and he knew it. *You're going to speak to him without me there anyway, aren't you?*

Probably, I admitted. *I can't expect him to be honest with me if you're listening to every word we say.*

You can't expect him to be honest with you anyway! Get it through your head, Hashi, he's got only his own self-interest at heart. You're a curiosity to him, nothing more.

Well, that's the problem, because he's a curiosity to me, too. I shifted my tactics. *We spoke for hours before and barely touched on all the history he's lived through. Did I tell you he said he'd seen Twakh keep once?*

No. I could almost feel his curiosity. *Before or after the roo war?*

Before. I recalled Tori's account. *He evidently spent some time in Tinaros. He said he hadn't met you, that he didn't think introducing himself would have been wise.*

For him, *it wouldn't have been.*

He has about the same opinion of the roo as you do, you know.

I find that hard to believe.

I don't. They slaughtered an entire culture, wiped their history from the face of the planet. I think he finds that even more appalling than the killing of the populace.

*That *does* sound like a high elf's assessment of a genocidal war.*

Pointing out that Saraknyal might actually have something in common with Tori seemed to placate him. In truth, I just wanted him to leave me in peace. Despite my self-proclamation that I was done being afraid, my pending conversation with the high elf concerned me. I might not be afraid of anything in this world, but the next... I had no way to know if he was telling me the truth about my soul.

The carriage jolted to a stop, and I glanced out to find us parked at the gate to Tori's estate. A shout from Bromish opened the gate, and we rolled through.

Last chance to change your mind.

I ignored Saraknyal and took in the expansive grounds, the immaculate gardens, citrus trees, kiwi vines, cacao, breadfruit, almond trees, and two towering mangos heavy with fruit. We rumbled across the wooden bridge spanning the ornamental moat and stopped at the gravel court. A deep breath, an uneasy tug at my skirt, and I stepped down before anyone could approach.

"Stay with the carriage," I told my shade escort. I spotted Tori descending the steps to the manor with two footmen at his heels. A light breeze fluttered my blouse and skirt, and I patted them back into place.

"Lovely to see you again, Hashi!" His smile blazed, and I noticed he wasn't wearing his sword. "That's *another* new look!"

"I felt like a change."

Tori had suggested we stroll his gardens, and I remembered wearing light breezy outfits when I was young. Reinforcing my new resolution to stop being afraid, I'd gone shopping, determined to turn over a new leaf. I wore a blazing green silk shirt and a positively florescent yellow and orange ankle-length sarong. If nothing else, I thought it might throw Tori off his game, but his face showed more consternation than appreciation.

"You don't like it." I patted my clothes self-consciously.

"Oh, on the contrary, it's just so...*bright*." He blinked. I'd truly caught him flat footed. "I hardly recognize you."

Score one for the necromancer.

It wasn't my idea, Saraknyal said.

I meant me. "Well, you suggested that we stroll your gardens. Black's far too hot for tropical sun." He could hardly tell me I was dressed too casually; He wore a billowy shirt of light cambric the color of new snow, open at the neck, and a pair of doeskin riding pants tucked into soft boots. I unclipped Soul Drinker from the waist of my sarong and handed it up to one of my shades. "Keep that safe."

"Yes, mistress."

Do try to be careful, my dear, Saraknyal said as Bromish reined the team around toward the stables.

Careful is sometimes highly overrated, old man. I turned to face Tori. "Shall we?"

"By all means." He gestured and we walked, our shoes crunching on the gravel until we reached the winding stone walkway through the gardens. "You seem very different today, Hashi, and not just the clothes."

"I'm in a good mood," I admitted. "A project I've been working very hard on has come to fruition, and I feel like I've truly accomplished something."

"You mean the containment of the Death Stone?"

I jerked to a stop, staring at him open mouthed. "How the hell..."

He chuckled. "Oh, don't worry. I won't tell anyone. Malchi would rupture himself."

"Who told you?" My tone surprised me, as sharp as Soul Drinker's blade.

"Relax. Your people are models of discretion, but there are some wagging tongues among the Tinworthy clan that I exploit on a regular basis." He grinned maliciously. "Congratulations on your success." He gestured and we walked on.

"I should have known better than to think it would remain a secret, I suppose." I eyed him. "You aren't worried?"

"Oh, I think it was a brilliant idea. Certainly safer than a furnace that has to be tended constantly, and if anyone understands Void essence and how to contain it, I suppose a necromancer would." He smiled at me. "I don't suppose you'll tell me how you managed it."

I shrugged. "A rune-inscribed containment vessel with three layers of enchantments: reflective, transformative, and containment. It's closed for good."

"Well, Saraknyal's truly brilliant, then." He reached up to touch a dangling star fruit as we passed a tree. I would have sworn the tree's leaves shuddered. "Anything specific you wished to discuss?"

"Yes, but I thought we'd chat about history first. I've had some time to think, and I'm curious about a few things." Truthfully, I didn't want to broach a truly sensitive subject until we were well away from my carriage. Saraknyal could hear a pin drop across a ballroom.

"Such as?"

"Well, history is generally written by the winners, and that narrative isn't always accurate."

"True." He touched another tree in passing, his fingers caressing the smooth bark.

"The founding of Tsing, for instance. History paints it as an amiable alliance between Arianus Tsing and the dwarves who already inhabited the area, but I have trouble imagining that."

"Well, it certainly wasn't as peaceful as *that*, but it came up short of outright war. I wasn't there personally, and dwarves and elves don't exactly get along, but we did learn some details."

We walked and Tori assuaged my historical curiosity on many varied subjects, including the necromancer war with the reincarnation of Azrael. Saraknyal would have hung on his every word. That Tori had actually met the woodling Empress Shildra prior to the war shocked me; more so that he knew the elf who forged the blade that finally destroyed Azrael for good. He had little information about the early decades of Valaka, however, and the wars between cultists and dragonlords, which left me wanting. As we passed trees, he touched them, and every leaf fluttered as if in a breeze.

"What are you doing when you touch the trees?" I finally asked, nodding as he did so.

"Oh, just an elf thing. We tend forests and plants because we love them." He smiled and plucked a mango. "They transform sunlight, earth, and water into life itself. Don't you find that wondrous?"

"I never thought of it that way." I watched him draw a tiny curved blade from a pocket and deftly slice the mango into wedges. He held out a wedge to me, seemingly oblivious to the juice dripping from his fingers, and I took it. He ate one, and I followed suit, the flavor astounding, juice dripping from my chin. We paused and finished the fruit, wedge by wedge, tossing the skin and pit into the foliage.

"Here." He produced a handkerchief and handed it to me.

"Thank you." I wiped my hands and chin, and the cloth miraculously absorbed every sticky drop of juice. I laughed and handed it back. "That's handy."

"Mmm." He wiped his hands and tucked the handkerchief away. "Would you mind asking me what you really came to discuss, Hashi? Not that I'm not enjoying your company, but..."

"All right." I girded my nerves and threw caution to the winds. "How do you know my soul isn't doomed to be sent to Hell? No offense, but you're not a god, and you can't know the mind of Demia."

"Ah, that." He smiled and we resumed walking. "I know the feeling of good and evil, Hashi. You've felt the same, I'm sure."

I furrowed my brow at him. "I have?"

"Yes, when you make a shade." He met my scowl with a critical gaze, not judgmental, but analytical. "You take in a soul, and you feel its essence, then Saraknyal changes it into...well, for wont of a better word, *corruption*. You've experienced both."

"Yes, I've felt that, but..." I shook my head. "All the souls I've changed into shades felt the same to me."

"Well, I have the advantage of being able to feel a soul without drawing it out of its body." He raised a hand and carefully placed it on my shoulder. "I've felt tens of *thousands* of souls, Hashi, and yours is mostly good."

I looked at his hand, then into his eyes. "And how do I know you're telling me the truth?"

He shrugged and took his hand away. "You don't, but trust me when I tell you that I've felt souls that were just as corrupt and evil as those you put back into shades. Generally, people are more complicated than good or evil. They're a little of both and a lot of neither. You've done some horrible things in your time, Hashi, I'm sure, but so have many good mortals. So have *I*, to be honest. It's not what we're forced to do that defines us, but how we *feel* about our actions and the actions of others that makes us who we are."

I thought about that, and realized that I'd always regretted the necessity of destroying human souls. I'd never done it simply for power. Maybe he was telling me the truth.

"I can show you your soul, if you wish."

I stared at him, wondering if I'd heard him correctly. "You...what?"

"I can mirror what I'm feeling to others, which makes sex *really* a lot of fun, actually, but I can do it with any feeling."

I gaped at him, and a niggling mistrust gnawed at my mind. "I don't think so, Tori. No offense, but I don't know if I trust you to show me the truth."

"Someone else, then?" he suggested.

Again my brow furrowed. "Who?"

"You saw the elf woman at Fancy's Folly, didn't you? The one with Longbright's first mate?"

"Oh, yes, I noticed her. She'd seemed such a strange match for a pirate."

His brows knitted. "Why?"

I shrugged. "Longbright's crew seem so...hard. Not grim, but...violence is their business. That elf woman didn't look like she'd hurt a fly."

"Ha, well, appearance can be deceiving, no?" He gestured to my attire. "You hardly look the necromancer today."

"Valid point."

"Her name's Illian, and as far as I know, she's the only other true elf in Haven." Tori shrugged. "We know one another from the Northlands. I can introduce you if you like."

"No." I said it innately, my defenses rising like a shield. "I don't trust strangers that much."

"Suit yourself." We walked on. "Let me know if you change your mind. You might consider dropping by the Folly to watch her perform. She has an astounding voice."

"I may. Thank you." I couldn't remember the last time I simply went out for a night of music, and the emptiness felt like the Tinworthy mine full of Void essence. *Music...dancing...color...life...* It had been decades.

"You're welcome." We walked on.

"Can I ask you about something else?" Another thought had been eating at me for weeks.

"Of course."

"The potion you gave me after the Tinworthy Mine incident."

"The restorative. Yes. What about it?"

"Something strange..." I told him about Saraknyal's condition after our exposure to Void essence, and how he seemed to perk up later without taking any soul energy, then his claim that he'd used some of the residual energy from the potion to revive himself.

Tori stopped dead in his tracks. "What again?"

"He said there was left over energy from the potion, and he used some." I shrugged. "I wondered if you thought that was possible."

"I've never heard of it happening before, but...Saraknyal is...unique." Tori blinked at me, wide eyed. "Hashi, if this is true, the implications are..."

"I know."

"I can give you another vial of the same restorative, to test, if you like. It may be possible because you're soul bonded with him. This is...unprecedented."

"I appreciate the offer, but..." Another problem loomed. "You said you felt a void in his soul. If he lied to me, and found a way to consume a part of his *own* soul, but didn't want to tell me...forcing him to reveal his lie could cause serious repercussions. I don't think I should risk it."

He looked startled. "Is your relationship with Saraknyal so fragile?"

I smiled ruefully. "Well, it's been strained lately. He seems to think I'm suicidal, and I think he's too controlling. He's...overly protective."

"Because he cares for you," Tori said.

"Or because I'm his only conduit to wield his magic." I shrugged. "Either way, I can't alienate him. We've had some real rows in the past, and I don't want to—"

Shouts from the gate interrupted us, and we both turned. I felt suddenly naked without Soul Drinker at my side. If there was trouble, I was defenseless.

"Nothing to worry about. One of my people, I think." Tori gestured, and we started back toward the courtyard.

The gate opened and a rider entered, their horse lathered. Horse and rider cantered across the bridge to the courtyard where they pulled up and began to dismount. Then she spotted us, and wheeled around to trot toward us. Uneasy with an armed rider coming at me, I stepped off the path beside a tree.

"It's all right, Hashi. She's one of mine." Tori raised a hand, and the horse stopped some strides away. "What news?"

"Lord Blackbriar, ships approach the harbor from the south. Three of them." The rider dismounted and led her horse over. "One's the *Golden Harlot*!"

"Captain Tan?" Tori turned to me. "Well, this *is* good news!"

I stepped to Tori's side. "And the other ships?"

"A smaller one, maybe a smuggler, and a big fat warship! They're all flying Haven colors and parlay flags."

Tori looked at me askance. "Tan's found some allies?"

"Or she met up with the ship Que-Chen sent to Sariff to buy a hull for Patak." I grinned. "Our navy's growing!"

"Oh, we simply *must* be the first to greet her!" Tori crowed. "I won't have Malchi getting the news first!" He snatched the reins from his messenger and leapt into the saddle as graceful as any dancer Mati had ever produced. Then, to my shock, he held a hand down to me. "Ride with me?"

I barked an incredulous laugh. "I think it'd be more prudent to arm ourselves first, and I'm hardly dressed to ride. We can take my carriage."

"Oh, well, I *suppose*..." He looked crestfallen, his hand drooping.

On impulse, I grasped his hand. "But I could manage as far as the stable."

"Excellent!" He moved his foot from the stirrup, and I mounted behind him. "Hang on!"

I did, and endured a jouncy ride over the two hundred yards to the stable. As he reined up, I slid off the horse's rump, laughing and straightening my twisted sarong. "Bromish! We're going to the waterfront." I held up a hand to my shade and took Soul Drinker. "Lord Blackbriar's accompanying us."

"He is?" Bromish looked a little stunned.

He is? Saraknyal echoed.

I gave Tori a challenging look. "Well, if he's not afraid to ride in a coach with a necromancer."

"Just let me get my blade." Tori kicked his mount and rode right up to the front door before dismounting, calling for his butler to bring him his sword.

Captain Tan looked more astonished with the transformation of Haven's waterfront than the arrival of two Lords of the Council dressed for a country picnic emerging from black coach manned by shades. As Tori and I stepped down, I reminded myself that Tan hadn't been in Haven for almost two months. As we watched her launch approach the quay, she stared at the uniformed harbor watch, armed merchantmen, siege engines, and bustling shipyard as if she'd found herself magically transported into a fairyland. I'd never met the woman, but she had that "serious sea captain" look that's hard to define.

"Captain Tan! Welcome back to Haven!" Tori held a hand out to her as the captain climbed the ladder onto the quay.

Tan looked at him, at his hand, then at me and the carriage behind us, then again back at Tori. "Forgive me, sir, but I don't...think I know you."

"Ah, my apologies. Lord Blackbriar, and this is Lady Hashi Severn. I'm afraid your arrival caught us in the midst of a pleasant stroll in my gardens. We're hardly dressed appropriately."

"Lord Blackbriar, of course." She bowed and shook his hand,

then bowed to me. "Lady Severn. Well met. I imagine the Council has questions."

"We do." I caught Tori's eye and raised an eyebrow. "But Lord Blackbriar and I thought to spare you the agony of facing the entire Council. You've undoubtedly got work to do."

Tori flashed his disarming smile. "Yes, Admiral Longbright gave us his account of your actions, and it was clear to us that they were correct and appropriate."

"Well, remind me to thank Admiral Longbright." Tan seemed to relax somewhat.

"You may have to wait for that; he's out recruiting privateers." Tori grinned again. "We can take your account of your mission to Sariff to the Council and save a lot of nonsense."

She smiled, but it looked a little strained. "I don't have any problem speaking to the Council, but thank you." She waved to the other ships, the larger warship now rafted up with *Tiger Lily*, surrounded by smaller boats. "Que-Chen's messenger ship, *Violet*, found me in Mati, and I sailed for Sariff the following day. I sent *Violet* to Valaka with the same instructions the Council gave me; spread the word of the threat to the Blood Sea, and pitch the offer of a protectorate. I know it wasn't within my authority to do that, but it seemed prudent, and *Violet*'s captain seemed capable."

"More than prudent," Tori greed.

Longbright was right. Tan has a level head and shows initiative.

She does, I agreed. *I wish we had a dozen more like her.*

"I found another of Que-Chen's ships in Sariff Harbor, *Snapdragon*, with Captain Harig commanding. He'd just purchased *Sea Drake*," she pointed to the huge warship, "and told me the Council had recruited Captain Patak. They were short-handed—the *Drake*'s a bit of a beast, I'm afraid—and my visit with the Jaguar King was brief, so we agreed to split our crews and sail back in company for safety."

"And how did the Jaguar King respond?" I asked.

"Belligerently, at first. He accused Haven of starting a war. They have a lot of trade with Toki, and more with Mati. I explained it wasn't Haven, but Jhavika, but I don't know if he believed me. He seemed more receptive when I told him the piracy on his country's shipping would end if Sariff joined the protectorate, and that we were already recruiting a privateer fleet. He wouldn't commit, but said he'd discuss it with his advisors." She shrugged. "Two of them were present, and didn't seem opposed, but I can't predict how they'll go."

"Well, that's as much as we can hope for, I guess," Tori said. "Well done, Captain."

"Thank you, Lord Blackbriar." She glanced over her shoulder at the harbor.

"Do you know if the Mati parliament learned of their ambassador to Toki?" I asked.

"Not that I know of, Lady Severn, but Mati's an incredibly busy harbor. Ships come and go from all over the world. If a message came from Toki, I had no way to know. I didn't hear any rumors."

You need to find out if they've been told, Saraknyal said.

I shared a glance with Tori. "Well, I imagine the Council will send someone to spy on—"

An elaborate carriage escorted by a score of cavalry soldiers rumbled onto the quay a block away, and the unmistakable form of Reginald Malchi stepped out. He spotted us, shouted something to his driver, and climbed back aboard. The carriage lurched into motion toward us.

"There goes the party," Tori grumbled.

"If you'd prefer to see to your ship, Captain, we can deal with Lord Malchi."

Tan shrugged at my offer. "Thanks, but I can handle Lord Malchi just fine."

And his son, Maurice, too, Saraknyal quipped.

Oh, hush. I suppressed a smile. I couldn't blame her for indulging herself. *From the sound of it, she well might have been playing Reginald as much as he was playing her.*

Well, if she was, she's even more wily than he is.

That's not difficult, I thought.

Malchi's coach clattered to a stop and he got out, his eyes wide, flicking between the three of us and my carriage. My four shades still rode up there, attentive and grim as always. "Tori, what's going on here? Why are you two are dressed like a couple of *trollops*?"

"We were relaxing in my gardens when we received word of Captain Tan's pending arrival, Reginald." Tori didn't sound happy.

I wasn't happy either. I stepped around Tori and glared the pompous ass down. "And you need to stop thinking with your *mouth*! It's ill-mannered and not very intelligent! How I dress is none of your gods-damned *business*!"

Careful, Hashi.

He's the one who needs to be careful! I seethed. *I'm sick of his bullshit!*

Malchi bristled. "And I don't think—"

"No, you *don't*! At least not about anyone but yourself, *Lord* Malchi!" I clenched my hand on Soul Drinker's hilt. "Insult me again, and see how it goes for you!"

"Guards!" He snapped, and his mounted force jostled forward, hands reaching for weapons.

I laughed in his face and thought, *Chill of fear.*

Malchi's face drained of color and his soldiers' horses balked and bucked. Two riders were thrown, and the team harnessed to his carriage reared. My own team jerked their traces, but they were used to me and Bromish had them in hand. Malchi staggered back, his hand white on his sword.

"Draw that and you're my next shade, Reginald!" I growled.

"Hashi." A hand settled on my shoulder.

I turned to glare, and found Tori looking concerned like I'd never seen him. "I'm sick of his pompous bullshit and insults, Tori." I glared back at Malchi. "He needs to be taught a lesson."

"And I think he's learned it. Please." Tori's hand remained on my shoulder.

I gritted my teeth. "I'll have your apology, Lord Malchi."

"I meant no disparagement," he sputtered. "I've...simply never seen you dressed like that before, that's all."

That was a weak-ass apology, but you should let him off the hook. He's terrified, and fools do dangerous things when they're scared. As much as I dislike him, Haven needs him.

Saraknyal had a point. I nodded to Malchi and took my hand off of Soul Drinker's hilt, my anger ebbing away. "Weak-ass apology accepted. Now, we were *about* to tell you that Captain Tan has given us a summary of her mission to Sariff. If you'd like to *listen*, the news is rather mixed."

"I can speak to Captain Tan myself, thank you." Malchi recovered some of his poise and attitude.

"I'll speak to him, Lady Severn." Tan stepped around me and shot me a look over her shoulder, one eyebrow cocked in amusement. "Thank you for the offer, but Lord Malchi and I are well acquainted."

Longbright was right; she's no fool.

"Very well, Captain, and again, welcome home." I nodded to her and turned to Tori. "Can I offer you a ride home, Lord Blackbriar?"

"I can think of nothing better!" Tori turned to my carriage and opened the door for me, bowing with a flourish. "After you, Lady Severn!"

He just wants to look at your ass, you know, Saraknyal quipped.

I suppressed a smile and thought, *Let him look,* before I climbed in and took my seat. I glanced back just in time to catch Tori averting his gaze.

Told you.

As Tori took his seat and closed the door, I said, "You know one of the *best* things about soulblades, Tori?"

His eyebrows arched. "There are quite a few, I imagine."

"There are, but the *best* one is that they can look behind you and tell you when someone's ogling your backside."

His face flushed. "I...was...merely appreciating beauty, Lady Severn."

"And I was just reminding you that I'm *always* talking to Saraknyal." I cocked an eyebrow and swept my gaze down, then back up to his eyes. "And he sees *everything.*"

"*Everything?*" He swallowed hard and crossed his legs. "Well, *that's* a little embarrassing."

154

Chapter Fifteen
Difficult Propositions

From the journal of Preel Longbright —

One thing I never learned during my life as a slave was the art of negotiation. Slaves obey or are punished; I learned *that* lesson too well. We also learn to hide our true feelings. Now, as with Jhavika, I'm faced with dealing with a dangerous adversary without giving away any secrets. I feel like I'm in Jhavika's clutches all over again.

After an entire day of fretting about how to deal with Brilla, I sent a note to Lady Severn, begging an audience. I stared at her reply now, my hands shaking so hard I could barely read.

> Preel:
>
> I believe it's time to nip this bothersome weed in the bud, but I'd like to speak with you in person to discuss how you want it handled. To be frank, there has to be more afoot here than a plea for commiseration. Please come to Ash Keep this evening. I'll be happy to talk this over with you. I personally guarantee your safety, but you may bring as many bodyguards as you wish. I suggest discretion. If you agree, I'll expect you an hour after sunset.
>
> I also have other news you may want to relate to your husband that has nothing to do with your current dilemma.
>
> Sincerely,
> Lady Hashi Severn

My instinct told me not to trust the invitation. It sounded too much like Brilla's. Logically, I knew I could trust Lady Severn's discretion. I couldn't tell her *all* of the truth, of course, but there were enough possible ulterior motives in play to validate my concerns without going there.

I discussed it with Lewin, of course, and he encouraged me to go. We came up with a list of legitimate concerns that had nothing to do with Brilla's true motivations, and certainly didn't reveal the real reason Jhavika had me abducted. Then I drafted a letter to Lady Severn accepting her invitation, and had Busashi deliver it.

"I'll need a carriage and an escort," I wrote to him in my notebook. "I'll leave security up to you."

"Of course, mistress." Busashi bowed and pressed a clenched fist to his chest. "You'll be perfectly safe. You have my word of honor."

I nodded to him and fretted. I hated being afraid, and hated myself for blaming Kevril for leaving me here. I couldn't help but think that I'd be safer aboard *Scourge*, even if we did have to battle pirates. I was so worked up that I could barely eat dinner, and finally broke down and poured myself a glass of wine. I dressed befitting an audience with a member of the Council, and fretted some more. When Busashi finally knocked the door to our sitting room, I was calmer, steady, and prepared.

Or so I thought.

"Come in." I downed my wine and picked up the enchanted silk gag.

The door opened, and Busashi entered with his entire cadre, none of them looking anything like nokitu. They were dressed in formal Marathian garb, complete with head dresses, scimitars, and flowing robes. Ghiti wore a beautiful sari, headscarf, and matching veil. She looked to all the world like a Marathian Princess' lady in waiting.

"Ready, mistress?" Busashi bowed in perfect Marathian fashion, and Ghiti curtsied. Damn me if she didn't even wear eye makeup and a gem-studded headpiece.

"What's all this?" I gestured to their garb.

"You left security in my hands, and I deemed it best to take on these guises to match your own." He shrugged and bowed again. "Rest assured, we're prepared for any eventuality, but this will give no observer any clue who is visiting Ash Keep."

"You're...brilliant, Busashi." I held out the enchanted gag. "Please."

He tied the gag, and we trooped downstairs, robes swirling like a tribe of dervishes. Busashi had rented a huge carriage, and the driver was one of ours, formerly Jhavika's. Busashi, Miaki, and Ghiti got in with me, two rode on the boot, and one with the driver. I tried to relax as we rolled down the ramp from our gatehouse into the streets of Haven.

Ash Keep, as it turned out, wasn't far, but we took a circuitous route. When we finally stopped before the torchlit gates, night had fallen in full. Our driver simply called up that we had an appointment to meet with Lady Severn, and the gates opened. We rolled through into a courtyard of midnight black stone lit with the glow of torches. Human figures with skin as black as coal and eyes of crimson stood guard around the periphery of the open space, as still as stone. I shivered and clenched my hands in my lap.

"They're undead shades, mistress," Ghiti whispered. "Many are Jhavika's former house guards. The spoils of war. Don't fear them. They follow only Lady Severn's commands."

I nodded, wondering how anyone lived amongst such horrors day and night. Then again, I'd lived amongst horrors of my own, though not undead ones.

We jolted to a stop before a pair of high arched doors, jet black against black stone, more grim guards posted beside them. Busashi and Miaki got out and made a show of helping the ladies down, as is the Marathian custom. I nodded to Busashi, and we approached the steps to the entrance.

The doors swung inward, and an older man in a black jacket, waistcoat, and trousers, smiled and bowed to us. "Mrs. Longbright." His eyes flicked to my three companions. "You and your retainers are most welcome. Please come in."

Well, at least all of her retainers aren't undead, I thought. Of course, Lewin had told me this.

I nodded and we followed the butler into a high, vaulted entry hall of polished black stone from floor to ceiling. Glow crystals lit the area with soft golden hues from two overhead black iron chandeliers. Alcoves between branching corridors were filled with glowering, life-sized statues of komei, resplendent in full armor and weapons. They were so lifelike, I half expected them to move.

"Lady Severn will be down shortly." The butler bowed.

I nodded, disconcerted by the monochromatic décor, but intrigued by the statues. I stepped closer to inspect one, the garishly painted lamellar armor incongruously bright. The horrible crimson-painted mask scowled down at me, so intricate and dreadful, it made me shiver.

"Mistress," Ghiti whispered, and I turned to find the lady of the keep descending the stairway at the end of the hall.

For a moment, I didn't recognize Lady Severn, dressed in a flowing skirt of purple and black, a deep crimson blouse, and a light silk jacket with voluminous sleeves and intricate gold stitching. She looked like an entirely different woman than the grim necromancer who had visited Longbright Keep. She descended the steps gracefully, as if flowing instead of walking.

"Do you like my sculptures?" She gestured to the grim komei likenesses, her lips curved in an amused smile. "They're sixth century Toki, recovered from a shipwreck in Hyko harbor. I reconditioned them myself."

We all bowed and curtsied appropriately. I nodded and withdrew my notebook from the fold of my robe, scribbling and handing it to Ghiti, who had agreed to be my voice tonight.

"They're amazing. So detailed. I half expect them to come to life."

"Well, they haven't *yet*." Her teeth flashed and she extended a hand to me. "Welcome to Ash Keep, Preel."

I took her hand and curtsied again, surprised at the gesture. I expected the legendary chill of the necromancer's touch, but her hand was warm and her grasp firm.

"Please, no formalities tonight." She gripped my hand a bit longer than a simple greeting warranted, a far-off look flashing across her features, then she shook her head minutely and released me, gesturing to the statue looming over us. "Your husband said you were a student of history."

I nodded and took my notebook back to scribble. Ghiti read it. "Yes, history, magic, poetry, and western traditions."

"Western?" She looked curious. "But you're from Fornice, yes?"

I wrote, "My family moved to Chen when I was young. We lived in Marathia, and my father sought a more egalitarian home for his four daughters, since I had no brothers. In Marathia, women cannot own property."

"And he relocated across the continent for that? That speaks well for him."

A long-harbored pain scored through me, and I wrote, "Until he sold me into slavery to support his family."

Lady Severn blinked at me, her eyes wide. "I'm sorry, Preel. That's..." She paused, taking on another absent look for a moment before shaking her head and gesturing toward the stairs. "I thought we'd chat in the library. It's private, and, as a student of history, I thought you'd appreciate it. We have much to talk about, and I have news."

I nodded enthusiastically at any chance to visit a library, and I wondered what news she might have. We followed her up, and I felt graceless amongst her flowing gait and my nokitu. At the top of the stairs, we passed a marvelous sculpture of two entwined merfolk, life-sized and incredibly detailed, each scale distinct. I paused to admire it, dashing off another quick note.

"This is beautiful."

"It's from Valaka." She looked the sculpture up and down with a wry smile. "I deal in antiquities, and Valaka has a rich history."

"I've been there," I wrote. "This reminds me of the Serpent's Children."

"Well, then you have more experience with them than I do." She chuckled, as if remembering some private joke, and shook her head. "I found this beautiful as well, and put it up without knowing exactly what it depicts."

I looked at the two sinuous shapes and shrugged. "And what is that?"

"An...acquaintance of mine recently informed me that this is how merfolk...um...reproduce." She smiled and shrugged.

I gaped and looked at the statue again in a new light. I wrote, "Still, it's beautiful."

"It is." She continued on, and we followed.

The library shocked me.

Vaulted and packed with shelves, lit with glow crystals, and furnished with a single long table sporting two comfortable chairs, the room seemed to glow with the knowledge contained herein. Lady Severn must have seen the amazement in my eyes.

"Many of these were Jhavika's. She had quiet an extensive collection, and I couldn't resist pillaging it after..." She paused again and shook her head. "Please take a seat, and we'll discuss things. Can I offer you something to drink?" She gestured to a chair and pulled a bell rope beside the door.

I wrote, "No, thank you Lady. Forgive me, but I'm still a little uncomfortable speaking to a Lady of the Council. I don't want to seem too familiar. As you said, we're allies, not friends."

"Very well. You'll forgive me if I indulge myself." A footman appeared at the door and she told him. "Bring me a brandy, please." He nodded and hurried off, and she strolled over to the other seat. She leaned back and crossed her long legs, folding her arms, like a cat curling into a comfortable position. With our eyes on the same level, I felt a little more at ease. "So, Brilla's being a nuisance."

"Yes. I don't believe her sincerity for one second. She wants something, but I don't know what."

"Well, she certainly hates your husband, though I honestly can't understand why. She should be as grateful as the rest of Jhavika's former slaves for her release from the enchantment."

"Brilla was conditioned to love her," I wrote. "She may think she still does. Jhavika seduced Brilla before she enslaved her. She arranged for Brilla's husband to be murdered at her request to get close to her."

"How..." Severn cocked her head curiously. "Did Lewin tell you this?"

"Yes, but I have first-hand experience as well." This was my first attempt to steer the conversation away from the truth of my nature.

"How so?" A knock at the door and a footman delivered a snifter of brandy on a silver tray.

I waited until he left, then wrote, "Because Jhavika used Kevril to assassinate Brilla's husband. Kevril was unknowingly ensorcelled by Jhavika at the time. After he carried out his orders, he found me chained in Captain Nightspinner's cabin."

Her eyes widened. "Chained?"

I simply pulled up my sleeves and showed her the old scars on my wrists.

"Motherless son-of-a...." Severn's face clouded over, and her lips tightened. "Your husband said you were a slave, but... If Brilla knew about you..."

"I don't think she did at the time," I wrote. "But she may have learned from someone who served aboard Nightspinner's ship."

Severn nodded. "Which would give her cause to hate you."

I shrugged and wrote, "Maybe, but Brilla already hated Nightspinner and her brother for arranging the marriage. She preferred the company of women, and had many affairs whenever her husband was at sea, which was most of the time."

Severn's eyes narrowed. "And how did you learn this?"

I wrote. "From Nightspinner. He found out, and took out his jealousy on me. He may have planned to end the marriage, which might have been another of Brilla's motives for murdering him. Nightspinner owned four ships, and they went to the Balshi fleet when he died. Minus the one that Kevril burned."

Severn shook her head and sipped her brandy. "That's a tangled web indeed. More-so because you don't know how much of this Brilla actually knows. She could simply want to use you to pressure your husband, as Jhavika did."

"Yes, and informing Brilla of any of this, if she doesn't know, could set her off."

"Yes, it could." She sipped again and swirled the snifter under her nose. "Frankly, I don't think it would take much to set Brilla off. She's pretty close to bat-shit crazy already."

"So Kevril told me," I wrote, smiling at the euphemism. "Which is why I'm also hesitant to simply refuse to meet or correspond with her."

Severn sighed and got up to pace, a panther in a cage. "Well, short of murdering her, I don't see much of an option."

"Not murder, please," I wrote, then added, "Can you warn her off for me? Tell her you'll invoke the Council and have her sanctioned for harassing me? Tell her I'm afraid, which is true enough. Brilla's got an army." I didn't have to fake looking worried.

"Well, I can certainly do that, but I don't know how she'll handle it coming from me." Severn smiled ruefully. "She hates me just as much as she hates your husband, I'm afraid."

"Lewin told me."

"Yes, well, I was much younger and very angry. Her father was a pompous ass." She grinned. "I *improved* his temperament, I think, when I transformed him into a shade."

I didn't know how to respond to that. The thought of that kind of power pacing only feet away terrified me.

Severn surprised me. "Don't worry, Preel. I do what I have to do to protect myself, that's all. In fact, if anyone in Haven knows what I'm capable of, it's Brilla Balshi." Her grin morphed from friendly to feral. "I'm the one person she doesn't *dare* fuck with. I'll warn her off for you."

"Thank you, Lady," I wrote, breathing easier. "You said you had some news for Kevril?"

"Oh, yes! Ha! I'd nearly forgotten." She delved a fold of her voluminous sleeve and withdrew a roll of parchment. "I've outlined it here. In short, Captain Tan returned this morning. She sent our messenger ship to Valaka to inform the Dragonlords of developments, and contacted the Jaguar King with our offer. He's consulting his advisors, but seemed receptive. Oh, and Captain Patak's new ship arrived with Tan. The *Sea Drake*'s a beast of a vessel, and needs some refitting. Patak and the shipyard foremen are working up an estimate on how quickly they can get her into fighting trim. The Council's going to send Tan to Ton Chi, then Black Point, since your husband's headed north."

I took the scroll and nodded. "That's all good news! Things are coming together quickly."

"They are." She finished her brandy. "Now we just have to hold this place together long enough to solidify our protectorate."

"Yes." I stood. The audience was clearly over. "I can't thank you enough for what you're doing for me."

Severn waved it off. "You're husband's vital to putting this whole thing together, Preel." She grinned again, which caught me off guard. For someone who'd stated flatly that she didn't want friendship, she seemed very friendly. "And I find myself enjoying the company of another student of history." She waved to her vast library. "Most of Jhavika's collection has to do with political and military matters but she had a few historical references on Chen, if you're interested."

I nodded, still stunned. This seemed such a different woman than the grim necromancer who'd been so standoffish before. I wondered why. "I'd love to borrow something."

"Well, let's see what we can find, then, shall we?" She gestured to the looming shelves and I followed, my nokitu close behind. "You lived in Chen, so you know its atheistic laws. Did you know about the sects who fled the east and built temples in the foothills of the Ironwalls?"

"Only that they exist," I wrote.

She grinned and nodded to my escort. "You might find it interesting. They were warrior monks. They've developed some amazing martial arts and can channel their qi to an astonishing degree. Here's a good historical account." She pulled down a thick tome. "Oh, and here's a history of the building of the Sky Temples translated from dwarvish." She pulled down another. "And an account of the Long March through the Empty Quarter, and the battle of the sect of Koss Godslayer against the emperor's army." She pulled down yet one more book.

I gaped at her generosity, unsure how to thank her. I left some time later with a stack of books and an entirely altered opinion of Lady Hashi Severn.

Chapter Sixteen
Intervention

From the journal of Hashi Severn —

I've visited Balshi Keep many times. Only during two of those visits was I forced to kill anyone. I can only hope this visit turns out to the good.

I crafted a careful note to Brilla the next morning. Cordial, respectful, but firm, I told her that I needed to speak with her on a matter of mutual importance at her earliest convenience. I hadn't slept well, pacing my sitting room late into the night discussing our revelations about Preel with Saraknyal. Call me a suspicious old crone if you wish, but my curiosity is a dangerous thing. I'd invited Preel to Ash Keep for the single purpose of greeting her with a cordial handshake.

The instant our hands touched, Saraknyal told me, *She's innately magical, Hashi. I don't know what it is, but it's powerful. She's also got something on her face, a magical cloth covering her mouth.*

A magical cloth? My mind had raced, but I managed to keep my sudden unease hidden. *Can you tell what the cloth does? Or what she does, for that matter?* Innate magic was entirely different than being capable of wielding magic. Nahli Twince was innately magical, but a wizard or alchemist isn't. *She isn't a fae, is she?*

No, no, and no, Saraknyal answered. "And you're still holding her hand.*

Shit! I'd snapped my attention back to my guest and diverted the conversation to history, a subject I knew we shared interest in.

I didn't like the notion of being deceived, but whatever Preel's secret was, I couldn't just come out and ask. Talk about an awkward subject. As we'd settled into the library, and she refused my offer of refreshment—of course, she had something magical covering her mouth—I forced myself to check my curiosity. She was clearly scared, in need of my help, and I'd already agreed to give it. She was obviously no stranger to abuse, either.

The scars on her wrists confirmed her slave past, but also made me wonder about her innate magic once again. Why would a sea captain keep an enchanted pleasure slave? Had she actually been a pleasure slave, or something else entirely? I'd read stories of powerful people keeping fae captive for their own pleasure, and the thought revolted me.

I resolved to help Preel any way I could. Her secrets were exactly that; hers. She and her husband had put their trust in me. I couldn't betray that. I knew how it felt to be betrayed.

Saraknyal, of course, was no help. *The woman's magical, Hashi! She could be dangerous! For all you know that cloth on her mouth's the only thing keeping her from breathing fire, or—*

Shut up, old man. If she had that kind of power, she wouldn't need nokitu to protect her, or my help for that matter.

Okay, probably true, but if she reaches under that veil, I suggest you duck.

Enough! We're helping her. End of story!

And so we did, though my curiosity wouldn't let go so easily. Late that night I wondered if Brilla's fascination with Preel, or Jhavika's abduction of the admiral's wife, for that matter, might have more to do with her magic than jealousy, vengeance, or manipulation. I'd finally given up and gone to bed, resorting to brandy and my old mental exercises to finally fall asleep.

Brilla's response to my letter surprised me.

Lady Severn

I will meet with you at noon today in my home. Your undead abominations will not be allowed within Balshi Keep.

Lady Brilla Balshi

And so, I prepared myself.

I would wear Soul Drinker openly as a deterrent, for Brilla had witnessed first-hand more than once what both the blade and I were capable of. Yes, she had an army, but that hadn't kept me from exacting retribution from her father. I wore basic black and comfortable boots, clothes I could move in. I'd bring an escort, but they'd stay with my carriage outside the keep. I would have no way to summon them if things went wrong.

Diplomacy... I muttered to myself as my coach approached the estate's outer wall. Even in the daytime, being here reminded me of the fateful night of Jhavika's party. Oh, how the future would have changed if I'd simply killed her that night. How many lives could I have saved? How many souls? But what might have happened if Jhavika had taken up Soul Drinker?

I'd never asked Saraknyal what he would have done if I'd died and Jhavika had taken him. I didn't think I wanted to know.

The other even more blood-curdling question was, what would have happened if I'd taken up Jhavika's scourge? I shivered at the thought of what I might have become.

Bromish announced us, the gate opened, and we rumbled through. Soldiers stood in formation to either side of the entrance, obviously meant to intimidate me. They didn't. The endless roar of the falls filled the air, and I could taste the pervasive mist with every breath. The cascade of snow melt kept the temperature here much cooler than elsewhere in Haven, and I wondered if that was why they built a palace here.

Personally, I preferred the heat.

I exited my carriage and strode for the entrance to the looming palace, ignoring the soldiery.

Like game tiles lined up on edge, ready to be knocked over, Saraknyal quipped.

Let's not knock the game board over just yet, I thought to him. The doors opened to reveal more soldiers and a butler.

Hashi, their crossbow bolts have silver heads, Saraknyal warned.

Well, well. Someone's been doing their homework. Saraknyal couldn't dissolve silver like he could iron or steel. *Good thing I'm not here to start a fight.*

And if she's invited you here to end the necromancer threat? he posited.

Then I should have put this off until Hipshill finished my next project. With the containment vessel finished, I'd put my armorer to the task of crafting light mail to be sewn into an overcoat. It wasn't finished, so I'd settled for wearing my steel-lined waistcoat. I doubted it would stop a hail of crossbow bolts, however.

The butler bowed. "Lady Severn, Lady Balshi will receive you. This way, please." He started off, and I followed.

Soldiers fell in behind me, a full score of them. *More silver?*

The crossbows, at least. If things go pear-shaped, we're in trouble.

I followed my escort through the ground floor of the palace to a room that might have once been cozy, situated with a bank of windows overlooking the lake and the falls, a fireplace in one wall. My escort of soldiers filed in behind me, filling in to my left, right, and behind. The room sported only one piece of furniture, an elaborate chair of red and gold. It sat facing the room, its back to the windows and the stupendous view. In that chair sat Brilla Balshi.

The butler announced me and backed away.

She looks like she swallowed something sour, Saraknyal observed, and I couldn't disagree.

She also looked like she was still in mourning, clad in a frumpy black gown with a high neck and lace collar and cuffs. Her hair had been pulled back, and she wore a lace veil over her head. Skeletally thin hands clutched the ornate arms of the chair, her mouth quirked into a moue of something between amusement and distaste. Her eyes assessed me coldly.

I wasn't going to be the one to break the silence, and I'd be damned if I let her intimidate me. Finally, she spoke.

"What do you want?"

Rude, but to the point. Fine, I can play that game.

"I want you to leave Preel Longbright alone." I watched her for a response, but there wasn't one. Her expression didn't change at all, but the tendons in the backs of her hands flexed, her nails digging into the red brocade upholstery.

"And what makes you think for a moment that I'm causing the woman the slightest distress, or that I'll consider doing what *you* tell me to do?"

"I have an agreement with Admiral Longbright to act as his wife's liaison with the Council in his absence. Preel contacted me after receiving your letters requesting to meet her. She's not in a position to accept your hospitality, and it would be pointless anyway. She's mute. You can correspond with her by letter, but not in person."

Her face shifted into a sneer of distaste. "And what gives *her* the right to refuse *my* hospitality? She's nothing but a slave! A pirate's whore!"

Well, now we know she's not trying to spark up a friendship with Preel.

Or she knows Preel used to be her husband's pleasure slave, I hypothesized. "She's neither, Brilla, and she's been through enough."

"You'll address me as Lady Balshi, you base-born witch!"

Base-born? Does she really think she's royalty?

"No, I won't." I rested a hand on Soul Drinker. "And I'm a *necromancer*, not a witch. Your father made the same mistake. I would *think*, having witnessed how that worked out for *him*, that you'd learn from his error."

Careful, Hashi.

"How *dare* you threaten me!" she seethed, shaking with rage.

"I'm not threatening you, Brilla, I'm simply telling you that while Admiral Longbright is at sea, Preel enjoys *my* protection. She doesn't want to meet you, and after your outbursts at the council meeting, and your clear opinion of her, I can't blame her." I smiled thinly. "If you continue to harass her, I'll speak to the Council. Admiral Longbright is vital to our efforts. You're interfering with those efforts."

"I'm doing no such thing! I merely want to talk to the woman!"

"Why?" I asked flatly. "Are you *jealous* of her?"

She looked mildly perplexed. "What could I *possibly* be jealous of her for?"

I don't think she knows Preel was Nightspinner's slave.

"You tell me," I countered. "Why do you want to speak with

her?"

"That's my business and Preel's! I don't answer to *you*!"

I shrugged. *Well, it was worth a try.* "Very well. I've said what I've come to say, Brilla. Leave Preel alone, or it won't go well for you."

"You'll leave this palace immediately, and you'll stop interfering where you're not welcome!" She sneered at me. "Or it won't go well for *you*, Hashi Severn!"

I smiled at her threat, then at the nervous guards surrounding me. "You *do* have a short memory, don't you?"

"I have a *perfect* memory!" Spittle flew from her pale lips. "I remember how you murdered my father!"

"I didn't murder him, Brilla. I took him into my service in retribution for his attack on me." I bared my teeth. "Think of it as indentured servitude, a direct consequence of his misbehavior."

"Leave this *instant*!" She seethed.

I nodded once, turned on my heel, and walked out. Soldiers stumbled out of my way, and had to trot to catch up with my long-legged stride. I wasn't exactly angry, just troubled.

So, what the hell was that about?

She clearly wants something from Preel, but I have no idea what that is, Saraknyal said. *Oh, and she's barking mad, by the way.*

I suppressed a snort of laughter. *I don't need a necromancer to tell me that, old man.*

Chapter Seventeen
Recruitment

From the diary of Kevril Longbright —
More negotiations...but at least these are my kind of people.

Two days into our search for Nonny Brethwite and Terence Caul, *Scourge*'s crew had mostly recovered from the pirate revel, though a few still sported cuts, bruises, and sprains. We were scooting along two miles to leeward of some of the smaller islands, far enough to sea to maintain good wind, when Boxley shocked me flat footed by reporting for duty with her hair cut in the exact style Preel sported. When I had recovered enough from the shock to be able to speak, I asked her what possessed her to do such a thing.

"Um...too much ale and ribbing from one of the Ravens, sir." She looked sheepish and ran her fingers through her bobbed hair. "It looked worse, but I asked Hemp to touch it up."

I hadn't seen her since the revel and wondered if she'd been hiding from me. "Well, it could be worse, I suppose. You could have shaved your head entirely."

"I thought about it, but I didn't want to offend Miko." She brushed her scalp again. "It's taking some getting used to, but at least I won't get it caught in a block or some such."

"True, and it can't be grabbed in a fight." I started to send her off to her duties, but my curiosity got the better of me. "So, what *ribbing* induced you to cut your hair?"

"Oh, *Blood Raven*'s third lieutenant, Zackary Balzack, called me a liar, and I threatened to shave his head with a boarding axe." She grinned. "He didn't believe I'd killed Jhavika Keshmir, you see, and I'd shown him the axe that clove her skull. He told me he'd let me shave him head to toe if I let him cut my hair."

I narrowed my eyes at her. "And…"

"And he's lucky I'm a better barber than he is, sir!" She laughed. "I had to sharpen my axe twice! He's a hairy fook, or *was*."

At that point in our conversation, the foremast lookout called down that he'd spotted two brigs in the lee of a tiny island named Bird Rock. I mentally thanked the man for rescuing me from my conversation with Boxley, and ordered a parlay flag hoisted and sails trimmed to windward. I raised a spyglass and espied *White Lady* and *First Light* hunkered in a cove, hard to spot against the rocky cliffs and flocks of birds aloft. The island was a popular stop over for foragers, for terns, boobies, and even frigates rooked there. Few ships stayed long, however, for the smell of guano could curl your eyebrows. It took us hours to work upwind into the bay, so both ships had plenty of time to prepare. Parlay flags flew and boats were launched before we even dropped anchor.

"Ahoy, *Scourge*!" Nonny Brethwite stood in the stern of one of the launches and waved his much bedraggled tricorne, grinning gap toothed, his white beard bristling. "Ain't seen you in a tree's age!"

"It's been a while, all right!" I waved. "Good to see you still sailing!"

"Aye, pickin's are slim, but we're survivin'." He gestured to the other launch. "This here's Terence Caul, captain of *First Light*. We been parnerin' up for half a year, now."

"Captain Caul, good to meet you!"

"And you, Longbright." A wiry man with a narrow face and beak nose, deeply pox scarred, Caul wore a striped shirt and a bright green jacket that made him look like a scarecrow. "Your reputation precedes you! We ran across an armed merchant not long ago lookin' for you."

"Aye, there's a story that goes along with that, and I've got news. I'd be happy to stand you both to dinner tonight to talk it over. My cook, Bert's, top notch!"

"As long as you don't feed us eggs or fowl!" Nonny laughed and Caul grinned.

"I'll make sure of it! Sunset, then?"

"Sunset it is!" They both waved, sat, and ordered their crews to row back to their ships.

"Boxley, inform Bert that we've got company, and tell Kivan and Miko they'll be expected to attend."

"Aye, sir." She snapped a salute and hurried off.

I raised my spyglass to look over the two brigs. They both appeared seaworthy, if a little worn, but they'd probably give *Scourge* a run for her money on any point of wind, and could undoubtedly outmaneuver us. They wouldn't haul a fifth of the cargo we could, but they could each sport a crew of thirty or so, valuable additions to our fleet if I could talk them into joining up.

I closed my spyglass and began to formulate my plan of attack.

Bert put on a full saddle of mutton with all the fixings that literally brought tears of gastronomic joy to my guests' eyes. While we stuffed ourselves within an inch of being able to walk away from the table, I filled Nonny and Terence in on the situation. Neither of them took it well, but Nonny was more pragmatic.

"Was bound to happen sooner or later." Nonny drained his glass and nodded to the decanter. "It's all about money. We been bleedin' Toki and Mati dry for almost two centuries. Empires run on trade."

"True enough." I filled his glass and offered the bottle around. Miko accepted, but Kivan's eyes had started to glaze over with the food and drink. Caul had no taste for wine, but a decanter of my finest rum sat at his elbow, much reduced in volume. Good food and drink had been the first phase of my plan, and seemed to be working well.

"Seems like a drop in the bucket what we take," Terence argued. "Maybe thirty or forty pirate ships in all the Blood Sea. That's maybe four thousand souls, and ain't none of us gettin' rich."

"Which is why I hooked up with Haven," I put in. "Steady work and a home port. And you can't tell me you both wouldn't benefit from the shipyard."

"True enough." Nonny sipped and eyed the mauled saddle of mutton. The grease pooling beneath had congealed, but he dredged a piece of soft tack through it and popped it in his mouth. "Beats livin' on eggs and bird shit."

"Death of a thousand cuts," Miko said, and when both of my guests looked at her askance, she explained. "That's what the pirates of the Blood Sea are doing to Mati and Toki. Sariff, too, to a lesser degree. The truth is, they're already supporting every island and city state in the archipelago indirectly, though Haven more than the rest. Sooner or later, rich merchants would band together and complain."

"Aye. Used to be we preyed on each other as much as the main trade routes, but that's pissin' in yer own bathwater." Nonny reached for the bread again, but I raised a hand.

"Save room. Bert's got a tartberry pie."

"Bloody devils drag me down, how do you keep from gettin' fat with a cook like that!" Terence shifted in his seat and loosened his belt a notch.

"It's not easy."

"I'm surprised Mati hasn't taken action sooner," Nonny said, still on subject. "They're more isolated and dependent on trade. All of the Empire of Tira flows through there."

"Navies cost a lot," I put in, "and Mati's not an empire. They've no standing army, and their navy's more for harbor defense than chasing down pirates. The princes like their money in their pockets, not supporting soldiers or sailors. Hemp!"

"Sir!" Hemp ducked in and eyed the table. "Ready to clear?"

"Yes, and open another bottle of the Beriknor Red."

"Aye, sir!" He called in a scullery lad and they cleared, then he opened another bottle of wine and decanted it.

"So, we get to prey on shipping of anyone not signed into this protectorate, and use Haven's shipyard once a year." Terence stuffed a pipe and lit it, filling the air with fragrant smoke. "What's the catch."

"The catch is, we defend our allies." I nudged my dozing lieutenant under the table, and she started. "You can bow out if you wish, Kivan."

"And miss pie? No, sir!" She sat up straight and blinked herself awake.

"Youngsters these days got no stamina!" Nonny grinned at my young officer and laughed at her scowl. "Why, when I was yer age, I could eat a whole sheep, drink a keg of rum, and rut my way through half the brothels in Black Point before breakfast!"

"Only half?" I grinned as Kivan blushed. "And don't underestimate the lieutenant, Nonny. She's tougher than she looks."

Kivan's blush deepened.

Hemp returned bearing a steaming pie the size of a barrel lid, the filling still bubbling hot, and the aroma vying with the pipe smoke. I topped up glasses as he cut and served with military precision, the deep purple juice of the filling dripping like blood onto the plates.

"So, if we don't join, what happens?" Terence asked as he picked up his fork and set his pipe aside.

"Nothing at all." I sampled the desert and rolled my eyes. "My complements to Bert, Hemp. She outdid herself."

"Oh, aye, sir!" He grinned and hurried out.

Terence scowled at me. "I don't believe that, Kevril. If we don't join your privateer navy, there's got to be a down side."

"Well, you'd have to steer clear of preying on the shipping of our allies, and you'd be less than welcome in Haven. I can't speak for the other islands or city states, but your choices of ports to sell your booty would probably thin." I narrowed my eyes at him. "But if you were caught preying on allied shipping, there'd be repercussions."

"But you'd still be free to prey on shipping from Toki or Mati, unless they capitulate." Miko sampled her dessert and chased the bite with a sip of wine.

"*Capitulate?*" Nonny scratched his whiskers. "You're mad as a hatter if you think either one's gonna roll over and play nice."

Miko shrugged. "Maybe not initially, but an organized privateer navy would be able to put a lot more pressure on shipping than pirates currently do. War's expensive, and would cut merchant shipping to nil. Eventually, they'd crack."

"Crack how?" Terence said, his scowl undiminished.

"Details haven't been worked out yet. If it comes down to blockading shipping entirely, they'll either go to war, or some kind of agreement will be reached. The Blood Sea Protectorate gets recognition and takes tithe from every merchant to sail through our waters." I raised my glass to Nonny. "You're right that it's all about money, and if we do this right, we get paid without having to risk our lives."

"*Tax* collectors," Terence grumbled around a mouthful. "What's the fun in that?"

"Nobody's required to stay in if they don't like it," I added. "Every captain commands their own ship."

"Well, I for one don't see a down side." Nonny raised his glass. "I'll talk it over with my crew, but count me in."

"Good!" I raised my glass to his, then looked sidelong at Captain Caul. "You, Terence?"

"Oh, aye, I'll give it a go, but if I get bored, I may just sail for the horizon." He raised his glass and we all toasted.

"I've drafted a letter for you to take to Haven. Two, actually, one for the Council, and one for my wife."

"Wife?" Nonny blinked at me. "When did *that* happen?"

"Some months ago. I owe her my life. We thought it best if she stay safe in Haven for now."

"Safe in *Haven*?" Terence snorted a laugh. "That's what they call an oxymoron, ain't it?"

"Well, safer than sailing around aboard a pirate ship, anyway." At least I hoped so. I broached the subject of Hyko, and listened half-heartedly to the sparse news from the north, but my mind and my soul slipped away from the conversation to the woman I loved hundreds of miles away.

Chapter Eighteen
Suboptimal Outcomes

From the journal of Preel Longbright —

I should have known better than to try to warn off a madwoman. It didn't work for Kevril when I was raving, and he'd honestly tried to help me. I met his entreaties only with scorn, hatred, and violence. I doubt this will turn out any better.

A tap at my door brought my bleary eyes up from the tome. It was late, and my nerves were shot, so instead of a futile attempt at sleep, I'd immersed myself in one of the books Lady Severn had loaned me. I found the history of Chen fascinating, troubling, and heartwarming all at once. The monastic sects of the Gods of Light had truly overcome impossible odds, all in the name of faith. I had never had much faith in the gods, believing myself cursed for so long. I wondered about this mystical inner power of qi the warrior monks had mastered, but none of the books I'd delved so far had defined it.

"Come in." I put the thick book down without closing it and stood as the door opened.

Busashi stepped in and bowed. "I'm sorry to disturb you, mistress, but Lady Severn's here and wishes to speak with you if you're not indisposed."

"Lady Severn?" I glanced at the clock; nearly midnight. I opened my mouth to ask what on earth she could want so late, then realized that, whatever it was, it had to be important. "Yes. Give me ten minutes to get ready, then bring her here." I snatched up the enchanted gag and hurried to the door. "And please put this on me."

"Yes mistress." He complied, and left.

I dashed to the bedroom, threw off my light robe and pulled on a longer one, then picked out a headdress and veil that matched. A quick dab of makeup to cover my tattoo, and I was ready. I went back to the sitting room and searched frantically for a minute to locate my notebook, then paced.

Another knock at the door and I opened it.

Busashi stepped in, then to the side. "Lady Severn, mistress."

She came in, tall, dark, and imposing as hell, clad in black from collar to toes, a wicked-looking bone-handled dagger at her belt, a completely different woman than the one I'd met in Ash Keep, clad in flowing silks. Ghiti and Whapo entered behind her, Ghiti moving quickly to my side.

"Preel, I'm sorry to come so late, but I had to think this over, and I saw your light on, so I..." She stopped and looked around the sitting room as if suddenly troubled, then shook her head. "Sorry. I just...remember this room."

A little stunned by her arrival and strange behavior, I scrawled, "You've been here before?" which Ghiti read aloud for me.

"Yes. I went through the whole keep after...the fight with Jhavika's guards." She shook her head again and smiled weakly. "You have much better taste than Jhavika did."

"Thank you," I wrote, then prompted, "You're troubled, Lady Severn, and you wouldn't be here this late if it wasn't important."

"Yes, to both." She sighed and began to pace, her hands flexing at her sides with her long-legged strides. "It's about Brilla. I'm afraid all I did was make things worse. I warned her off, and she..." She stopped and fixed me with her dark eyes. "She's all but psychotic, Preel. She threatened me, used a most *shocking* insult in reference to you, refused to tell me why she wanted to speak with you, and ordered me out of her home."

Shit! I thought, biting my lip behind my enchanted gag. I wrote, "Do you think there's anything the Council can do about her?"

"If she actually comes out and threatens you, or does something to endanger you, yes, but it would get messy." Lady Severn shook her head and resumed pacing. "She's not in a frame of mind to back down from a confrontation, and she's got a large force of soldiers and runs half the crime in Haven. Protection rackets, thugs, spies, you name it."

I thought furiously but came up blank. I knew why Brilla wanted to meet with me, but I dared not tell Severn why. I wrote, "What should I do?" and Ghiti read it.

"Frankly, short of having her killed, I don't know." She scoffed a dry laugh. "I walked every rooftop in Haven, and couldn't think of a single course of action that wouldn't have serious repercussions. I can't walk in and murder her without provocation, and I don't think your nokitu could do it cleanly. She's surrounded by an army, and is clearly paranoid. If it's any consolation, I don't think she knows you were Captain Nightspinner's slave. I asked her if she was jealous of you, and she just seemed confused."

"Well, that's something," I wrote.

"Anyway, she also knows that you're under my protection, so if she fucks with you, she fucks with me." Severn turned to face me and grinned. "And *trust* me, Preel, *anyone* who fucks with me loses."

"Thank you, but do you think that will deter Brilla?"

"It should at least keep her from trying anything overt. She wants something, and..." She paused again and her face went blank. "Um...look, Preel, your secrets are your business, not mine, but..."

I stiffened, and so did my three bodyguards, but Lady Severn raised her hands, open and empty.

"I'm...sensitive to magic, so I know there's something special about you. I don't know what it is, and frankly I don't care, but I'm guessing *that's* what Brilla wants."

My blood went cold. I should have known better than to let someone with her skills into my presence. Whapo caught my eye from behind Lady Severn, clearly poised to strike.

"Preel, you're scared, that's obvious, but you needn't be scared of *me*." Severn's pleading tone brought me up short. "I won't tell a soul, but you've *got* to play this closer to the vest if you intend to keep this secret to yourself." She started ticking off fingers. "Don't come to any Council meetings, don't take an audience with Lady Twince or Lord Blackbriar, and be *careful* with Brilla. I'd suggest you don't go out for at least a few days."

I breathed easier, my tension melting away. My talent had picked someone truly worthy of my trust. I scribbled, "Why Twince or Blackbriar?"

"Because they're both also sensitive to magic, Twince far more so than I am." She smiled weakly. "She felt the scourge's enchantment upon Jhavika. She even *warned* her."

"Warned her of what?" I scrawled.

Severn's mien sobered. "That there was magic about her, and she should have a care, lest it consume her. She told me the same, after the fashion. You should take that warning to heart. You're young, and you may not understand the seduction of magic. It can...be a bit like black lotus. The more you use it the more you *need* to use it."

I nodded, fully aware of the danger of my own talent. "And Brilla? What can we do about her?" I wrote.

"I'll try to keep an eye on her, but House Balshi controls about half the criminals in Haven, which is why you shouldn't go out." She bit her lip and spread her hands in a helpless gesture. "I'm sorry, but that's all I can offer you right now."

I nodded. "Thank you for the warning."

"It's the least I could do." She flashed a smile and nodded to the open book on the reading table. "Are you enjoying the books?"

Her non sequitur question took me aback, but I nodded. "Yes, very much. They're fascinating."

"Good. I'll pick some others out for you." She nodded to Busashi. "Keep your nokitu close, Preel. They're your best defense right now."

"I will."

"Good. I'll be off then." She nodded to me. "Sorry to ruin your evening."

"No, thank you for coming."

"Be safe." She flashed another dazzling smile and whirled for the door.

"Escort the lady," Busashi ordered Whapo, and the nokitu ushered Severn out.

The door closed, and I felt like a tornado had swept through my sitting room. I collapsed into a chair, staring at nothing, unsure what to do. I felt trapped, abandoned, and helpless. Rubbing the scars on my wrists, I recalled the feeling of manacles there. If Brilla found out my nature, those chains would return. No keep's walls, no force of soldiers, could keep it from happening.

"Mistress?" Busashi took a knee before me to bring our eyes on the same level. "How may we help you?"

I clenched my hands into fists to keep from shaking. *How? That's the question, isn't it? It's always about the questions... You're a gods-damned truthsayer, Preel! You're not helpless!*

I lurched up, my mind spinning. Discarding my veil, I tapped the gag insistently.

"Of course, mistress." Busashi untied the gag and stepped back.

"Ghiti, bring Lewin here. We need to talk this over and formulate a plan. All of us. Everyone who knows I'm a truthsayer."

"At once, mistress!" She dashed out.

I started to pace. "Busashi, I want your honest assessment of whether you and your team could eliminate Brilla Balshi without being caught or leaving evidence that leads back to me."

"It's possible, mistress, but there's always the danger of discovery." He shrugged helplessly. "Unfortunately, the entire Council knows we pledged our service to your husband. Brilla will have guards stationed to protect her at all times. It's likely we'd be seen, if not identified. We could *remove* the guards, but that sometimes only increases the risk of discovery. No matter how careful we are, there's always evidence left behind."

"Blast!" I paced, wracking my brain for an alternative.

"There's also the risk of failure. If we try, and the target survives, there would be serious repercussions."

I fixed him with a surprised look. "You think there's a chance she'd survive the attempt?"

"No assassination is without risk of failure." He shrugged again. "If, as Lady Severn says, Brilla is psychotic, that could lead to paranoia. She could have someone pose as her, or arrange some kind of trap."

I nodded and resumed pacing. I was feeling a little paranoid myself. But was I being paranoid *enough*?

A tap at the door and the rest of my nokitu entered with Lewin. The sage looked bleary eyed. I'd forgotten it was so late.

"Lewin, I'm sorry, but there have been developments."

"No matter, mistress." He flashed a weary smile. "When you're old as me, sleep's the least of your concerns."

"Well, I hope you're not too tired to put your mind to work." I looked everyone over. "Now, I want everyone to speak freely, but above all, be *careful* what you say. I intend to use my talent to discern the best course of action tonight, and a careless question will ruin that."

They all nodded, lips sealed, eyes fixed.

"Good. So, you all know Lady Severn just paid us a visit, and her warning to Brilla Balshi evidently didn't go well." I filled them all in on as much as I could remember of what Severn said. I prompted Busashi for anything I'd missed.

"One other thing." He glanced from Lewin to me. "Lady Severn detected an aura of magic about you, which is concerning. If that news gets out, the consequences would be dire."

I nodded. Memories of chains, beatings, and worse raced through my mind. I clenched my hands over my stomach to keep them from shaking. "Which is why we need to invoke my talent."

"It's only been three days since the last time we posed you a question, mistress." Lewin looked concerned for me. "Do you think it's safe?"

"It should be. The last question wasn't very taxing." I forced a deep breath and resisted the urge to pace. "I can gauge how much the question pressed me by how long I sleep after. I should be fine."

"Very well, then it's not a question of whether or not to invoke your talent, but what question to pose." Lewin's pragmatic logic calmed my nerves a little. "We can ask how best to eliminate her, what she knows, what she intends—which is tricky—or what she's currently planning."

Options clicked through my mind. "Asking how best to kill her is problematic, because the word 'best' can have many connotations. Wording is everything. If we want to know how Busashi and his people can kill her with the most certainty of success, that's one question. How to do it with the least chance of being discovered, observed, or traced back to me, may be a completely different one, or more than one. And never forget that my talent only gives an answer of what currently is, not what will be. I can't look into the future."

"There are too many variables and considerations, I think," Busashi said. "Pick one, and let us deal with the rest."

I nodded and sighed. "What else? If we ask what she knows, we have to be specific, and the answer might not help us."

"I think it's safe to assume that she doesn't yet know of your talent, mistress," Ghiti said. "If she did, she would have acted."

"Probably. That leaves us with her intentions, which is always a tricky subject."

"What Master Lewin said last," Busashi put in with a raised finger, "what she is currently planning. That's specific and would give us an immediate course of action."

"*Maybe*," I countered. "If she's planning a picnic on the lakeside, it won't help us."

Lewin wagged a bony finger. "But if we asked what she's planning with regard to *you*, mistress, it might. She wants to know what makes you special. You're not going to tell her, and neither are we. She'll try to find out some other way. How she plans to do so should at least warn us if she's planning something dangerous."

I bit my lip, struggling to think of problems with that question. "I need paper and pen." I whirled to the small writing desk and sat down, fishing implements from the drawers. "Wording is *everything*."

We worked through it word by word until we had a question I was happy with. I wrote it down on a clean sheet of paper and handed it around. "Tell me if any of you can find a problem with this."

One by one, the nokitu read it and shook their heads.

Lastly, Lewin read it carefully, his wizened lips pursed. "I believe this is a solid approach, mistress, but before we ask, we should take some precautions. You'll be sleeping until late morning, and there may be developments."

"Well, I—"

"Two of my people in your room with you while you sleep, mistress. I insist." Busashi sounded adamant, and I couldn't disagree.

"I suppose that's prudent. We should also warn the entire household." I recalled Bert's poisoning of the food aboard *Scourge* when they were taken by Jhavika. "The food should be tested for poisons, and all the doors checked and bolted from the inside."

Busashi nodded. "We already do those things, but double checking would be wise."

"And Lady Severn was right about going out," Ghiti added. "I'm sorry, mistress, but no shopping trips for a while."

I sighed and nodded. Shopping was truly one of my few delights. "I suppose." I looked around. "Anything else?"

Silence.

"All right. Let me use the washroom, then you can ask me that question, Lewin." I pointed to the paper in his hands.

Lewin bowed shortly. "Very well, mistress."

I started to turn, then a thought came back to me, and I turned back. "And I want to thank you all from the bottom of my heart. I'd be in dire straits without your help."

"It's our honor to serve you, mistress." Busashi bowed, and the others followed suit.

"Still, thank you." I smiled to myself. Less than a year ago, I had been a slave chained in a sea captain's cabin, gagged, questioned, and abused as I lay unconscious every four days. Now...I wondered what I'd done to deserve all this.

Simple, I thought. *I fell in love with a pirate.*

I freshened up, readied myself for the question, and lay in bed with my hands folded over my stomach, Lewin at the bedside, and two nokitu at the door. "You should write the answer down, Lewin. Sometimes they're complicated."

"Oh, yes." He snatched up paper and pen and sat at my dressing table. "Ready?"

"Yes, but be sure to put the gag back on me after."

"Of course, mistress." He cleared his throat, dipped his pen, and asked. "What is Brilla Balshi currently planning to do to discern what made you so valuable to Jhavika Keshmir?"

My talent gripped my soul, and the voice so unlike my own answered. "Abduction and hard interrogation."

Once again, deep dread chased me down into a pit of darkness and oblivion.

Chapter Nineteen
Welcome News

From the journal of Hashi Severn —

I must admit, our admiral is persuasive and knows who to approach. I find myself liking Red Moll, though I don't know why. I hope we can find more like her, and soon.

"Thank you, Captain Moll, Captain Jaris." Malchi dropped the letter of introduction from Longbright onto the table, insufferably satisfied with the arrival of two new recruits to our privateer fleet. "We'll inform the shipyard foreman of your needs, and begin work immediately!"

Thank the gods, Saraknyal groused. *One more council meeting and I'm going to go insane.*

Or murder Reginald Malchi, I thought. The man continued to posture and bluster, even though few of the other members paid him much attention. *You must admit, the Council's hardly the same mob of crime lords they were before Jhavika kicked the hornet's nest. They're playing the long game now. Your idea, remember.*

Don't remind me.

"Bloody fine!" Captain Moll stood and grinned lopsidedly, chucking the younger and less exuberant Captain Tunny Jaris on the shoulder. She'd stumbled upon Jaris' ship, *Rogue*, on her way to Haven from Twin Capes, and talked him into entertaining Haven's offer. After an excruciating hour of questions, he'd agreed. "Cheer up, Tunny! We're privateers!"

"Aye, fine enough." He stood, his dark features set in the same dangerous scowl he'd sported when the two walked into the impromptu council meeting. "This is my *happy* face; can't you tell?"

Red Moll laughed and hitched up her belt. "Oh, and I near

184

forgot! I got a letter for Admiral Longbright's wife." She patted the breast of her sharp red and black jacket. "Know where I might find her?"

"I'd be happy to—"

"I'll take it to her." I shot Malchi a smile and stood. "I've agreed to act as the admiral's wife's liaison with the Council in his absence."

Eyebrows rose around the table, except from Brilla, who just scowled at me.

"You have?" Tori looked at me as if I'd just admitted to devil worship.

"I have." I grinned at him and looked around the table.

"Well, I suppose there's nothing wrong with that," Malchi grumbled.

"I think it's a wonderful arrangement." Nahli stood and arched an eyebrow. "If that's all, I have other matters to attend to." She looked around the table but nobody interjected. "Farewell, then, and welcome, Captains. We *do* appreciate your efforts."

"Well, thank you, Lady Twince." Moll nodded politely to Twince as she exited the establishment's banquet room, then looked to me. "You're Severn, aren't you?"

"Yes." I rounded the table and held out a hand. "The letter?"

"Will stay right here in my pocket until I hand it to Preel Longbright." She patted her jacket again and looked me up and down. "I promised Kevril I'd put it in her hand, and I intend to. I've also got a burning curiosity about the woman who managed to put a noose around Longbright's...um...*heart.*"

She's a piece of work, Saraknyal observed.

She is, I agreed. *And I think I like her.* The captain didn't mince words, and certainly wasn't intimidated by anyone, including me. I found that refreshing. "She's not what you might expect, Captain, but I'll be happy to make the introduction." I waved to the door. "Do you mind walking? I didn't bring a carriage."

"Not at all. I could stand to stretch my legs." She sent her escort back to *Blood Raven* with orders to ready the ship for a haul out, then followed me out of the rooftop establishment, a club owned by Malchi, of course. I turned us southeast, and my two shades fell in behind us. "How far is it?"

"About a mile." I glanced at her boots, hard soled with a thick heel. "Will you make it in those boots?"

"I'll manage, if you don't outpace me with those long legs of yours." She looked up at me, then back at my grim escort. "You're the necromancer, aren't you? Those are...undead, right?"

"Yes, and yes." I caught her eye. "Is that a problem?"

"Not if you don't sic them on *me*, it ain't." She smiled sidelong. "Longbright speaks highly of you, by the way. I trust his judgment, as least as far as people goes."

"Oh? I thought pirates weren't big on trust."

"Well, I trust him more than most, anyway." She waved a hand at the rooftops. "Just like you probably don't trust many here in Haven, I guess."

"True." I wasn't much for small talk, so lapsed into silence. When we approached the first bridge, I asked her, "Do you know Haven well?"

"Well enough to keep a hand on my sword when I'm crossing one of those." She nodded to the flat stone span. "Bloody gnomes..."

I smiled and nodded. "Good." I ordered my shades to walk in front and behind, and started across with one hand on Soul Drinker. *Keep an eye on her for me, old man.*

Of course.

I walked without looking back, keeping to the middle of the span. Nothing untoward happened, and we resumed our side-by-side stroll.

"You aren't what I expected from a necromancer," Moll said.

If she uses Maurice Malchi's 'too full of life' line, we'll have to kill her. Saraknyal grumbled.

I stifled a smile and looked at her. "How so?"

She shrugged. "Dunno. You're cautious, amiable, and...younger than I imagined."

She's observant, Saraknyal said.

"Only a fool isn't cautious in Haven," I said.

"Well, only a fool crosses a necromancer, so why the caution?"

"Because there are no shortage of fools here, or anywhere." I eyed her again, trying to figure out if she was curious or just talking to pass the time. "And I'm older than I look."

"Well, you fooled me there." She grinned. "Kevril told me you took down Jhavika's whole guard complement all by your lonesome. That's not a very careful thing to do."

I shrugged. "Sometimes extreme measures are necessary."

She barked a laugh. "You're talkin' to a pirate. We're *specialists* in extreme measures."

I smiled at that and nodded. "Perhaps that's why Longbright and I understand one another. We're both willing to do what's necessary."

She caught my eye and arched an eyebrow. "Necessary for what?"

I thought about that for a moment, then realized the answer. "To protect what we love."

"Love?" Her other eyebrow arched to match the first. "Well, Kevril's in love with his wife. I know that as well as I know my own name. Who are *you* in love with?"

"I didn't say 'who,' I said what."

"Okay, Lady Severn, *what* do you love?"

Tell her you love to be left the hell alone, Saraknyal suggested.

I shrugged and thought about it. "As crazy as it may sound, I love Haven. It's the only place I've been able to carve out a home for myself without someone trying to destroy me for being what I am."

"Yeah, necromancers don't have a very good reputation." She chuckled low. "Kevril told me it didn't make you a bad person. I find that...hard to believe, I guess."

"Maybe he's wrong." I fixed her with narrowed eyes. "Maybe I *am* a bad person."

"And maybe I am, too." A lopsided smile spread slowly across her lips. "Pirates don't have a much better reputation than necromancers, you know."

I couldn't help but smile. "True enough. Maybe *that's* why I get along with Longbright."

"Maybe."

We walked along in silence for a time, crossing three more bridges, before she asked. "Mind if I ask you a question?"

"That *is* a question." I glanced at her and shrugged. "Go ahead."

"Why take up necromancy?"

I opened my mouth to tell her it was complicated, then shrugged. "Why take up piracy?"

"Fair question." She stuck her thumbs in her belt and took up a piratical swagger. "Pirates have one irrevocable motto: free and beholden to none. That's what we live for. We're our own masters, our own lords, and we make our own rules."

"I've heard that." I looked at her. "Then why join Haven's fleet?"

"Because there's a storm comin', and that's the only way to weather it." She looked at me with knitted brows. "You didn't answer me. Why necromancy?"

"It's complicated," I said with a sigh. "It was...my only option."

Moll looked nonplused. "*Really?*"

"Really." I sighed. "Call it a forced career decision, one of those moments in your life when you have to make a choice to survive or die screaming. I chose to live the only way I could."

"Well, slap my ass with a porcupine and call me prickly!"

I snorted an involuntary laugh at the ribald comment and shook my head. "That was inventive."

"It's a gift." She chuckled.

We walked along in silence for another while, crossing two more bridges, the last a swinging rope affair that left my heart pounding. Moll, I noticed, seemed more at ease on the moving platform than the stone.

"Mind if I ask you why you're so keen to meet Preel Longbright?" Call me suspicious, but I had agreed to see to Preel's well-being.

"Just curious what kind of woman Kevril could fall for. I've known him off and on for years, and as far as I've known, he's never loved anything but his ship and freedom." She looked to me again, and I saw something different in her eyes, something I couldn't name, and didn't know if I wanted to know. "He told me she was a slave when he found her."

"So I understand. She's had some hard knocks."

"So have we all, I suppose."

"Did he tell you she was mute?"

"No." She looked a little startled. "That's...odd."

I shrugged. "She's also from Fornice, raised in Marathia. Wears traditional clothes."

"You mean like a *veil?*"

"Yes." I glanced at her. "You find that odd?"

"I find it odd that Kevril Longbright would fall ass over teakettle for a veil-clad slave from Fornice, yes." She looked honestly perplexed. "That just doesn't seem his type."

"Well, she's also quite a scholar."

"A slave scholar?" She looked even more perplexed. "That's...even stranger."

"I told you she's not what you'd expect, didn't I?" I shot her another smile.

"That you did."

We lapsed into silence again, then came to the gatehouse that guarded the flying bridge to Longbright Keep. I pulled the bell rope.

Moll gaped at the expansive keep. "*This* is Kevril's?"

"Yes. It used to be Jhavika's. The Council didn't know what else to do with it, so we gave it to Longbright." I shrugged. "He needed someplace to call home, after all."

"Never needed anything before but a ship and the wide open sea," she said.

"Well, he never *had* anything before but a ship, did he?"

"You saying this Preel woman's worth it?" she asked.

I fixed her with a challenging stare. "Longbright thinks so. That's all that matters, isn't it?"

She shrugged. "I suppose. Just never thought I'd see the day."

Two soldiers crossed the bridge to answer the bell and unlocked the gate. One recognized me and bowed. "Lady Severn." His eyes slid sideways to take in Captain Moll, her sword, and her garb. "Who's this?"

"Captain Moll of the corsair *Blood Raven*. She has a letter from the admiral for his wife." I shot Moll a glance. "She insisted upon delivering it in person, so I offered to make the introduction. Is the lady of the keep present?"

She better be, unless she's got a death wish, Saraknyal quipped. *Did you see the thugs watching the bridge gate?*

No. How many? I didn't look, but put a hand on Soul Drinker's hilt. *Show me!*

He did, and my head swam with the mind's eye view. *Five or six at least. They're not very subtle.*

Remind me to inform Busashi.

"Lady?" The guard looked at me askance, the gate standing open.

I'd missed something. "Sorry." I turned to my shade escort. "Stay here. Guard the gate."

"Yes, mistress." They stood facing the rooftop, arms folded.

"Huh, I didn't know they spoke." Moll followed me through and we started across the bridge.

"Only when they need to, and then not much."

"Ha! Sound like the perfect male companions. Maybe I'll borrow a few from you!"

I chuckled. Moll had a quirky sense of humor.

The guard ushered us into the keep, then bowed. "I'll send someone to inform the mistress, Lady Severn, but it may be a moment. Can I offer you refreshment?"

"An iced tea would be welcome." The walk had been warm.

"Straightaway." He hurried off.

"Nice place," Moll observed, looking around.

Nicer now that Jhavika's gone, Saraknyal said, and I couldn't help but smile.

"What?" Moll looked at me curiously.

"Oh, nothing. I remember the place before Longbright got it. Jhavika had too much money for her own good and crappy taste. Preel's given it a nautical flavor."

A footman arrived with two tall glasses of iced tea with mint. I accepted one and thanked him.

"Damn me, that's good!" Moll exclaimed after a long drink.

"Isn't it?"

"Where do they get ice?"

"I wondered the same thing. Seems the Brickhammer clan has a sideline business mining ice from a glacier halfway up one of the mountains. They pack it in straw-filled barrels and sell it." I sipped and sighed. "I told them they should consider shipping it to the outer islands, or even Toki."

"Ha, maybe we could bribe the god-emperor into leaving the Blood Sea alone with a steady supply of ice."

I chuckled at the thought. "Not a bad idea."

The guard returned with one of Preel's nokitu. "Lady Severn, Captain Moll, Mistress Preel will see you. Please follow me."

We handed our empty glasses over to the hovering footman and followed. They ushered us to the same sunroom were I'd first met Preel. She stood with Busashi and another nokitu, wearing yet another colorful sari and matching veil, and curtsied as we entered.

"Preel, this is Captain Moll of the *Blood Raven*. She met with your husband some days ago at Twin Capes." I gestured to Moll, and she stepped forward, reaching under her jacket.

"I have his letter right—"

Instantly, the two nokitu stood between Moll and Preel, weapons drawn. They'd moved so fast that not even Saraknyal had warned me. Luckily, Captain Moll froze, her eyes suddenly wide.

"Captain, please remove your hand from your jacket!" Busashi ordered, his two kamas poised.

Hashi! Tell her to do as he says. They're serious!

I can see that! I swallowed hard and said, "Moll, do as he says. Preel's bodyguards are very protective, and have reason to be cautious."

"Bugger me to the *balls*!" She slowly pulled her hand from her jacket, a letter held between two fingers. "Nervous types, you are."

Preel clapped her hands, and pointed to the letter. The nokitu put their weapons away, and Busashi took the letter, inspecting it before handing it over to Preel.

"Sorry," I told Moll. "I should have warned you."

"Hell *yes*, you should have." She swallowed hard and stepped back to my side. "Should'a known Kevril Longbright wouldn't've married a woman who didn't know how to take precautions. My pardon, Mrs. Longbright."

She stepped forward between her nokitu and curtsied again, then drew the notebook she used to communicate from a fold of her sari. She scrawled something quickly and showed it to the female nokitu I'd met before. "I apologize, Captain, but as Lady Severn said, I have reason to be cautious."

"No doubt." Moll grinned and nodded. "Well, I've got to say I'm pleased to meet the woman who finally landed Kevril. Congratulations to you. He's one of the good ones."

Preel wrote, "I know, and thank you. How is he?"

"Oh, right as rain and strong as a summer squall. No doubt that note gives you all the details, but he signed me up at Twin Capes, then headed north toward Hyko. Might have a couple more volunteers sail into Haven in a few days. Smaller ships, but good captains."

"That's good news," she wrote, and for some reason her response seemed less enthusiastic than I'd expected.

I looked closely at Preel and noted beads of sweat under her eyes. "All's well, Preel?"

She wrote quickly in her notebook and stepped up to show me the page. I read silently, "Not really. I learned through Busashi's contacts that Brilla's planning on kidnapping and interrogating me. I can't prove it, but I don't know what to do."

I swore under my breath, my teeth grinding. *Gods damn Brilla Balshi to all Nine Hells!*

You should make that woman a shade, Hashi. You'd have a pair of Balshi bookends.

Don't tempt me, old man. "I'll look into this, Preel, but without proof, I can't do much."

She scribbled, "If I can secure some proof, can you do something?"

I nodded. "Yes, I can, with or without the Council. And there are people watching the other end of your bridge." I nodded to Busashi. "There not very subtle."

Preel pressed her hands together and curtsied in the traditional Fornician gesture of thanks. It made me smile.

"All right, then," Moll said. "I've delivered my note, and it was right nice to meet you, Preel. If you need anything a randy old pirate can do, just let me know."

Preel scrawled and her nokitu read, "Thank you for delivering the letter, and welcome to the Haven Privateer Fleet, Captain Moll!"

Moll grinned. "Never thought I'd ever hear those words, I tell you true."

"I'll speak to you later, Preel. Be safe." At Preel's enthusiastic nod, I turned to follow Moll out.

"Well, you were right about one thing, Lady Severn: Preel wasn't what I expected!"

I chuckled under my breath. "Yes, well, few of us are, are we?"

"Truth there, or I'm a kimono-clad geisha girl!"

I laughed at that, trying to imagine the brash pirate captain dressed like Mah Hatsu. For some reason, Moll amused me. She seemed to have a bawdy quip for everything, and never the same one twice.

We crossed back to the roofs of Haven and Captain Moll turned to me and extended a hand. "Thanks for the introduction, Lady Severn, even if it did nearly get me killed!"

I shook her hand, her grip hard. "My pleasure, Captain." I thought for a moment and added, "If there's any way I can help you deal with the Council, just send a note to Ash Keep."

"Dunno if I'll ever need the services of a necromancer, but I'll keep the offer in mind." She released my hand and grinned. "And if you ever want to forget you're a high-falutin' Lady of the Haven Council of Lords, and just want to kick up your heels, drop me a note."

"I may just—" I paused, a crazy notion coming into my mind in a flash. *Music...dancing...color...life...*

Hashi, what are you thinking?

Shut up, old man. I was through being afraid. "As a matter of fact, there's a singer at a club I've been told I should see. Do you know Fancy's Folly?"

Moll's eyebrows arched. "I know *of* it, but never been there. Members only, ain't it?"

Hashi, are you actually asking this woman out on a date? What the hell are you thinking?

It's not a date. Tori told me about this elvish singer, and I thought I might go, but I'd rather not go alone. To Moll I said, "Well, that's one advantage of being a high-falutin' Lady on Haven's Council of Lords. The singer's an elvish woman, and I've been told she's quite something. I'm not much for social engagements, but..."

"But with *me* along, you don't have to be." Moll laughed.

"Well, yes, I suppose." I felt suddenly uncomfortable. "Going alone just seemed..."

"Creepy. I get it." She stuck her thumbs in her belt and nodded. "Not to worry, Lady Severn. Been a while since I been out to a fancy club, and I'd be happy to accompany you."

This is a bad idea, Hashi. She's a pirate! She'll stab you in the back!

Don't be ridiculous, old man. "Thank you, Captain, and please, call me Hashi."

"And you can call me Red." She grinned broadly again. "What time?"

"Oh, I think her first act begins around eight. I'll arrange a table near the stage for us."

"Excellent! It's a date, then!"

I told you it was a date.

It's not a date! "I'll see you there."

Moll shot me a salute and whirled on her heel, striding away with a piratical swagger and not a care in the world. I watched her go and felt strange, jealous or something I couldn't quite place. The woman just seemed so full of life, overflowing with exuberance. I wondered what my life would have been like if I could have been like that.

Music...dancing...color...life... A memory flashed of the dancers I'd seen in Mati, whirling and undulating, graceful and sensuous. The chance of that life had been utterly crushed by my mother's resentment.

"Hashi? You're standing like a statue, and people are starting to stare.*

Let them stare, old man. I strode forth through the rooftops of Haven toward Fancy's Folly. I had a date to arrange...my first.

Chapter Twenty
Hyko

From the diary of Kevril Longbright —
When did I become such a trusting soul? I should really know better.

"Quiet here," Miko said as she swept her spyglass across the harbor of Hyko.

"A bit." I counted five merchantmen and one small Toki warship, which wasn't uncommon. There seemed to be few of the usual fishing cogs and independent cargo ships. There was, of course, the typical tangle of barges along the river mouth, for the twin cities used that artery to distribute goods from both the sea and the upland Jungle of Nin into the city. A wide sand bar kept deeper draft vessels from venturing upriver, but barges transferred cargo in vast quantities. At the moment, there weren't many barges moving. "Maybe we missed some festival day or something."

"Maybe. Don't like the look of that warship, though."

"Well, *Scourge* doesn't have a price on her head here, and it's a small one. They'd be fools to start trouble in a foreign port."

"Plenty of fools in the world, sir." Miko lowered her spyglass and gave me a sidelong look. "Plans?"

I considered, but my mind was elsewhere. We'd met with *Gull* two days before. Tan had arrived with a warship for Patak, and Preel said she was dealing with unwelcome attention from Brilla Balshi, but that Lady Severn was helping her. Worry vied with my scrutiny of the harbor until finally I simply shrugged. "Anchor well to leeward of the warship, close to shore. No pirates to recruit here, so I'll just take a launch upriver with an escort and set up an audience with the governors."

"Shore leave, sir?" she asked.

"Not until I get the lay of the land and find out how long the governors are going to make me wait." I scanned the walls that surrounded the two halves of Hyko on the landward sides, but we were still too far to see much detail. The city was actually two, Hy, and Ko, which had long been abbreviated. They were independently governed but closely allied, separated by the river running between them. Things looked peaceful, at least, and the surrounding farmland placid as ever. "See to anchoring, Miko, and pick a shore party for me. I've got to put on some decent clothes."

"Aye, best to look like a diplomat instead of a pirate, I suppose. The governors enjoy their arrangement with Toki; telling them a war's brewing won't be welcome news."

"They also like their *independence* from Toki." I shot her a grin. "But you're right; it's best to look less than piratical." I fingered the scars on my face. "I don't suppose you'd like to—"

Miko barked a laugh. "*Hell*, no, sir! I don't get along with politicians very well."

"Fair enough." I left the quarterdeck and yelled for Hemp the moment I stepped inside the sterncastle.

"Sir!" The word had been shouted through a mouthful of something, and his scraggly head poked out from the door to the galley, cheeks bulging.

"How in all Nine Hells and Seven Seas do you stay so thin eating day and night?" I strode down the length of the corridor toward my cabin.

He chewed and swallowed forcefully. "Tapeworms, sir! Or so my old dad used to say. I don't know about that, 'cause I never seen any—"

I cringed and waved him to silence. "Never mind, for the sake of all that's holy! I need a shave and a trim, then I want you to lay out some clothes. Nothing flashy, but official business. I'm trying to put on a first good impression."

"Oh, aye, sir!" He brushed the crumbs from his chin and clothes, snatched up a steaming kettle from within the galley, and followed me into the great cabin.

While I doffed my shirt, Hemp worked up hot lather and

stropped my razor. By the time I sat down, he was ready, draping a towel over my shoulders and lathering up his brush. As he sliced a day's growth off my face, I considered my strategies for approaching the governors of Hyko. I'd never met either of them, but knew them by reputation, and the interviews would be a far cry from my talk with the chiefs of Twin Capes. *Tactics...like taking on a galleon versus a junk...* The governor of the western city of Hy, Natik Haav, had fae blood, they said. The other, Alassa Rokiri, governor of Ko, was third generation descendant of a ridiculously wealthy Toki merchant who had irritated the god-emperor just enough to earn exile but not execution. Both harbored a smoldering hatred for the empire to the north, which played to my favor. Unfortunately, they also reputedly hated each other.

Which one first? I thought, ignoring the razor scraping along my throat. My choice might not matter much unless the governor I approached second found out I'd approached the other first. Powerful people, I'd learned, had fragile egos.

"Finished! Now for a little snip!" Hemp snatched up his scissors and comb, and brandished them like weapons.

"Not too short," I ordered. "I don't want to end up looking like my senior midshipman."

"Oh, no worries there, sir. That was an emergency operation." He started in, pushing my head this way and that, the scissors snipping dangerously close to my ears. "You should'a seen her when she came aboard. Looked like a dandelion after a lightning strike, she did!"

"I just wish you'd have made it look a little less like Preel's."

"I didn't have much to work with, sir."

I let him do his job, focusing on my own. I probably wouldn't get to speak with either of the governors today, but I had to make my pleas the right way. I was, after all, the designated emissary from Haven.

Politics... I had to remind myself that dealing with pirates was nothing like dealing with politicians; my one and only meeting with the Haven Council had been an eye-opener.

By the time Hemp finished with my hair, I'd decided to put in my request for an audience with Alassa Rokiri first, then hurry across the river to do likewise with Natik Haav. I could always deny approaching Rokiri first if Haav became jealous.

"Done!" Hemp wadded up the towel and shook it out the stern gallery windows. "I'll see to your clothes straightaway."

"Thank you, Hemp. Now remember, nothing too fancy. I'm talking to politicians today, not pirates."

"Aye, sir! You just scrub off the salt, and I'll have your rig spit and polish. I'll get hot water." He dashed out.

I bathed, dried, and emerged from the quarter gallery clad in a damp towel to find my clothes laid out on my bunk, a deep navy blue jacket with epaulets and gold braid on the cuffs and collar, black pants, and a lily white shirt with plain cuffs and a broad neckcloth. Perfect.

I dressed, dabbed on a bit of cologne that Preel had bought me, and stomped my feet into my glossy black boots. I checked myself in the mirror, shot my cuffs, and picked out a cutlass and dagger.

"Hemp!"

"Sir!" He burst through the door, took one look at me, and grinned.

"Well done." I gave him a nod and a smile. "If there's shore leave, you're on the first launch."

"Thank you, sir!"

I strode out, endured a whistle from Bert as I passed the galley, and stepped out onto the busy deck of my ship. Grins, a few whistles, and one anatomically impossible suggestion regaled me before my bosun silenced the row with a bellow that rattled my eardrums. A glance confirmed that my launch awaited, Boxley and a dozen stout pirates headed up by Tansy lined up in their shore rigs awaiting my arrival.

"Miko!"

"Sir!" She snapped me a salute from the quarter deck.

"Keep an eye on things, would you?" I nodded to the distant Toki warship. "A *sharp* eye."

"Like a hawk, sir."

I turned to my escort. "Boxley, let's get them aboard."

"Aye, sir! Shore party, aboard the launch! Smartly now!" Her shrill commands were followed with no nonsense and due alacrity. I boarded last and took my seat amidships, Boxley at the tiller acting as coxswain. "Oars out. Cast off!"

I sat and watched the shore as twelve pirates bent their oars. The harbor was smooth, our track a bee-line for the river mouth. Thankfully, the falling tide made the way smoother, if somewhat slower, and we shipped not a drop of water. The stone-girded riverbanks seemed remarkably quiet, with only a few workers moving cargo on and off barges. A few city guards strolled unconcernedly, barely giving us a glance from under their wide-brimmed helms.

"Eastern shore, Boxley." I pointed to a wide gap on the bank that sported ladders descending into the running current. "That looks like a good spot."

"Aye sir. Bow there, ready a line."

"Aye, sir." The two forward sailors shipped their oars and readied lines to tie off the launch.

Boxley executed the maneuver smoothly, and a crewman scrambled up the ladder. We tied off with the starboard rail bumping the algae-covered ladder. I climbed up and accepted a rag from the crewman ashore to wipe the slime from my hands.

"Boxley, pick two to stay with you to watch the launch. Eyes open, mind you."

"Aye, sir." She picked the stern-most pair and steadied the launch as the rest clambered up to join me. "Good luck, sir!"

"All right, form up and look sharp." I shot my cuffs, got my bearings, and set off toward the governor's palace, ten stout pirates at my heels.

We made it three blocks.

My mind was so fixed on my task that I didn't notice anything amiss. The streets were quiet, but that didn't trigger any warning in my mind. My first inkling that something was dreadfully wrong came when Tansy's hand closed on my arm.

"Sir! Trouble."

"Wha—" I turned to find her looking behind us. My eyes widened at the squad of Toki soldiers filling the street, five with bows, five with drawn swords, all of them fully armored. "What the—"

"Sir!" Another of my party snapped in a hissed whisper.

"Ahead!"

Another ten-squad, this one with an officer in red-lacquered armor, filed in ahead of us. The officer drew his sword, and the archers nocked arrows. "Captain of the *Scourge*! You will drop your weapons, or we will shoot you down!"

My mind shifted from politician to pirate in a heartbeat. We were outnumbered two to one, and they had bows. They were also in each other's line of fire, but that wasn't much of a disadvantage. They had obviously set this up carefully, but they'd missed one detail.

"Wait!" I shouted to the soldiers, raising my hands. I whispered to my squad, "Shop to the left. Window. When I say 'surrender,' we go through, out the back, and run for the launch."

"No waiting! Drop your weapons now!" The archers had not yet drawn their bows, which gave us maybe two seconds.

"But I'm not captain of the *Scourge*!" I called out.

The officer's eyes widened. "What? Then who are you?"

"I'm *Admiral* Kevril Longbright, of the Haven Free Privateer Navy!" I proclaimed, making up the name as I spoke. "And unless you want to start a war with the entire Blood Sea, you better rethink arresting me."

"There is no such navy!" The officer exclaimed.

"There *is*, and you're either ill-informed or your commanders are lying to you, sir. I'll peacefully meet with whoever's in charge here, captain," I saw the soldiers relax a trifle, exactly what I was hoping for. "But I'll walk straight into hell before I surrender."

At my final word, my entire squad bolted left and dove through the wide shop window, bowling over mannequins and displays in a shower of shattered glass and wood framing. We landed in a tangle, but rolled to our feet and charged through to the back of the shop even as shouts of alarm rang out behind us. I thanked Odea as we smashed into a back room and found a back door. Two of my pirates kicked as one, and the stout portal disintegrated, flying into the narrow alley in pieces.

"Left! Swords out. Soldiers get in our way, we cut and run! GO!"

We ran for it.

A street opened up before us and we dashed straight across into the next alley. More shouts rang out, but I didn't even bother to look. We were moving too fast.

"One more block, then left!" I said as we neared the next street, trusting that unarmored pirates could run faster than fully armored soldiers.

A ragged flight of arrows clattered on the cobbles as we crossed the street, telling me there were more soldiers stationed around the city. My mind spun. Toki soldiers in Hyko could mean only one thing: the god-emperor had already moved against the Blood Sea, and intended to use Hyko as his base. A solid strategy, since it was the only city state accessible by both land and sea from Toki. What this really meant to me was that we had to win free to warn the rest of the Blood Sea.

That, of course, meant getting back to *Scourge* alive.

A flight of arrows zinged down the narrow alley from behind us. One of my crew yelped, and I glanced back to see a crewman stumble, an arrow piercing his arm. He didn't fall, and his mate grabbed his good arm to steady him. We pounded out of the alley onto the wide stone avenue abutting the river, and I allowed myself a glimmer of hope.

That hope dashed to shards as I heard Boxley's cry of alarm half a block to my left. She and her two crewmen stood on the quay above the launch, eyes wide and hands empty as a squad of soldiers poured out from the street only yards away.

There was only one option.

"Boxley! Cut loose and make for *Scourge*!" I bellowed. Half the Toki soldiers turned to face us, the other half fanning out to hem in Boxley, even as she and her two crew turned and leapt down into the boat. Then to my party, I hissed, "Into the river! Stay under and let the current take you downstream. Surface and swim for the launch."

Gods bless them, they followed my order without a moment's hesitation.

We hit the turbid water of the river in a flailing ragged splash. I didn't think until after we hit that some of my squad might not be able to swim. As strange as it sounds, some sailors never learn, and can barely stay afloat if they fall overboard. Luckily, all but one of us could.

I dove deep and took a moment to kick off my boots. I could

barely see my own hand before my face, but could feel the outflowing tide and river's current pulling me downstream. I shucked out of my jacket and swam with the flow, to slam right into a flailing pirate. I didn't recognize them at first, but knew from his thrashing arms and legs that he couldn't swim. I grabbed him by the collar and pulled him with me, praying to Odea he had the sense to kick off his boots.

When I felt my lungs would burst, and my companion's thrashing became more desperate, I kicked for the light overhead. Bursting through into the air, I found I held the collar of a long-time foremast jack aptly named Bug-Eye Pete. His eyes were even wider than his moniker suggested, and he promptly began thrashing like a hooked marlin, trying to grab hold of me.

"Pete! Stop, or I swear I'll let you fucking drown!"

He froze, either in stark terror of being abandoned, or so conditioned to follow orders that he did so reflexively. Either way would suit me fine. I maintained my grip on his collar and looked around for the launch. More heads popped up around me, and arrows began to hit the water. One found its mark, transfixing one of my pirates through the head. She rolled over and floated face down with the flow. I cursed under my breath.

"Sir!" Boxley's shrill cry brought me around to find the launch with two oars out only ten yards away. Arrows stood out from the hull sides, and more arched from both shores. Some of the archers wore the distinctive armor of komei.

"Stay down, Boxley! We'll come to you!" I swam side-stroke for the launch, the rest of my squad out-pacing me due to my burden.

Boxley and her two crewmen started hauling pirates aboard as they arrived, some sporting arrows from arms, legs, and one lodged deep in someone's backside. I finally reached the launch, and handed Pete over. They hauled his miraculously un-riddled form up and over the railing.

Boxley stood and reached down for me. "Welcome aboard, sir! I thought for a moment you—"

She jerked, and I saw the arrow exit from her stomach, long and black, with a forked head. It passed cleanly through her to splash over my shoulder. Boxley looked down at the blood spreading through her white shirt in astonishment.

"Boxley, get down!"

I don't know if she followed my order or collapsed, but when I hauled myself up and over the rail into the boat, she lay crumpled in the stern, one bloody hand clutching the tiller, the other her abdomen. The rest of the crew clutched oars, rowing madly downriver, hunkering as low as they could. I scrabbled aft to Boxley, her face ashen, but her jaw set in a determined grimace.

"Boxley, let me look." I drew a dagger and parted her shirt.

"Fuck-ing komei, sir." She gasped as I examined the wound.

"I saw them. Hold still." The blood was dark, not bright red, and she was still alive, so I gauged she might survive, but a belly wound usually didn't bode well. If the bowel was violated, she'd die of fever in a matter of days. More arrows whistled by and impacted against the hull. One actually pierced the hull and speared one of the crew in the thigh. She swore, snapped the shaft off, and kept rowing.

"I can steer, sir," Boxley said, nodding forward. "Take an oar. We...need to get to *Scourge*. They've cut their cable."

"What?" I glanced forward and saw that *Scourge* had indeed cut her cable. Canvas billowed from her bow, and crew swarmed aloft to rig the squares. I looked to Boxley in wonder. Fourteen years old, shot through the guts, steering a launch under deadly hail of arrows, and she still took note of our ship and what was happening. Damn it, she was going to make one hell of an officer...if she survived. I cut a swath from her shirt and wadded it up to staunch the bleeding. "Keep one hand pressed here." I took her right hand and placed it on her stomach. "Steer downwind as soon as we clear the river mouth."

"Aye, sir."

I took up an oar and rowed for our lives, trusting this amazing young woman to steer us true.

By the time we cleared the river, all of us had been marked by arrows, though only one worse than Boxley. Another of my cherished crew lay dead in the bilge, shot through the chest. His name was Moili, an islander from Black Point, and a talented fiddle player. I cursed every curse I knew, and, when the hail of arrows finally fell silent, sat up straighter to look around.

All of the merchant ships were under sail as well as the Toki warship. I could see the colorful armor of Toki soldiers aboard them all. *Scourge* was gaining speed, but spilling wind intentionally to allow us to catch up. I could see Miko at the taffrail focusing on us with a spyglass, and crew lined up on the leeward side with heaving lines. A cargo net had been rigged over the side.

"Pull like you mean it, lads and lasses! Boxley, steer for the cargo net. Tansy, take the bow line when they throw and make it fast."

They grunted their answers, all of them straining, injured, and sodden, but determined. Boxley sat with one hand pressed to her stomach, her lower lip clenched between bloody teeth, her face deathly pale. But we were gaining.

"Heaving line away!" Wix's bellow sounded like music to my ears, and I craned my neck to watch Tansy catch the perfect throw and lash it to the bow cleat. "Haul forward. Lifting lines over the side!"

"Ship oars!" I ordered as the forward line came taut, and we raced along surfing *Scourge*'s wake.

Miko bellowed for more canvas aloft, and Rauley echoed the orders with encouragement to trim smartly. We took lift lines and secured them fore and aft, and those crew who were able swarmed up the cargo net. Boxley, of course, wasn't able.

"Well done, Boxley. Now just hold fast for a moment longer, and Bert'll see to that scratch."

"Sorry I got shot, sir." She grimaced with bloody teeth, and her eyes fluttered.

"Stay with me, Boxley." I cradled her in my arms and looked up to my crew. "Lift the boat and call for Bert."

"Haul away!" With only three of us aboard, the launch lifted easily, and as we rose, Wix reached out his brawny arms. "Hand her over, sir."

I did, and he took her as gently as if he cradled a chest of gold. I vaulted the railing and helped Variki Tau, who still had a broken arrow in his arse, aboard. Bert was already there seeing to Boxley, and Wix had ordered every able-bodied sailor to their duties. I accepted a jacket from Hemp and climbed to the quarterdeck.

"We walked right into a trap," I told Miko without delay. "The entire city's been occupied by Toki soldiers."

"Aye, and they manned every ship in the harbor as well." She handed me a spyglass, her face grim. "But that's not our biggest problem." She pointed south.

"Don't fucking tell me..." I turned to scan the horizon and spotted several lug-rigged ships rounding the southern point of the nearest island. I counted seven, then an eighth emerged from behind the island. They were hull down, but so many could only mean one thing. "Warships?"

"Lookout says so. An entire Toki armada, and they're coming around northwesterly." She accepted the spyglass from my limp and bloody fingers. "Rock and a hard place, sir."

She wasn't lying; with half a dozen enemy ships to the northeast, and who knew how many fanning out to the southeast, we had nowhere to go. I ground my teeth and tried to think of options.

"*Scourge* can beat any junk on the sea to windward." I gauged the closing ships innately. "Can we shoot the gap between the two and beat east?"

"It'd be tight, and we'd have nowhere to go. They'd fan out, cut off our escape, and close in."

I looked at the angle of the sun. "Can we hold them off until dark?"

"No way, sir. They'll pin us against the shore in about three hours."

"Blast!" I gritted my teeth and thought frantically for a way out. We had to get word to Haven somehow.

"How's Boxley?" Miko asked.

I winced. "Not good. Komei arrow through and through her stomach." I didn't have to tell Miko what that meant. "I'm sorry, Miko. I shouldn't have taken her ashore."

"I'm the one who assigned her to the party, sir. Not your fault."

I looked at her and saw the anguish. "Not yours either. Tell me the truth; she volunteered, didn't she?"

Miko nodded and looked away. I cursed beneath my breath and looked again to the horizon. There were ten sails now to the south, six to the north, and a rocky shore to the northwest. We had nowhere to go.

"Sir?" I whirled to the stairway and found Bert wringing her bloody hands.

I could see from her face that the news wasn't good. "Tell me."

"Arrow pierced her bowel. Bleedin's not terrible, but..." She sniffed and wiped her nose, leaving a bloody streak. "She'll be fevered in short order, and it'll only get worse."

"Is there *nothing* you can do?" My voice didn't sound like my own.

"Short of magic?" She shook her head. "I heard once of a surgeon who opened up a man's belly and stitched the bowel, then rinsed it all with willow bark and tincture of bread mold, but..."

Magic, I thought, recalling the tale I'd heard from Bikka Patak. "How long does she have?"

Bert shrugged. "She's young and strong. Can't feed her, of course, and even water'll make it worse. I could work up an infusion that might buy her some time, but..."

"How many *days*, Bert? I need to know!"

She blinked at my tone. "Three, at least. Four, maybe."

I nodded, and turned to Miko, a mad plan forming even as I spoke. "Rig both longboats for sea and provision each with enough to keep twenty sailors alive for four days. No weapons, no extra weight. We'll launch them on the leeward side when they're ready. You'll take Boxley, Bert, and the wounded to Haven as fast as you can possibly sail, and Kivan will take the other to Twin Capes to warn the chiefs."

I saw realization strike, and she nodded. "Aye, sir!" She whirled away to comply.

I turned to Bert, and strode up to take her by the shoulders. "Roberta, I want you to do everything in your power to keep Boxley alive, and when you arrive in Haven, go to Preel and have her summon Lady Severn. She's on the Council."

"Severn?" Her eyes widened. "Ain't she that sorceress?"

"Necromancer, and Bikka Patak told me she cured his wound fever with a simple touch. If you can get Boxley to her alive, she has a chance."

"Yes, sir." Her head bobbed, her tear-streaked jowls jiggling. "I'll do my best."

"Thank you." I drew her in and squeezed her hard. "It's been a pleasure, Bert. Tell my wife I love her."

"But..." She looked stunned. "You're comin' with us, aren't ya?"

"No. I'm staying aboard *Scourge*. They won't execute me, I'm too valuable a prisoner, but I don't like my odds of ever seeing the outside of a prison cell again." I grinned at her. "Just tell Preel..." I couldn't say it.

Bert's head bobbed again. "I will, sir." She whirled and descended to the main deck, calling for the scullery lads to collect her gear.

I paced and watched the opposing forces as my crew scrambled to prepare to abandon ship. I did the math; forty would sail free, thirty-two would remain to be captured. Maybe a few more could fit aboard the launches if they took the youngsters. I ordered the helmsman to steer a point to port, which would give the longboats a better angle on the southern cape. I had little doubt that Miko could outmaneuver the Toki warships, even if it meant sailing close to shore.

Half an hour slowly crept past. We lengthened our lead on the northern ships, but the southern ones fanned out and closed in, ten war junks in a precise line, one of them a monstrous three-decker flagship.

"Sir!"

I turned to find a red-faced Kivan advancing upon me as if she meant me bodily harm. I hadn't expected her to take the news well. "What is it, Lieutenant?"

"I'm not leaving, sir!" She took a stance a step away, her hands behind her back, her jaw set. "Put the launch in Rauley's command. He's a better sailor than I am by half."

"Kivan, you're going. They'll *interrogate* officers." I fixed her with a cold stare. "I won't have you go through that again."

She swallowed hard and shook her head. "And I don't *want* to go through it again, sir, but I'm not leaving this fucking ship!"

I glared at her. "Refusing a direct order is *mutiny*, Lieutenant Kivan."

"Then I resign!" She wrenched off her jacket and threw it on the deck. "I'm a common sailor guilty of refusing a direct order from her captain! Clap me in irons and have me flogged, but I will NOT leave this ship!"

I narrowed my eyes at her. "And if I have Wix hogtie you and throw you in one of the launches?"

"Then someone's going to get hurt, sir!" Her hand clenched on the komei sword she'd earned in battle.

"Kivan, I want you to stand down right now."

"I will if you agree to let me stay, sir." Her knuckles whitened on the hilt of her sword. "You can dress me as a common sailor, knock me around and put me in chains. Tell them I'm a mutineer. I'll spin some kind of tale to make them believe me, but don't make me *leave* you!"

I gritted my teeth, but realized there was no way short of violence I could make Kivan leave the ship. Also, her posing as a mutineer wasn't exactly a bad idea. My mind raced with the possibilities as we glared at each other.

"Lieutenant Kivan, you're stripped of your rank." Her eyes widened, but I matched her horror with a conspiratorial grin. "You'll report to Wix for five lashes, and you'll be chained in the hold as a mutineer...who signed on recently, planning to murder me because I killed Jhavika Keshmir, whom you sailed with before you went ashore with her five years ago. You'll fabricate the wildest tale you can think of, but you'll keep to the facts as much as possible, including the enchantment of Jhavika's scourge, and keep your story *straight*. You have two hours to concoct that tale; then you'll tell it to me so our stories match." I took a step toward her and held out my hand. "Now hand over that sword and tell me you understand my *orders*, Lieutenant."

Her mouth fell open, then closed, and she nodded. "I understand perfectly, sir." She slipped the scabbarded katana from her belt and handed it to me.

"Good." I took the sword. "Report to Wix and fill him in. I have no doubt he'll be staying aboard, and all of our stories have to match up. Have him spread the word of your mutinous actions."

"Aye, sir!" She dashed off.

I picked up Kivan's jacket and wrapped it around her sword, cinched the sleeves in a knot, then strode to the forward quarterdeck rail. "Master Rauley!"

"Sir!" He looked up from his work rigging one of the launches.

"Here!" I tossed him the wrapped sword. "You're a temporary lieutenant. You'll be taking command of the launch to Twin Capes. You will *not* get caught. Do you understand me?"

He gaped at me, then stared at a jacketless Kivan as she dashed across the deck toward Wix. "I understand, sir." He saluted me. "Best of luck, sir!"

"And to you." I saluted. "Carry on! Time is short, and I want the longboats well away."

"Aye, sir!"

"Hemp!"

"Sir?" He looked up at me askance.

"Load everything of value from my cabin into Miko's launch, then bring me a bottle of wine and some biscuits with tartberry jam." I grinned to him. "I *despise* the notion of surrendering on an empty stomach. Oh, and bring me my best jacket and a pair of boots."

"Aye, sir!" He grinned and dashed off.

I pulled a spyglass from the locker and watched the fifteen ships arrayed against us. Half an hour later, the longboats were ready to launch. Rauley's departed first, packed to the rails with supplies and crew, the gaff-rigged sail straining as they bore away. Boxley, drugged and wrapped in canvas, was stowed in the bow of Miko's longboat with Bert at her side. Miko shot me a salute before she descended the boarding ladder, the last to board. I returned the gesture and lifted my wineglass to her. There was nothing left to say.

The two craft raced away on diverging courses, spray flying from their bows with the rolling swell, Miko's surfing wildly. As I watched, two warships changed course to chase the launches, but I doubted they'd catch them. Both Rauley and Miko knew their business.

"Wix, how are we situated?"

"Right enough, sir. Thirty heartless pirates ready for blood, and one traitorous mutineer chained below." He glared at the approaching armada. "Seems a shame not to put up a fight."

"I'm afraid I can't indulge you, Wix." I cleared my throat and gave the order I never thought I would utter. "Heave us to and strike the colors! Raise a white flag on the foremast! Lay down arms, and prepare to surrender the ship."

They complied without so much as a grumble.

As *Scourge* rounded up into the wind and settled on an even keel, Hemp climbed up onto the quarterdeck, dressed in his best white steward's jacket, bearing a second bottle of wine.

"Found this hidin' in the bottom of your locker, sir." He showed me the label, a Nolshir red older than me by a decade. "Seems a shame to hand it over to some Toki fook who don't know rice wine from vinegar."

"Join me in a tot, then, Hemp!" I emptied my glass.

"Aye, sir!" He pulled the cork with expert ease and withdrew a second glass from his inside pocket. He filled my glass first, then his own. "Here's to randy women and wide open seas, sir!"

"I'll drink to that."

We touched glasses, drank, and watched the Toki armada bearing down on us.

Chapter Twenty One
An Untenable Situation

From the journal of Preel Longbright —

I know the limitations of my talent; ambiguity is always a problem. How many times have I preached that to my masters, to Kevril? How ironic that, in my haste, I failed to build sufficient specificity into my own question. My short sightedness has come back to bite me.

I clutched the letter in my hand, blinking back tears, reading and rereading the bold hand of the man I loved. The note brought little new news, the recruitment of two new pirates to our growing privateer navy, Boxley's misadventure and resulting haircut that disconcertingly resembled my own severe bob, the running of the ship, and Kevril's intention to sail north to Hyko next, as the Council had recommended. None of it mattered much to me, though I smiled imagining Boxley with short hair. The only line that truly mattered was the last.

"I love you with all my heart and soul, and miss you as a drowning man misses breath. Yours always, Kevril."

I heard his voice in my mind when I read that line, smelled the scent of him, felt his touch. "I miss you as a drowning man misses breath." My heart ached with love and longing. I folded the note and held it to my nose, inhaling it, imagining him, knowing that he'd touched it only days before. I gritted my teeth and bit back a sob.

Gods damn you for ever leaving me alone, you fucking pirate!

A knock at my door interrupted my tryst with self-pity. I tucked away the letter, wiped my eyes on the sleeve of my robe, and said, "Come in."

Busashi, Ghiti, and Miaki entered. The latter two had been

stationed outside my door; two nokitu were always stationed outside my door, and stood guard in my sitting room while I slept. Busashi bowed and advanced, his face emotionless.

"We have visitors, mistress. A...contingent from Balshi Keep."

"A *contingent?*" I didn't like the sound of that.

"Yes, some thirty armed troops commanded by one officer. He says he has a letter for you from Brilla Balshi, and that he'll only place it in your hand." Still, his face remained expressionless.

Mine, on the other hand, undoubtedly showed an entire range of emotions, from fear to suspicion to annoyance. "She doesn't learn, does she?"

"Or there have been other developments," Busashi suggested.

"Or it's a trap," Miaki added.

"If it is, it's a clumsy one." My mind raced. What could have happened in the last three days that would precipitate a new message from Brilla? If there was a message. "Have you seen this letter?"

"Yes, mistress. It bears the seal of House Balshi."

"And whatever's inside, Brilla sent it with an escort of thirty soldiers." I bit my lip. *Thirty solders...* My entire guard complement barely numbered fifty, and she had hundreds. *But what's so important that she escorts it with such a force, and will only hand the letter over to me?* Curiosity burned in my gut like a hunger. "Tell the officer I'll come down to receive the letter. He'll come in alone through the postern door, under guard, and hand it to me."

"And if he refuses those terms?" Busashi remained emotionless, but I knew if I told him to murder the man and take the letter, he would, and he might even get away clean, but I couldn't do that without starting a war with Brilla.

I could, however, make my displeasure clear. "If he refuses, tell him he can take the letter back to Brilla, roll it up, and stick it up her ass."

The corner of Busashi's mouth twitched as he bowed. "I'll relay the message, mistress."

"I'll be down in ten minutes."

"And I'll arrange our forces along the courtyard and wall for the exchange," Busashi assured me. "If this is a trap, they'll regret it."

"Good. Thank you." As Busashi hurried out, I retrieved my

enchanted gag from the pocket of my robe and held it out to Ghiti. "Please."

"Yes, mistress." She affixed the gag and I hurried to my bedroom to change. I picked the first sari my fingers touched, pulled it on, and chose a matching headscarf and veil. I applied a quick layer of makeup to my tattoo, checked myself in the mirror, and descended to the courtyard of the keep with Ghiti and Miaki hot on my heels.

The heat of the afternoon tropical sun pounded into the courtyard, the flagstones warm through the thin soles of my sandals. What looked like our entire complement of soldiers stood in a broad semicircle around the gate and upon the curtain wall above. Each one carried a heavy crossbow loaded and readied. Busashi and our other three nokitu stood waiting for me. I strode across to join them.

"The messenger has agreed to your terms, mistress."

I nodded once to Busashi, and he motioned two of his cadre forward. Kofuut and Liant jogged to the postern door. Another gesture, and every single one of our soldiers raised their crossbows to aim at the postern door. A moment later, Kofuut and Liant escorted an armored soldier in, a tall man wearing an open faced helm, chainmail, and a tabard bearing the crest of House Balshi. They brought him across the open space, and fifty crossbows followed him.

"Mrs. Longbright, I assume," the soldier said politely.

I nodded.

"Lady Balshi sends her respects, and this." He fished a sealed envelope of fine white parchment from his tabard and held it out. "For your hand only."

I took a moment to look him over closely. He seemed unafraid of the weapons trained upon him, and his stance remained relaxed, not poised for sudden action. Sweat streamed down his face, but tropical heat and armor would cause that. His other hand hung far away from any weapon. If he tried to hurt me, he'd be dead in an instant.

I took one step and snatched the letter from his grasp.

The man bowed shortly, his lips twitching in a faint smile. "I've discharged my duty, Mrs. Longbright. Should you wish to send a reply, Lady Balshi has requested that you send it under guard to keep your correspondence private."

I nodded, turned on my heel, and walked away, trusting Busashi to see to our guest. In the comparative cool of the entry hall, I paused to look closely at the letter. Only my name and a wax seal impressed with the Balshi crest graced the surface. I took a deep breath and let it out slowly, calming my trembling hands before I broke the seal and opened the envelope.

The missive was short, but every word felt like a kick in the stomach.

Preel,

I know what you are. If you do not meet with me, I will tell your secret to the entire Council and everyone else I can think of. If you tell Hashi Severn, or even have me killed, the Council will know that Kevril Longbright has his own private truthsayer. You will meet with me, or you will be enslaved once again.

Lady Brilla Balshi

My knees trembled so badly that I feared they might fold. I read the message twice over, panic rising up to smother me. I couldn't breathe, couldn't think. The words "you will be enslaved once again" rang in my mind like the toll of a bell at my own funeral.

Never, I vowed to myself. I would throw myself off of the keep's highest tower before I let anyone enslave me again, but how could I keep Brilla Balshi from exploiting what she knew, from using it to blackmail me into capitulation? Then another question rose up within me. *How? How in all Nine Hells and Seven Heavens did she find out?* I could count the people in Haven who knew my secret on two hands, seven of them in this keep, the two *Scourges* who manned the *Gull*—they had returned from sea this very morning—and Doctor Yiv. Someone must have betrayed me, but who? Who could I trust?

I glanced at my escort, but felt in my soul that the six nokitu were loyal. Lewin hadn't left the keep in a week, or at least not that I knew of. But I had to be sure.

I dashed for my rooms, my paralytic panic resolving into action. My escort didn't say a word until the door of the sitting room closed behind us.

"Preel, what's happened?" Ghiti sounded more tense than worried as I tore my veil off and tapped frantically at the enchanted silk girding my mouth.

The knot came free, and I spouted, "Brilla knows about me. I don't know how, and other than you and your brethren, I don't know who I can trust. Bring everyone here right now."

"Everyone? You mean—"

"Just the nokitu," I corrected. "I don't even know about Lewin. If he—"

"Preel." Ghiti put a hand on my arm. "Breathe and focus. See everything. Poise and calm are your allies." Her steady tone and firm grip calmed me, the familiar lessons soothing.

I breathed and nodded. "Bring your brethren here, Ghiti. We have to make some decisions."

"Yes, mistress." Ghiti nodded to Miaki, and he dashed out without a word.

In less time than it took me to walk to the sideboard and pour myself a bracer, all six nokitu stood in my sitting room. I thanked them and handed the letter to Busashi.

"I'm in trouble."

He read it aloud to the others, and once again I felt those words tightening around me like the coils of a great serpent.

"So, your professional opinion, Busashi; can I trust Lewin?"

"Nothing is absolutely certain, mistress, but I believe you can. Even if he wished to betray you, he hasn't left the keep in eight days. He doesn't correspond with anyone that I know of either." He glanced at the others, and they nodded. "There are others who know your secret. Three others."

"Yes, Doctor Yiv and the two *Scourges* manning the *Gull*, but they only returned today." I sipped my drink and let the spiced rum burn the panic away from my throat. "I made a mistake. I thought the answer to my last question meant abduction and interrogation of *me*. It didn't, did it?"

"That may be the case, mistress. It should be a straightforward matter to find out if Lady Balshi has abducted any of them, or others for that matter. Its exceedingly unlikely that Brilla knew exactly who to interrogate. She may have cast a wide net."

"Gods and devils, I'm a fool!" I knocked back my rum and swallowed, drawing a deep cleansing breath. "Bring Lewin here and find out if any of the keep staff have gone missing."

"At once, mistress." Busashi pointed to three of his people, and they left the room, then he turned back to me. "May I point out a critical piece of information, mistress."

I glared at him. "Of *course* you can! Now stop being so damned polite and tell me. I need your help, not your kindness!"

"How Brilla found out is less important than what she plans to do with the information, and perhaps who she's already told. Your one advantage, still, is your talent, even though Brilla already knows."

"Yes, I know, and I don't intend to waste my talent on discovering how Brilla found out." I resumed my pacing, reminding myself that Busashi and his people didn't truly understand me. They might have heard what I'd gone through, but they didn't know my inner determination, my utter refusal to ever be anyone's slave again. "The true question is how to best employ my talent, and to answer *that*, we need to think this through."

"Exactly, mistress."

A tap at the door, and Liant escorted Lewin into the room. The old sage looked unruffled. Sequestered in the library, he probably didn't even know we'd had visitors.

"Mistress, I'm informed there's been some dire news, but—"

"Read this." I handed him the letter.

He did, and I could see by the widening of his eyes that he saw the implications. "It wasn't you she was planning to abduct and interrogate. That was very short sighted of us." He handed the letter back to me. "She's undoubtedly abducted either Doctor Yiv, or one of the sailors your husband left here."

"The *Gull* only returned from sea today, but we should send someone to find them. We're trying to find out who's unaccounted for already. Brilla may have taken a number of Jhavika's former retainers, thinking they might know something. I'd like to know who she's taken, but that's not my primary concern. The result is, she knows I'm a truthsayer. If I refuse her, and she outs me, I won't have many options."

Lewin frowned. "Only one, I would think: flee Haven."

I grimaced. "Gods and *devils*, I wish Kevril was here!" But what would he do if he was? Likely, he'd storm into Brilla's palace and cut her throat. I needed a more measured approach, but I also had to start thinking like a pirate. Being married to one had taught me a great deal. I knew how pirates responded to threats: lie, cheat, steal, or kill if necessary.

"That would open up more options, mistress, but there would be even more dire consequences if Brilla outed you to the Council."

I flicked a glare at him. "More dire than me ending up in *chains*?"

"Well, perhaps not from your perspective, but from Haven's, yes." He lifted his gnarled old hands in a helpless gesture. "How do you think the members of Haven's council would react if they were told what you are?"

The answer seemed obvious. "They'd all want to own me, of course. They'd stop at nothing, including storming this keep. Word would spread, and might eventually even reach Toki, which would result in an armada of warships being deployed to hunt me down."

Lewin nodded. "War would break out, from within and without."

I gritted my teeth and clenched my hands.

"We could flee now," Busashi suggested. "We could have you in Hyko in four days to reunite with Admiral Longbright."

"Tempting." I tapped a finger to my pursed lips and continued to pace.

"I wouldn't recommend immediate flight, mistress," Lewin cautioned. "You're not without resources, and information is key to making the right decision." He nodded to Busashi. "By all means, we should be ready, and have the *Gull* poised to sail at a moment's notice, but escaping by night would be preferable, and tonight will be four days since we last employed your talent. We must consider what piece of information is most vital to our decision making process, and how to respond to the answer."

I nodded. "Yes. Busashi, send one of your people to the *Gull*.

She should be moored in the harbor. If the crew hasn't been abducted by Brilla, tell them to prepare for a voyage, and that we may be departing as early as tonight."

"Tonight, mistress?" Busashi looked mildly shocked. "If you employ your talent, you'll be unconscious."

"Yes, tonight, depending on the answer to the question. If the answer leaves us no alternative, I may have you bundle me up and haul me aboard disguised as cargo." I had little doubt that the nokitu could get me out of the keep and aboard *Gull* without a soul knowing. I turned to Lewin. "Our primary concern is to craft a question that gives us the most vital information."

"Yes, mistress, that's where our efforts are best put to use, but there is one other player in this game."

I cocked an eyebrow at him, thinking furiously. The answer came to me. "Severn."

"Precisely."

"But Brilla specifically warned me not to tell..." My mind spun. "Because she's *afraid* of Severn!"

"And rightfully so," Lewin agreed.

"But...what can she do to help me? If Brilla's already set up a contingency to out me even if she's killed, murdering her won't do any good."

"*If.*" Lewin smiled. "We need to consider Brilla's motives, her state of mind, and her level of desperation. She must know what would happen if she outed you to the Council."

"But she's got the biggest force of soldiers. If it comes down to war, maybe she thinks she can win!" The thought of an all-out war between the council members nauseated me. All of Haven would burn.

"Against any one, two, or maybe even three houses, yes, she *might* win, but not against all of them." Lewin shrugged. "And while they fight one another, you might slip away. She can't discount that possibility. Brilla may be psychotic, but that doesn't mean she's a fool."

"You think she's lying?"

"I think she *may* be lying to prevent you from taking...preemptive action. There are other possibilities, but crafting a question to discern Brilla's intent may be difficult, especially if she's deranged."

"This is getting complicated, as always." I paced. "We need to know as much as we can before we decide on the final question. That will help us."

"Tell me what you need, mistress," Busashi bowed low. "We are at your disposal."

I thought furiously. "First, find out who's gone missing. Second, give me your best plan for eliminating Brilla without getting caught, and your honest assessment of the likelihood of success. Third, work up a plan for getting me aboard *Gull* tonight, and another for covertly notifying Hashi Severn that I need to meet with her in private. Pick a location for that. Someplace we can get to without anyone knowing. Set that meeting for tomorrow midmorning." I looked to Lewin. "What am I missing?"

He addressed his response first to Busashi. "Brilla controls a wide network of racketeers and thugs. Caution would be warranted in our inquiries, but if rumors spread about Brilla and her machinations, that's where they'll spread first." Lewin turned to me again. "We must also consider whether or not we could...negotiate with Brilla. Would she do as she says and keep your gift a secret if you agreed to answer questions for her."

Remembering Lady Severn's warning, I shook my head. "I don't think trusting Brilla is an option. No, we either kill her or flee, I think."

"Knowing who else she's already told of you would be invaluable in making that decision," Lewin said.

"It would." I bit my lip hard enough to bring tears to my eyes. "If that's fifty people, we're already sunk."

"But if she doesn't intend to out you publicly, telling a large number of people would be dangerous for her." Busashi scowled. "As Master Lewin said, she may be psychotic, but she's no fool. I doubt her people are as loyal as your husband's crew. Word would eventually get out."

"Well, that's to our advantage, then." I looked between everyone present. "Anything else at all?"

They all looked at one another and shook their heads.

"Okay, then Busashi, put your people to work. Lewin and I will be in the library. I think one guard would be sufficient, considering the circumstances. I mean, we know Brilla's not going to try to abduct me now."

"Very good, mistress." Busashi bowed again, motioned Ghiti to stay, and hurried out.

"All right, then, Master Lewin, let's get to work!" I waved to the door.

"Mistress?" Ghiti stepped forward before I could take a step. "Are you armed?"

"No, I..." I shrugged like a child caught without clean underwear. "With what you've been teaching me, I've stopped carrying my dagger. It seemed...I don't know, superfluous."

"But a blade can be used as other than a weapon. Please, arm yourself."

I nodded and knew she was right. I hurried to my room, retrieved the slim stiletto Kevril had given me, and tucked it into my sari. I returned to the sitting room and patted my waist. "Ready. Let's go. There's no time to waste."

"Yes, mistress," they both said in unison, and followed me out.

Lewin and I worked all afternoon, through a cold supper, and into the night to craft a foolproof question that would tell us what we desperately needed to know. As we did, news trickled in from my nokitu.

First, Kofuut came in to report that the *Gull*'s crew, Morelie and Sauncey, were aboard their vessel and ready to depart at a moment's notice. Welcome news.

Next, Busashi came in with less welcome news. "Two of our guards and one scullery boy went missing yesterday while in the city. No one's seen or heard from them. We can only assume that Brilla had them abducted." He handed me a slip of paper. "Their names."

"Blast! How could we not know they'd gone missing?"

"The scullery lad wasn't reported to cook because his friends didn't want to get him into trouble." Busashi frowned. "The soldiers'

220

absence was reported to their superior, but not to me, as it should have been. I've rebuked the superior, and demoted him to common guardsman. His replacement won't make the same mistake."

"Closing the barn door after the cow's gotten out, but thank you." I sat back down and we got back to work.

As we finished up the last of cold ham, mustard, and bread for our supper, Busashi returned with the worst news yet. "Both Doctor Yiv and Eias Lavo went missing suddenly yesterday, and a number of soldiers currently serving as harbor watch who were once Jhavika's."

"Doctor Yiv is the leak, then." Lewin looked stricken. "We should have taken precautions."

"Yes, we should have, but now all that matters is our next step, not what we should've done weeks ago." I pushed my plate aside, my stomach clenching on what little I'd eaten. "See to all the preparations, Busashi. We're close to having our question nailed down. The answer will either be yes or no. Yes will mean we flee. No will mean we attack. I'm drafting two different letters to Lady Severn, depending on our answer. You'll deliver one tonight without anyone seeing you."

He bowed deeply. "Very well, mistress. We're ready."

Lewin and I got back to work. An hour later, we had our question, though I wasn't very happy with it.

"I still think we need to know who else she's told." I tapped the page I'd written the question upon.

"You're correct, but I believe this is more vital. It gives us an immediate course of action."

"Yes, fight or flee." I stood and picked up the two missives I'd drafted for Lady Severn. One wax seal bore a scratched 'Y', and the other an 'N' so that we wouldn't mix them up. When I answered the question, Lewin would heat our bronze seal and press it into the appropriate envelope for delivery. "Shall we?"

"Yes, mistress."

Lewin followed me up to my chambers and waited in the sitting room while I readied myself for bed. I dressed in loose pantaloons and a short nightshirt, comfortable enough, but more modest than my usual nightgown if my nokitu had to bundle me up for our escape. With no small amount of trepidation, I lay down, folded my hands on my stomach, and nodded to him. I'd either wake up aboard the *Gull* at sea, or in this very bed. The answer would determine which.

I took a deep breath. "Ready."

"Very well." Lewin cleared his throat and read the question. "Has Brilla Balshi put into place a mechanism to inform anyone of your truthsayer talent in the event of her own death?"

The room went dark as my eyes rolled up and the answer gripped me. The emphatic rasp of "No" escaped my throat an instant before oblivion took me.

Chapter Twenty Two
Pointed Questions

From the diary of Kevril Longbright —

In my experience, things always look darkest right before they go completely black.

It had been a very long time since I'd worn manacles, and I can't say that I missed the experience. At least this time I wasn't locked in the lower hold of a rat-infested ship. The dungeon of Governor Rokiri's palace did have rats, but they were timid creatures compared to the marine variety.

Something clanked, and Hemp crowed in triumph. "Ha! Got another one! That makes four!"

"I'm at six, but that last one tasted funny," Wix countered.

Several others groaned or called out their own scores, but I didn't reply. The competition was good for my crew's morale, but not mine. My ship had been taken, my crew imprisoned, and I didn't know how those who had escaped fared. I prayed to Odea that Boxley might survive. She was in the best of hands, and had a chance, if a slim one. Probably a better chance than I did, all things considered. Rauley would arrive in Twin Capes in another two days, and Miko would make Haven by that evening or night.

Three and a half days, I thought. *Just hang on, Boxley.*

Then there was Kivan to consider.

Unlike the rest of us, my mutinous lieutenant hadn't been brought to the dungeon. That could be good, or very bad. The tale she'd spun, imaginative and fitting into the facts nicely, might buy her softer treatment than the rest of us. She also intended to find out as much as she could from our captors. I had no way to know what had come to pass, but she wasn't here. I'd last seen her when we confirmed our stories with each other. She'd changed into common seaman's garb, her shirt filthy and bloodstained from Wix's lashes and a split lip he'd given her for good measure.

With all these concerns, and chains and a hard stone floor and rats to boot, I hadn't slept well. Our cells didn't have windows, but my stomach and yearning for blackbrew told me it was morning. I leaned my head back against the cool stone and closed my eyes, letting my mind drift, sifting through everything plaguing me, guilt and anger at myself rising up to drown me.

Stupid, Kevril, I thought to myself. *How hard would it have been to ask Preel, "Is it safe to go to Hyko?"*

That, of course, led my thoughts to Preel. I longed to see her again, but saw no path to that future. I told myself she'd be fine; she had money and security. If Haven survived, so would she.

A clank and a rattle of keys snapped me from my misery. The tromp of heavy boots and the rustle of lacquered armor told me we had company. Lamplight flickered down the hallway. I didn't stand.

A man in a rough tunic, leather pants, and worn boots stepped into the light of our guttering lantern, escorted by two Toki soldiers. Not the jailor I'd seen upon our arrival, but he held a lantern of his own, a ring of keys, and a leather oilskin hung from his belt. He hung his own lantern, lowered ours, and filled it with practiced motions.

His escort squinted into the cells at us and settled on me.

"Longbright?" one said.

"Yes," I replied.

The soldier grunted, nudged the jailor, and pointed to me. "That one."

The jailor finished with the lantern, rehung it, and fumbled the proper key into the door of my cell. The door screeched open, and he stepped inside to unlock the ring bolt in the wall over my head from the chain to my manacles.

One of the soldiers stepped inside the cell. "Stand up."

I did, stiffly. "I'd like to speak to your commander."

"Fortunate, then, for General Koto would like to speak to you." He nodded to the jailor who secured the long chain of my manacles snugly around my waist and locked it there. "Come."

I shuffled through the door, thanking the powers that be that they hadn't put leg irons on as well.

"Give the general a kiss for us, sir!" Wix called out, and I couldn't help but smile. My escort didn't.

By the time we climbed four flights of stairs and traversed about a quarter mile of hallways, all heavily guarded by Toki soldiers, I'd worked the kinks out of my muscles and joints. We reached a pair of ornate double doors framed by two komei. They didn't move as my escort first knocked, then opened the doors.

I'd never seen a throne room before, and Governor Rokiri wasn't queen, so she hadn't actually had a throne. I supposed, as I stepped through the doors into the ornate chamber, that this qualified as an audience chamber, but it sure as all Nine Hells looked like a throne to me.

In that throne, instead of the middle aged woman I'd hoped to meet here, sat a man clad in elaborate armor sans helm. Two fully armored komei stood at each side of the throne, armed with long naginatas, as well as the traditional two swords My escort gripped me by the arms and marched me forward until we stood about three strides from the raised dais.

"You're the pirate, Longbright," the general said. A statement, not a question.

"No, I'm *not* a pirate, though I have been in the past. I'm now a privateer, and admiral of the Haven Free Privateer Navy." I nodded respectfully. "Very pleased to meet you, General Koto."

His eyes had narrowed as I spoke, his lips tightening. "The soldiers I sent to apprehend you said as much, and we found a paper in the cabin of your ship signed by ten people calling themselves the Haven Council of Lords."

"Yes, that's my letter of marque."

"It's not. It's a piece of paper written by a gang of criminals and exiles who have no legal status and no legitimacy. Haven is not recognized by the God-Emperor of Toki as a legitimate city-state. Therefore, this *supposed* council cannot bequeath letters of marque. You are nothing but a pirate."

I shrugged. "I would argue that point, but it'll do me no good. If you don't recognize Haven as a city-state, you're not going to recognize me as admiral of their navy. The navy *does* exist, and I am it's senior officer. By taking my ship and invading Hyko, you're committing an act of war.

"Hyko is now part of the Toki Empire, Mr. Longbright."

I didn't reply. There seemed no point to contesting his claim.

"What was your mission here?"

"To speak with the governors."

"About what?"

"About joining the Blood Sea Protectorate." I was proud of that name, but the general didn't seem impressed.

His eyes narrowed again. "The *what?*"

"The Blood Sea Protectorate." I gave him my best look of bafflement. "Surely Toki's intelligence service has informed the god-emperor that the city states are allying into a protectorate."

The hint of a sneer tugged at his upper lip. "There is no such alliance."

I sighed and shrugged. "I assure you, General Koto, there is, and if your empire continues its conquest into the Blood Sea, there will be repercussions."

"From this so-called *navy* of yours." Koto's sneer evolved into a mien of derision.

"Yes, from our navy." I kept my temper in check. "May I tell you something that might help clear up this misunderstanding, General?"

"I doubt there's any misunderstanding, Mr. Longbright, but feel free to spin another tale. We don't get much *entertainment* here."

I ignored the snide comment. "You're here because Jhavika Keshmir sent a spy to the god-emperor's court. His name was Fawahah. I know this because, at the time, I was working with Keshmir, and acquired Ambassador Fawahah for her."

"You attacked a Toki ship, killed six komei assigned to protect that ship, and kidnapped the ambassador."

"Actually, I picked him up floating in a barrel, but that's neither here nor there. Keshmir was using a magical scourge to control people, you see, which was how she made Ambassador Fawahah her spy. That was before Keshmir betrayed me, then attempted to stage a coup on the Haven Council of Lords. That didn't work out so well for her."

The general's sneer had faded to simple dislike. "And what became of this enchanted scourge and Jhavika Keshmir." He said it like he already knew these facts, which he well might.

"The scourge was destroyed, and Keshmir is dead. The subterfuge perpetrated upon your emperor and the Haven Council alike is ended. There's no need for continued hostilities between the Empire of Toki and the Blood Sea Protectorate." I didn't mention the fate of Hyko, and didn't ask what had happened to the governors.

"It might entertain you to know that I've heard this tale before, Mr. Longbright. Twice before, in fact, though the versions vary somewhat."

"Once from Ambassador Fawahah, I suppose."

"Yes, though second hand from my superior. The other was from a young woman we found chained in the hold of your ship." He smiled thinly. "She's been most forthcoming, and has a rather...poor opinion of you."

I snorted a laugh. "Well, most people who've tried to murder me have that opinion. She was one of Jhavika's loyalists."

"Yes, so she told me. She said it was *you* who betrayed Keshmir, murdered her in cold blood, and that she infiltrated your crew to exact revenge."

"She was ensorcelled by Jhavika's scourge, General. From what I understand, most people who were have exhibited some...mental instability with the cancellation of the enchantment."

"She seemed perfectly sane to me."

"I'm sure she did." I smiled. "She seemed less than perfectly sane to me when she tried to put a dagger in my heart."

"I imagine so." The general pushed himself up from his seat and stepped off the dais. He stood half a head shorter than me, but looked broader, though that might have been the armor. "Let *me* tell *you* why I'm here, Mr. Longbright."

"Please do," I said with a polite nod.

"I'm here, with the support of Admiral Miaku of the Imperial Toki Navy, to apprehend the pirate who abducted Ambassador Fawahah, find Jhavika Keshmir, and retrieve the enchanted scourge she used to enslave him. The god-emperor wants it." He smiled.

"I've accomplished one third of my mission."

I shuddered at the thought of the god-emperor as the master of Jhavika's scourge. "Actually, your mission is complete, because Jhavika and the scourge are both gone."

He grinned without humor. "So you say."

"I do say, because I'm the one who destroyed the scourge and killed her." I sighed, not honestly expecting him to believe me. "And taking Hyko for the god-emperor? Was that not part of your mission?"

"It was a necessary first step in my mission, which I'm afraid is not finished until I confirm that the scourge is, in fact, destroyed, and that Keshmir is dead."

"That's going to be difficult, general," I said.

"Why is that, Mr. Longbright?"

"Because they're both rotting on the bottom of the sea in the middle of the Serpent's Eye." His eyes widened with incredulity. "Which I don't expect you to believe, but every single member of my crew will verify it."

"Oh, I *will* ask them, each and every one of them, Mr. Longbright, but first I think I'll introduce you to someone else." He nodded to one of his komei, and the masked warrior strode for a side door.

The komei opened it and barked an order. A soldier entered with Kivan, who wore finer clothes than I'd ever seen her in, a blouse of red silk and a pair of sharp black trousers tucked into high cuffed boots. Her lip was still swollen, and the bruising had darkened, but she otherwise looked hale. Her eyes flung daggers at me as the three strode to the general's side with Kivan between them.

"Miss Kivan, I believe you know Mr. Longbright."

"I do, General." She sneered at me. "He's a fucking pirate!"

"Yes, so you've told me." He smiled to her. "You've also said you wanted revenge against him for killing Jhavika Keshmir."

"You *know* I do!" Her hands flexed at her sides.

"In fact, I don't know you do. You've told me you do. You could be lying."

She blinked at him in shock. "Why the hell would I lie about that? He murdered Lady Keshmir! She was our *queen*!"

"Yes, so you said." The general unsheathed a tanto from his belt, examining the short blade closely. "It occurred to me that a clever captain might place a loyal crewmember in chains, even order her whipped and beaten, to fool me into believing her account of events. I can think of only one way to confirm your story is true." He flipped the dagger in his hand and held it out hilt first to Kivan. "Exact your revenge upon the pirate Longbright."

Kivan looked shocked for a moment, then reached out and took the dagger from him. "Really? Right here?" She looked at the soldier and komei standing beside her suspiciously.

"Really, Miss Kivan. Right here and now. Prove to me that you're telling me the truth."

I struggled in earnest at the soldiers' grips on my arms. "If you think for one second I'm going to stand here and let that crazy bitch knife me, you're delusional!"

General Koto grinned and took a step back. "I don't expect you to do anything but die, Mr. Longbright."

Kivan swallowed hard and took a short step forward, well within reach. Her minders stepped with her. She forced a grin, but I could see the strain in it. "All right then."

I tried to kick the dagger away, but my guards were ready. They twisted me, and my kick went wide, then they slammed boots into the backs of my knees to force me down. I grimaced as the hard stone floor cracked my knees.

My mind raced for a way out of this trap I'd laid for myself. "Don't let her do it, Koto! Killing me will only buy you trouble!"

"Oh, but I'm not killing you. She is." He grinned at me. "I can't be held responsible if you're killed by one of your own crew."

"But your mission is to bring me to your emperor!"

"Your corpse will have to do." He nodded to Kivan. "Go ahead."

Kivan shifted her grip on the dagger for an underhand thrust, her knuckles white on the hilt. I saw the rising panic in her eyes, and feared she'd do something monumentally foolish. I knew she wouldn't stab me, or if she did, not lethally. Her eyes shifted left and right once, then she drew back the blade and thrust.

Maybe she knew something I didn't, or would have pulled the

thrust, but it certainly looked to me in earnest, I tensed and tried to twist, but my captors held me fast. The instant before the blade would have plunged into my chest, the komei's hand shot out to snatch her arm. The tip of the blade pricked my skin through my shirt.

"NO!" Kivan thrashed and cursed, trying to wrench her arm free, but the komei gripped her hard.

"Well, well!" Koto stepped up and relieved her of the dagger.

"You lied to me!" she raged.

"Yes, I did, to make sure you weren't lying to me." The general smiled and raised a hand to run his knuckles along her cheek. She didn't flinch away, and I wondered what might have happened the previous night. "You understand, don't you, that this man is far too valuable to me alive?"

"I..." She shook her arm free of the komei's grasp. "I suppose so." She glared at me. "I wish he wasn't."

"I'll make it up to you, Miss Kivan." He smiled again and nodded to the komei, who guided Kivan away. Before they reached the door, he stopped her with a question. "I'd like to know, however, how you received those scars on your back. The recently healed ones?"

She turned, her eyes wide. "They...were a gift."

"A *gift?*" Koto sounded utterly perplexed. If so, he and I had something in common.

"Yes, from Jhavika." She gestured to me. "I found out where they were going, you see, so she marked me as her favorite." She grinned wide, her eyes taking on a maniacal look. "She told me the pain would be the most wonderful thing I'd ever felt, and it was." She lifted her chin, her face an image of rapture. "She was...like a *goddess.*"

"I see." He nodded to the komei again, and they ushered her out.

My guards lifted me to my feet. "Does she seem perfectly sane to you now?"

"Well, perhaps not *entirely*, but she's valuable in other ways." He made a dismissive gesture. "You'll forgive the pretense, Mr. Longbright, but I had to make sure you weren't spinning some fanciful tale."

"I understand *perfectly*." I glared at him.

"Good." He gestured me away. "Now, if you'll pardon me, I have about thirty more interviews to go, and I'm sure they're going to be tedious in the extreme." He sheathed his dagger and turned away.

Before I reached the ornate doors, he said, "Oh, and I lied to you earlier, too, I'm afraid."

"Oh?" I paused to look back at him. "About what?"

"There's one more element to my mission." The smile that creased his face reminded me of a shark.

I swallowed. "And that is?"

"I'm to eradicate piracy from the Blood Sea, subjugate the islands, and reduce Haven to a pile of rubble."

I barked a laugh. "Good *luck* with that! You'll find Haven a hard nut to crack, and you'll never catch every pirate in the Blood Sea."

"I don't *need* luck, Mr. Longbright. I've got an armada, two thousand fighting sailors, and a hundred komei at my command. Now throw him back in the dungeon and bring me his highest ranking sailor."

I considered silently as they pulled me away that such a force might just be enough to do exactly what he'd said. *Preel...* I prayed silently that she would learn of the pending attack in time to flee, but where could she go? Valaka? Would she go back to Shepherd? I hoped so. The dragonlord might be able to keep her safe.

Then I realized that, even if the Toki navy could occupy Haven, they'd find at least one of the council members a worthy adversary. I recalled my meeting with Lady Severn and smiled to myself.

Chapter Twenty Three
The Services of a Necromancer

From the journal of Hashi Severn —
This is what I get for fostering a bad reputation, I suppose.

I woke from the strangest dream, deeply disturbed, wondering how my mind could conjure such things. I lay there for a moment, remembering it as clearly as if it had been real. I was out at the Folly with Red Moll, sitting at our table, much as it had happened. We watched the singer, Illian, performing, her amazing voice filling the entire space, enthralled. Then, *not* as it had happened, Red took my hand and pulled me up on stage.

"Dance," she'd said in my dream. "Dance with me."

With the eyes of the entire room upon us, and Illian singing, her luminous eyes rapt upon us, we danced an intricate Mati duet that I remembered from childhood. It's called Serpents in Water. Our dance flowed, fluid and undulating, flawless and erotic, and it ended with us entwined in each other's limbs, our lips a hair's breadth from touching.

Red smiled at me, and said, "A kiss to die for."

I kissed her, and felt complete rapture. The crowd cheered. Then Illian's voice faltered, and Red Moll crumbled to ashes in my arms. The entire room silenced, the crowd staring at me accusatively as I stood in a pile of cinders.

"Gods, I'm going mad." I lurched out of bed and flung off my sweat sodden nightgown.

Pardon? Saraknyal sounded startled. *Are you okay?*

"Fine." The sultry morning air prickled my skin as I changed into fresh scanties and pulled on a robe, morning light just hinting at the eastern sky outside my open balcony doors. The dream returned, and I felt like I needed to wash off the ashes. "Mad as a hatter, but fine. I need tea."

Bad dream? Saraknyal often asked me to relate my dreams, since he had none of his own.

"Yes, and the sooner I forget it, the better." Thankful that Saraknyal couldn't read my mind, I snatched up Soul Drinker and stalked into my sitting room to pull the bell rope for a footman. "What's on the agenda today?"

Oh, the usual. Murder Reginald Malchi for being an ass, slaughter thousands, and raise and army of undead. You know. Business as— Hashi!

"What?" I froze, knowing that tone all too well. My hand went to Soul Drinker's hilt. "Where?"

The balcony window.

I whirled and gaped at the rectangle of fine white parchment that seemed to float in the air, stuck to the door's glass pane at eye level with a blob of glue. "What in the names of all the..."

It would appear that someone's left you a note.

"Motherless son of a *bitch*!" I crept to the doors, but they were secure. "Up a seventy foot sheer wall?"

Or down from above.

I peered through the glass in all directions, then turned the lock, pulled open the door, and snatched the letter. One glance at the seal explained everything, a dragon skull and crossed scourges. *Preel... Fucking nokitu!*

At least it's not a love note from Lord Blackbriar.

I snorted a rueful laugh. *And it pointed out that our security isn't as secure as we thought.* Nokitu were preternaturally skilled at stealth, but I hadn't ever dreamed one could climb up a sheer seventy-foot wall.

You could station shades on your balconies.

I'll think about it. But the note in my hand demanded all of my attention at the moment. What was so important that a note had to be delivered in secret? I cracked the seal and opened it.

Lady Severn,

I apologize for the manner of this missive's delivery, but

secrecy is paramount. Brilla has threatened me directly, and I need to discuss my next course of action with you privately. I'm turning to you in desperation, for I have no other option.

Please meet me at Rolly Molly's Public House at ten this morning. My head of security, Busashi, has arranged an appointment for you with a trollop named Lola Marie Tonce, who was once one of Jhavika's slaves. She's been paid well for discretion, and Busashi has confirmed that she is trustworthy. She will bring you to a room where we will meet, and I will explain everything.

Brilla has spies and thugs watching, probably both of us. She warned me directly not to contact you about this, but I have no recourse. My nokitu can get me to our meeting in secret, but it would be best if you attend this assignation as if nothing is amiss. I apologize in advance for the implication that you consort with trollops, but this one instance should cause no lasting damage to your reputation.

Thank you for your discretion and your commitment.

Sincerely,
Preel Longbright

Well that throws a wrench into the machinery, doesn't it?

"It certainly does." I sat at my desk, put the letter down, and tried to think. *A brothel, of all places? Could this be a trap, do you think?*

Honestly, no; not if you trust Preel. That's her signature, and the seal's genuine. You should be prepared for trouble, but I think she's sincere. Saraknyal rarely dismissed the chance of danger so readily, but his attention to such details far exceeded mine. *Frequenting brothels isn't exactly your style. It might draw unwanted attention.*

I thought about it, then shrugged. *If Brilla's having me followed, let her spread rumors that I'm a whoremonger. As long as no one knows the real reason I'm there.*

You're already socializing with pirates, I suppose. He'd groused about my trip to see Illian, but he'd enjoyed her singing as much as I had."

A knock at my door announced my breakfast. My footman place a pot of tea, a cup, a small pitcher of milk, and a covered plate before me. Lifting the cover revealed porridge, toasted bread, and a single poached egg doused with pepper sauce.

"Anything else, mistress?" The footman poured my tea and lightened it perfectly.

"Yes. Notify Bromish that I'll be going out this morning. Have the carriage ready by nine. Tell Joss that I want to speak with him."

"Yes, mistress." He nodded respectfully and left.

So, you're going, I guess.

I sipped tea. *Yes, we are.*

Brilla's a problem, you know. Not only to Preel, but to the Council.

I know. I ate my breakfast slowly, thinking. I finished my breakfast as Joss arrived, prompt and somber as a magistrate.

"You rang, mistress?"

"I'm going out this morning. I have an appointment at a public house by the name of Rolly Molly's at ten. I need to know where that is, and I need you to keep your inquiry quiet. Bryce should know." Bryce knew every dive in Haven.

"Right away, mistress." He took the tray of dishes and bowed out.

I had hours to spare, so I exercised, bathed, dressed conservatively, and read a tome on the ancient dwarvish history of western Chen. Tori's tales of the Sky Temples had piqued my interest. Joss arrived at half past eight with my information, and a rather puzzled look on his face.

"Are you sure about this public house, mistress?" He handed over a note with directions. "It's...a..."

"A brothel. Yes, I know." I leveled a stare at him. "Is there a problem?"

"No, mistress."

"Good." I glanced at the directions, straight forward enough. "Tell Bromish he'll be dropping me off at the waterfront. I'll get a lift and walk from there. We leave in an hour."

"Very good, mistress." He left, his puzzled look unchanged.

You're going to get a reputation, you know, Saraknyal chided.

I've already got one.

*True, but not *this* kind of a reputation. Tori Blackbriar's never going to let you live it down if he finds out you're consorting with trollops.*

I considered how Tori would respond to learning I visited a brothel, and smiled. *Icing on the cake, old man.*

I found Rolly Molly's without difficulty, down one floor from the rooftops, two blocks from the waterfront. Two bleary eyed bouncers the size of two-legged oxen framed the door. They eyed me professionally, then my escort.

One raised a hand the size of a dinner plate. "Um, sorry, but those...*things* can't come in. Bad for business."

Tell him that turning him into a shade would probably also be bad for business, Saraknyal suggested.

I considered it, then thought better of the notion. I was supposed to be acting like this wasn't anything dangerous or secretive. "Of course." I turned to my escort. "Return to the carriage. Wait for me there."

"Yes, mistress." They strode off without pause, and the bouncer opened the door for me.

Inside, the place was warm, welcoming, and gaudily decorated in red velvet with gold trim. A hefty woman in a kimono that matched the décor greeted me with a blazing smile. "May we be of service to you?"

Other ladies and men lounged around a common room to my left, variously clad in silks and robes, all of them amply fleshed and beautiful. The brothel's name took on new meaning. I cleared my throat. "I'm Hashi Severn. I have an appointment with Lola Marie Tonce."

"Of course." She raised a finger, and a young man appeared as if by magic at her side. "Lola," she said without looking at him, her smile unaltered.

He bowed and dashed off.

"May I offer refreshment, Lady Severn?" the hostess asked.

"No, thank you." I tried to keep my eyes from wandering while I waited.

Nauseating décor, Saraknyal commented.

Not here for remodeling ideas, old man.

Before I could become truly uncomfortable, the young man returned with a curvy woman clad in a silk robe. She looked me up and down. "Lady Severn, I presume."

"Yes." I tried to smile.

"*Well!*" She looked me up and down again, and grinned. "You're tall enough to wrap around me *twice*, you are."

I opened my mouth, then closed it, an unwelcome image forming in my mind. I clenched my teeth and forced a smile. "Shall we?"

Lola curtsied. "Just follow me, honey." She turned and undulated away, her ample backside cavorting beneath the thin silk.

I followed.

Don't bite off more than you can chew, my dear, Saraknyal quipped.

Oh, shut the hell up!

Lola led me through labyrinthine halls, past numerous doors, then opened one without knocking. "Just come on in and relax, honey."

I stepped into the tidy bedroom, my eyes drawn to the high four-post bed that dominated the space.

Lola closed the door behind me, her pretense suddenly dropping. "Sorry about the come-on, Lady Severn. Just window dressing, you know." She bustled to another door, opened it, and four ebony-clad nokitu entered, their dark eyes sweeping the room, taking me in. They all wore black face coverings and snug hoods, only their eyes exposed. One nodded back through the door. Three more nokitu came in, one much shorter than the others, but identically clad.

The short one curtsied to Lola and pressed her hands together.

That's Preel, Saraknyal observed, but I'd already suspected.

"Take your time." Lola looked to me again. "Just knock when you're done. Wouldn't do for you to leave too soon."

"Of course." The door closed, and I could hear music from beyond. I nodded to the arrayed nokitu. "Preel. So what's this about?"

They all dropped their veils, and Preel removed her hood as well. Her hair, surprisingly short, stuck up at all angles. Under the veil Preel wore a swath of ivory silk that covered her mouth, gold stitching clear on the cloth in patterns I couldn't read.

That cloth on her mouth is the magic I felt before, Saraknyal said, but again, I'd already suspected.

Can you tell what it does?

Rune magic. Yes, it keeps her from speaking.

I opened my mouth to speak, but Preel raised a hand and produced the small notebook she carried. She handed it to me, the page already filled with her flowing script.

I read aloud, "Please, at the risk of my life, hold your questions. I will explain everything, but you must just listen. Don't ask. If you do, I will die." I stared at her. "Die?"

She nodded emphatically.

"Please, Lady Severn," Busashi interjected, "Miss Preel speaks the truth. Just listen. All will be explained."

I suggest we listen.

I nodded. "Very well, I'll listen."

Preel nodded, then tapped the silk covering her mouth and turned her back to Busashi. He deftly untied and pulled it away. Preel turned to face me. She looked very different without a veil, her full mouth giving her an exotic look. She smiled and flashed lovely white teeth.

"I'm sorry for the deception, Lady Severn, but it was for my own protection."

She speaks.

Of course she does. She wouldn't need a magical gag if she couldn't, would she?

Oh, sure, go and use logic!

I opened my mouth, then closed it, remembering my promise to listen.

"I wear the enchanted gag to keep me from speaking because of my very nature. I possess a gift that's dangerous to me in more ways

238

than one. If I'm asked a question I don't know the answer to, I'm compelled to answer truthfully. The answers tax me, knocking me unconscious. If I'm asked another question too soon, I'll fall insensate and die."

Unholy mother of every demon in Hell, she's a truthsayer!

I gaped at her, my mind spinning. I knew what a truthsayer was, how rare they were, and what it meant. Wars had been fought over them, assassinations committed, warlords and even *kingdoms* toppled. The implications of what stood before me in the guise of a young woman struck like a hurricane, chilling me to the bone. *We are so fucked, old man.*

We?

Yes, we. If this gets out, you know what will happen to Haven, the Blood Sea...everything.

*War, of course, but it answers the question of why Brilla's interested in Preel, doesn't it?"

It certainly does.

"In case you haven't figured it out, I'm a truthsayer," Preel admitted. "The rest of what I've told you is basically true. Kevril found me enslaved and freed me in exchange for helping him break Jhavika's enchantment. Falling in love, we didn't intend, but..." She shrugged helplessly, her subtle smile enchanting.

Glad I dodged that arrow, I thought with a nod.

"And you may have figured out, too, that Brilla Balshi has somehow learned of my talent." Preel bit her lower lip, and I could see the tension rise into her face, the terror. "She sent me this yesterday." She pulled a letter from her dark clothes and handed it to me.

I read it, and clenched my jaw on the questions it evoked.

"It's a lie," Preel said. "At least the part about outing me to the entire Council."

"How—"

"Please! No questions!" Preel snapped. "One slip, and I'm dead. You can ask my *opinion*, or what I *think* about something, but no direct question that I might not know the answer to."

I nodded. "What makes you *think* this is a lie?" I tapped the letter.

"Because I invoked my talent to find out." She smiled thinly. "She should have known better than to lie to a truthsayer. She has no mechanism in place to spread the word of my talent in the event of her death."

"But...she might have told others already."

"Maybe, but that would be dangerous for her. She wants me for herself, and Brilla's no fool."

"True. Even her loyal guards might murder her for...um..."

"For *me*. Yes. It's the curse of the dove that laid diamond eggs, if you're familiar with that story."

That's quite an apt analogy, Saraknyal commented.

I nodded. "I am." I considered another point. "Yet you trust *me* with this?"

"I do. Kevril and I used my talent to find out who, among the Council, we could trust most. The answer was you. Lewin confirmed it. You have no aspirations to power at all, it seems."

"Other than a soft bed, good brandy, and peace and quiet, no." I chuckled at the irony, *I never wanted magic, and here stands a truthsayer before me, trusting me with her secret.*

Serendipity's a bitch, Saraknyal agreed.

I phrased my next statement carefully to avoid a question. "So, please, tell me what you want from me."

"Your opinion, first of all." Preel clenched her hands and began pacing the tiny space. "It's unlikely, but not impossible that Brilla's told others. Do you think she can be eliminated without risking my secret?"

So, her own question doesn't invoke her talent, Saraknyal observed. *Interesting!*

"Probably, and you're right, she's not likely to have told anyone. Brilla's not only psychotic, she's paranoid." I considered. "Do you know how she found out?"

Preel nodded. "She abducted several of Jhavika's former retainers and soldiers. One of them, a physician named Yiv, knew of me. Brilla must have...gotten it from her somehow."

Money, coercion, or torture, I wonder?

I gritted my teeth, remembering Dr. Yiv. "If they're not dead, she'll have the prisoners in her home. She'd never risk letting them out of her sight. If she didn't...question them personally, someone else knows."

Preel nodded. "Yes. But if this other person knows, Brilla may have had them killed. The truth may have taken her by surprise, but she'd have silenced anyone who could betray her."

I nodded. "But she hasn't told anyone to spread the news if she's killed."

"Yes, as of last night, she hasn't planned to. My talent can't look into the future, so she may have put something in place this morning."

"But you only received the letter yesterday."

"Yes." She nodded again. "What are you thinking?"

"I'm thinking Brilla Balshi has worn out her welcome, but there are complications." I wagged a finger. "The *one* stipulation of becoming a member of the Council of Lords is to never go directly after another member, either by assassination or attacking their interests. That was basically why the Council was formed in the first place.."

"So Brilla's untouchable?" Preel scowled. "That's a problem. Busashi's looked into removing her, but there's a chance of failure. If I try to have her killed, and fail, it would be disastrous."

And her army's too big for you to tackle alone, Saraknyal said.

I don't need to tackle her whole army, old man, just her. She has no heir, no one to take over House Balshi. She dies, and the house dies.

Unless she's named an hier.

I frowned. *I don't know who she would trust, other than maybe Jhavika.* An idea formed in my mind. "I think you should make Brilla an offer, Preel."

"What?" She looked shocked, but I raised a forestalling finger.

"Write out a sincere *sounding* offer, but one that you know she won't agree to. Make something up about the limitations of your talent."

"Okay, and?"

"And then send it to me, and I'll deliver it to her as your agent." I smiled. "That's why you asked me to help you in the first place, after all, to liaise with the Council, and Brilla's a council member."

"But.. what if she refuses to speak with you?"

"I won't take 'No' for an answer."

"And what if she accepts my offer?"

"That's why you have to make it a *really* crappy offer. Whatever you can think up. Insist her questions be submitted in writing for your approval. Insist on a written contract. Only one question a month. Fill it with legal verbiage. Lewin can help you with that."

"Okay, I can do that. But...what then?"

"Then I piss her off." I let my smile devolve into an evil sneer. "She's unstable, and it wouldn't have taken much the last time I talked to her to push her over the edge. I'll provoke her into attacking me, then it's all over. That's one thing I'm *sure* I can do. Brilla thinks she's invulnerable, above every other council member because she's the richest and has the biggest army. I'll tip her over the edge, and she'll try to kill me."

She looked a little shocked, but nodded. "Okay. When?"

"Oh, let her stew for a couple of days at least. Maybe send a preliminary letter telling her you're considering her proposal, and will arrange a meeting. Just don't tell her it's with *me*. Her temper will already be simmering, then when I show up on her doorstep, she'll be ready to boil over."

And you're very good at making people angry, Saraknyal commented.

Why thank you. I'll take that as a compliment.

"I don't..." Preel bit her lip again. "I'm asking you to commit *murder* for me, Lady Severn. It seems..."

"Evil?" I shook my head. "No, it's self-defense, Preel. She's *threatening* you, and not only you, but all of Haven. You *know* what would happen if word got out about your talent."

"Yes. War." She nodded. "And word would spread about me, even if I fled. Trust me when I tell you I'll die before I become a slave again." She bit her lip again, her dark eyes swimming with unshed tears. "I don't know how I can ever repay you for this."

I chuckled. "Maybe I'll have a burning question that I just can't answer myself one day."

She nodded, a sad smile tugging at her mouth. "Very well, Lady Severn. We have a deal." She held out a hand to me.

I took it and squeezed firmly. "Please, Preel, call me Hashi. And you've already answered one burning question. I've been wondering what the magic was that I felt in you, and now I know. You're unique, you know. The legends of truthsayers all agree that only one can exist at any given time in the world." I smiled and released her hand. "Now, you better go before someone blunders in here."

"Oh, no one will. Lola's been paid for a full hour, and she assured us that she's never disturbed." She held out the enchanted silk cloth to Busashi. "Thank you again, Hashi. I'll send the contract to you in two days."

"Very good." I watched the nokitu affix the silken gag over her mouth. They all refitted their face coverings, and Preel pulled her hood back over her hair. She nodded once again to me, and they left the room, her nokitu checking the hall then ushering her out quickly and silently.

Well, that was certainly interesting, Saraknyal quipped.

It was. I looked around the room, my eyes once again inexorably drawn to the bed. I wondered how many clients Lola had entertained here, and why she'd chosen such a life. *I should go, but leaving too soon could cause suspicion.*

Well don't ask me how long it takes to...um...you know.

I almost laughed at his unease. *Don't worry, old man. We'll be out of this den of iniquity soon.* I stepped over and knocked on the adjoining door.

Lola answered directly, robe clad and smiling, the room behind her a dressing chamber, plinky music playing from an ornate music box. "Done already? Well, that barely took a quarter glass." She closed the music box, eyed me, and licked her lips. "What*ever* will we *do* with the rest of our time together?"

I backed away and looked for a chair, but there weren't any in the tiny room. I clenched my hands at my sides and gave in to my own curiosity. "Would you mind if I asked you a question?"

"Ask away." She undulated past me, moving with more raw sensuality than anyone had a right to own. And she *owned* it. Even the woman's curves had curves. "I've been paid for my time." She sat on the bed and crossed her legs, the robe parting to reveal an ample thigh. "And I don't have *any* secrets, except the ones I've been well paid to keep."

243

"Are you a free woman?" I asked.

"Yes, I'm free."

"Then why choose this life?" I gestured randomly.

She laughed a peal of jiggling mirth. "Oh, honey, you just don't get it, do you?"

"Get what?"

"I *enjoy* sex, I'm very, *very* good at it, and it's earning me quite a fine living." She waved around the room. "I choose the people I entertain and I enjoy making them happy. A roof over my head, gold in my pocket, and I love my work. What could be more fulfilling?"

"I...just can't imagine...being intimate with strangers, I guess."

"Oh, they might be strangers when they come in, honey, but they aren't when they leave!" She laughed again, and eyed me once more. "You're as nervous as a long tailed cat in a room full of rockin' chairs, honey. Why don't you just sit down and relax." She patted the bed beside her.

"I'll stand, thanks." I realized every muscle in my body had tensed up and tried to unclench. "How...long do you think I should stay?"

"You better stay at least another half an hour or I'll lose my reputation."

"Okay." I leaned against a wall and folded my arms.

She stared at me.

I stared back.

"You sure I can't do *something* for you, honey?" she asked. "Maybe just a *little* something? It'd be my pleasure, really."

The memory of my morning nightmare surged up in my mind. "I...no. I don't think so."

"Well, you better at least rumple up your clothes a bit, or people will think you just came here to watch me pleasure *myself*." She slipped a hand under her robe. "Unless you might like that..."

"No, thank you." I realized I was sweating and blew out a breath. "I don't...generally trust people."

"Oh, now you know whores and priests are just about the only people you *can* trust, don't you, honey?" She grinned. "And I ain't even a *little* religious."

To that, I had no comment. To my relief, neither did Saraknyal.

Chapter Twenty Four
Shock and Horror

From the journal of Preel Longbright —
I thought the threat of having my secret revealed to be my greatest horror. Never in my life have I been more mistaken.

Two days after my meeting with Hashi, my nerves were in tatters. I'd sent the preliminary letter to Brilla the same day as our meeting, vague and forestalling, and Lewin and I had drafted a contract so convoluted and restrictive that even a crazy woman wouldn't have signed it. Appropriate, we thought, considering Brilla Balshi's mental state.

Exercise, training, yamshi, and wine were the only things that kept me sane. That and being thoroughly pampered by my staff.

Right after breakfast, I handed the thick contract to Busashi for delivery, and began pacing the floor of my sitting room. He returned and reported the packet delivered into Hashi's hand. I thanked him and resumed pacing, awaiting news. By mid-morning, I was a wreck. I didn't know how it could be taking so long. Finally, Ghiti insisted that we do a yamshi routine to settle my nerves. We moved to the patio and had barely begun, when Busashi burst into the day room with none other than Miko at his side.

At first, I thought that the reflection on the windows and my own overactive imagination had fooled me. Then they stepped onto the patio, and I nearly fainted. I clawed at my gag, and Ghiti promptly removed it.

"Miko?" She looked wretched, salt-caked and exhausted, and the dismay on her face spoke volumes. My mind flooded with dread that drowned my former anxiety. I knew, even before I spoke, what had happened. "Kevril's dead, isn't he?"

"No, but he was taken prisoner." Miko crossed the patio and gripped me by the shoulders, her hands trembling with fatigue. "Hyko's been taken by Toki. They trapped us, and *Scourge* couldn't escape. He sent me here with the injured, and sent Rauley to—"

"Injured?" Hope that Kevril might still live, and several new shades of dread hammered at me like crashing waves upon a fragile shore. "Who? How badly? What—"

"Preel! It's...Boxley. She's in bad shape, but still breathing. She took a komei arrow in the stomach. Bert's taken care of her the best she can, but..." She forced a breath, and I could see the strain of holding herself together slipping into despair. "She's *dying*. Fevered."

"Why not take her to a healer?"

"Kevril told Bert to bring her to Lady Severn, that she could help her, banish the fever with magic. *Then* we can find a healer. Kevril gave me...everything he had, so we can pay."

"Shit, shit, *shit!*" My mind raced. Hashi was currently committing murder on my behalf, and Toki taking Hyko was a matter for the Council, and Kevril... And Boxley... The dam broke within me, and my panic flared into action. "Busashi, have Brindal ready the coach. Send for Lewin. This is an emergency. I'm taking Boxley to Ash Keep. Lady Severn should be there, if not when we arrive, soon. And the Council has to be notified of what's happened."

"At once, mistress."

I whirled to face Miko. "Where's Boxley?"

"We brought her. Rented a wagon. Bert's taking care of the others. We took them to an inn near the waterfront."

I strode for the sitting room, and Miko followed. "Can she be moved into a coach? It'd be faster."

She nodded. "Probably. She's lived through three days hard reaching in a longboat."

"Good." I snatched my silk gag from a pocket. "Tie this for me. I need a veil. You'll have to speak for me."

"Yes, milady." She affixed the gag and I dashed to my bedroom to don a veil.

I took half a minute to apply makeup to my tattoo and emerged to find Miko with my nokitu and Lewin. I pulled my notebook and dashed off a note for Lewin. "Get word to Lord Malchi, or whoever else on the Council you can think of. Tell them Toki has taken Hyko and captured *Scourge*. Have them convene a meeting. I'll attend with Miko."

He read it and paled. "Mistress, Lady Severn warned you not to meet directly with the Council."

I scribbled. "Fuck that! Do it! They've taken my husband! Meeting at Fancy's Folly in one hour, or I'll burn this whole gods-damned city down!"

He read my note and nodded. "I'll do it, mistress."

I nodded, gestured to Miko, and we dashed out, five of my nokitu on our heels. In the courtyard, we found Busashi helping our stableman and driver with the coach. A bedraggled wagon full of sea-worn pirates stood just inside our gate. I dashed to the wagon, and caught my breath at what I found.

Boxley lay wrapped in salt-crusted canvas, looking like a corpse. Her face was more gray than pale, sheened with sweat, her eyes sunken and dark, her lips almost blue. I put a hand on her damp forehead. She had a raging fever.

"We're moving Boxley into the coach," Miko ordered, and half a dozen pirates leapt to help. "We'll take her to Lady Severn. You all get with Bert and give her any help she needs. We're meeting the Council at Fancy's Folly in an hour."

A chorus of "Aye, sir!" and they lifted Boxley carefully, transferred her to the coach, and lay her on one of the plush cushions. Her chest barely rose and fell, and she didn't stir. I wondered if Bert had drugged her. Six months aboard a pirate ship had taught me the prognosis for a belly wound. The end usually came with screaming agony.

Miko, myself, and Busashi boarded. "Ash Keep!" Busashi bellowed to our driver as the rest of the nokitu swarmed up onto the carriage. "And don't spare the whip!"

The driver yelled, "Hah!" and the whip cracked. We lurched into motion, the clatter of hooves and iron-shod wheels on cobbles deafening.

All three of us steadied Boxley on the opposite bench. I brushed her short hair, even shorter than mine, now. *Please, please, please be there, Hashi.* I pressed a hand to Boxley's face, and prayed to every god I knew for her survival. No one spoke; there was no need. We each had our own mountain of terrors to deal with.

Gods damn you, Kevril Longbright, I found myself thinking. *If I'd been with you...*

Then I realized that if I'd been with him, I'd probably be in chains right now in a Toki dungeon, awaiting shipment to the god-emperor himself. As we tore along the cobbled streets, a cold resolve settled upon me. I would find a way to secure Kevril's release even if it killed me. Even if I had to trade my freedom for his.

When we entered the courtyard of Ash Keep, however, surrounded by a grim crowd of ebon-skinned shades, my resolve faltered.

Busashi stepped down from the carriage. "We need Lady Severn at once!"

I stepped down, and my nokitu escort helped maneuver Boxley out. The cordon of shades surrounding us stared at us unmoving, red eyes fairly glowing in the sunshine. Then Hashi's butler emerged from the entrance, a puzzled look on his face, his eyes wide.

"Mrs. Longbright? What's the—"

"We need Lady Severn. The situation's dire." Busashi gestured to Boxley. "A life hangs in the balance!"

"I'm sorry," the butler said gravely. "She's...still at Balshi Keep."

My heard fell in my chest.

"What?" Miko glanced at me, then at Busashi. "Why..."

I snatched out my notebook and scrawled. "It's complicated. We have no time! Busashi, take a horse and bring Hashi here as fast as you possibly can! Tell her what's happened."

He read it and nodded, turning to the butler. "We need a horse at once!"

"Well, it'll take some time to saddle—"

"No saddle, just a bridle! *Please!* This young woman doesn't have long, and only your mistress can save her!"

I had no idea Busashi could be so persuasive.

"Very well." The butler turned to a pale skinned man with black eyes, who I realized must also be undead. A wraith. "The fastest horse in the stable, at once."

"Yes, master Joss." The wraith hurried off.

Moments later, a man emerged leading a leggy gelding that didn't seem to mind the crowd of grim undead filling the courtyard. Busashi took the reins, vaulted aboard, and rode out of Ash Keep without a word.

"Mrs. Longbright, please, bring your friend inside out of the heat. We can arrange cool compresses to soothe her."

I nodded and we followed the butler into Ash Keep.

Chapter Twenty Five
Baiting the Bear

From the journal of Hashi Severn —

I've had almost fifty years to perfect my skill at pretending I'm a heartless necromancer. You'd think I'd have more confidence, but I feel this a paper-thin lie. Killing another council member was the one thing I swore never to do, but, like Jhavika Keshmir, I think this is justified. I just hope the Council agrees.

My carriage pulled to a stop at the outer gates to the Balshi estate, and Bromish announced me to the guards.

"You have no business here!" someone bellowed back.

"Lady Severn has business to discuss with Lady Balshi!" Bromish shouted back.

"No, she doesn't. We've been told not to admit you!"

Not exactly a warm welcome, is it? Saraknyal wasn't comfortable with my plan, but hadn't come up with anything better.

What did you expect? I opened the door and stepped down, tugging my new jacket straight and working my shoulders with the unaccustomed weight. "I'll handle this, Bromish. Shades, stay with the carriage"

"Thank you, mistress." He'd been through so much with me over the years that this probably seemed just another day of work.

I strode up to the gates, inch thick wrought iron bars secured by a heavy locking mechanism. Two small stone gate houses flanked the portal, and a dozen guards stood in two staggered ranks facing me, a nervous officer in the fore. They hefted crossbows, the tips of the bolts gleaming in the sun.

Silver?

Yes.

Then I'm glad I dressed appropriately.

"Open the gate," I said with all the warmth of a glacier.

"My apologies, Lady Severn, but I can't. I have direct orders not to allow you entry."

I sighed. "I'm a member of the Council of Lords, and I'm here to discuss a business arrangement with your lady. A business arrangement *Brilla* requested with Admiral Longbright's wife, whom I'm representing. Open the gate, or I will."

"A business arrangement?" The man looked puzzled.

I sighed. "Yes. I have a contract for her to sign."

The officer's puzzlement doubled. "A...*contract?*"

"Yes, for Mrs. Longbright's services. Your mistress will understand." I glanced right and left at the gate. "I'll wait here."

The nervous sergeant thought it through, then ordered his squad to lower their weapons. I tried not to look relieved. The officer sent one of his people to deliver the message. The young woman jogged off up the graveled drive toward the looming palace.

I waited, enduring the heat of the day baking through my heavy jacket. The soldiers remained where they were, their weapons lowered. My carriage's team shifted, and Bromish hauled on the reins to calm them down. We all began to sweat, save the six shades riding on my carriage. They simply stared at the guards, probably thinking only how they would taste.

You should ask the Tinworthys who built this monstrosity, Saraknyal said.

The palace? I looked up at the soaring spires, looming walls, and ornate leaded glass windows. *It certainly doesn't look gnomish, does it?*

No, it doesn't. He fell silent, then asked, *Are you sure you wouldn't like to live here? The view's stupendous.*

I glanced over my shoulder at the view of the city, the bowl-shaped harbor, ships at anchor, and the sea beyond, then back and up at the looming mountains behind the palace. *No, thank you. The damp and the roar of the waterfall would drive me insane.*

You'd get used to it.

I like the home I have, old man. It's all I've ever wanted.

All? Amusement tinged the single word. *What about Lola Marie Tonce?*

Don't be an ass. I suppressed a smile, knowing it would be misinterpreted by Brilla's soldiers. The muscles in my shoulders eased slightly, and I mentally thanked Saraknyal for breaking the tension.

Finally, the messenger returned and reported to the sergeant in a voice so low that even Saraknyal couldn't pick out his words over the roar of the waterfall. The sergeant looked relieved, which I found odd.

"Lady Balshi will see you."

"She...will?" *That was way too easy, old man!* I'd been fully prepared to bully my way in just short of violence.

You're right. And not like Brilla at all.

"Yes, but only under strict conditions. None of your escort will be allowed on the grounds. You'll be escorted by Balshi guards throughout your visit. At one hint of aggression, you will be shot down. If you accept these terms, I'll escort you to the keep."

At least she didn't insist you left me behind, Saraknyal said.

I was worried she might, actually. You think this is a trap?

Now that's more like Brilla's style. She kills you and can make up any story she likes.

Nothing to do but walk right into it, then. I forced a pleasant smile and nodded to the officer. "I accept those terms." I turned and called to Bromish. "Relax in the carriage, Bromish. This shouldn't take long."

"Thank you, mistress!" He set the brake and climbed down.

I followed an escort of guards up the long gravel drive, our boots crunching along. I fought the urge to match their stride. We passed more guards at the lofty entry, and the comparative cool enveloped us. Here, the gate guards exchanged duty with six more in different attire but similar weapons. Their crossbows were also cocked and loaded, the silver tips of the bolts glinting.

All that silver must have cost Brilla a fortune.

She can afford it.

We strode through the vast place, through halls I'd never seen before, but not climbing any stairs. It struck me what a monumental waste of space it all was. The former Lord Balshi hadn't any children, and neither did Brilla. *All this, for one person... What a waste.*

At least you'd get your exercise walking around the place, Saraknyal suggested.

We're not living here. That's final.

Think of the library this place must have.

I haven't even read all the books in my library.

You can never have too many books, my dear, he quipped.

I didn't remember finding a library in Tawkh keep, but didn't press the point. Our conversation had eased my nerves a bit, but I had to focus.

Finally, we arrived at a pair of doors, and my escort opened them. *Another throne room? Really?*

The room wasn't particularly large, but the expansive view through the wall of leaded glass made it seem so. Beyond the glass loomed White Rock Falls, cascading off the high bluff to crash down into Mirror Lake. In front of the awesome vista sat Brilla Balshi upon a high-backed chair, clad in black as before. Of course, I wore black, too, but I looked good in it, whereas she looked like an emaciated hag.

I glanced at the guards to her left and right, hard-eyed and armored, hands on the hilts of their swords. Five more guards stood against the left and right walls, these hefting crossbows.

More silver-tipped bolts? I asked Saraknyal.

Yes, and the guards' swords are enchanted. Not elvish, but enchanted. Brilla's also wearing a magical amulet, but I can't tell what it does from here. This is the trap, and you are in it, Hashi.

Wonderful. I fixed Brilla's eyes with mine and gave her a respectful nod. "I trust you're well, Brilla?"

So polite. I thought you wanted to make her angry.

It never hurts to start out being polite, I countered. *And it also never hurts to be ready to slaughter everyone in the room. Are we ready?*

Always, my dear.

"Why are you here?" Brilla's monotone left no doubt to the anger that simmered beneath her stoic façade. "I *specifically* told that whore not to contact you."

I smiled thinly at her. "First, using that slur is not only inaccurate, but also not as derisive as you obviously intend. Preel has, to my knowledge, never bartered her favors for money, and some of my most pleasant acquaintances are whores. Second, and more to the *point*, I'm here as Preel's agent. She's drafted a contract for her services that she hopes you'll find agreeable."

"A *contract*." She sneered as if she found the idea of a written agreement offensive. "She can't be serious."

"She is *completely* serious." I unbuttoned my coat and pulled the bound document from an inner pocket. It was thick enough to stop an arrow. "I haven't read it, since it's between you and her, but I know its basic tenets." I refastened my coat and held out the document. "I suggest you read and sign it."

"Why should I? I have all the cards in this game, and she knows it. She'll drag her fat ass up here, or I'll spread her secret far and wide. She'll be in chains by nightfall, as she deserves!" Her tone escalated as she spoke, her bony hands clenching the arms of her chair, tendons distending from her neck.

Barking mad, Saraknyal quipped.

And also not very bright, I agreed with a tired sigh. "Brilla, you hold exactly one card in this game, and it's a dreadfully weak one. Preel knows for a fact that you're bluffing."

"I'm *not* bluffing!" she spat.

"You are." I kept my voice neutral for no other reason than to infuriate her. "If you're wondering how she could possibly know that, please put your tiny little mind to the task and figure...it...out."

"How *dare* you insult me in my own home!" she raged.

As her if she'd prefer you insult her on the patio.

I smiled, and did exactly that, enjoying the rage it evoked. "Come on, Brilla, if you do as you threatened, you'll get nothing. Less than nothing, in fact, since all of Haven will probably end up in flames as a result. If you've even told any of your own *retainers*, you're a bigger fool than I thought, so read the contract, sign it, and shut the *hell* up."

Her guards exchanged worried glances. My mention of Haven in flames had shaken them.

She seethed in silence for a moment, then flicked a hand. "Bring me that document!"

The soldier to her right strode forward, took the bundle from my hand, and handed it to her before resuming his position.

Brilla broke the seal on the contract and began to read. The muscles of her jaw bunched and writhed under the skin as she flipped a page. I waited, my hands behind my back, fingering the smooth bone pommel of Soul Drinker under the ruffled cuff of my sleeve.

*When she springs the trap, you need to move. Don't let them get a head shot, and you *might* just survive this.*

Good advice. I examined the guards through my mind's eye view from Saraknyal. They looked nervous, but not terrified. They clearly thought they had me dead to rights. They didn't know my true intentions in coming here, or that I'd spent four of my shades to ensure Saraknyal had enough soul energy to face the pending conflict. I also hoped they didn't know I'd spent a good bit of money on my armorer and tailor to prepare for this. I rolled my shoulders and waited.

I watched Brilla. Every page she flipped, she became angrier. Soon she flipped them too quickly to be reading much at all, and her bony hands were trembling.

Finally, she rolled the entire document up and threw it at my feet. "That's rubbish!"

"Well, I'm sorry you think so, because it's the only agreement you're going to get."

"Ridiculous! She'll come here herself, or I'll reduce her pitiful keep to rubble!"

I gave her a cold smile. "No, you *won't*, Brilla."

"And why not!" She lurched to her feet, hands clenched at her sides. "I have ten *times* her forces! I have—"

"No, you do *not!*" I finally put some steel into my tone. "You have *nothing!* You have a herd of lambs lining up for slaughter!"

"*What?*" She blanched to an even paler shade.

"You may have soldiers, Brilla, but Preel has *me.* You kidnapped and tortured members of her household. You threatened our admiral's wife! Threaten her again, and I'll inform the Council. Attack her, and I'll annihilate your army and raise them into my own." I grinned at her. "Sign that contract."

"You wouldn't dare! You can't! I'm a member of the Council of Lords!"

"No, you're a petulant, half-crazed little rich bitch who needs to shut the *fuck* up! You're grasping for power you can't have! Why don't you ask *Jhavika* how that worked for her?" I barked a derisive laugh, just enough to send a pulse of terror through the room. "Oh, *right!* You can't. She's *dead!*"

Finally, her temper boiled over. I saw it in her eyes even before she spoke, and drew a deep breath.

"Shoot her down!" Brilla screamed.

As the crossbows raised, I drew Soul Drinker and dropped into a roll. Ten crossbows cracked in a ragged volley, and enchanted steel hissed from the scabbards of Brilla's closest guards. Five of the bolts hit me squarely. I felt the impacts like punches, but the tips didn't pierce the fine mail that Hipshill had fashioned for my tailor to sew into my coat. One silver arrowhead left a crease along my neck, but the pain didn't arrive before I screamed out my deadly retaliation.

Winter!

The arc of my icy breath caught both of Brilla's guards and her, transforming flesh to blue death and frosting the leaded glass wall behind them. The guards fell and shattered into shards, their enchanted swords still gripped in their dead blue hands. Brilla stood encased in frost, her mad eyes fixed in a mien half-terror, half-rage. I lunged to my feet and whirled to face the soldiers.

"STOP!" I bellowed even as they drew their swords. "Your mistress is dead! House Balshi is no more! You serve no one!"

They hesitated, steel gleaming in their hands, aghast at the sight of Brilla standing frozen solid behind me.

Their swords are silver plated, too, Saraknyal warned. *You need to convince them to give up. I don't have enough energy to freeze them all.*

I stood as if untouched by the barrage of bolts, though I ached in several places, and my neck bled into my collar. I chuckled and fear swept through the room. "Don't waste your souls on *nothing.*" I shoved Brilla's statue and watched it shatter upon the stone floor.

Their swords wavered and they exchanged terrified looks. Their lady had just attacked a necromancer, and I stood apparently unhurt by their weapons. The door burst open, and the six soldiers who had escorted me earlier barreled into the room, weapons raised. The sight of me sanding amid the shards of their liege, however, brought them up short.

"Don't be fools!" I pointed Soul Drinker at them. "There *is* no House Balshi any longer! Brilla ordered me killed and paid the price! Don't force me to destroy you."

After a long tense moment, their weapons lowered.

"I hold no rancor for your actions." I pointed to Brilla's remains. "By ordering you to kill me, Lady Balshi broke the one rule that all members of the Council of Lords must live by."

They all looked at one another, clearly stunned and adrift, then one older man stepped forward and sheathed his sword. "We...surrender, Lady Severn." The others nodded and sheathed their weapons, relief clear on their faces. "Lady Balshi was...um..."

"Deranged from her ordeal." I slipped Soul Drinker into my forearm sheath and drew a handkerchief to press against my bloody neck.

Pick up Brilla's amulet. It's about a foot from your right toe.

I stooped and scooped up a silver and sapphire amulet on a chain, then the discarded contract as well, and stuffed both into my coat. My fingers brushed a tender spot, eliciting a wince. "You won't be held responsible for her actions. Now, where are the prisoners?"

They all looked at one another again, and the older man shrugged. "Some people came and delivered...some captives. We were told not to ask questions. Lady Balshi had them all brought to her chambers. She doesn't let anyone in there anymore. Not even the maids, but..." He glanced at his comrades, who looked ill. "We heard screams."

Well, as grim as this may sound, that's good. Nobody else will know Preel's secret.

I felt wrong for agreeing with that horrible truth. "Take me there!" I strode forth. "The rest of you, spread the word to the rest of the soldiers and staff what happened here. Brilla attacked me and perished."

They all muttered agreement and scattered. The older fellow bowed to me and said, "This way, if you please, Lady Severn."

I followed him, trying not to grimace at the pain from the crossbow impacts. *Remind me to thank Hipshill, old man. Those bolts would have skewered me.*

I will. You're still bleeding.

I looked at my sodden handkerchief, folded it and pressed it to the gash. It came away stained, but not drenched. *Not badly.*

We'll have to find a good surgeon to stitch you up, or your beauty will be forever marred.

I suppressed a chuckle. *Oh, shut the hell up, would you?*

You're lucky to be alive, my dear. That was...close.

I considered where the bolt had creased my neck, and agreed. An inch to the left and it would have severed an artery. *Close indeed.*

We arrived at Brilla's chambers and the soldier waved to the door. "It's locked, I'm afraid. None of us has a key."

"No problem." I placed a hand on the latch and reduced it to dust. "I'll just have a—"

As I swung the door open, the stench of old blood and worse almost knocked me down. I gagged and pressed my bloody kerchief to my nose and mouth. The room within resembled an abattoir that hadn't been cleaned in days.

"Gods and devils," I muttered.

Looks like Brilla found a hobby, Saraknyal quipped.

I stepped cautiously into what had once been a sitting room, now a torture chamber. Several corpses had been piled in a corner, days dead from the smell, and obviously tortured. A woman hung from a nail that had been hammered into the wall, also clearly dead from horrific wounds. I took a closer look at her, and barely recognized the alchemist Eias Lavo. Another form sat tied to an armchair, slumped and bloody. When I lifted her head, however, Dr. Yiv's eyes flung open wide, and her bloody mouth gaped to scream.

"No! No! Please! Don't!" She strained against her bonds, rough hemp rope cutting at her forearms. Her hands had been broken, a pair of bloody pliers on the floor at her feet. "I told you *everything*! I told you! No more!"

"Shhh, Yiv, it's Hashi Severn. You're safe." I touched the ropes and dissolved them to dust. Her arms jerked up in a defensive posture. "Brilla's gone. You're safe. We'll get you out of here."

Her eyes focused on me, and she wailed anew. "She...she *made* me! She made me *watch*! Oh, gods, just kill me! My hands! I'm..." She crumpled forward and I caught her, lowering her trembling to the floor.

I turned to my escort. "Do you have a healer?"

"Yes, lady. I'll get him."

Yiv continued to wail, her shattered hands quavering like leaves in a hurricane. I tried to comfort her as best I could. Perhaps Tori or Nahli Twince could heal her, but as far as her mind, and the secret it still held, I didn't know.

Killing her would be a mercy, Hashi, Saraknyal said

No, I'm not doing that. I held Yiv as still as I could. *She might recover.*

And she might rave and reveal Preel's secret.

I gritted my teeth. *She might, but I can't just kill her.*

An old man arrived with a brown leather case, several soldiers with him. He paused at the door, drew a horrified breath, and promptly threw up.

"Stop that and get over here!" I held Yiv until the man's retching subsided. "She's alive, but in pain. Do something for her."

"Yes, Lady. Opium will ease her pain." He opened his case and produced a brown glass bottle from within. "Drink this, miss..."

She thrashed, trying to avoid the bottle.

"Yiv," I told him. "She's a physician."

"Yes, well, now she's a patient." He held her face and force the bottle between her lips. "Drink now. It'll ease your pain."

Yiv drank greedily, some portion of her mind regaining cognizance. I hoped it remained so. Shortly, her trembling eased, her breathing steadied, and her eyes sagged shut. I released her and stood.

"Do what you can for her. I'll try to send someone who can heal her hands."

"Nothing short of magic will—" he began, but then obviously realized who he was talking to. "I'll see to her, Lady Severn."

Outside the room, I found the captain of Brilla's house guard standing waiting for me with a squad of soldiers. She wore gleaming armor, held a helm under one arm, and stood taller than me by a hand, her shoulders broad, black hair cropped short, stark blue eyes like ice.

She bowed to me, her face grim. "I'm Captain Farlay, Lady

Severn. At your service."

"*My* service?" I strode past her and the detachment of soldiers. "I just killed your liege, Captain."

"Justifiably, from the account of the ten surviving soldiers who were there, and I hold no grudge. Lady Balshi was clearly deranged, but we couldn't...do anything about her."

They could have killed her, Saraknyal pointed out.

I bit my tongue. Recriminations were pointless. "Did Brilla name an heir?"

"She has a will, but I've not read it." She winced. "Her scribe told me that she bequeathed everything to Lady Keshmir in the unlikely event of her death."

That meant House Balshi had no lord. "Well, I'm going to have to deal with repercussions from this, and I'll need the testimony of those ten soldiers." I trundled down the stairs, the clatter of armored feet hot on my heels. "Right now, I'm going to find a healer to tend to Brilla's single surviving victim. Please leave the others where they lay for now. The Council will probably want to see this." A room full of tortured corpses would certainly add credence to my story.

"Yes, Lady Severn."

"Keep order here until someone from the Council tells you to do otherwise. Dealing with the Balshi estate's going to be a mess, but there's nothing for it." One thing I'd already considered. "I suppose the Council will find places for you all, and I don't imagine House Balshi has any shortage of funds to support you."

"Not for the short term, milady. Thank you."

I didn't even try to consider what she was thanking me for. Maybe for disposing of Brilla. On the way down the stairs I asked Saraknyal about the Brilla's amulet.

A little disappointing, actually. It's supposed to protect against enchantments.

Stands to reason after being enchanted by Jhavika for so long, I thought.

Fat lot of good it did her in the end.

Guilt welled up within me at the thought of all the things that had driven Brilla to madness; watching her father transformed into a shade, a loveless marriage, ensorcellment by Jhavika, and finally being cast adrift. I wondered how Demia would gauge her soul.

We reached the ground floor and headed for the front entrance. More guards stood there, and they snapped to attention at my approach. Word had spread quickly.

"Someone will be here from the Council later today, I'm sure, to straighten things out."

"We'll maintain order here, Lady, you can—"

The front doors of the keep burst open before we arrived, and more Balshi soldiers bustled in.

"Lady Severn, there's a man here who insists he must speak with you. He said his name's Busashi, and that he—"

"Busashi? What the..." Dread welled up, but speculation was pointless. "I know him. Where is he?"

"At the gate, milady. Under the circumstances, we thought it best to deny him entry."

"I'm surprised he didn't kill you all!" I hurried across the courtyard and down the drive, still aching from my injuries. At the front gate, I found Busashi holding the bridle of a leggy black gelding that I recognized from my own stable.

"Lady Severn! There's an emergency. The *Scourge* was taken in Hyko by Toki forces. Some of the admiral's crew escaped, and one's in dire shape. They're at Ash Keep."

"Taken? What of Admiral Longbright?"

"Taken captive, but alive as far as we know. Miss Preel needs you to see to this injured young woman. Belly wound some days old. She's near death."

We can purge the infection, Hashi, Saraknyal informed me.

"Gods and demons, this is quite possibly the *worst* timing I've ever..."

"Please, milady, take your horse. It'll be faster, and there's not a moment to waste. The girl's nearly gone." He held out the reins to my gelding.

"And not even a saddle?" I took the reins, let him sniff me, and allowed Busashi to give me a leg up. "Bromish, bring Busashi to Ash Keep. I'll meet you there."

"Yes, mistress!" He climbed up into the driver's seat. "How did the negotiations with Lady Balshi go?"

"About as badly as I expected." I reined my mount around and kicked him, pointing him in the general direction of home.

Hell of a day, Saraknyal quipped as we clattered along at a reckless pace.

It certainly has been so far, I agreed. *And I don't think it's over yet.*

Chapter Twenty Six
A Concerted Effort

From the journal of Preel Longbright —

Never in my life have I been so out of my element, even sailing aboard a ship in the Serpent's Eye. Watching these people decide the future of the man I love felt like watching someone slowly thrust a knife into my heart.

I could do nothing but hold Boxley's hand, think of Kevril, and feel helpless. We'd removed the canvas wrappings, but Boxley still had a wide bandage across her stomach that emitted a fetid odor. A maid pressed cool compresses to her brow, but her breathing remained a fragile thread, her color terrible, her eyes unmoving behind their lids. Twice, I thought she'd expired, but the thready pulse at her neck remained. Miko sat to Boxley's other side, her forehead resting on her clenched hands, her muttered prayer too soft to catch.

A clamor from the hall outside, and Hashi Severn entered the sitting room like a dark storm, clad in a close-fitting black coat, blood coloring her hands and the frilly collar of her shirt. Her eyes took us in as Miko and I stood.

Miko bowed shortly. "Lady Severn, I'm—"

"I recognize you." She strode over to the table, unbuttoning and handing her coat to her butler, her eyes drawn to Boxley. This close, I caught the scent of clean sweat and horse. "You're Admiral Longbright's first mate. I saw you with Illian at the Folly."

Miko looked a little stunned. "Yes, and this is my shipmate, Midshipman Boxley. She...took an arrow in the stomach."

"So I was told." Hashi placed a hand on Boxley's brow.

I thought to ask about Brilla, but at this point it seemed trivial.

Instead, I retrieved my notebook and scrawled. "Can you help her?"

She glanced at the note, and nodded. "I can destroy the infection, but I can't heal the injury or the damage that the suppuration's caused." She took on a distant look, and Boxley gasped suddenly, her eyes fluttering, her color flushing pink. "There. I've taken the infection and the poisons from her blood, but—"

Boxley's mouth opened to emit a horrible wail of agony.

"What happened?" Miko gripped Boxley's hand. "What did you *do*?"

"I took the infection, as I said," Hashi insisted.

I realized she'd also said poisons before, and wrote furiously, "She was given opium for the pain."

"Damn! I didn't think to ask." She looked around. "Joss, see if we have anything for pain. *Not* alcohol."

"Yes, mistress!" The older fellow hurried out.

Boxley's eyes opened, her head thrashing as she looked around, her gaze darting between Miko and Hashi. She shifted away from the taller woman, focusing on Miko. "Sir, I... It...*hurts*." Her face twisted into a mask of agony. "I can't..."

"Hold fast, Boxley. This is Lady Severn. She took the infection. You're going to make it. We're in Haven. We'll get you something for the pain."

"I need to contact Tori Blackbriar. He can help. Maybe Nahli Twince." Severn started to turn, but I grabbed her arm.

At the mention of the other council members, I scrawled madly in my notebook. "Toki has taken *Scourge* and arrested Kevril. I had Lewin call a Council meeting at Fancy's Folly. They should be convening soon. Can we take Boxley with us?"

Hashi opened her mouth, then stopped as if remembering something important. Then she shook her head sharply. "You shouldn't go, Preel. Remember what I told you about Blackbriar and Twince. They can help your friend, but they can sense—"

I shook my head sharply, and wrote. "I have to be there! I need to know what they're going to do for Kevril, if anything. I've got to free him! I can find him!"

Hashi looked thoughtful, then sighed. "Yes, you *can* find him, but I don't know how you can get him out of a Toki dungeon."

"I don't either," I wrote, "but I can find out! I can answer *any* question!"

"But..." She paused again, perhaps considering my potential. "Preel, if you're captured, they'll find out what you are. They'll take you to the god-emperor. They may know about you already."

She didn't understand. "If they know about me, that would change everything. The god-emperor would stop at nothing to find me. They would invade, sweep across the Blood Sea. But I can find out if they know my secret! If they do, I'll offer myself in exchange for Kevril."

"Preel, no. You're much too—"

The elderly man reentered the room with a small pot. "Mistress, cook said this would help pain. It's hemp resin mixed with henbane. He uses it for his back, said not to give too much, a pea-sized ball under the tongue."

Hashi waved to Boxley. "Give her some." She turned back to me. "Preel, Toki's *already* invading. They won't stop with Hyko. We're already at war, and we're not ready!"

"Then Haven needs her admiral!" I scrawled. "I'm getting him back, Hashi. Whatever it takes. He sailed into the Serpent's Eye for me. I can't abandon him!"

She stared down at me for a very long time, then finally nodded. "I can't stop you, Preel, but if you walk into a Council meeting, whatever you do, don't let Tori Blackbriar or Nahli Twince touch you. If they do, they'll know."

I nodded and gestured to Boxley. "We need them to help Boxley, yes?"

She nodded again. "Let me do that. You and Miko can address the Council. I'm going to have to explain about Brilla, too. It's going to be a nightmare."

I'd almost forgotten about Brilla, and wrote, "What happened with Brilla?"

Her teeth flashed in a brief and dangerous smile. "She had her soldiers attack me. She's dead. Her soldiers surrendered." Her smile faded, and her face went grim. "She was completely deranged, Preel. She...tortured several people she'd abducted. Dr. Yiv was the only one who survived, and she's in bad shape. I don't know if she'll recover."

I swallowed hard and wrote. "Thank you. I owe you a great debt."

"You don't owe me anything, Preel. Brilla was a menace. Someone would have had to deal with her eventually." She put a hand on my shoulder and turned us to where Boxley lay, Miko and the necromancer's butler stooped over her. "How is she, Joss?"

"Resting easier, mistress." He stood and shrugged helplessly. "She'll need magic to heal properly. She's torn up inside. It's a wonder she's alive."

"Then let's bundle her up and take her with us." Hashi shrugged her shoulders and twisted her neck, wincing. "Maybe a wet cloth to clean my hands and neck?"

"At once, mistress! And the carriage has arrived."

"Then let's be at it." Hashi had one of her shades lift Boxley and carry her out to the waiting carriages.

We put her in mine, and my nokitu boarded. Hashi accepted a steaming wash cloth from a silver tray and did a quick wash of her hands and neck. She then called together a force of shades as our escort.

"Best speed to Fancy's Folly. We'll get a lift on High Street, then it's only one bridge." She spoke as if she'd walked all of Haven. As long as she didn't try to keep me from getting Kevril back.

Miko and I boarded my carriage to tend Boxley in transit, and I dropped my veil and tapped the silk gag so we could speak.

"That woman's scary," Miko commented as she untied the binding.

"Yes, she is, but she's on our side."

"So far." She checked Boxley, who seemed to be insensate, but her color and breathing were much better. She then looked at me curiously. "She knows, doesn't she?"

I nodded. "It was necessary." I filled her in on what had happened with Brilla, and my solution. "None of that matters now. We need to figure out how to get Kevril out of there."

Miko blew out a breath, and I could see the exhaustion wearing on her. "I'm sorry I left him, Preel, but..."

I put a hand on her shoulder and squeezed. "You *didn't* leave him. He ordered you to go."

She nodded. "They won't execute him. He's far too valuable."

"I know." Another thought came to me. "How many Scourges are with him."

"Thirty. Are you serious about trying to get him out?"

I narrowed my eyes at her. "*Deadly* serious."

"I don't see how it's possible, Preel. They've got an army and an armada of warships. Haven's got...what?"

I shrugged. "Maybe eight warships, or so. A few more armed merchants. Now that Brilla's dead, her soldiers can be conscripted. Then there's the council members to consider. Some wield real power, and Twince is fae. We might even ally with the fae. They hate Toki. And Lady Severn is..."

"Bloody scary," Miko finished for me, and I nodded.

"She is. But she's *our* scary." Then I thought of one more advantage. "And we've got a truthsayer, Miko."

"True enough, but we've got to play that card close to the vest." She seemed to solidify slightly, hardening with determination. "And who knows what support we might get from Sariff or the other islands. Kevril spoke to the Chiefs of Twin Capes. They hadn't decided about the protectorate yet, but told him they were always ready for trouble."

I looked at her dubiously. "Canoes and spears against warships and komei?"

"Don't sell the islanders short," she assured me. "They come off as fun-loving and peaceful, but they're fierce warriors."

I swallowed hard. "War, Miko. It's happening."

"It is, and if Mati weighs in too soon, we're in deep trouble."

"It's all about naval power." I fixed her with a hard look. "You've *got* to help me convince the Council that they need Kevril."

She sighed and rubbed her face. "I'll try, Preel, but they're not going to commit their entire navy to try to save one man."

"Then we'll just have to do it ourselves," I told her.

She met my gaze and shook her head. "As much as I'm on your side, I just don't see how it's possible."

Neither did I, but there had to be a way, and if I was good for one thing, it was finding answers to difficult questions.

Chapter Twenty Seven
Council of War

From the journal of Hashi Severn —

Negotiating has never been my strong point. It always seems to end up with people's souls torn from their bodies. Saraknyal has no problem with this strategy, but I do. I took solace in the fact that no souls were destroyed in dealing with Brilla. Maybe I'm learning.

Ten sea-worn pirates met us outside Fancy's Folly, looking as hard as nails. A scarred woman in the fore snapped a salute to Miko, her eyes fixed on the injured young woman being carried by one of my shades.

"Sir! How's Boxley?"

"Better, Tansy, but not healed quite yet." Miko nodded to me. "Lady Severn here helped her, but we need magical healing. She said two of the council members could help us. Stay outside."

I didn't break stride at the door, and with shades and nokitu flanking me, the two massive bouncers simply stepped aside. The din from inside warned me.

We walked into a hornet's nest. Captain Patak and the three new captains were arguing with the council members, primarily with Reginald Malchi and Ingrid Brickhammer, though Tori was holding his own. The rest of the Council looked about ready to join in.

I touched Miko's shoulder and nodded to Preel. "Give them your account while I see to your friend, then I'll join in. I'll get their attention."

"Yes, milady," Miko squared her shoulders.

Time to call order to this free-for-all.

Right. I drew a deep and painful breath, my ribs still aching from my encounter with Brilla's guards, and screamed at the top of my lungs. "QUIET!"

The Folly's surprisingly good acoustics helped amplify my voice, and the verbal assault fell silent. Everyone in the club looked at us, and the sight shades and nokitu backing us seemed to make an impression. Malchi went pale and motioned his personal guards forward, but before he could open his mouth, I interjected.

"We have a serious situation, but I need Tori and Nahli to help me with this young woman first. It's urgent. She's near death. Miko, here, is Admiral Longbright's first mate, and this is his wife, Preel. They'll fill the rest of you in."

I gestured the shade bearing the young officer to follow me, and strode away from the rest. The farther I could keep Nahli and Tori from Preel, the better. Thankfully, with a firsthand witness to interview, none argued. Tori and Nahli hurried over, and the rest listened as Miko began relating the events at Hyko.

My shade lay the young woman on a table, and she stirred. "She needs healing desperately," I told them.

"And who's this?" Tori looked perplexed but intrigued.

"Does it matter?" Nahli stepped around him, her eyes fixed upon Boxley.

"She's an officer from *Scourge*," I told them, sparing a glance at the others. The Council seemed to be listening to Miko, and Preel joined in with Busashi reading her hastily scrawled notes. "A belly wound. I destroyed the infection, but..."

"How long?" Nahli placed a hand on the young woman's brow.

"Four days."

"Hashi, you're injured." Tori raised a hand to my bloodstained collar. "How..."

I drew away. "One of Brilla's guards. We had a...disagreement. I'm fine."

"A *disagreement?*" He shot me a skeptical look. "And she *attacked* you?"

"She ordered her guards to, yes."

Nahli looked up from our patient. "And she *survived?*"

No point in beating around the bush now, my dear, Saraknyal said.

I started to sigh, but it hurt. "As a matter of fact, no, she didn't."

They both gaped at me.

"Look, I'll fill everyone in as soon as we're finished saving this young woman's *life*, okay?"

"Of course." Nahli leaned down to open Boxley's eyes. "She's drugged, yes?"

"Yes. Hemp and hensbane. When I banished the infection, she woke in agony. We had to give her something."

"Yes..." Nahli closed her eyes. "This should be straightforward."

"Straight..." Tori started to ask, but his question faltered as Nahli took a deep breath, muttered something wispy, pinched the unconscious patient's nose, and pressed her mouth over Boxley's.

Nahli exhaled, and the young woman's chest rose, and with it, her back arched and her limbs quivered.

"The breath of life," Tori muttered.

"The what?" I looked at him askance.

Magic. I'm surprised even you can't feel it.

"Fae magic." Tori's eyes took on a far-off look. "Not many can do this. It's..."

Nahli held the breath in Boxley's lungs for what seemed a long time, until her rigid muscles relaxed, and the tremors eased. Then Nahli released her and rose, one hand still resting on the young woman's forehead.

"That should do." Nahli sounded spent. "She'll rest until the medication wears off. Her body will do the rest, but she needs food and liquids desperately."

"After four days at sea without, I suppose she does." Tori hailed one of the Folly's wait staff and told them to bring water, then turned to me. "Now what's this about Brilla?"

"I'll tell everyone once they've heard what's happened to Admiral Longbright."

"I'll watch over her," Nahli assured us. "I'll get the news later, I'm sure."

"Thank you." I strode back to the table where most of the Council sat, Tori at my side. Thankfully, we took seats far from where Preel and Miko stood. We hadn't missed much. Toki had occupied Hyko without much of a siege, and had an armada of warships.

"Can you estimate their forces?" Malchi asked when the details wound down.

"Eleven war junks, four of them small, six two-deckers, and a flagship, three good sized merchants, and now *Scourge*." Miko shrugged. "I don't know how many soldiers landside, but sailors alone...at least two thousand. To occupy the city, they'd need at least that many more."

"But Hyko has *walls*," Ingrid Brickhammer argued. "How could they take the city without an extended siege?"

"By the river, I'd guess," Miko said with another helpless shrug. "It doesn't matter *how* they did it; they have."

Preel scratched a note and handed it to Busashi, who read. "What matters is that they can't come any farther south by land. We need to plan how to respond."

"*We?*" Malchi made a face. "There is no 'we' here, Mrs. Longbright. The Council will—"

"Don't be an *ass*, Reginald," Ursula Roque snapped with a glare at Malchi. "Our admiral, Preel's *husband*, and the crew of *Scourge* have been taken by Toki! She has a vested interest in this!"

Her vehemence surprised me.

"Exactly," Miko agreed. "And we need a plan not only to deal with their armada, but to get Kevril out of there, either through negotiations or...other means."

"That's insane!" Malchi retorted. "He's undoubtedly in a dungeon or halfway to Toki by now."

"They're not likely to waste a ship to send him back," Miko countered. "Fifteen ships in all is not an overwhelming force considering they're facing the entire Blood Sea."

"They could be receiving reinforcements even as we speak, both by land and sea." Tambris Matesh still wore an eye patch, but seemed to have recovered from the rest of his injuries, half of his face a mass of healed scars. "They must intend to use Hyko as their base of operations."

"Which is why we have to strike *now!*" Miko raked the table with her dark eyes. "Muster every ship we can, man them with every solder we can spare, and hit them hard."

"And leave Haven defenseless?" Malchi barked a laugh. "No.

We don't have the solders to..." He looked around the table suddenly. "Where the hell is Brilla? She's got—"

"Brilla's not coming." I stood and put my fists on the table. "You're not going to like this, but Brilla's dead."

The Council took a collective gasp, but I held up a hand to forestall them.

Cat's out of the bag now, Saraknyal quipped.

"*Listen*, please!" I'd been thinking hard about how to pitch the news. "Brilla kidnapped several of Jhavika's former people and...tortured them for information about Preel. One survived, her physician, Dr. Yiv. Brilla was completely deranged. She tortured these people to death in her own chambers. I saw it after. The bodies are still there, decomposing in a *pile*. Look for yourself, but I hope you have a strong stomach."

The younger members of the Council turned pale, and Roque pressed a hand to her mouth.

Tori nodded. "I'll see what I can do for Dr. Yiv once we're finished here. Frankly, Nahli's probably the better choice." He looked from me to Preel. "What were Brilla's intentions?"

I broke in before Preel could scratch an answer. "I don't know what her *exact* intentions were, but Brilla clearly attempted to extort Preel. I tried to talk her down. She became violent, ordered her solders to attack me, and I defended myself." I touched the bloody collar of my shirt.

"Gods and devils," Malchi cursed. "You *murdered* a member of the Council of Lords!"

"No, I *defended* myself!" I fixed his eyes with a cold stare. "Ten of Brilla's soldiers witnessed the exchange and will corroborate my account. Instead of slaughtering her entire force of guards, I chose to end the conflict before it could escalate. House Balshi is now leaderless."

"Bloody Nine Hells," Ingrid muttered. "That'll throw half of Haven into chaos!"

Now tell them the good news, Saraknyal said.

"It will, but more importantly, it gives the Council access to Balshi's soldiery *and* resources." I raked the entire council with a cold, hard, stare. "Six hundred soldiers, I don't know how many ships, and enough money to support them and build more, are now at our disposal. I propose we *use* them!"

"Balshi has three merchantmen in port," Captain Patak cut in. "And as I was telling the Council, *Tiger Lily's* still outfitted for war, and *Sea Drake's* near finished. We can do the rest underway." He looked to Miko. "All we need is captains."

"And sailors," Miko added.

"Two thirds of Balshi's soldiery just spent a month at sea, and many of our own forces as well," Ursula Roque put in. "They have *some* experience. We have Captain Patak, Red Moll, Captain Tan, and Captains Jaris, Brethwite, and Caul, each with ships of their own. If Captain Niland takes *Tiger Lily*, and *Captain* Miko takes one of Balshi's ships, we're two captains short. Their captains can *sail* the ships, but they're not military minded."

"If we put our first mates aboard, they'll be able to advise," Patak offered.

"Two of my smugglers are sailing lookout," I put in, grateful that the conversation had drifted away from Brilla's death to general strategy. "They should be dispatched to Sariff and the islands. We need every ship we can get. We need to spread the word."

"It'll take *weeks* to muster a fleet!" Malchi argued.

"No, it won't!" Miko insisted. "It'll take days, and we can join forces at sea. We sent a longboat to Twin Capes. The Chiefs have been informed, and assured Admiral Longbright they were prepared for conflict. If Captain Moll's already at Black Point, I can't imagine by now that they aren't making preparations."

Preel tugged at Miko's sleeve and held out her notebook.

Miko nodded. "And we have to figure out how to get Admiral Longbright away from them. Even if we destroy the Toki Armada, simply besieging Hyko won't free them."

"I'm afraid I see no way to free them, Mrs. Longbright." Malchi stood, looking grim. "We must direct our efforts—"

"I do." I pressed my hands flat on the table and leaned forward. *You what?*

"I'm sorry, you do *what?*" Malchi asked with a glare at being interrupted.

"I can get Admiral Longbright, the rest of his crew, and maybe even *Scourge* out of Toki hands." Even as I spoke, a plan formed in my mind.

*Hashi, what the hell are you *thinking*?*

Slaughter thousands, raise armies of undead, take over the world... You know, the usual.

Really?

No, not really. I suppressed a smile at his incredulous tone. It wasn't every day that I could put one over on Saraknyal.

"How?" Tori asked at my elbow.

I grinned down at him, then nodded to Preel and her entourage. "Mrs. Longbright has a small fishing smack. Six nokitu, myself, and a select crew of seasoned pirates should be enough to rescue Admiral Longbright, and take *Scourge* back."

"Are you insane?" Malchi spouted. "You don't even know where they're holding them!"

"Leave that to me." I grinned at Preel, and her eyes widened. "We get Longbright and his crew aboard *Scourge*, sail south, and draw the Toki armada right into a trap!"

Everyone in the room just stared at me.

You're not kidding, are you?

Nope.

Why, Hashi? Saraknyal sounded both terrified and baffled.

The reason came to me from nowhere. *Because I can.*

"You know," Bikka Patak said with a piratical grin, "that's just fookin' crazy enough to *work*!"

The room exploded into a dozen different arguments, some lauding my plan, others calling it insanity.

Tori stood beside me and leaned in close. "You can't expect to succeed, Hashi. Don't do this."

I looked him square in the eye, our noses barely an inch apart. "Who's going to stop me? You?"

"No, not me, but I'd think two thousand Toki soldiers might try."

"Let them." I grinned at him. "When we're finished, *I'll* have an army. One powerful enough to face down Toki."

"Hashi, that's—"

Someone pulled on my sleeve hard enough to turn me around,

and I found Preel there with her nokitu. She pressed her notebook into my hand and I read, "Are you serious about this?"

I laughed and put a hand on her shoulder. "Yes, Preel, I'm serious."

She snatched the notebook and wrote, "Then you'll need my help!"

"I know, but we have to be—"

"Mrs. Longbright, I don't believe we've met. I'm Tori Blackbriar." Before I could intervene, Tori slipped in beside me and took Preel's hand in his. His suave persona devolved to shock in the span of a heartbeat. "By the Tree! You're a—"

Busashi and two more nokitu moved. Even as I grabbed Tori's arm as hard as I could, there were two blades pressed into vital spots, both shielded from view by the five of us pressed so closely together.

"Silence would be wise, Lord Blackbriar," Busashi hissed.

"Or at least thinking it through before you speak!" I pulled him close and whispered into his ear. "If you sense the *truth* here, you know what Brilla was using to blackmail Preel. If you speak a word of it, I'll murder you, elf blade or no."

Preel, for her part, looked suddenly terrified, her hand still grasped in Tori's.

He slowly released her, then cleared his throat. "I...understand completely, Lady Severn. Mrs. Longbright, you can be assured, I'll not speak of this." Tori turned to me. "This is the *nexus*, Hashi. It *has* to be. This is the moment when it all comes together! The Death Stone, a necromancer, and now...this? It's a conjoining of forces!"

He could be right, you know, Saraknyal said.

"Okay, maybe it is," I whispered. "If so, your mission is complete. You can go home now."

"Oh, I don't think so, Lady Severn." That disarming smile flashed and he turned back to Preel. He couldn't bow with two nokitu blades pressing into his gut, but he smiled an inclined his head. "In fact, I'd like to offer my services in the rescue of your husband, Mrs. Longbright."

"You *what?*" Busashi flicked a finger, and the nokitu withdrew their blades.

"I'd like to help." Tori shot his cuffs, inspected his jacket for damage, and gave me a glance. "Hashi can attest that I'm capable, and I do have...other skills that could be of use."

Like appearing as anyone he wishes? Saraknyal mentioned.

The thought had merit, especially since we'd be infiltrating a city full of Toki soldiers. I released my grip on his arm and nodded to Preel. "He's not lying. He would be useful."

Preel wrote furiously in her notebook and handed it to me. I read, "We need to discuss this!"

I showed the page to Tori, then Busashi, and both nodded. The arguments still raged around the room, so few had noticed our quiet confrontation.

"Let me speak with the Council, then we'll met at Longbright Keep," I said.

Preel nodded, and her nokitu collected Boxley and carried her out. Miko and the three pirate captains were holding their own against Malchi, Que-Chen, and several other council members. Nahli seemed to have vanished, and Ursula Roque and Tambris Matesh were arguing with Ingrid Brickhammer and the Tinworthys. Mah Hatsu sat watching it all from her seat, looking slightly horrified.

"Do you want to call order, or should I?" Tori asked with a sly smile.

I drew Soul Drinker and hammered the pommel onto the table until the arguments stilled, then sheathed it.

"Tori has agreed with my plan and will accompany us." I caught Miko's eye. "We'll be leaving as soon as we square away the details."

"You're both insane," Malchi proclaimed, his hubris intact.

"You're just jealous, Reginald." Tori hitched up his sword belt and grinned. "Sailing off into the sunset with a beautiful necromancer to save the Blood Sea... What could be more fun?"

"Sun*rise*," I said. "Hyko is north*east*, Tori."

"Well, of *course* it is! Figure of speech!" He barked a laugh and waved a hand. "We'll have *someone* along to find the way, I'm sure! We'll leave all the other details in your capable hands, but please *do* arrange to come to the rescue." He snatched up a crimson cloak from the back of his chair and flung it on in a dramatic arc. "It would be *embarrassing* if you didn't."

Chapter Twenty Eight
Desperate Council

From the journal of Preel Longbright —

I can't believe I'm considering this, but at least I can savor the solace that it's not the craziest thing I've ever done.

Boxley regained consciousness as we were carrying her into Longbright Keep, groggy but insistent.

"I'm fine! Lady Preel, I can walk. Please!" She struggled weakly. "Put me down!"

I nodded and the two nokitu carrying her eased her feet to the floor. She went pale and wavered on unsteady legs, but didn't fall down.

I wrote her a quick note. "You need to recover. Food and rest. We're planning to rescue Kevril and we'll need your input." Boxley was the only one currently in the keep who knew the situation in Hyko.

"Yes, Lady Preel!" Boxley brightened, wobbling on her bare feet. "I'm thirsty and starving, and I could use a wash, but I'll be right as rain in no time!"

I caught Brindal's sleeve and dashed off a note. "Third floor guest room. Food, drink, and a bath."

"Yes, mistress!" He grinned and took Boxley by the arm. "Now come along young miss. We'll find a nice dress for you to wear."

"You just *try* to put me in a dress, you tight-laced twit!" Boxley teetered up the stairs, accepting Brindal's help despite her complaints. "I'll have your liver on *toast*! Why, I've *killed* men for less!"

Her shrill protests made me smile. I gathered my nokitu with a glance and we hurried up to the day room. I tapped my gag as the door closed, and Busashi untied it.

I turned to him immediately. "I need you to tell me if this rescue is even possible, Busashi."

He looked grave. "*Possible*, mistress? Knowing what I know of Lady Severn's capabilities, I'd say yes, it *is* possible, but dangerous in the extreme. I have no idea what Lord Blackbriar's capable of, or if I trust him to accompany us on such a mission, let alone with the knowledge of your talent."

"Well, that cat's out of the bag, I'm afraid." I flung off my veil and wrung my hands. "Six nokitu, myself, Hashi, Lord Blackbriar, and...four pirates, maybe? Will we all *fit* aboard *Gull*?" I'd never seen the little smack, but had heard descriptions from Kevril.

"Yes, but not comfortably." Busashi replied. "She has a small forward cuddy cabin with room for four to sleep, and a small galley. Storage is sufficient for our needs. She has a small fish hold."

"We'll get by, then, but that means nine of us in the weather at all times." Kevril had assured me *Gull* was weatherly and fast, but she was also low and we'd be beating to weather. I started a mental list. "We'll need black sails and dark clothes for everyone. Weather cloaks, of course, weapons, some medical supplies, and enough food to get us there, all wrapped water tight. We have no way to know what they left aboard *Scourge*."

"They'll leave stores, certainly, but they may also have a sizable force aboard. They likely intend to use the ship, pose as pirates to hunt other pirates. Taking her will be difficult. We must decide whether to rescue the Admiral and his people first, or take *Scourge*."

I paced, trying to think like a pirate, like Kevril. Rescuing the pirates first would give us a larger force to take *Scourge*, but there could be unforeseen problems. "*Scourge* first, I think. I can't imagine getting everyone out without raising an alarm. Just getting everyone to the ship will be hard enough without fighting our way aboard."

"Indeed," Busashi agreed. "Taking *Scourge* without raising an alarm will be challenging."

We discussed the details—at least the non-nautical ones—and Busashi sent four of his nokitu to start procuring everything necessary for the mission as well as informing Morelie and Sauncey of our plan. I didn't even know if they'd been informed of Kevril's capture yet, but I felt sure they'd be willing to go. I graduated from mental lists to paper and pen, but before we got far with our plan, Lady Severn, Tori Blackbriar, and Miko arrived together.

Miko looked least happy of the three.

"They put me in command of *Temoin,* Balshi's bloody flasgship!" Miko swore and strode for the sideboard without asking, grabbed a bottle, and poured a measure into a glass. "A slug of a galleon manned by twenty pirates, two dozen merchantmen, and three *hundred* lubbers! Odea's sweet tits, she won't sail to windward worth two pennies in a tin cup!"

I let her rant and faced Hashi and Lord Blackbriar. "I can't thank you enough for this, Hashi. Really, I don't know why you're doing this, but..."

"Lord Blackbriar asked me that same thing, and I had no good answer other than because I can." She cocked an eyebrow at Tori. "In fact, I'm the *only* one who can do this."

"Admittedly, Lady Severn's probably correct." Blackbriar stepped closer, but not too close—wary now of my protective nokitu—and executed a graceful bow. "And rest assured, Mrs. Longbright, your secret is *most* secure with me." He grinned widely. "I have a few of my own, in fact."

"Thank you, Lord Blackbriar, but—"

"Tori, please." He straightened, that dazzling smile intact. "Titles are *such* a bother."

"Tori, then. Please call me Preel."

"*Delighted* to meet you, Preel."

I nodded and took a deep breath. "And, if you *do* know what I am, I must warn you to guard your speech. An incautious question could—"

"Kill you, yes, I know." He barked a laugh. "You can't imagine my shock! I've only ever met three other truthsayers in my entire life! By the Tree, it's *such* a pleasure!"

"*Three?*" I gaped at him. That seemed impossible if, as Hashi had said, only one could exist in the world at a time. "How..."

"Suffice to say I'm older than I look." He grinned again.

"A *lot* older," Hashi commented.

I looked between the two and felt like they were sharing some secret. Then again, we all had secrets we weren't willing to share.

"Pardon, Lady Preel, but I came to check on Boxley." Miko put down her empty glass and tugged her salt-stained jacket straight. "I've got a lot of work to do to get the *Temoin* ready for sea. The Council's buzzing like a hornet's nest!"

"Of course. She's awake, and probably eating us out of a month's provisions." I gave her directions to the guest room, and told her to feel free to ask the staff for a meal and a bath for herself. "Tell Boxley as soon as she's feeling up to it, I'd like her opinion on the situation in Hyko. You've obviously got your hands full. I'm sure we have a chart of the harbor around somewhere."

"I will, lady, and thank you." Miko turned to Hashi and nodded. "And thank *you*, Lady Severn for tending to Boxley. She means a lot to me."

"The least I could do."

Miko nodded and turned away, then turned back at the door. "She's actually the one who killed Jhavika, you know."

"*Her?*" Hashi looked startled, then at me. "But she's just a child."

"Pirates grow up quickly," I explained. "She was also on the team that infiltrated an alchemist's stronghold to rescue *me*. She's going to be a fine captain one day, Kevril tells me."

"One never knows who will aspire to greatness, does one?" Tori cocked an eyebrow at Hashi. "Even a necromancer can—"

"Shut up, Tori. I'm not aspiring to anything. I'm just helping save my own home." She turned away from him to give me a hidden smile. "It's purely self-interest."

"Well, send word before you go, Lady Preel. I'll be aboard *Temoin*." Miko shot us a farewell salute and left us alone.

"So," I turned to the two council members, "What happened with the Council? They didn't seem very...cooperative."

"Oh, they argued like cats in a sack, but there's no alternative, is there?" Tori looked to Hashi, then to me again and shrugged. "The fulcrum has tipped. Events are moving with their own impetus. War is upon the Blood Sea."

"To be more specific and less *prophetic*," Hashi added, "we at least agreed to use all the resources of House Balshi, and much of what the rest of us could muster, to man every ship in the harbor and send messenger ships to Sariff and the islands. Timing is the issue. We won't know how many ships will be able to meet *Scourge*, even if we *can* win free. Patak promised at least eight to ten."

My nerves had tightened with their every word, and I felt ready to burst. Ten ragtag ships against a Toki armada? And that was *if* we could rescue Kevril, retake *Scourge*, and escape Hyko in one piece. I gritted my teeth and nodded. "*Well*, good enough, I suppose. Before Boxley arrives and gives us much needed details, I need to know what you think of our rudimentary plan." I turned for the sideboard. "Can I get anyone a drink? We have much thinking to do, and I find my mind always works better when I'm relaxed."

"Brandy if you have it." Hashi said. "And before we settle on a plan, we should all know our strengths and weaknesses."

"A good idea." I filled and handed Hashi a snifter and looked to Tori, who seemed suddenly very quiet. "A drink, Lord Blackbriar?"

"Nothing for me, thank you." His aplomb had diminished, as if he'd just realized what he'd volunteered for.

"Very well, let's all sit, at least." We did, though Busashi and Ghiti hovered over my shoulders protectively. I sipped spiced rum and cleared my throat. "As far as our capabilities go, I'll start. I can only answer a question that invokes my talent every three to four days, depending on the difficulty of the question. I imagine we'll be asking where they're keeping Kevril, but we should wait until the moment before we try to free him. I can't tell the future. Ambiguity in the questions usually yields ambiguous answers. We might have time for one more question before we ask Kevril's location, depending on how long it'll take us to sail to Hyko."

"And if there's trouble, can you fight?" Hashi asked.

"Yes, but not very well." I gestured to Ghiti. "My nokitu have been training me in unarmed martial arts."

"And we *all* know the legendary prowess of nokitu," Tori said with a lesser smile.

"And what, exactly, is *your* prowess, Lord Blackbriar?" Busashi asked.

Tori barked a laugh. "Well, aside from seducing beautiful women, I'm an accomplished swordsman, have a knack with people, and I'm *remarkably* good at disguises."

"*Oh?*" I couldn't imagine him looking like anything but a dandy.

"Tori, like you, is much more than he seems." Hashi fixed him with a pointed stare. "Show them."

Blackbriar sighed. "If you insist."

And suddenly, a woman in a low-cut dress sat where he'd been. I jumped in startlement, and Busashi and Ghiti both drew weapons.

"Please," the woman said with an utterly feminine flip of her hand. Even her voice was feminine, the dress, her hair, every detail. I even caught a whiff of perfume. "I'm no threat to your mistress." She gave me a sweet smile, then was Tori Blackbriar again in the blink of an eye. "So, I should be useful."

"I told you he had magical talent," Hashi sipped her brandy. "It's illusion, but a very good one. He's been fooling Nahli Twince for years."

"And you can look like *anyone*?" The possibilities scurried around my head like mice in a maze.

"Anyone I've seen close up, yes." He looked to Lady Severn. "Your turn."

"Okay." She swirled the liquor in the snifter. "I'm not invulnerable, as you may have guessed from the gash on my neck. Silver, gold, and magical weapons can injure me, as well as flint, obsidian, and stone. I have a number of spells, but they all require soul energy to cast, which I don't like to...harvest. Once we're in the city, I can create a force of shades and other undead to fight for us or create diversions. I can also scare the living daylights out of people." She took a far off look for a moment, then continued. "Unfortunately, my abilities are tied directly to this." She drew the obsidian dagger that I'd seen at the Folly from her sleeve, holding it by the pommel. "If I'm separated from it, I'm powerless."

I tried to digest all that while I sipped spiced rum. "Okay, so we'll get there aboard the *Gull*. It won't be comfortable, but it'll be fast and all but invisible. She's painted black, and we'll outfit her with black sails." I gestured to Busashi. "We'll dress everyone in black. Busashi suggested we strike in the dark."

Hashi lifted her snifter to me. "Preel, I've got more black clothes than all the nokitu in Toki. What can we expect when we arrive in

Hyko?"

"Warships in the harbor, and soldiers patrolling heavily in the city. Boxley should—"

As if conjured by my mention of her name, the door opened and Brindal ushered a robe-clad, freshly scrubbed, and pink-faced Boxley into the room. Tori stood.

"She insisted she was strong enough, mistress," Brindal said.

"I am." Boxley shuffled forward, clutching the robe. "Not quite myself, if you please, but good enough to discuss Hyko. Miko explained what you need."

"By all means join us, Midshipman." Tori stepped aside with a flourish toward his vacated seat. "Please. A gentleman never stands when a lady has no seat."

Boxley snorted a derisive laugh. "Thanks." She sat and fiddled with the robe. "So, what do you need to know before we set sail?"

"*We?*" I must admit my mouth fell open. "No, Boxley, you're staying here. You're far too weak to come with us."

"With all due respect, Lady Preel, I'm going." Her jaw clenched, and she shifted in the seat. "I'm weak because I haven't *eaten* in days. I'll be fine by the time we get there. It's a four-day sail anyways, and you gotta have someone along who can navigate."

"Morelie and Sauncey can find Hyko well enough. You're *staying*," I insisted.

"No, I'm coming along." Boxley set her jaw and glared at me. "No offense, Lady Preel, but you're not my captain. Your husband saved my life. I'll see him free or die trying."

"That's *exactly* what I'm worried about!" I snapped.

"*You're* going, and you can't fight for sour seagull shit!" she snapped back.

"I'm necessary for the success of this mission! And Kevril's my husband!"

"And *I'm* necessary for your *survival*." She retorted. "None of you knows the least bit about sailing or handling a ship. I do. And your *husband* is my *captain*! I pledged my life to him before he even *met* you!"

We glared at each other for a full minute.

"Do you realize," Tori said in a note of amusement, "That you both have exactly the same haircut?"

"Long story," we both said in exactly the same tone.

I glared at Boxley with all the venom I could muster, but I could think of no argument to make her stay behind.

"So," Boxley said, fiddling with her robe again, "when are we leaving?"

Chapter Twenty Nine
Sea Change

From the journal of Hashi Severn —

All these years, and I've never voyaged by sea. If I ever do again, it'll be in a bigger boat.

I arrived at the quay in the pre-dawn hours by coach. My baggage consisted of one waxed canvas duffel. I knew how to pack for the wilderness, but not a voyage at sea. A spare pair of boots, clothes, tooth brush, and, because I didn't have to lug it on my back for a hundred miles, several books. I stepped out of my carriage and shouldered my bag.

"Farewell, mistress," Bromish called down. "Do be careful, please."

Careful? I almost laughed at the notion; four days sailing on the open sea in a fishing smack, then facing down the Toki army and navy. "I'll be fine, Bromish. Joss is in charge until I return. I've left him instructions if I don't."

If you don't, you'll have more to worry about than what happens to your retainers, Hashi.

Hush, old man. Saraknyal had barely let up long enough to let me sleep. He'd accused me of being insane, suicidal, stupid, and, in his opinion the worst of all, an altruist. I had only one argument against him. *There's no alternative, and no better time to fight.*

To that, he had no rebuttal. If Toki got a foothold in the islands, it would be all over but the crying. I'd read enough military history to know the endgame; Haven would be blockaded by a fleet of warships, and everyone would starve to death or surrender. If I surrendered, I'd be burned at the stake, and Soul Drinker would be taken to the god-emperor. So would the Death Stone.

285

"Take care, milady." Bromish tipped his hat to me and wiped his nose on his sleeve.

I turned to where *Gull* lay snugged against the quay wall, her deck well below street level. Perhaps thirty feet from stem to stern, if one didn't include the long bowsprit, she looked like a tidy little ship, though what I knew of ships would barely cover a sheet of paper. I squinted down at the deck. Preel sat on a bench seat in the large cockpit while her nokitu and the two pirate crewmembers stowed gear in the hold amidships. Boxley sat in the stern, looking slightly less drawn. She'd won the argument to come along by means of sheer stubbornness and logic. She was, after all, a naval officer, if only a fourteen-year-old one.

I thought it would be bigger, Saraknyal groused.

Truth be told, so had I, but I wasn't going to give him the satisfaction of admitting it.

Tori sat cross legged on the top of the cuddy cabin forward, watching the entire operation with an air of amusement.

"Ahoy, *Gull!*" I called down.

"Hashi!" Tori lurched to his feet and held out his arms. "Jump, fair maid! I'll catch you!"

That earned him laughs from the pirates, but only scowls from the nokitu. I snorted a laugh and threw my bag at him, which he did actually catch.

"Welcome aboard, Lady Severn," Boxley tipped her hat to me, but didn't rise from her seat.

Preel wore a veil, and, I assumed, the silken gag beneath, but raised a hand in greeting.

I descended the ladder and stepped aboard carefully. The vessel tipped with my weight.

"Oh, she's a tall one, ain't she! Dunno where yer gonna sleep, yer ladyship." The thin young man, Sauncey, touched his brow with one knuckle.

I opened my mouth to tell him I'd manage, but the other pirate, Morelie, chimed in, "Not with you, so don't get your hopes up!"

Sauncey blushed furiously, and I thanked my dark complexion. "I'll manage, and call me Hashi." I accepted my bag from Tori and handed it to the pirate to pack away. "Where will I be out of the way?"

"Join Tori on the coach roof, if you please, Hashi." Boxley remained seated, one hand resting on a tiller rigged with ropes and pulleys.

As I complied, folding my legs to sit tailor fashion, I took in the layout of the little ship. Boxley sat on a step that led to a low hatch behind her, another small cabin, or compartment. The ropes from her tiller led to a longer one in the very stern atop the deck. The forward hatch slid into the coach roof, and I glimpsed a tiny wood stove and four bunks built into the hull sides. None of them looked long enough for me, or Tori for that matter.

"Sauncey wasn't lying about nowhere to sleep, was he?" I said to Tori.

"It's been a while since I've voyaged on such a...nimble craft, but if you bend your knees and press them against the leeboard, you'll not only fit, but it'll keep you from tumbling out."

I leaned to look inside. *Do you know what a leeboard is?* I asked Saraknyal.

Not a clue, he replied.

I leaned closer to Tori. "What's a leeboard?"

"Oh, sorry. The board along the edge of the bunk." He gave me a curious look. "You've never sailed before?"

"Across Mati harbor once when I was a girl. A boat about this size, actually." I remembered thinking it a grand adventure, though I was only aboard for few hours.

"Well, sailing the open sea, I'm afraid, is an entirely different kettle of fish, so to say." He gave me a shallow smile. "You may regret volunteering for this in a few hours."

I told you, Saraknyal grumbled.

Is that you agreeing with Tori Blackbriar, old man?

Yes, as a matter of fact. I never said he was a fool, just dangerous.

We lapsed into silence as the crew finished stowing.

"All right, then, passengers into the cockpit if you please," Boxley ordered. "Three of you in the cuddy to make room until we get settled. We'll have to learn to accommodate each other, so get used to it. Sauncey, cast off the bow and hoist the jib. Morelie, ready astern."

I forced myself not to smile at the command in the young woman's tone as everyone complied. Sitting beside Preel, I watched the sailors work, nimble as cats, arms corded with lean muscle. Sauncey flipped a rope off one of the big iron bollards, coiled it neatly, and then untied something from a bundle of canvas, clipped on another rope, and stepped back to the mast.

"Ready on the halyard," the pirate announced.

"Haul away smartly!" Boxley reached for another rope I hadn't noticed that led from the cockpit along the deck forward. She flipped two loops over a bronze drum set into the deck.

Sauncey pulled on a rope that led up the mast, and a black triangular sail emerged from the canvas bag on the bow to soar aloft on the forestay. As the sail's front edge came taut, he heaved on the line hard and tied it off on a cleat. Boxley hauled on her rope, which led to the corner of the sail, and it came taut, flattening the sail and catching the wind. *Gull*'s bow drew away from the quay.

"Cast off astern," Boxley ordered, and Morelie complied.

We drew away, nosing out into the bay.

Preel touched my arm. She'd lowered her veil and tapped the silk band on her mouth. I reached back and untied the knot.

"Thank you." She slipped the cloth into a pocket. "Your first time to sea?"

"Yes." I realized my stomach felt as if I'd swallowed a swarm of butterflies. "A little nervous, I guess."

"She's a sound ship, milady," Boxley said. "You needn't worry."

"I'm more worried for the *passengers* than the ship," I replied.

Tori coughed a laugh, but Preel patted my arm. "I'm sure you'll be fine. Sea travel takes some getting used to."

"Aye, and if you don't get used to it, yer in for the four most miserable days of yer life!" Morelie and Sauncey laughed.

"Enough!" Boxley barked. "Ready the main. We'll hoist in the anchorage. One reef."

"Aye, sir!" They hopped to, stepping amongst us nimbly as they untied short lines that bound the black mainsail to the boom.

"If you don't mind my asking," Preel began, "how did you arrive in Haven if you've never been to sea?"

"Over the mountains." I made sure to say it loud enough for everyone to hear. "Six days from northern Sariff. If this voyage is worse than *that*, I'll eat my boots."

Even Boxley barked a laugh at that.

Don't tempt fate, my dear, Saraknyal warned.

They hoisted the huge mainsail, and *Gull* tipped dramatically as the canvas caught the wind. Boxley hauled on another line that ran through a network of pullies to haul the sail in. We picked up speed and tipped even more.

Is it supposed to tilt like this? Saraknyal sounded worried.

My knuckles cracked with my grip on the seat. *Nobody else seems concerned.*

"Shift to the windward side," Boxley pointed to the uphill side of the ship.

We all shifted, and the deck leveled somewhat.

"Fly the outer jib!" Boxley barked. "Smartly now! We're passing for review!"

"Review?" I asked.

"Sailing past the other ships in the fleet," Preel explained, pointing to the anchored ships. "That's *Temoin* with Miko in command."

I looked to the lofty galleon, a beamy ship, but well kept. To my surprise, a number of people stood at her rail despite the early hour, and some high in the rigging. I recognized Miko as she took off her hat and waved to us.

Boxley raised a hand.

As the larger forward sail soared aloft and cracked full, we picked up even more speed and raced past the ship's towering stern.

Miko cupped her hands and bellowed. "Good hunting, Captain Boxley!"

Boxley flushed pink and yelled back. "And to you, Captain!" She snapped a salute, and Miko returned it.

"Sailors are such a curious breed," Tori commented. "Rowdy and rough, but steeped in tradition and protocol."

"Protocol?" I asked.

"He means the chain of command," Preel explained, nodding to Boxley. "She might only be fourteen years old, but Boxley's our lord and master for the next four days. We live or die by her command."

We're in the hands of children, Saraknyal grumbled.

That child killed Jhavika Keshmir, I reminded him.

All right, she's admittedly a determined and capable young woman, but...

But what?

She's just so very young, I guess.

Well, as Preel said, pirates grow up fast.

I just hope she knows where we're going, he replied as we cleared the anchorage and tacked south for the harbor entrance.

Boxley snapped more orders, and we shifted to the new windward side. The crew hauled on ropes, the nokitu lending a hand here and there. The horizon opened up beyond the bluff, and we began riding over the rolling swells. I squinted into the crimson glow of the sunrise and spotted whitecaps farther out to sea.

"Red in the morning, sailors take warning," Tori said.

"Aye, we're in for a trouncy ride," Boxley agreed. "Weather cloaks on deck. We'll be taking quite a lot of spray. Sauncey, a pot of blackbrew and a biscuit, if you please."

Busashi handed out weather cloaks and I struggled into one, my stomach feeling uneasy, either nerves or the building swells. We tipped sharply at the mouth of the harbor, wind howling around the eastern bluff, and I grasped the railing desperately.

"Just the cape effect, Lady Hashi," Boxley assured me. "Nothing to worry about."

"Not worried." I braced my feet against the opposite seat and leaned back. "Just a little uneasy." My mouth watered and I swallowed forcefully.

"Well, if you're gonna puke, do it downwind!" Boxley grinned as we mounted a white-capped swell and pounded through. Spray lashed us, and Preel and the others ducked away. I was too slow, and saltwater drenched the back of my neck. Our captain grinned and crowed, "We're in it now!"

"After four days of this, we won't be in any condition to fight!" I said.

"Oh, we're beating close hauled right now," Boxley explained. "As soon as we clear Snomish Bay, we'll tack to the north and level out some. The trades have clocked a bit south of east, which will help, but we'll be beating the whole way, and taking spray. Just a little trouncing. Nothing dangerous."

I nodded and swallowed again, determined not to be sick.

Game of chess to pass the time? Saraknyal quipped.

Oh, shut the hell up. I swallowed hard as another breaking swell slapped the boat, drenching us with spray.

Well, at least I don't rust.

We sailed on, seemingly straight into the wind, until the cliffs of the headland receded behind us. Sauncey came up with blackbrew served in tin cups. I shook my head. My stomach roiled, but I hadn't yet succumbed. Finally, Boxley adjusted the tiller, and we turned through the wind to the north. She gave some nautical orders, but I wasn't in the mood to pay attention, though I managed to shift my seat.

After some adjustments, we seemed to be riding more smoothly, more of a roll and less of a pitching, pounding, torture session.

"That's our heading!" Boxley tied off the tiller and flexed her hands. "Off watch, in your bunks. I'll take the morning watch, Sauncey the forenoon, Morelie the afternoon, and we'll have a hot meal for the dogs watch. Two of your people on each watch, Busashi. Lady Preel, it's time."

She nodded and slipped below, sure footed on the unstable deck.

"Time?" I asked as Preel descended into the tiny cabin and shrugged out of her weather cloak.

"For a question."

"Oh, right." With my concentration focused on not vomiting, I'd forgotten our plan to employ Preel's gift to answer a question. We'd discussed it for some time the previous evening, and Saraknyal had been fascinated. "Would you mind if I observed?"

She shrugged. "Not at all, though there's not much to watch." She seemed a bit surly, or perhaps worried.

Thank you, Hashi. This is a unique experience for me, you know.

Me too. Of course, Saraknyal was centuries older than me.

As Preel climbed into one of the lower bunks, and Busashi

secured her in place with a canvas covering that clipped to eyes in the hull and leeboard, I eased down the companionway into the tiny space. I had to stoop, for the overhead caught me square at nose-height. I found the confines a little stifling, but braced myself out of the way and watched. Tori leaned through the companionway over my shoulder, equally intrigued.

Preel settled herself and finally nodded to Busashi. "Ready."

"Yes, mistress." He cleared his throat. "Do the Toki authorities in or around Hyko currently have plans to send Admiral Kevril Longbright away in less than five days from today?"

Preel surged up against the restraining canvas, her back arched, her eyes rolled back. A voice so unlike her own as to be startling rasped, "No!" She then went utterly limp, breathing hard.

Busashi quickly affixed the silken gag back over her mouth and checked her breathing.

"Is she all right?" I asked.

"Yes. She'll sleep until evening." Busashi ordered two of his people to bunk down, and Morelie did also, each securing themselves into their bunks.

I clambered out of the close confines of the cabin and gulped fresh air, wedging myself into my seat with feet braced.

Are you feeling all right? Saraknyal asked.

No, I'm feeling ill. I swallowed hard.

"Hashi, are you well?" Tori asked. "You look—"

"I'm trying not to throw up at the moment, thank you."

"Cup of tea and a biscuit will settle your stomach," Sauncey suggested, seated with his back against the hull beside the stove, a cup in his hands.

I nodded. "I'll try anything."

"Look at the horizon, lady," Boxley said, pointing downwind. "It helps."

I tried, but the swells were large enough to block my view half of the time, and spray lashed us regularly, preventing me from standing.

It could be worse, you know.

Shut up. I accepted a tin cup of tepid tea and a rock-hard ship's biscuit from Sauncey. The former soothed my stomach a bit, but the biscuit was so hard I nearly broke a tooth. I worried off a corner and chewed the bitter and slightly salty biscuit, chasing it with a swallow of tea. I started to take another bite, but Saraknyal interrupted me.

You should throw that away, Hashi.

What? Why? I looked down at the biscuit in my hand.

Don't!

Saraknyal's warning came too late to prevent me from spying the wriggling weevil squirming free from the biscuit I'd been eating. My stomach rebelled, my mouth flooding with saliva in imminent warning.

I dropped the biscuit and my cup and lurched across the cockpit. The coaming struck me in the chest, and I retched into the scuppers. A hand gripped my belt from behind, a safety measure, I supposed, but I was too busy puking to see who it was. After my stomach was empty, I retched again for good measure, spitting up bile, my throat on fire. Finally, my stomach settled slightly.

A hand clapped my back. "Better?" It was Tori.

I nodded, hawked and spat, trying to clear the vile taste of vomit. "Shouldn't have eaten breakfast, I guess." I allowed him to help me back in my seat, expecting a saucy quip. Instead he offered me a handkerchief. "Thanks." I wiped my mouth.

"Best keep something in your stomach." Sauncey offered my cup back to me, this time filled with water. "Sip this. It'll help."

It did, and though my stomach still complained, it settled.

"The closer we get to the islands, the calmer the seas," Boxley informed me. "Most get their sea legs in three days or so. Just try to keep water down."

Three days... I sipped and tried to watch the horizon. *You're allowed to tell me this was a bad idea again, Saraknyal.*

Well, I never said it was a bad idea, I just said it was dangerous. Ridiculously dangerous, and probably insane, but not a bad idea.

I chuckled and shook my head.

"What's funny?" Tori asked.

"Nothing. I just thought it would be ironic if I died of seasickness before I got a chance to be killed by a komei. It seems so..."

"Undignified?" He smiled and laughed. "Few die from ship's sickness, Hashi. Here." He fished a small vial from a pocket.

"Ginger. It'll settle your stomach."

"I can put that in a cup of tea for you, lady," Sauncey offered.

I wondered why everyone was being so solicitous. Maybe they just didn't want me to throw up on them. "Thank you."

I accepted a cup of tea and inhaled the strong ginger aroma. Sipping experimentally, my stomach decided to accept it. I stared at the horizon, reverting to the old mental exercises I used to do to keep my mind occupied. In time, the cup ran empty, and I felt slightly better.

Are you going to live? Saraknyal asked.

What am I, a fortune teller? I considered, then thought, *Unless I'm killed by a komei, I suppose I will.*

For three days I survived on ginger tea, salty jerky, and bland porridge. We endured one squall that I was sure would swamp us, amazed how calm the sailors remained. Boxley ate like a ravenous beast, almost to the point where it made me ill to watch her. I took little sleep, for the close confines of the cabin made me nauseous. Saraknyal read to me, and Tori told me tales of history. Preel seemed grimmer by the day, as if the closer we got to our goal, the less emotion she allowed herself to feel.

The seas calmed, as promised, and I ate a decent meal which stayed down. As the sun neared the distant mountains on the fourth day, Boxley pointed to a smudge to the northeast and proclaimed our destination in sight.

"That's Hyko. Five hours. Maybe four if we shake the reef in the main and don't run into a warship."

Tori stood, bracing one hand on the boom, shading his eyes. "Not much smoke for such a large city."

"You got sharp eyes," Sauncey said.

"Sharper than yours, for certain," he said without a hint of bravado.

"Spyglass," Boxley ordered, and Sauncey handed up a small telescope to Tori. "You can be our lookout. Step up and brace your back to the mast. Warships usually run with lamps lit at night."

"Aye, aye, Captain." Tori grinned and scrambled up on deck with a grace even the sailors hadn't exhibited.

"We should eat a good meal and keep a dark ship," Boxley said, then looked aloft. "And shake the reef."

"Maybe we should have asked the armada's deployment," Preel said.

I shook my head. "We wouldn't know if they'd kept it the same. Can we—"

"No questions!" Preel barked.

"Sorry. We use patrol ships in Haven." I looked to Boxley with a raised eyebrow.

She nodded. "They'll have at least two, I'd wager. That's what Sariff always did. I'd guess smaller ships. They shouldn't spot us in the dark."

We hope, Saraknyal grumbled.

"If we're spotted, we pose as fishermen." I patted Soul Drinker at my belt. "Get me aboard, and I'll take care of it."

"Unless they have komei aboard," Preel said.

"I can handle a few, but that *would* complicate things."

"If we have to deal with a warship in the dark, we'll go aboard with you," Busashi insisted.

I nodded to him. "Just don't get between me and any Toki soldiers."

With little else to do for the last three days, we'd discussed our strategy for retaking *Scourge*. We'd settled on a simple plan of stealth, surprise, and lethality. Any Toki soldiers or sailors not killed would be brought to me to be made into shades. Boxley doubted there would be any komei aboard the captured corsair, but there was that possibility. Of course, if *Scourge* wasn't there, we'd have to make other plans.

We ate—I'd had two meals of salt pork stew, and was already tired of it—watched the sun set, and the growing glow of Hyko.

"Ship," Tori said conversationally from his perch, pointing east. "Some miles away. I can't tell what direction they're sailing."

"Sauncey, have a look," Boxley ordered.

"Aye, sir." He lurched up and took Tori's position and the spyglass. After a time, he reported, "Hull down, easterly course. If she maintains that heading, she'll pass our stern by some bit."

I stood and scanned the horizon, but saw nothing. *Can you see it, Saraknyal?*

Just a distant light. I've no idea how he determined its heading.

Best not ask any questions. I glanced at Preel. The muscles of her jaw clenched and relaxed rhythmically.

"Keep an eye on them," Boxley instructed. "Tell me if they change course."

"Aye, sir!" Nobody smiled at Boxley's orders any longer.

We sailed along in silence, and Morelie handed up tea and blackbrew. I inhaled the aroma of ginger and sipped.

An hour passed before Sauncey announced, "Coming hull up," and pointed.

I stood again and saw lights, one higher, and more lower that dipped below the swells occasionally.

A small ship, Saraknyal said, and I told Boxley.

"A picket, just like we thought." She grinned. "We're well past them."

"Shadows in the dark, invisible and anonymous," Tori intoned.

I sat back down. "We'll have to sail past them aboard *Scourge.*"

Preel nodded. "If we win free of the harbor, yes." She sounded worried, and I realized why; she'd be unconscious during our escape.

"No worries," Boxley proclaimed. "The admiral's a fox. Unless the whole fleet cuts us off, we'll slip through."

I wish I shared her confidence.

"We'll be short-handed if it comes to a fight," Preel said.

"After Hyko, I'll have some allies for us, I'm sure."

They all looked at me with wide eyes, realizing what I meant and clearly uncomfortable with the thought of recruiting undead.

"It's why I came along," I said. "Don't get squeamish now."

"And all along I thought you came along to regale us with song and story," Tori quipped with a smile.

Oh, yes, tales of bravery and regurgitation, Saraknyal added.

I couldn't help but laugh, and repeated the quip. It drew smiles and low laughter, breaking the tension.

"She's worn," Sauncey announced, and I wondered what he meant. He pointed to the lit warship well astern. "She's close hauled now."

Worn? Saraknyal muttered.

No idea. "Tell me what *worn* means."

"When a ship turns around with the wind astern, it's called 'wearing ship.' We're in the clear now." Boxley pointed forward. The glow of Hyko had resolved into distinct lights. "Two hours. We're right on time; moon won't be up till morning watch. Now all we have to do is find *Scourge*."

"How many—"

"No questions!" Preel snapped with a scowl.

"Sorry." I bit my tongue. That was twice I'd nearly ruined everything.

"I'd better wear this." She withdrew the silk band from a pocket and handed it to Busashi. "It's too dangerous."

"Yes, mistress." He tied the band and then raised his own face covering. He handed out snug hoods and face coverings to the rest of us. "It would be best if we ready ourselves. Darken your faces and keep silent."

"How many ships?" I waved away the garments. My dark skin made them redundant. The others applied black grease paint around their eyes.

"A lot." Sauncey replied. "Maybe a dozen."

"They must have pulled in their armada. They may be preparing to take them south." Boxley unlashed the tiller and took it in her hand. "Sharp eye for *Scourge*."

We sailed on, tension rising among us. The seas calmed even further as we proceeded behind the headland, and the wind eased.

"Furl the outer jib and reef the main," Boxley finally ordered. "We'll go in slow."

"I'll watch while they work," Tori offered, accepting the spyglass from Sauncey again.

They worked quickly and quietly without any calls. When they were done, everyone but Tori took seats either below or in the cockpit. I craned my neck to peer over the deck, the harbor opening up before us. The confusion of lamps, both on the water and ashore, baffled me. How anyone could pick out one ship among those anchored against the backdrop of the city, I had no idea.

"There!" Tori hissed, raising a black clad arm to point. "Near shore. East of the river mouth."

"Sharp eyes indeed," Sauncey muttered.

"That's good and bad." Boxley altered course by Tori's direction. "Easier to get everyone aboard, and harder to get out of the harbor."

"With luck, their attention will be on the city when we're through." I put a hand on Soul Drinker. *You ready for this, old man?*

Just don't fall in the sea wearing that heavy coat. You'll sink like a stone.

Good advice. I fingered my chainmail enhanced coat and reconsidered wearing it aboard *Scourge*. I turned to Busashi. "What do you think the chances are of a komei being aboard *Scourge*?"

"Low. Most will either be stationed near the general's quarters, or aboard the greater warships."

"Okay, good." I doffed my heavy coat, folded it and handed it below.

"Wardrobe adjustment at this hour?" Tori asked.

"It's mail-lined. Weighs a ton. If I'm not facing komei I don't need it. It's not worth the risk if I end up in the sea." The dark water still made me nervous, and the little sleep I'd gotten aboard *Gull* had been plagued by nightmares of drowning.

"Ah, good thinking." He redirected his attention back toward our quarry, and I picked out the lower profile of *Scourge* against the lights of the city.

"Everyone ready!" Boxley hissed. "We furl the main and ghost in astern. Busashi, you're up first with your people to take the deck. Hashi and Tori, through the stern gallery windows and forward below into the hold. We'll follow with Preel and secure the sterncastle."

Everyone agreed and I settled a hand on Soul Drinker. *Time to be bad, old man.*

Music to my ears, my dear.

I smiled without showing my teeth. *If you had ears...*

Oh, shut up!

Chapter Thirty
Home Again

From the journal of Preel Longbright —

Seeing *Scourge* again smote my heart in a way I wasn't prepared for. So much joy, so much pain, so much love and hate. This ship was where I fell in love for the first time. This ship will always be my true home.

I had to hand it to Boxley; she handled *Gull* like a musician playing a favored instrument. We ghosted along like a shadow in the night. The lanterns on *Scourge's* deck seemed to stab out at us, but they found nothing to touch. Black sails, black hull, distant black cliffs far behind us, black-clad assassins drifting closer, death and worse nearing undetected.

I glanced at Hashi Severn and shivered. She seemed suddenly so dreadful after three days being so fragile with ship's sickness. I found myself glad that I wouldn't witness her in action, see the harvesting of human souls. Such evil from a woman I'd grown to like and respect, a woman to whom I owed my freedom and my life... I wondered if that made me evil.

Focus, Preel! I forced myself to take deep steady breaths as we drifted closer...closer... I could see figures on deck, strolling slowly, soldiers or sailors on watch. Their gazes passed over us without seeing. We were invisible.

"Now!" Boxley hissed in a bare whisper, and Sauncey and Morelie lowered the jib slowly, furling it with barely a sound more than the scrape of the bronze clips along the forestay.

We drifted with only the momentum of the ship toward *Scourge* swinging slowly on her anchor. Another whisper from Boxley, and the nokitu moved into position, two forward, two amidships, and two aft, their slipper-clad feet clutching the cockpit coaming with perfect balance.

We closed... Twenty feet...fifteen...ten...

Three nokitu leapt into the night, flying like shadow-harbingers of doom in the darkness. *Gull* rocked with their leaps. They scrabbled up the ship's quarter galleries and transom like black spiders trailing ebony webs. Without a sound, not a whisper of hands or feet on wood, they flowed over the taffrail like shadows, securing their thin silk ropes. The other three nokitu tied off to *Gull*'s cleats, fended off to keep us from thumping into the ship, then ascended, vanishing over the rail.

"Hashi, Tori!" Boxley hissed, and the two taller figures rose.

Tori reached up to grasp the frame of the stern gallery windows, and pulled himself up with astounding strength and agility. The windows were open for ventilation, and he slipped through. The length of his sheathed sword clacked against the window frame in passing, eliciting a startled gasp from within. Hashi grasped the frame and levered herself up with less grace, scrabbling through the opening. I saw the interior of the cabin in my mind. She would find herself crawling across the navigation table.

A clatter, and we all cringed, but heard no outcry.

"Sauncey, Morelie, up!" Boxley stood and slipped a blackened boarding axe through her belt as the pirates clambered up and through the windows with only a few more clatters. *Gull* now drifted astern of *Scourge*, current and wind holding her off.

I stood and accepted Boxley's help in climbing to the wobbling deck. A soft glow of a lamp suddenly lit the glass above me. A figure emerged, black clad.

"Clear!" Sauncey hissed, reaching down a hand.

"Up you go, lady." Boxley grasped me at the waist and lifted as I leapt to take the proffered hand.

Sauncey hauled me up and through the window. I clambered over the table and landed on the floor without too much noise. At a glance, so many memories returned, the bed, quarter galleries, Kevril's locker... I stood for a moment, stunned.

Focus, Preel! I moved to the starboard side, opposite Morelie, who had drawn her cutlass and faced the door to the passage forward.

The door was closed, and Tori and Hashi weren't in the cabin. There was blood on the bed, and a spatter on the deck toward the door, but no body.

Boxley joined us with a clatter as her boarding axe cracked against the window frame, and glanced around. "Where?"

"They went forward, sir." Sauncey drew his cutlass.

"Right." Boxley drew her boarding axe and a dirk. "We secure the sterncastle. Quiet as we—"

"Captain, I thought I heard—" The cabin door opened to reveal a Toki naval officer in a kimono. His eyes swept the cabin and widened, his hand snatching at the wakizashi at his waist and his mouth opening to cry out.

I don't know if he deemed the three armed pirates a greater threat than me, or if he didn't even see me standing to the side, clad from head to toe in black, unarmed. Regardless, his attention focused upon the others, and countless hours of training kicked in before I could even think.

As his sword cleared its sheath, I lunged into low roll, *monkey in grass*, and lashed out with both feet at his ankles, *scythe cuts wheat*. A startled yelp escaped his throat as he fell. He hit the deck hard, cracking his head against the wood. Before I could even stand, Morelie thrust her cutlass through his neck. It was over in less than two seconds.

"Forward!" Boxley hissed, and the two pirates leapt over the convulsing body. "Lady Preel, are you all right?"

I nodded and motioned her forward, my nerves singing like harp strings.

"That was...*something*." She stooped to snatch up the officer's weapon in lieu of her dirk, and stepped over the corpse I'd helped to make. "Never knew you could do that!"

I tried not to look at the man's staring eyes as I followed, unable, of course, to answer. The others cleared cabin after cabin, finding only two more officers, both bewildered enough to be taken easily. Passing the galley, I noted more bloodstains, but no body.

The door to the deck opened, filled by a figure in black. "The deck is ours," Busashi whispered.

"Sterncastle's clear," Boxley replied, pointing to the

companionway down to the lower decks. "Hashi and Tori went below."

He nodded. "Hold here. We'll take the foc's'le and meet the others below."

As he hurried off across the mid deck, I spotted several fallen sailors. I thought for a moment they were *Scourge*'s crew lying dead, but they weren't. Boxley must have caught me staring, and put a hand on my arm.

"It's war, Preel. They started it. We're just fighting back." She let go and nodded aft. "We'll hold here. Check on *Gull* for me, please."

I knew she was just getting me out of the way, but I nodded and turned back to the great cabin, glancing around the familiar yet subtly changed environment. Most of Kevril's personal effects were gone; a few books, some art, and a sword over the stern gallery windows that he'd told me he'd received at the age of eight from his first captain remained. I checked on our little boat, so seemingly insignificant now, and felt a pang. *Gull* had served us well, Boxley's first command. She bobbed there, abandoned.

I snatched up the bloody blankets from the bed and draped them over the officer's corpse. It blocked the door, so I left it open. Looking into Kevril's locker, I saw that his store of liquor had been much diminished, though a few bottles remained. I would have loved a tot, but couldn't with my mouth bound. A captain's jacket hung in the locker with a kimono and several other outfits in the Toki style. A katana hung from a peg by a shark-skin strap. I didn't touch it, but turned to inspect the rest. The chart locker hadn't been looted, but my own locker stood completely empty, nothing left of my six months of bliss but shadows and blood.

"Preel?"

I whirled to find Hashi Severn standing in the passage. She held Soul Drinker in her hand, white mist trailing from the obsidian blade. Her clothes were slashed, but she seemed unhurt. Her face looked set in stone.

"You're unhurt? Boxley said you..." She gestured to the covered corpse at her feet.

I nodded to her.

"Good! *Scourge* is ours, and we're ready to go ashore. They're putting the launches in the water now." At her gesture, the corpse under the blanket sat up, then stood, the blanket falling away to reveal the man's very dead face, the gaping wound in his throat that had killed him. "Go forward," she said, and the undead thing shambled past her.

I stared at it, my mind stumbling. I'd known she was a necromancer. I'd even seen her undead minions. I'd just never seen a dead man stand up and walk away.

"Sorry. I know it's horrible." She shrugged and sheathed the dagger. "Please, come with me. We need to ask your question. There's no time to lose."

Kevril... I nodded and followed.

Upon the middeck we found everyone assembled. Everyone included all six nokitu, Boxley and her two pirates, Tori Blackbriar, and the entire thirty-soul skeleton crew who had been stationed aboard *Scourge*. Of course, the latter were dead...undead. Some were the dark-skinned, red-eyed shades like I'd seen at Ash Keep. The rest were simply animate corpses. My skin crawled.

"We're leaving ten shades aboard to guard the ship," Hashi explained. "They won't bother you. They'll only attack Toki soldiers trying to come aboard."

I nodded and waved to the rest.

"We're taking them with us. They'll serve as a diversion while we find and release Admiral Longbright."

"But first we need to know where he is," Tori turned away from the walking corpse he'd been inspecting and suddenly changed into a perfect likeness of a Toki captain, complete with naval officer's uniform and sword. He snapped a precise bow to me. "I'll also act as a distraction."

I swallowed my astonishment, nodded, approached Busashi, and tapped my gag.

"At once, mistress." For the first time since I'd known him, he smiled to me. "We're honored that you trust us to see to your husband's release. Rest assured, you'll awaken in his company." He untied my gag and bowed.

I glanced to Boxley, and she waved Sauncey and Morelie forward. They'd take me to the cabin once the question was answered. I cleared my throat. "I want to thank you all for this. I can't in a million years repay you."

"Oh, I'm sure we can arrange *something*!" Tori, incongruously now a Toki captain, wagged an eyebrow.

"Shut up, Tori." Hashi snapped.

I smiled to them both, so different, yet my champions. "I know you're both doing this for Haven, as much as me, but...thank you, just the same."

"We must move, mistress," Busashi insisted. "Lady Hashi, please see to the...loading of the launches."

"Of course." She turned away and the dead began shuffling forward.

I turned to Busashi. "Ask."

He glanced to Sauncey and Merilee, who stood ready, and asked, "Where precisely is Admiral Kevril Longbright being held prisoner by the Toki forces occupying Hyko?"

My back went rigid, the world went black, and the answer tore from my throat. "In the dungeon of Governor Rokiri's palace, three floors below ground, in the cell at the end of the eastern block." I felt myself falling, strong arms enfolding me, then oblivion.

Chapter Thirty One
Night of Screams

From the journal of Hashi Severn —

I don't know how I feel about unleashing Saraknyal like this. Part of me thinks I'm damning myself to hell, while the other thinks I'm coming to the rescue of an honorable man and foiling a tyrannical act of war. Maybe I'm splitting hairs. I hope the gods don't judge my actions too harshly.

Zombies, it seems, can't row worth a damn. The required coordination is beyond them. That left eight of us, four per launch. So we rowed, with one zombie to keep the rudder of each launch straight.

"Manual labor," Tori grunted beside me. "My ego is taking a beating tonight."

"Shh!" Busashi hissed.

I glared at Tori, but he didn't look like himself, so I couldn't tell if my ire scored. I wasn't in the mood for his quips. Not after slaughtering ten sleeping men and turning ten more into shades. Taking *Scourge* had gone off more easily than any of us could have hoped, owing mainly to the skeleton crew. I'd felt worst about the cook, but he'd come awake with a cleaver in his hand, and swung at me. One thrust, and Saraknyal had done the rest.

I'm not so sure about this plan of yours, Hashi, he complained, not for the first time. *Steer left a bit.*

I relayed his guidance in a whisper. Seated backward, we couldn't see our destination, the river mouth. *Suggest something different, then.*

I did. Several times.

We're not slaughtering the entire populace of Hyko.

How about just the occupying army. Send them marching back to the god-emperor's palace as a warning.*

I told you, we don't know how many komei are stationed here. If it's hundreds, we can't take them all on.

True, but I can't imagine there are more than a score, maybe, fifty.

Your imagination has never impressed me, I snapped. *We're sticking to the plan. Now a little guidance, please!*

More left, and there's no reason to get snippy.

Snippy? We're sneaking into a city occupied by who knows how many Toki soldiers! I'm allowed a little snippy!

We rowed on in blissful silence until the stone bastions of the river mouth passed us on both sides, then Saraknyal warned us.

Guards on the east shore walking patrol.

"Guards," I hissed, then. "Zombies, lay flat."

They did, forcing two of us to steer. I took our tiller, and Tori stood and turned to hail the patrolling guards.

"You there! Lend a hand!"

"Who's there?" one of the guards called out, motioning for the others to come.

"Captain Toshiri. My crew's come down with some sudden illness. Bad food, I think." I had to admit, Tori put on a good performance.

I spotted six soldiers, but at low tide I couldn't see farther than the edge of the quay. The stone bastion stood ten feet over our heads. I kept my face down, trying to avoid scrutiny. I didn't look Tokiri, but in the faint light, I might go unnoticed. Busashi and the other nokitu had removed their hoods, and would pass for sailors dressed in black. Or we hoped they would. Between Tori and twenty zombies playing dead, rather than undead, we should at least get close enough.

"We don't want your sickness in the city! I'll send word to the general. He'll send a physician."

Or maybe not.

"It's not contagious, you idiot! It's food poisoning! Two-year-old salt pork gone bad." Tori waved us forward and we sculled closer to the ladder out of the main current of the river. "Now you'll help me with these sailors, or I'll report you to the general myself!"

The guards exchanged glances, then the one who'd spoken cursed and stepped up to the edge of the bastion. Tori threw a line from the bow, and I managed to toss a stern line without looking too much like a lubber. The other launch tied up on our other side.

"Hashi, climb up and help take these poor sailors ashore."

Ready, old man? I thought as I grasped a slimy rung and started to climb.

Of course, I'm ready. Just wipe your hands before you touch me.

Right. I feigned a slip at the top rung—not difficult with half an inch of algae on the ladder—and said, "Damn slimy... Give me a hand up, mate." The nearest soldier held out a hand. "Thanks." I took it and gripped hard, clambering up onto the quay wall.

The man gaped up at me, head and shoulders taller. "You're not —"

Death's chill, I thought, then said, "Look into my eyes." The man froze, gripped by terror, unable to refuse the compulsion. I breathed him in—*Shade*—exhaled the profaned soul back into the man's body, and drew Soul Drinker.

Busashi and his nokitu materialized as if by magic beside me, their blackened blades whispering through the night. One of the soldiers managed to free their sword and slash, but the nokitu facing him flipped over the stroke, then buried his kama in the man's throat. He went down grasping the gushing wound.

Take him, Hashi. I need energy.

Don't lie to me, old man. I can feel your power. Even so, I stepped up and thrust Soul Drinker into the twitching man. *Feed.*

He did, and energy crackled along my nerves. *Thank you, and I'm not lying to you, Hashi. The more power I have, the more likely you'll be to survive, and less likely I'll be to end up in the god-emperor's palace under a glass case.*

The rest of the soldiers were dead; I raised them with a thought. The nokitu had melted into the shadows. No shouts or alarms rang out, so I assumed our arrival had gone unnoticed. I stepped to the edge of the quay and hissed down into the boat. "Zombies, climb up."

They did, though not very adroitly.

Tori joined me and handed over my armored coat. "That went well, all things considered." He wiped his hands and rolled his shoulders. "It's been a while since I rowed a boat. Now I remember why I have servants."

I huffed a quiet laugh, then beckoned my shade. "Take these zombies and walk the perimeter of the city along the outer wall. Attack and kill any soldiers you find."

"Yes, mistress." It bared its shattered and jagged teeth. I'd just given it freedom to feast.

"Zombies, follow this shade. Kill soldiers." They shambled forth to follow my simple orders.

"That ought to create a nice diversion." Tori drew his sword, the elf blade looking a little incongruous in the hand of a Toki naval officer. "Shall we stroll to the governor's palace and rescue poor Admiral Longbright?"

"Fine." I slipped Soul Drinker into my sleeve and put my hands behind my back. We'd worked out a simple ruse which we hoped would allow us to get past any soldiers we encountered, and allow us entry into Governor Rokiri's palace. "Just stop being so gods-damned cheerful, okay?"

"I promise to be grumpy and judgmental throughout the rest of the evening." Tori loosely wrapped a short piece of rope around my wrists, then grasped my arm and tugged me toward the palace. "Now, come along you!"

I glared at him, but followed along, the nokitu pacing us in the shadows. We'd only made it one block into the city when distant screams echoed through the night. Our diversion, it seemed, was working.

We arrived at the governor's palace with four additional shades in company, courtesy of two unlucky squads of soldiers responding to the growing turmoil near the wall. After a quick ploy from Tori, stealthy assassinations by the nokitu, and a few strokes of Soul Drinker, I'd added the four to our personal guard and sent the rest of the shambling corpses to create more mayhem. Busashi's nokitu—virtually invisible until they attacked—aided my harvest of souls by immobilizing with strangling cord and crippling cuts rather than killing. The alarm was spreading, but most of the conflict still focused near the defensive wall where I'd sent my undead.

Consequently, the palace defenses hadn't been fully called out yet, but the guards were nervous. So was Saraknyal.

There will be komei stationed here, Hashi.

You think? I eyed the four armored soldiers, each armed with a long naginata as well as the usual swords. None of them wore komei masks.

I'm just suggesting caution.

"Halt!" one of the soldiers snapped. "What is this, Captain?"

"A prisoner." We slowed but didn't halt. "You've heard the commotion. This is one of the culprits. She's a necromancer."

"A *what?*" The officer made a snapping motion, and all four leveled their weapons at us.

"A necromancer." Tori hooked a thumb at our ghastly escort. We'd supplemented our original plan with a new tactic; the truth. "Those are hers, but they won't attack as long as I have her captive. Now step aside. I must show this to the general."

"Are you insane? Just kill her and be done with it!"

We stopped, the tips of their weapons only inches from my chest. "Yes, well, we *did* try that. The problem is, she won't die."

"Won't die?" The officer's eyes widened. "That's ridiculous!"

"Try for yourself," Tori dared.

I grinned at the officer. "You're pathetic."

He sneered, shifted his weapon, and stabbed me in the throat. The instant the blade touched my flesh, it puffed into dust. As he staggered in shock, we sprang our trap.

Two nokitu dropped from the sculpted stonework above the entry, silencing and immobilizing two of the soldiers with strangling cords. I stepped forward and buried Soul Drinker in the officer's gut. *Feed!* The man stiffened and died, his soul tingling along my nerves. A naginata slashed into my side, and my armored coat stopped the blade from touching me, which hurt more than if it had. I folded sideways over the blow, clasping the weapon and dissolving it. Tori stabbed my attacker under the chin, his elf blade stifling a strangled cry.

"Hashi, are you all right?" Pulling his sword from the soldier, Tori put a steadying hand on my arm.

"Bruised." I straightened with some pain and raised the man Tori had slain. "My coat stopped it." The nokitus' victims weren't dead, so I transformed them both into shades. I pressed the gash in my coat experimentally. Breathing hurt a little, but I could move. I'd rather take a dozen bruises than one komei blade through my chest, so I counted myself fortunate. I tapped one shade and a zombie. "You, and you, stand guard here and let no one enter. The rest of you, follow me."

"We're in." Tori took a moment to examine one of the guards and changed his appearance to match. The entry hall was vast, but quiet. The nokitu faded into the shadows. "Now all we need to do is find the dungeon."

"Right." Preel's answer had been precise, but hadn't included directions. The palace was big, and we didn't have time to waste. I turned to my newest shade. "Do you know where the prisoners from the *Scourge* are being held?"

"Yes, mistress."

"Take us there. Avoid guards if possible."

The shade started off at a brisk pace, and we fell in behind.

At this hour, the palace was quiet. Guards were stationed at stairways, exits, and important locations such as armories. Our way twisted and turned, but Tori assured me he'd be able to find our way out. When my shade approached a door manned by two armored guards, they didn't react immediately to my shade, probably due to the dim light. I was nearly as dark as my undead minion. Tori walked behind as if escorting us.

"Who are these people?" They both reached for weapons.

"New prisoners," Tori said.

They didn't buy it, but ruse got us close enough. A throwing star flew past me to strike the nearer one in the face. Tori drew and thrust so fast I didn't see the blade until it stuck the man through the gut.

Feed them both to me, Hashi!" Saraknyal insisted. "I need energy. Things are going to get dicey on the way out.

Now wasn't the time to hold back, so I did as Saraknyal suggested. In seconds, I had two new zombies and Soul Drinker fairly sang with unspent power.

My shade pointed to the locked doors. "Dungeons."

Tori looked down the three corridors that intersected at the doors. "This is a choke point. We should hold it while Busashi frees the admiral and his crew."

"He's correct, Lady Severn," Busashi confirmed.

I nodded and turned to my shade guide. "Are there any more guards between us and the prisoners?"

"Two and one jailor, mistress."

"Busashi, take the weapons from the zombies and the guards you encounter for Longbright and his crew. The jailor will have keys. Leave the naginatas. I'll station the guards here and Tori and I will wait just inside the doors with the others." I stuck a finger into the lock's keyhole and destroyed the mechanism. That way, it would at least look secure.

"Yes, milady!" He pushed the door open cautiously to reveal a short landing and a dark stairway. The other nokitu took the weapons and followed him down the stairs.

"Alone at last," Tori gave me a wink.

"Except for a few shades and zombies." I stationed the two zombie guards at the door and we slipped inside to swing the portal closed. The stairs were pitch dark, so I withdrew my light crystal from my pocket and lit the stairs with starlight. I twisted my torso and winced.

Tori's face went serious. "How bad is it, and don't lie to me?"

"Just bruised. Maybe a cracked rib." I took a deep breath and held it before letting it out. It hurt, but not horribly. "I'm fine."

"I have an elixir if you—"

"No. Save it." I flexed my hand on Soul Drinker. "If we get out of here unscathed, I'll be surprised."

"So far, it's been far easier than I imagined. If all the Tokiri are this lackadaisical about security, we should be able to win free."

Gods and devils, he's an insufferable optimist, Saraknyal grumbled.

I snorted a foreshortened laugh, wincing only slightly at the pain in my side.

"What?"

"Saraknyal said you're an insufferable optimist."

"Guilty as charged." He grinned. "After two thousand years, how could I be anything else?"

That seemed an odd thing to say. "What do you mean?"

"Despair is easy for elves, Hashi." He shrugged and looked strangely forlorn. "One of the down-sides of living so damned long, I suppose. We...see too much, and often...leave life behind."

He's right, you know. Immortality's not all it's cracked up to be.

I'd never thought of immortality that way before and shook my head. "One more thing you and Saraknyal agree on."

"Oh, I imagine there's quite a lot we'd agree upon, if we took the time to chat, but..." He cocked his head.

Trouble. A distant shout. I think someone's discovered your door guards.

"Someone's fighting." Tori drew his sword, the blade shimmering green in the dim light.

"Saraknyal heard it." I cracked the door and glanced down the three halls. "How long before they find us, you think?"

"General alarm, martialing the barracks... Maybe ten minutes."

I glanced back down the stairs. "Come on, Busashi..."

A minute passed, and I heard a clatter from down the right-hand hallway.

"I may have over-estimated how much time we had."

"Time to stall. Zombies, go that direction. Kill anyone you find." I pointed down the hallway where we'd heard the commotion.

Three living corpses shambled off. At the first corner they rounded, a shout rang out.

"Back," Tori hissed.

I ordered my shades, and we backed onto the landing and eased the doors closed.

At least six, Saraknyal estimated, then a scream rang out. *Maybe five.*

I relayed the information to Tori in a whisper, and he nodded. Then another shout echoed down a different hallway. Armor clattered.

Several more coming the other way.

How many?

At least four, maybe more.

I held up five fingers and pointed the other way.

"Of all the rotten luck! With the guards gone, they'll investigate."

"Shades," I hissed, "when we're discovered, attack the soldiers."

They bared their teeth and readied their weapons as the clatter of armor neared.

I doused my light and turned to Tori. "When they're at the door, we open them. Let the shades go first."

He nodded, and we flattened ourselves against the walls, the shades standing between us. I reached out to grasp my door's pull ring, and Tori did likewise.

"The guards have been taken!" A voice rasped from beyond the door. "You, and you, stay here."

Something rattled in the destroyed lock.

Tori and I wrenched the doors open.

A fully armored komei stood in the doorway, keys in hand. My minions charged forth. One lost its head, but the other two struck, bowling the warrior backward with two swords through him. As he went down, he struck again, and one shade lost an arm.

I started to move, but Saraknyal warned me, *Wait! Another!*

A second komei stepped into view, sword slashing through the other shade. I surged out of the darkness and planted Soul Drinker in his side.

Feed! It only took an instant, and I raised the corpse before it fell. There were four more soldiers, though they didn't wear komei masks. I was down to one one-armed shade. I released a peal of laughter that staggered the soldiers and extinguished the lamps. Tori's elf blade flared green in the sudden darkness, and Saraknyal filled my mind with his enhanced view of our enemies.

More soldiers charged from the right. "Hold them off, Tori."

"Rather a lot of them."

I sent my komei zombie at the four soldiers facing me, and whirled. Four more soldiers led by two komei charged from the other direction.

"Switch, Tori!" As he slipped past me without a word to face the others, I screamed winter at the charging soldiers.

My icy breath froze three solid, but one komei escaped, rolling under the icy blast. As his comrades toppled, the komei lurched up to thrust at me. I parried with Soul Drinker, and the blades grated, but the komei sword didn't disintegrate. The tip of the blade caught me in the stomach, but didn't pierce my fine mail coat.

Thank you Hipshill! I slashed the komei's wrist, and Saraknyal wrenched his soul away.

The remaining two soldiers leapt the frozen corpses, their swords slashing. But these weren't komei.

I blocked one with an outstretched hand and parried the other with Soul Drinker. The fine blades disintegrated, both soldiers staggering with the shock of their suddenly absent weapons. I waded in, slashed one, then took a hard blow to my other arm from the other one's shorter sword. He'd drawn it so fast I'd missed it. My arm went numb, but the blade didn't penetrate my coat. He stabbed at my face and his blade disintegrated. I closed my eyes to keep from being blinded by the dust, and snatched his wrist.

Death's chill. He stiffened, and I pulled him in. "Look into my eyes." Seconds later, I had another shade. I turned to find Tori standing among four dead Toki soldiers and one partially dismembered komei zombie trying to stand. I raised the dead, and found that I could move my left arm, albeit painfully. Tori had blood on his arm, and had abandoned his Toki disguise.

"Are you all right?" I asked.

"Fine. Just a scratch." He turned and cocked his head again. "More on the way. I do believe we've drawn their ire."

"Wonderful." The first komei hadn't risen, so I assumed he lived. I knelt. *Enough for a shade, old man?*

*Make him a wraith! Komei are fearless, so it will work, *and* I get some energy from it.*

Do I have time?

If you hurry.

"Tori, warn me if we get company. I'm going to be busy for a minute."

"We may not have a minute."

"Which way are they coming from?" I asked.

Tori pointed, and I sent all the zombies shambling and crawling in that direction.

"That should slow them." I lifted the mask of the unconscious komei to reveal an attractive young man's face. I pushed back his eyelids and gazed into the dark orbs. *Look into my soul.* Saraknyal shredded the warrior's soul, consuming everything unnecessary.

The komei's slack features suddenly contorted and he screamed.

Chapter Thirty Two
Deliverance

From the diary of Kevril Longbright —

So much effort, so many lives risked and spent on my behalf, is humbling. I hope I live long enough to deserve this, and I pray to Odea that I'll never disappoint those who put such investment in me.

I woke from a nightmare to the jangle of keys; another day in prison. My wrists and shoulders ached abominably, and my backside had long ago gone numb. I'd torn the sleeves from my shirt, binding my wrists to keep the manacles from wearing me raw, but the cold iron and stone had their way in the end. Each successive day brought less hope, more despair, and the recollection of General Koto's offer: good food, comfort, a bed to sleep in, an end to the chains, if only we would cooperate. His tactic was simple, wear us down until we broke. I felt myself slipping closer toward the breaking point with every passing day.

So when, instead of our jailor delivering the meager gruel that had been our mainstay, I found darkly clad nokitu outside my cell, I could only stare in shock.

"Admiral Longbright?" Keys rattled, and the door opened.

"Who..." Recognition struck, and I squinted at Busashi in the wan light of our guttering lantern. "Gods and devils, Busashi?" I tried to stand and failed.

"Yes, Admiral." He hurried up and worked a key into my manacles. My arms fell free, welcome pain lancing through my shoulders. He handed the keys to one of his companions. "Free the rest quickly!"

"How..." The others were stirring, some muttering epithets of

316

disbelief. Busashi helped me to my feet. I staggered and rubbed my wrists. "How in all Nine Hells are you *here*?"

"Your wife and the aid of her most amazing friends." He pulled a scabbarded katana from his belt and handed it to me. "Lady Severn and Lord Blackbriar accompanied us."

"Okay, Severn I understand, but *Blackbriar*?" I checked the blade and jammed it through my belt. "And how? Did Haven mount an attack? How did you get through the fleet?"

"Aboard *Gull*, sir, in the dark." He ushered me out of the cell. I staggered. "Your midshipman, Boxley, commanded. She brought us here with no trouble."

"Boxley's alive?" Others stumbled from their cells, some armed, most not. "How many do you have?"

"Twelve in all, including your most determined lady wife."

My knees nearly folded. "Preel's *here*? Where? She shouldn't have—"

"She's safe aboard *Scourge*, sir. Sleeping. We took the ship first, then asked her a question to find you."

"Gods and devils!" I stomped my feet to return some feeling to my backside. "I assume you have a plan to get us out of here?"

"A vague one, sir. Lady Severn has caused a considerable diversion, but it won't last long. Follow quickly. We have boats waiting."

"Fookin' right!" Wix crowed, brandishing two short daggers. "Come on you cutthroats! Time to raise some hell!"

The Scourges grumbled curses and grinned. Hemp hobbled up to my side, his thin face bristling with joy. They were ragged, worn, starving, and madder than a sack of wet cats.

As we started to form up, a thought came to mind. "Release all the prisoners you can find. Just open a cell and hand them the keys. There's no point in leaving anyone incarcerated. We can't take them all, but they can cause trouble for the Toki."

"Yes, Admiral!" A nokitu dashed off, keys in hand.

I nodded to Busashi. "Let's go."

We hobbled out of the dungeon behind Busashi. The stairs challenged my legs, but feeling returned by the time we reached the first landing. Then a scream unlike any I'd ever heard echoed from above. We froze.

"Sounds like someone bein' tortured," Hemp muttered.

"Well, it can't be good. Come on!" We hurried up, and I rested a hand on the unfamiliar weapon at my waist.

At the top of the stairs, we found the most incongruous sight I think I've ever seen. Hashi Severn and Tori Blackbriar stood with two Toki warriors facing an oncoming force of soldiers, two komei at the van. Then a fallen komei at their feet got up, turned, and charged the onslaught.

"Fookin' hell!" Wix muttered at my side.

Severn and Blackbriar turned as one, and grim expressions transformed to hope.

"Admiral! Well met!" Tori saluted with his sword.

"And just in time!" Severn turned and strode toward the fray.

"Form up!" I snapped to my crew. "Arm yourselves if you don't have a weapon! Double ranks, tight formation. Move!"

"Here, Admiral!" Blackbriar flicked up a sword from the floor with his toe and held it out to me. "A finer weapon than the one you carry."

I took it, a komei katana. Staring at it for a heartbeat, I remembered Kivan. "Bloody fine!" I handed my previous weapon to a crewmember and drew the lustrous blade. "Scourges, with me!"

We charged down the corridor, Lord Blackbriar, Wix, and I in the van. Hashi Severn and the komei that seemed to be fighting on our side had already made a serious dent in the Toki forces by the time we arrived, and every slain enemy rose again to fight for us. As the last fell, Severn knelt beside a fallen soldier and pulled him up face to face. My blood chilled as a fine white mist issued from the wounded soldier's mouth. She inhaled it like a draft of opium, then exhaled it again into her shuddering victim. His skin darkened to flat black, and his eyes flared blood red. A crackling noise like dice on a marble floor shocked me to my bones. Bits of broken teeth fell from his black lips as he stood.

"By all the Nine Hells..." I muttered.

Severn looked to me, her face a mask of determination. "Rethinking your choice for liaison with the Council, admiral?"

"Not in the slightest, Lady Severn!" I sheathed my new sword.

"I can't thank you enough for coming to free us. Both of you. I'm forever in your debt."

"That's almost exactly what your wife said." Blackbriar grinned.

I nodded to them both. "I hate to say this, but we have one more thing to do before we go."

They both gaped at me. "We do?"

"Yes, my second lieutenant, Kivan, contrived a deception, posing as a mutineer to get close to the commander here, General Koto. It worked, though he thinks she's mad. We have to find her and get her out." I looked around at the palace walls. "Though I've no idea where she is."

Severn turned to the komei she'd somehow recruited. "Wraith, do you know where this woman, Kivan, is?"

He turned to face us, and I saw that his armor had been pierced several times. In fact, the broken blade of a sword protruded from his torso, though he seemed unconcerned. "No, mistress."

"I daresay the general would know." Blackbriar flourished his blade again. "Shall we pay him a visit?"

"If we can find him," I said.

Blackbriar shook his head. "The general alarm only sounded a few minutes ago, and generals aren't called out to fight. The captain of the guard would *inform* the general, but would secure the palace first." He seemed certain of his claim.

"Do you know where General Koto's quarters are?" Severn asked the komei.

"Yes, mistress."

"Take us there!" Severn snapped. "Zombies, drop your weapons. Go that way!" She pointed down another hallway. "Kill Toki soldiers!"

"Why split our forces?" I asked as weapons clattered to the floor and the abominations shambled off.

"Diversion," she said. "If we're all in one place, we'll be surrounded. We need to *move*."

"Everyone arm yourselves." I drew my new katana. "We're in for a fight."

Severn looked down at the icy obsidian dagger in her hand then nodded. "Let's go!"

We followed the komei wraith in a tight formation; Severn, Blackbriar, Wix, Hemp, and myself in the fore, then several shades and my rag-tag band of thirty pirates filling the corridors behind us. The six nokitu took up the rear. Not an insubstantial force by anyone's reckoning.

The two guards manning the main stairs took one look at us and shouted an alarm. They backed up the stairs, naginatas leveled as several more guards descended from above with two more komei in the lead. As we formed up and started to advance, Severn held up a hand.

"We don't have time for this nonsense!" She lunged up the stairs three at a time and screamed.

I wondered for a moment if she'd lost her mind, then gaped in awe at the torrent of killing frost that issued forth. The two soldiers and one komei unlucky enough to be in the van were petrified solid, and those behind them staggered back, several screaming as eyes and hands were frostbitten. Four recently living warriors toppled forth to shatter like blue crystal goblets on the stairs.

"Remind me never, *ever*, to piss her off," I muttered.

"Good advice for anyone," Blackbriar agreed with a grin.

"Forward!" I bellowed, for Lady Severn had already carried her attack into the midst of the remaining warriors.

The surviving komei lunged to the attack ahead of his support, and I thought Severn would be killed. His sword clashed hard on her coat, but didn't penetrate. She slashed, and his armor parted like a torn sheet. White mist trailed after her blade, and the komei fell.

We arrived, Wix and I on one side, Blackbriar on the other, his elf blade a blur. The soldiers fought to the end, but every one that fell, Severn raised. The last soldier thrust desperately at Severn. She blocked with an open hand, and his blade puffed into dust. She gripped his wrist, stepped up, and transformed him into yet another shade.

I cringed inwardly at the dreadful power she wielded, but kept my reservations to myself.

"Onward!" Severn commanded, and we continued up, then up again, encountering no more guards.

At the third floor, our komei wraith turned left and strode down a carpeted hallway lit with glow crystals. Around another corner, we found two komei, swords already in hand, stationed at an elaborate door. They faced us, a clearly overwhelming force, without fear.

"Stop!" Severn raised a hand, and her undead minions stopped.

The rest of us did too, and I glanced questioningly at Blackbriar. He just shrugged.

"Stand down, or perish. You need not be destroyed here!"

"We cannot." One of them said, his voice firm and emotionless.

Severn sighed, clearly frustrated. "Very well. Shades, kill them."

Five undead warriors dashed forth, teeth bared, hissing like beasts. The two komei met them and fought to the death. In only seconds, just two shades remained standing, the others twitching in pieces on the floor.

"Come on." Severn strode forth, and we followed. She paused for a moment to touch her dagger to the fallen shades, and their twitching stilled, the magic that sustained them evidently broken. "All right, let's find out where this lieutenant of yours is and get the hell out of here." She put a hand on the ornate doors and they ceased to exist, crumbling to rust and splinters.

"Handy that," Wix chimed in. "Though it do take the fun out of kickin' the door down."

We surged into a vast and opulent sitting room, three doors and a spread of windows that gave an impressive view of the city.

"Wix, go left. We'll—"

The door to the right opened. "What in the names of all the—" General Koto stood in a robe, staring at us in open-mouthed shock.

"Take him!" We charged, but he retreated and slammed the door.

Wix arrived first and reduced the door to splinters. We followed him through, weapons at the ready, but skidded to a halt.

"Mr. Longbright! I see you've found some allies." Koto grinned from the corner of the room, a gleaming wakizashi pressed to Kivan's throat. "Come to recover this little slut for your own entertainment?"

Kivan gritted her teeth in pain, for he had her arm behind her back. She wore a silk robe, hastily donned from the look of it, and the bed that dominated the room was rumpled. I saw shame in her eyes, through the pain, and it kindled my anger.

"No, I've come to recover my second lieutenant, General." I lowered my sword. "Mission accomplished, Lieutenant? I trust the general wasn't *too* difficult to manipulate."

Her shame melted away, replaced by grim determination. "Not at all, sir, though a little *disappointing*."

"One step and I'll cut her throat!" The trembling blade in Koto's hand quivered, drawing a line of blood. "You best take your freedom and leave her here with me. I'll have fifty komei here in minutes."

"Hurt her, and I'll—"

"What? Kill me?" Koto barked a laugh.

"No." Severn took a step toward the pair, raising her icy smoldering dagger to point at him. "If you kill her, I'll consume your *soul*, General. Harm her, and I'll only consume part of it, as I did your komei, here. But I swear, as a member of the Haven Council of Lords, if you release her, we'll let you live."

"The Haven Council of Lords?" Koto spat at her but it fell short. "The Haven council of *criminals*, you mean!"

Severn laughed at him, and a wave of terror gripped me by the guts. Staggering, I saw it I wasn't alone; all my comrades—save Severn, Blackbriar, and the undead—shivered and quailed at the unearthly noise. Koto blanched bone white, and the blade in his hand wavered, drooping an inch.

Kivan's heel came down hard on his bare toes as her free hand snatched his wrist. As Koto's eyes widened in agony, she snapped her head back hard into his nose. His eyes rolled back, and she wrenched his sword arm down, freed her other wrist from his limp grasp, and twisted to plunge the wakizashi into his stomach.

We all stood stunned for a heartbeat. Either Kivan hadn't been affected by the necromancer's terrifying magic, or she'd been long past fear. Regardless, the move had been worthy of any pirate on the Blood Sea.

"Call me slut again, why don't you, General!" Kivan took the blade's hilt in both hands and gutted him like a fish. He collapsed griping the flood of blood and intestines, a wail of horror rising from his throat. Kivan turned, the bloody sword in hand, shaking, but unhurt. "Reporting for duty, Admiral Longbright."

"And remind me to not ever piss *her* off," Blackbriar quipped.

I stepped past Severn and clasped my lieutenant in a crushing embrace. "Gods and devils, that was beautiful."

She coughed a laugh. "Thank you, sir."

I clutched her shoulders and held her to arm's length. "I might suggest some clothes before we leave."

"Oh! Right, sir!" She scrambled over the bed to a clothes press. "Out of uniform and all that! Two seconds, sir!"

I hurriedly turned my back as she flung off the robe, and gestured toward my gawking crew. "Everyone out! Give her some privacy! Wix, guard the corridor. We're leaving as soon as the lieutenant's properly attired."

I cast a glance at General Koto, but Kivan must have cut a major artery, for he was clearly dead. I would have liked to have taken him prisoner, but, all things considered, I'd call it even.

I never imagined being aboard my ship again, and the welcome we received made it all the sweeter.

"Sir!" Boxley broke all propriety and clasped me in an embrace that staggered me. "Sorry sir. I just..." She broke away looking mortified, hastening to salute.

"No harm done, Midshipman. Good to see you alive."

A glance around the deck startled me, for ten red-eyed shades stood along the bulwarks, swords in hand, still as stone. Severn's minions, former Toki sailors, from the look of them. Our flight from the city had been tense and dangerous, but every fight left us stronger and cost the enemy. Between the preternatural abilities of the nokitu, Severn, and—much to my shock—Blackbriar's magic, the panicked patrols of Toki soldiers didn't know what hit them. Some were sailors sent ashore to help quell the disturbances. Others were army. Both were led by komei, but even those couldn't stand against undead. They were dragged down and transformed to unliving abominations, sent out to slaughter their former brethren at the orders of our necromancer.

"Good to *be* alive, sir!" Boxley's eyes swept the crew, and her face split into a grin at the sight of Kivan.

"Wix! Haul anchor and haul ass! Kivan, take the quarterdeck! Dark ship, and quiet as possible. I need a decent shirt and jacket. I'll be back up shortly, but don't hesitate to call down if you need me. Boxley, get the launches stowed, then pick a crew and take command of *Gull*. You'll sail in escort, but evade capture if we get cornered."

"Aye, sir!" Boxley slapped a spyglass into my hand. "Quite a lot of launch traffic from the warships to shore, and some ship-to-ship, but none came to inspect *Scourge*. There was only a skeleton crew aboard, so they probably didn't think to recruit anyone." She started to turn away, then stopped. "Oh, and Lady Preel's in your cabin. Safe and sound."

"Thank you, Boxley." I swept the spyglass across the harbor.

The warships and two of the merchants were lit up and busy, but all still swung on their anchors. Launches ferried more troops ashore. *As long as they're not paying any attention to us.*

I turned to the council members. "Lady Severn, Lord Blackbriar, we're out of the frying pan for now, but need to evade the fire, if you know what I mean. We'll ease out quietly, but there *will* be pursuit. We may need your skills if we're going to be boarded."

"We'll stay out of the way," Severn said.

I nodded in thanks. "I can offer you some accommodation if you'd like to rest and freshen up, though not to the standards you're accustomed to."

"Better than the *Gull* with twelve aboard, I'll wager." Blackbriar sighed. "I would kill for a cup of blackbrew."

"I'm sure we can arrange that, please follow me."

"I'll stay on deck for now, Admiral." Severn doffed her heavy coat and handed it to Blackbriar. "Stow that for me, would you, Tori? It's too heavy for aboard ship. I'd have some tea if it's possible, thank you, Admiral."

"Have a seat on the quarterdeck then. I'll send Hemp up with something."

"Thank you." She seemed troubled, perhaps the lapse in action from our running fights ashore left her feeling spent.

I knew that feeling. The pale-faced komei whom she'd transformed into a wraith followed her up to the quarterdeck, seemingly unhurt though his armor was dented and pierced. The creature unnerved me, but again, I'd rather have such a thing on my side than the enemy's.

"Hemp! Blackbrew for Lord Blackbriar and tea for Lady Severn. She'll be on the quarterdeck. See if you can rustle up a decent meal for everyone. I'll be in my cabin for a moment to change and...well..." The other half of my soul lay sleeping in my bunk, and I longed to see her.

"Aye, sir! No worries!" Hemp dashed aft, and I escorted Blackbriar to Miko's quarters.

"Here you are. I'm afraid I can't offer you a change of clothes or—"

"I brought some things; thank you, Admiral." He ducked under the door frame and took in the space. "I'm quite accustomed to shipboard life. You needn't worry on my account."

"Thank you." I headed aft, only one thing currently on my mind. Of course, there would be a fleet of warships to deal with shortly, but at that moment, I could only think of seeing Preel.

Chapter Thirty Three
Fight and Flight

From the journal of Hashi Severn —

I told the Council that I was the only one capable of freeing their admiral, and, with help, I've done so. I wonder now, however, if the ends justify my means, and what more will be required.

I accepted a cup of tea from Longbright's steward and sat on a locker beside the mast on the quarterdeck. My new komei wraith I stationed at the aft rail. Saraknyal insisted he needed more work, but I'd put it off. I couldn't make myself do it just yet. The look on Longbright's face when he watched me create my abominations loomed in my mind.

The first light of dawn had not yet graced the eastern sky, and moon had not yet risen. I watched the sailors preparing *Scourge* for sea, quietly and without lights, marveling at their skills. The amazing young woman, Kivan, seemed completely at ease, barking whispered orders and surveying the anchorage with a spyglass. I couldn't imagine what she'd been through, yet here she was, in control, in command.

How are you, Hashi? Saraknyal asked.

I feel like I spent a few hours in the care of an expert masochist, if you want the truth. I flexed my arm and twisted my torso experimentally; both hurt. My body, I knew, would heal. Nothing was broken and I wasn't bleeding. My heart, on the other hand, ached worse than my battered body. I hadn't counted how many souls I'd destroyed this night. Would Tori still gauge my soul as mostly good? I had my doubts.

You should rest. If we get out of this without another fight, I'll be astounded.

I'm too keyed up. It wasn't completely a lie, but it wasn't the whole truth either. As always after destroying souls, a thick depression had begun to settle upon me. I had to work myself through it or suffer a breakdown, and I had no lead box to put Saraknyal into.

I sipped my tea and eyed Kivan. She stood behind the wheel of the ship, watching everything, hands clasped behind her back. She gave orders in whispers, and they were followed without question. Dark sails rose forward and fell from the yards above, black against black. I remembered the scars on Kivan's back when she'd doffed the robe so hastily. She'd been through hell before, and probably endured General Koto's attentions for days, all for her captain, her ship, and her crew.

Scourge began making way, *Gull* scooting along beside us, and the activity settled down. As Kivan directed us out of the anchorage, I stood and surveyed the other ships. None were moving.

"Nobody seems to have noticed us yet," I said.

Like shades in the night, Saraknyal said with no small satisfaction.

"We're not drawing any attention, but the hell we raised ashore certainly is." Kivan pointed to the city. Fires had broken out, distant screams and bellows reaching us over the water.

Our diversions seem to still be working, Saraknyal said.

Releasing the prisoners was a stroke of genius. Busashi had told me of Longbright's command to open all the cells in the dungeon. They'd found Governor Rokiri in one. He'd given her the keys and a weapon, and she'd assured him they would cause all the trouble they could. *And killing Koto didn't hurt.*

I looked back to Kivan, and, on impulse, asked, "Would you mind if I asked you a question, Lieutenant?"

She looked at me and shrugged. "Of course not, Lady Severn."

"How do you do it?"

She blinked at me. "Excuse me? Do what?"

"Hold yourself together with..." I waved a hand at the ship, the city, "with all you've obviously been through. At your age, I would have been a shivering wreck about now." I'd fled my fears as a girl, not confronted them.

"You do what you have to do." She shrugged. "And it's worth it."

"Worth it?" It was my turn to blink at her. "What's worth that much pain?"

"The captain...er, *admiral*, that is." She smiled at me. "He's the best man I've ever known. If I can't be loyal to someone like him, I can't look myself in the mirror. I owe him everything."

Such loyalty... I wanted to ask what had earned that kind of devotion, but just then the subject of our conversation climbed the stairs to the quarterdeck, his steward a step behind.

"Report, Lieutenant Kivan."

She whirled around and snapped a salute. "Underway without a fuss, sir. No sign of anyone noticing, but they're all watching the city. I imagine that'll change with the dawn."

"Bank on it. Moonrise in about an hour." He looked around and accepted a cup and something from the steward. His calm made me feel safe, even though I knew we weren't. "Hemp's found some provisions, and I ordered them served out. Feel free, Lady Severn."

"I'll stick to tea for now, thank you. I learned aboard *Gull* that the sea doesn't agree with my stomach."

"Ah, well, I hope you find *Scourge* a bit more kindly. A ship is a completely different experience than a fishing smack."

"Refill on the tea, Lady Severn?" the steward offered.

"Please."

"Lord Tori offered some ginger for you, so I put a drop in the pot." He poured from a porcelain pot wrapped in a cozy, and the scent drifted to me. "Oh, and I can mend that gash in your coat good as new. Lucky you weren't cut izzard to gizzard!"

"It's mail-lined, thank you." I felt a little out of place on the quarterdeck, but didn't want to go below, remembering what the stuffiness did to my stomach. So far, I felt fine, but we were barely edging out of the anchorage, not yet in the open sea. The sails caught the wind, urging the ship along. "Now that we have some time, you should know, Admiral, there was some...contention among the council members over what to do in response to your capture."

"Oh, I imagine there was." He barked a laugh. "Did Brilla Balshi suggest I be left to rot in prison?"

Time to fess up, my dear, Saraknyal chided.

"Actually, Lady Balshi's dead." I kept my tone neutral and

sipped my tea, trying to figure out how to relate the facts. "She managed to learn your wife's...secret, you see, and—"

Longbright's face shifted from surprise to concern. "Her secret? So, you..."

"Know she's a truthsayer? Yes. So does Tori, though that happened by accident. We're both committed to *keeping* it a secret. If word got out, there'd be hell to pay."

"Indeed there would. And how did you learn of Preel's talent?"

"She came to me and asked for help. Brilla threatened to expose her if she didn't...capitulate." I shrugged. "Acting as your liaison with the Council, I presented a contract for your wife's services to Brilla. The contract was crafted more as a trap than a legitimate offer, so convoluted and contrived that even a madwoman wouldn't have signed it."

His eyes widened a trifle. "That's...interesting."

"My idea, I'm afraid. Brilla was completely psychotic. She'd abducted and tortured several of Jhavika's former retainers to learn why Preel was so valuable. She performed the interrogations personally, in her own chambers. I've never seen the like." I sighed and shook my head at the horrific memory.

And people think necromancers are evil, Saraknyal grumbled.

"I provoked her into a rage, and when she ordered her soldiers to kill me, I did away with her. She had no heirs. House Balshi is no more, and their assets have been confiscated by the Council."

"Her army?" he asked.

"Yes, and three ships that were in port. Your first mate, Miko, now commands *Temoin*, Balshi's former flagship."

"And the rest of the Council?"

"They agreed to spread word to Sariff and the islands as quickly as possible. What ships they can muster will be manned by Balshi soldiers and anyone else the Council can spare. I sent my two smugglers to Black Point and Ton Chi to spread the word. *Blood Raven* was on their way to Black Point when word of your capture arrived. Oh, Captain Moll recruited another corsair, *Rogue*, on her way back from Twin Capes." I pointed to the south. "Miko told the Council you sent your sailing master to Twin Capes with news of your capture. We thought if you could lead the Toki armada there, we might be able to surprise them with a fleet of our own."

"Arrange a *fleet* in seven days?" Longbright frowned. "That *might* work, if they can coordinate things, but it's a logistical nightmare."

"It is, and we have no way to communicate with them."

"Well, it's something, I suppose. We might—"

"Deck there! Three ships making sail!"

"Damn!" Longbright raised a spyglass and I turned to squint into the darkness. The moon was rising. "The jig is up! All the sail she'll bear, Kivan! We've barely got an hour on them."

"Aye, sir! Mightn't we send *Gull* ahead, sir? She's a fast little smack, and Boxley could find Rauley and warn the chiefs of our arrival."

"*Excellent* idea! Give her the word!"

As Kivan shouted orders, and more sailors scrambled aloft, I turned to Longbright. "Do you think we'll be able to outrun them?"

"Short-handed, I don't know, to be honest. Warships are faster than merchantmen, but *Scourge*'s no slouch on a beam reach. And they'll have picket ships." He shrugged.

"We spotted two smaller ships on our way north. How many aboard those, do you think?" I asked.

"Oh, two hundred at most, I'd guess. Half of those soldiers, the rest fighting sailors."

"And komei?"

"Perhaps a few aboard each ship."

What are you planning, Hashi? Saraknyal had that accusatory tone he used when he thought I was about to do something insane.

"If we come rail-to-rail with one of them, Admiral, I can help deal with their soldiers. Komei present a problem, but not an insurmountable one with my shades backing me up."

"I'll keep that in mind, Lady Severn."

"Do that." I downed my tea and handed the cup to the steward. "Now, I think I'd like to change and try to eat something. Jerky and porridge seems to settle well, if there is any."

"Oh, I'm sure we can rustle up somethin', Lady Severn." Hemp grinned and touched a knuckle to his forehead. "And we'll get that fancy coat patched up right as rain! Can't have you takin' on the whole Toki Navy in a slashed coat! It just ain't proper!"

I barked a laugh at his tone, unsure if he was joking or not. "Please keep me informed, Admiral. If they get close..."

"Rest while you can, Lady Severn. I'm sure we'll need your talents eventually."

My talents... I nodded, collected my new wraith, and followed the steward below. *Destroying human souls is a talent, I suppose.* But what choice did I have?

One that I've been perfecting for centuries, Saraknyal quipped.

Just don't get cocky, old man. I worked my aching left arm and winced. *I don't think I'll be wearing that coat anymore. It's more pain than protection.*

Unless you face a komei.

Yes, unless that, or I could fall overboard. I looked at the black water streaming past the ship and shivered.

Hashi! Someone's at your door!

I roused from a dead sleep and levered myself out of the narrow bunk. The cabin was comparatively dark, though I could see full daylight out the tiny port. *Past noon, then.* I'd slept in one of my silk shirts, unaware until my head hit the pillow of my utter exhaustion.

My komei wraith stood facing the door, a hand on his sword. I'd spent some time before bed, allowing Saraknyal to continue the man's transformation. Luckily, he was already past the screaming phase, well more than halfway to the end-stage, when his powers would come to their full. Even now, he was an invaluable weapon, retaining all the skills and knowledge of a komei, with the invulnerability and recuperative gifts of Saraknyal's necromantic magic.

"Stand aside, wraith." As he did so, I stepped to the door and opened it a crack. "Yes?"

Longbright's steward stood with a cup of tea and a bowl of steaming porridge on a tray. "Your pardon, Lady Severn, but Admiral Longbright requests your presence on deck when you're able. I brung you a cuppa and a nibble." His eyes darted to the wraith and back to me. "Does your...um...man need anything?"

"No, thank you, Hemp." I took the cup and the bowl from the tray. "Tell the admiral I'll be up shortly. Is there trouble?"

"One of the Toki picket ships is bearin' down on us, but we got maybe an hour before the...before they get close enough to give us a mauling."

I nodded. "I'll be up." I closed the door and sat down to eat and sip ginger tea.

You must be feeling well. You seem to have an appetite.

"Mmm, yes, not bad." The porridge was surprisingly good, with dates and nuts, and the tea strong and hot. I worked my aching shoulder and twisted my waist. My bruises hadn't miraculously vanished with eight or so hours of sleep. I finished my meal, stretched, and got dressed. Soul Drinker I wore strapped to my forearm, the hilt pressing against my skin. "Wraith, follow me."

"Yes, mistress." He fell in at my heels and we made our way on deck.

The sun shone down at a steep angle, not long past noon, and the entire ship's complement seemed to be staring to the east, uncharacteristically quiet. The seas were remarkably calm, considering the wind, and even though the deck tilted somewhat, there wasn't much roll.

I climbed the stairs to the quarterdeck to find the admiral, Preel—wearing a veil—six nokitu, and Tori Blackbriar already there.

"Hashi! You look positively *radiant* this morning!" Tori grinned with his usual self-satisfied air and bowed.

"And you're as insufferable as ever," I retorted. "Preel, good to see you up and well. Admiral, your steward said one of the..." I faltered as I glanced to the east. A warship bore down on us from the southeast, a lofty island behind them some distance off. Another ship angled toward us from the northeast at a greater distance. I looked to the north, and found the horizon studded with sails. "Ah, I see."

"It's not as hopeless as it looks, Lady Severn." Longbright smiled more brightly than I'd yet seen before.

The reason for his mood strode up to me and, to my shock and embarrassment, embraced me without reservation. I stood stunned for a moment, until Preel broke away and withdrew the small notebook she used from a pocket of her sari.

She showed me the page. It read, "Thank you for my husband."

"You're welcome, Preel." I found myself smiling without knowing why. "Now, I think we should figure out how to keep him and the rest of us free."

She nodded with smiling eyes and returned to his side, clutching his hand in hers. My stomach did a little flip at their obvious joy at being reunited. Love had only ever caused me pain, but had given them happiness. What I'd considered a curse, they'd taken as a blessing.

"So, as I said, we've only got *that* one to worry about in the short term." Longbright pointed to the warship to the southeast. "She's smaller than *Scourge*, but looks to be well-manned and her captain's no fool. We tried some evasions early on, but they have the weather gauge."

"The weather gauge?" *Saraknyal, do you—*

Don't ask me. The weather looks fine to me, and I've no idea why one ship would be able to gauge it any better than another.

"Sorry, that means they're upwind and have control over the engagement." He pointed to the west. "We could run downwind, but that would only prolong the chase and allow the rest of the armada to close."

"Yes, there's that inconvenient *continent* in our way. Such a bother!" Tori chuckled at his own witticism.

I knew he was just trying to break the tension, but I flashed him a sharp look before turning back to the admiral. "What you're saying is, they'll catch us, yes?"

Longbright nodded. "In about an hour at most, less if we don't veer to the west. Our lookouts estimate about a hundred fifty to two hundred aboard, and they've got a battery of four ballistae on each side. They can use those to fire our sails, or grapple us and pull us in. We can't fight them rail to rail and hope to survive, even with you and your minions' aid, I'm afraid."

"I see."

Ask him if they've spotted any komei aboard, Saraknyal suggested, and I did.

"Yes, two at least. We don't know for certain they don't have more." Longbright looked to his wife, then back to me. "We need your help, but..."

I gritted my teeth at his hesitancy. "*All* our lives are at stake here, Admiral. What do you need from me?"

"We've come up with a plan to get you and perhaps a small team aboard without coming rail to rail."

How? Fly?

I ignored Saraknyal. "All right. I'm game if you are, Admiral, but I'd probably be better off with just my wraith along."

"If you're certain, we can do that, but..." He traded another look with Preel.

"The real problem, it seems," Tori broke in, "isn't getting you or anyone else *aboard*, it's getting you back. That's much trickier."

"Ah." I glanced at the other ships, the closest perhaps three miles away. "You can't exactly stop and wait, or circle around to pick me up, can you?"

"Not without having to face at least two more of their smaller warships. In fact, if they fire our sails, we may not be able to bend new ones before they catch us." Longbright pulled his wife close. "We're between a rock and a hard place, I'm afraid. We do have a plan that *might* get you back, but it's not...pleasant."

Not pleasant? Ask him to define unpleasant.

"Exactly *how* unpleasant?"

"That depends on whether or not you can swim or not."

I looked at the sea racing past and swallowed. "I can swim."

"Then it might be workable, but you won't have much time once you're aboard. I'd suggest killing the captain, officers, and as many soldiers as possible, but the komei will undoubtedly be all over you."

I thought for a moment. "But you don't need soldiers killed as much as the ship disabled, right?"

"Well, yes, but I don't see how you could disable an entire ship."

Without getting slaughtered, neither do I.

I ignored Saraknyal's comment and looked around, spotting what I needed. "Can I have one of those wooden peg things please?" I pointed to the railing where a number of the things were lined up, some with ropes tied and coiled upon them.

"Goffrey, grab a bolt pin for us," Longbright said.

"Sir!" A weathered sailor snatched one of the pins and hurried over with it.

Longbright took it and handed it over to me without a word, curiosity written on his face.

"So, you remember General Koto's door, right?" I held up the pin and thought, *Dust to dust.* The shaft of hardwood dissolved in my hand, carried away on the wind in an instant. "I can do the same to a larger piece of wood." I gestured to the towering mast only feet away. "A *much* larger piece."

Longbright's eyes widened. "Gods and devils, I'm glad you're on our side!"

Sailors muttered and made warding signs.

"So, now all we have to do is figure out how to get me aboard and back without drowning." I dusted off my hands and shrugged. "I know nothing of ships or how you intend on accomplishing that, so I'm pretty much in your hands."

And barking mad.

Perhaps, I acceded.

"Yes, well, you may not like what we've come up with," Longbright warned me.

"I'm used to not liking things, Admiral," I assured him.

"Oh, but you're *really* not going to like this!" Tori said with a grin. "It was my idea, you see."

Can't we just kill him, please? Saraknyal grumbled.

Don't tempt me, I thought, peering once more at the approaching warship.

"You're *sure* about this, Master Wix?" I slipped my right arm through the leather strap and gripped the rope, my other hand firmly clenching another rope trailing up the topmast. I didn't have a problem with heights, but motion at the mainmast crow's nest had my stomach in knots.

"Oh, aye, Lady Severn. Sure as can be. Just some swashbucklery, as they say." He grinned horribly, his teeth rivaling a shades, and his scarred visage truly horrifying.

"And you've done this before?"

"Oh, never. But don't you worry. You'll land light as a feather. Admiral his-self's on the wheel, and I measured these lines personal. It's all about timing. You just gotta let go at the right time."

"Right." I swallowed hard and squinted at the onrushing warship, now only a couple hundred yards away, angled to intersect our port side.

You're insane, you know, Saraknyal grumbled.

Yes, well, it'll be a new experience, won't it?

So will dying.

We're not going to die.

Well, I'm not, but...

You're not helping. I stared at the approaching ship, the archers standing in ranks on the broad platform jutting from the bow. Junks evidently didn't have bowsprits like square rigged ships.

"You're sure they'll turn?" I asked Wix.

"Oh, aye, or ram straight into us, which'd kill more of them than us." He barked a laugh. "Don't you worry, lady. They'll come hard to port and rake us, sure as dragon breath reeks!"

"All right then." I cleared my throat, checked the straps securing Soul Drinker to my left forearm, and nodded. "Just give me a shove when it's time. I don't trust myself to get it right."

"Happy to help, lady!"

Foam flew from the warship's bow as it bore down on us. At a hundred yards, the archers fired a volley that whizzed across our deck, but all the Scourges were hunkered behind solid objects. Kivan's high-pitched cry sent a bolt streaking out from our forward ballista; it ripped through the ranks of Toki archers, felling three.

"Good shot!" Longbright bellowed from the wheel.

I spared the admiral a glance. He stood like a statue, hands gripping the spokes, eyes fixed upon the approaching ship. The crew manning the ballista behind him fired, but the bolt only holed one of the junk's sails.

Then, barely fifty yards away, the warship turned hard to port to bring us beam-to-beam. The instant the junk had committed to the turn, Longbright hauled the wheel to port and declared, "Helm's a-lee!"

"Let fly mainsheets and haul the mainbrace!" Wix's bellow rattled my ears.

The huge mainsail below us flapped free, and the great yard swiveled even as *Scourge* veered violently toward the warship. Cries rang out from the Toki quarterdeck, and I watched our bowsprit clip the platform that jutted off the junk's stern.

"Hold tight, lady!" Wix placed a hand at my back and pushed me off the crow's nest.

I may have screamed; I don't remember. I do remember the jerk of the rope, the other end affixed to the end of the mainsail yard as it rotated, fairly flinging me outward like swinging a cat by the tail. The sea swept by below, white with foam from both ships. Toki soldiers manning the junk's quarterdeck stared at me open mouthed. I gritted my teeth and blessed Wix for a saint as my bare feet cleared the stern railing of the warship and my swing came to its peak.

For a moment, I hung there in space some feet above their deck. *Now, Saraknyal!* The leather strap around my arm vanished in a puff of dust, and I landed in a clumsy roll.

So much for swashbuckelry, I thought as I staggered to my feet and drew Soul Drinker. *Now it's time for some necromancery.*

I laughed terror and charged the stunned soldiers.

I have to give them credit, they didn't bolt and scatter. I wish they had.

Swords puffed into rust, soldiers staggered, and Saraknyal fed. Three fell lifeless, soulless, with one broad slash of Soul Drinker. I didn't even bother raising their corpses, but plunged on through them, ignoring their weapons and laying waste to their ranks. Soul Drinker fairly sang with pent up energy when an officer fought to the fore.

Saraknyal warned me just in time. "Enchanted blade!"

I screamed winter, petrifying him and several others. Then, in the second of silence, I reached out and touched the aft-most mast. *Dust to dust.*

A ten-foot piece of the waist-thick spar vanished in a cloud of decayed wood.

I dashed forward as rigging came down in a deadly fall. Crewmen and soldiers screamed and scattered as I vaulted over the forward rail to the middle deck. Another officer slashed at me, but Saraknyal didn't warn me so I just held out a hand to intercept the sword. He stared at me in shock as his sword vanished. Instead of taking his soul, I punched him in the nose with Soul Drinker, then dashed on.

At the mainmast, two armored komei stood at the ready, weapons drawn. I drew a breath to scream, but a ballista cracked barely twenty yards to my left. A wrist-thick bolt whistled past to smash through the two armored warriors.

I spared a glance, and the dark-haired Lieutenant Kivan waved from *Scourge*'s bow, then dashed aft.

Focus, Hashi! Saraknyal screamed in my mind.

Right! I dashed on, touched the mainmast, and reduced it to sawdust. The huge sails collapsed to leeward, shrouds falling to the deck, some with sailors still clinging to them. I barely escaped the falling wreckage in time to meet a thick throng of soldiers led by another komei.

This time I did scream winter, freezing the forward rank solid. The others charged me, several ranks deep, and I couldn't sweep them aside fast enough. I lost my footing amid the fallen and went down.

Get up! You don't have time!

I slashed and stabbed and kicked to keep any of them from getting a solid grip, and each time Soul Drinker touched flesh, Saraknyal fed. My clothes were rent and torn from blades and grasping hands, but I managed to regain my feet. The few soldiers still alive backed away.

Run!

I laughed terror and ran, flying up the steps to the foredeck three at a time. More soldiers faced me there, but I sent a blizzard at them and dashed through before they even fell. Archers on the forward platform fired at me, but the arrows dissolved, and I didn't slow. Two of them leapt over the side rather than face me. The other four dropped their bows, drew swords, and perished with Soul Drinker's insatiable thirst.

I stood alone on the platform, the warship a wreck behind me, and *Scourge* fifty yards ahead, impossibly distant, unreachable.

"I hope this works, old man," I said.

It's a long swim home if it doesn't, he agreed.

A ballista cracked from *Scourge*'s aft deck, and the six-foot shaft flew right at me trailing a stout line behind. I stared at the projectile, gripping Soul Drinker so hard my knuckles popped, the wind fluttering my shredded clothes like streamers.

The iron tip of the bolt struck the bow of the warship beneath my feet, the line trailing behind splashing into the water. I knelt down, grasped the rope at the butt end of the bolt, and slashed once with Soul Drinker. The thick rope parted, and I sheathed the dagger. As the long line began to come taut, I wrapped it around my both wrists, gripped it hard, and jumped.

I hit the warm water hard, and the rope jerked me even harder, wrenching both of my shoulders. I surfaced and managed to gasp a breath before a wave buried me. The rough hemp bit hard into my wrists.

Just don't let go, Hashi!

You think?

I surfaced for another gasped breath and caught the next wave in the face, spitting and sputtering. I couldn't see, of course, but Saraknyal could, and filled my mind with images. Six stout sailors and my wraith-komei were pulling me in fast. I gasped one more breath without choking, and glimpsed the stern windows above me, Preel staring out at me wide-eyed. The rope pulled me up, and I rose from the water like a freshly landed fish, spitting and coughing, blood running down my forearms from the abrasions of the rope. The saltwater stung like fire.

Eager hands reached down to grasp me and help me over the railing, I didn't even touch the deck before someone had a boat cloak over my shoulders, others pounding my back.

"Welcome aboard, Lady Severn!" Longbright grinned. "I daresay the Toki will think twice before they tangle with a necromancer again!"

The crew cheered, and I realized the person holding me, pounding my back, was Tori Blackbriar. "Showoff," he whispered in my ear, but his grin softened the jibe.

The beaming Lieutenant Kivan shouldered through the crowd to take my hands in hers. "That was amazing!"

"And that was an amazing shot that took down those komei." I didn't want to tell her that she might have saved my life.

She blushed and looked down, then her eyes widened. "You're bleeding!"

"Just rope burns." I released her hands and pulled the weather cloak closed, since my shirt was literally in shreds. "Are we in the clear, Admiral?"

"Yes. We've got open water before us, and took little damage. A few arrow wounds, but no one killed." He pointed aft. "At least one of their ships will stop to help them, which will cut their number further. Let's get you below, cleaned up, and bandaged. You can use my quarter gallery for a proper bathe, then we'll bandage those wrists."

"Thank you, Admiral." I nodded to the rest as they broke out in another ragged cheer.

"And if you need any help scrubbing, just let me know," Tori crowed, obviously pleased at my embarrassment.

I glared at him, but the crew only laughed.

"Kivan, you've got the deck. Lady Severn, if you please." Longbright escorted me across the quarterdeck, down the stairs, and aft. He offered me a towel from the wet locker, and I took a moment to swipe off the worst of the sea, wincing at my wrists. "Come on. Hemp!"

"Sir!" His steward poked his head out of the galley. "Hot water?"

"Yes, and bandages after." Longbright took me to the aft cabin.

"Hashi!" Preel stepped up and took me in head to toe. "Are you all right?"

"Bruises and rope burns. That's all." I shrugged out of the weather cloak without too much of a wince. My shoulders had been wrenched badly.

Liar, Saraknyal grumbled. *I can feel your pain, Hashi.*

I'm fine, old man. Honestly.

By the grace of all the gods and devils besides, he said.

But I got to swing like a swashbuckler. Totally worth it.

You're fucking mad.

"Out!" Preel pointed to the door, and I thought for a moment she was talking to me. "Go do something nautical. I'll take care of her. Go!"

Longbright barked a laugh. "Yes, love. Thank you, again, Lady Severn. You literally saved every soul aboard this ship."

The comment hit me like a blow. *And destroyed...how many?*

Do you honestly want me to tell you? Saraknyal asked.

No.

"Here." Preel pulled me toward the tiny washroom set into the corner of the cabin, her eyes still wide as hen's eggs. "You can hand out your...um, well they're pretty much rags. Gods, I don't know how you weren't cut to ribbons!"

"Blades and arrows don't touch me, Preel. I'm okay. Truly."

"Just leave your things on the grating inside then. I'll have Hemp bring you new. Take your time. There's soap and a towel inside. Hot water in two shakes."

I stepped inside and she closed the door.

Silence...

For a moment, I just stood there staring at myself in the shaving mirror, wondering if I'd really just done what I remembered. I struggled out of my shredded shirt, then my pants, cut in a dozen places, but probably worth mending. I unstrapped Soul Drinker, placed it on the basin, and jumped at a knock.

"Yes?"

"Hot water, Hashi. I'll hand it in if you like."

"Thank you, Preel." I opened the door and took the buckets from her, smiling at her averted eyes. "I won't be long."

"Take your time." She closed the door.

I peeled out of my sodden scanties, and took a dipper of the lovely hot water to wash away the salt and blood. I blinked and stared at the woman in the mirror, and, out of the blue, remembered something Kivan had said. *We do what we have to do, and it was worth it...* I dipped more water and reached for the soap, wishing I could wash away my sins so easily.

Chapter Thirty Four
Grim Prospects

From the diary of Kevril Longbright —

It's good to be home, but being chased by a Toki armada puts everything I love in peril. I think it might have been better to leave me where I was, but I look into Preel's eyes and know that's an argument I can't win. My wife has become a force to be reckoned with. Then again, she always was.

A knock at the cabin door woke me from a dead sleep. Preel stirred beside me, and I disentangled myself from her embrace.

"Don't go," she muttered.

"Sorry, love. My watch." Kivan and I had been standing watch-and-watch on the quarterdeck all day and into the night. I slipped out of bed and padded to the door, cracking it just wide enough to tell Hemp, "I'm up. Blackbrew and a biscuit on deck in ten minutes."

"Aye, sir."

I closed the door and turned to my locker, flinging off my nightshirt and rummaging for something decent to wear. Hemp had done his best, but all of my clothes were gone. A light flared from beside the bunk as Preel turned up the lamp.

"You should assign Wix a watch. You're exhausted." She got out of bed.

"He's already standing double watches." I snatched some clean linens from a drawer and pulled them on.

"I just got you back." She strode over and clutched me in her arms. "I deserve a little more time with you."

"You do, but..." Truth be told, our reunion had been both cathartic and heart-wrenching. I wanted nothing more than to spend a week in bed with my wife, but lives depended on me, and more lives than those aboard *Scourge*. She knew that as well as I did. I held her for a moment, relishing the feel of her against me. "You could come up on deck for a while. Watch the stars with me."

"Okay, I will." Preel released me and flung off her nightshirt.

I couldn't help but watch her cross the cabin, the soft lamplight caressing her dusky skin. "You're torturing me on purpose."

"What?" She turned halfway, giving me a sultry smile. "Who, *me*?"

I glared and growled, "Yes *you*, Mrs. Longbright!" I snatched a pair of trousers and pulled them on before things went awry.

"Spoiled sport." Preel dressed in the dark nokitu garb instead of a sari. "Better?"

"Not better, but at least I'll be able to walk without injuring myself." I donned a jacket that had belonged to the Toki captain, altered by Hemp, and slipped the komei sword through my belt. "A stroll on deck, Mrs. Longbright?"

"Delighted, Admiral Longbright."

We left the cabin, and I paused long enough to tell Hemp Preel was accompanying me on deck.

"Cuppa tea, Lady?" He asked with a grin.

"Please."

We both donned boat cloaks and ventured out into the night. We were running without lights, the stern gallery windows draped, so we took a moment for our eyes to adjust before climbing to the quarterdeck. Kivan met us with a salute. "Evening, Admiral. Lady Preel."

"Kivan. Anything to report?" I swept the night horizon with my eyes.

"Our pursuers are persistent. Eight warships in sight. I think they sent the rest back to Hyko. No lights visible to the south. Open sea, fair winds, all the sail she'll bear."

"Very well. Hit your bunk. I've got the deck."

"Thank you, sir." She saluted again and hurried below.

Preel took my arm and we stood in silence while the watch changed. I gauged the sailors, tired but hale, their morale good. Once everyone was settled, and Hemp had delivered our midnight repast, I checked our heading and the logbook, ordered the log run, and scanned the horizon with a spyglass. Of course the lookout perched at the maintop would have a better view, but I found the simple routine comforting. The eight lights on the horizon behind us were less comforting.

Preel took my arm again. "Do you think we have a chance?"

"Yes, a better one than we had twelve hours ago." I put my spyglass away and pulled her close. "It all depends on whether or not a fleet has been assembled when we arrive at Twin Capes."

"And if there isn't one?"

"Then we have few options. Try to lose our escort in the dark, sail for Haven, Sariff, or Black Point, and hope some kind of armada has been assembled somewhere." I sighed and rubbed my eyes. "I don't have many more tricks left."

"What about Hashi?"

"I hate to rely on her too much," I admitted. "She can do things that...well, give me nightmares, frankly, but she's still mortal."

"I'm not too sure about that." Preel shivered, though the night was warm enough. "Her shirt was slashed to ribbons, and she didn't have one cut."

"But the rope sure left marks on her wrists. Hemp told me they were pretty bad, and she's moving stiffly, too, if you notice. Not like she did before."

"Bruised, she said, though I don't know if she's telling the truth. She doesn't...trust."

"Well, we're trusting *her*," I said. "With our lives, in fact."

"True, and she's proven worthy of that trust, but..." Preel shook her head, the wind ruffling her short hair. "I just don't know. It's like she...hates what she is, or something."

"What, being a necromancer?" I hadn't thought of that before, but it made a strange connection in my mind. "Maybe. I don't think I can help her with that."

"We could...try. I don't know, be friendlier. Show her she can trust us not to betray her."

"I don't know how we *could* betray her, love. She's a loner and likes it that way. She made that clear, remember?"

"So were you when you found me." She gave me a nudge and a smile. "Now look at you."

I chuckled and pulled her close, deep in thought. "We've got at least one more day before we reach Twin Capes. How about we have our two council members in for dinner tomorrow, talk out our options, try to pull her out a bit. That Blackbriar's certainly gregarious enough."

"Yes, and she's friendly enough with him, but..." Preel sighed and put her head against my shoulder. "Something's hurt her badly, Kevril. Maybe long ago, but it's left scars."

"Then let's have them to dinner and discuss our situation. Hemp's told me *Scourge* is well provisioned, and he's learned some skills from Bert. He could put on a dinner easily enough."

"Good." Preel squeezed my arm and yawned. "I think I'm going to turn in."

"All right." I kissed her. "Goodnight, love."

"Wake me when you come off watch." She reached under my jacket and teased me with her fingernails. "I'll make it worth your while."

"Now *that's* something to live for!" I laughed and kissed her gain, watching her go with an ache in my heart. Once again, she'd saved me, but it had put her in horrible danger.

Morning brought few surprises. Open sea and an array of sails in our wake, some of them significantly closer. I'd once thought *Scourge* could outsail any junk on the sea, but I'd only ever tangled with merchantmen and the Sariff Navy, not Toki warships. Toki shipwrights knew their business. When I handed the watch over to Kivan for the Forenoon, I asked her opinion, more as an exercise than anything, but she surprised me.

"I think we should spill some wind and let them close, sir."

"For what reason?" I asked with a raised eyebrow.

"Bait for the trap, sir." She waved a hand to the south. "This time tomorrow, we'll have Twin Capes broad to windward. Even if Haven hasn't gotten a fleet together, Rauley and Boxley are there, and the chiefs won't like a Toki armada off their shore. They'll be ready."

Chris A. Jackson

"Canoes and spears against warships?"

"Oh, it'll be a right mess, sir, but Islanders don't like empires."

"That's true. Thank you, Kivan. I need to get some rest."

"Aye, sir!" She snapped a salute.

I turned to go, then stopped. "And Kivan?"

"Sir?" She turned to face me, attentive and sharp, as I'd come to expect from her.

"You've matured into quite an impressive young officer. I'm pleased."

Her face flushed pink. "Thank you, sir."

"If we survive this engagement, you may very well end up with your own ship. Haven is desperately short of captains, at least ones with real naval experience. What do you think about that?"

She looked a little shocked, then surprisingly introspective before she answered. "All things considered, sir, I think you'll need a proper first officer. Miko's going to have her own ship, and you won't have anyone to fill her boots. I'd rather stay, if at all possible, sir."

"All right, then." I swallowed the lump in my throat and nodded. "Consider yourself my first. I'll expect you to live up to that position and whip our midshipmen into proper young officers. You'll speak your mind whenever you feel you need to, and inform me when I'm making a mistake. I'll *also* expect you to survive this encounter with the Toki Navy." I glared at her. "If you get killed, I'll be *quite* cross with you, young woman!"

She beamed and snapped me a salute. "Aye, sir! I won't disappoint you!"

"See that you don't." I left the quarterdeck, considering how things might play out in the future...if we survived.

Chapter Thirty Five
Among Friends

From the journal of Hashi Severn —
I never thought to have so much, nor to be so afraid to lose it all.

I knocked on the great cabin door with some mild trepidation, unsure why Longbright would go to the trouble to have Tori and I over for a dinner while we were being chased by a Toki armada. Naval officers seemed to exude calm in dire situations, probably leading by example to bolster the morale of their crews. Necromancers didn't have to worry about morale.

The door opened and Longbright waved me in with a smile. "Welcome, Lady Severn."

"Thank you, Admiral, and—" As I ducked under the door frame, I came up short. Preel was dressed in a beautiful sari, but no veil, the admiral wore a dress jacket with epaulets, and even Tori had managed to bring along a dress shirt and riding pants. The table had been arrayed in white linen, silver, and porcelain all lit by a blaze of candlelight. Thick drapes had been pulled to cover the stern gallery windows, giving the cabin a warm feel without being stuffy. I felt like a beggar dressed in flat black pants and shirt. "I wasn't expecting anything formal. I—"

"Oh, don't worry. I'm wearing a Toki officer's jacket!" Longbright laughed and strode for a locker that sported a fully stocked bar. "Luckily, they hadn't pillaged my wine cellar fully. I've got just about anything you'd like, I think."

"Brandy, please."

"And you look positively stunning in basic black, my dear," Tori assured me, his usual grin intact.

"I managed to tuck one sari into my sea bag." Preel greeted me with a two-handed clasp and a warm smile. "We're not standing on ceremony, so please be welcome. We want to thank you for what you've done, both of you, and just have a nice evening."

"Yes, tomorrow may prove challenging, so drink deep and live for today!" Tori raised his wine glass as Longbright passed me a snifter. "Here's to giving the Toki Navy another black eye!"

"I'll drink to that!" Longbright raised a tumbler, and we all toasted.

The brandy warmed my throat and filled me with a fruity glow. "This is very good, Admiral. You have good taste."

"I'm glad you like it, and please, it's Kevril." He waved to the table. "Please, everyone have a seat. I'm afraid Hemp's not quite up to my usual cook's standards, but we must make do, mustn't we?"

An array of soft and hard cheeses, sliced sausages, and thin crispy biscuits adorned a silver platter in the center of the table. They were laid out with the precision of a gnomish locksmith, as were the plates, glasses, and silver.

"I'm not used to such finery," I admitted.

"Especially from a former pirate!" Tori plucked a wedge of cheese and a biscuit from the platter. "You do well for yourself, Kevril."

"We enjoy a few comforts." He shrugged and stacked a slice of sausage on cheese on a biscuit for himself. "Please, feel free. Hemp's preparing a searaker for the main course. I hope your stomach has settled enough to enjoy it."

"I seem to be acclimating, thank you." I sampled a bit of cheese with a biscuit. The salty biscuit with the sharp cheese went down nicely. "You wanted to talk about our situation."

"Yes, but it needn't cast a shadow on our evening." He waved vaguely at the stern windows. "At Kivan's suggestion, we spilled a bit of wind from our sails to slow us down somewhat. If we're fortunate, they'll be in close company when we reach Twin Capes."

"And Hashi's trap is sprung!" Tori raised a glass to me. "Another brilliant idea."

"Brilliant until it goes wrong," I retorted.

"Which is why I wanted to talk to you both." Kevril constructed another stack of cheese, sausage, biscuit, and munched. "We can at the *very* least expect some help from the islanders, though I don't know exactly what form that help will take. Timing is everything, but if we don't meet at least six of our own ships there, I'll be astounded."

"I met *Blood Raven*'s captain, Red Moll. She seemed...enthusiastic." She'd seemed more than that after a few drinks at the Folly, but I wasn't about to mention that.

"She is, and I know we can depend on Miko, Patak, Niland and the two smaller ships, *White Lady* and *First Light*. The others..." Kevril shrugged.

"Tan will show up, I feel confident," Tori added.

"That's seven, but three are smaller ships." I sampled more cheese with cracker and sipped my brandy. "Against..."

"Eight warships. Three lesser, like the one you disabled, four three-masted ships that can fire twelve ballista on a side, with maybe three-hundred aboard, and the admiral's flagship." Kevril grimaced and sipped his drink. "That's a beast I'd rather not tangle with; twenty ballistae per side and likely seven hundred aboard."

Lambs to the slaughter, Saraknyal muttered.

Don't get cocky, old man.

"One other advantage we have is me," Preel piped in for the first time. "We can ask one more question late tonight, but we haven't decided if we should." She looked to her husband.

"It *would* be valuable to know how many ships will be waiting for us at Twin Capes," Tori said.

"Yes, it would, but it'd also leave Preel unconscious for twelve hours. If something should happen, she'd be defenseless."

"About that," Tori began, swirling his wine, "and you'll forgive me, Preel, but it seems to me that you should be in the possession of the god-emperor by now. Surely, during your slavery, word of your talents spread."

"Simple, Tori," she smiled thinly, "greed and fear."

"Fear of letting her secret out." I nodded. "Even Brilla wasn't fool enough to let *that* slip. It would have started a war in Haven, and anyone who has half a wit would see the same. If one of the god-emperor's truthseekers found out about you, the emperor's spies would stop at nothing to find and take you."

"Exactly. The curse of the dove that laid diamond eggs." Preel looked to her husband with an adoring smile. "I simply got lucky enough to be taken as plunder by a pirate who's not a rapacious scoundrel."

Tori coughed a laugh that nearly spewed wine, and I gaped at her remark.

Kevril just laughed. "A private joke, I'm afraid."

"And one that I'm not afraid to share with our new friends," Preel countered, reaching out to clasp his hand. "When Kevril found me, I thought I was doomed to yet another cruel master. I'd already had several, you see, and I expected nothing else."

"That's horrific," Tori said. "With your talent..."

"Some men like to own unique and dangerous things," I said. "It makes them feel powerful."

"Yes," Preel shrugged. "Anyway, when Kevril found out what I was, he at first intended nothing more than to sell me for a king's ransom, though he was smart enough to see the danger in that. While he decided what to do with me, he kept me safe right here in this cabin. He told me flat out that I didn't need to fear abuse from him. I'd heard about pirates, you see, and..."

"And I assured her that I wasn't a rapacious scoundrel." He squeezed her hand.

"Yes, and he was telling the truth." She gazed at him adoringly. "Then I struck a bargain with him; I'd help him free himself from Jhavika's enchantment, and he would free me in kind."

"And you did." I stared at Kevril Longbright in a new light, and began to understand how he'd deserved such loyalty from his officers and crew.

"Yes, well, I agreed to, but that was before..." He shrugged. "Seeing what Preel had gone through, then her willingness to help me...changed me somehow."

"You fell in love," Tori said, glancing at me. "The one thing that can change anyone."

I looked away from him and sipped my brandy, wondering if he was alluding to me or Saraknyal. Maybe both. I guarded my thoughts and sampled another wedge of cheese.

A knock at the door couldn't have come at a better time. Hemp entered with a platter the size of an infantryman's shield. A single fish lay atop that platter, raised on a mound of roasted potatoes, and surrounded by stewed vegetables, greens, and fruit.

"A noble fish!" Tori crowed.

"Aye, and tasty." Kevril stood to make room for Hemp to place and serve the meal, refilling glasses generously.

Hemp dished small portions onto my plate, at my behest. My stomach felt moderately steady, but a heavy meal and alcohol might prove disastrous. Kevril encouraged us to all begin as Hemp finished serving, and I tried a bite of the flakey white fish. Buttery, mild, and spiced with lemon, garlic, and pepper, it melted in my mouth.

"Delicious, Hemp," I complemented.

He beamed with pleasure. "Glad you like it, Lady Severn."

"Careful, Hashi, you'll give him a swelled head!" Kevril laughed at his steward's scowl.

"Kevril!" Preel swatted him on the flank. "Be nice!"

"Well it is nice to have a *bit* of appreciation now and again, it is! Not like some sea captains who go and get captured by a bunch of Toki goons and have to be rescued by *this* fine lady!"

Kevril just laughed at the remark, and I noted a hidden smile from Hemp as he turned away.

"Save room for dessert! I found a jar of Bert's tartberry preserves, and made a crumble."

"We stand forewarned! Thank you, Hemp!" Kevril sat and raised his glass. "Here's to surly stewards and sultry truthsayers! One captures the stomach and the other the heart!"

Preel blushed but raised her glass.

I found myself smiling and joined them in toast.

"And to the most striking Lady Severn!" Tori chimed in, ignoring my glare. "May her stern façade one day crumble to the humble attentions of an emissary to the house of Tree and Star."

"Tori, if you don't stop trying to..." I faltered at a loss for words.

I've got enough energy for you to freeze him solid, if you like, Saraknyal offered.

"House of Tree and Star?" Preel eyed Tori with a furrowed brow. "Isn't that the house of the Elvin Council?"

"It is," Tori admitted with a nod and a smile. "Of which I am a member, albeit a lowly one."

"But you have to actually be a pure-blooded high elf to be..." Preel's eyes widened. "You're not, are you?"

"Alas, I am." Tori just smiled and shrugged. "This countenance is but a façade, I'm afraid."

"Tori!" I nudged him under the table, astonished at his admission.

"Well, it seems only fair, don't you think?" He raised his glass again. "I mean we know Preel's secret, and truthsayers are much more rare in the world than elves! Why, there's a pure-blooded elf singing at Fancy's Folly! That's hardly caused a kerfuffle, has it?"

"Illian?" Preel looked startled. "You know her?"

"Only in passing. Not as well as your first mate, Miko, I daresay!" Tori nodded to me. "I suggested to Hashi that she go see her perform. Her voice is truly—"

"Astounding," I cut in. "Yes, it is. *She* is, rather."

Tori gaped at me. "You went?"

"Yes, with Captain Moll, as a matter of fact." I sipped my brandy and took another bite of the wonderful fish, utterly satisfied with the look of startlement on Tori's face.

"You went out to the Folly with Red Moll and didn't get into a brawl?" Kevril raised his glass to me. "Yet another achievement of note!"

"Well, she *did* offer to stick one young man's rapier up his arse if he didn't leave us alone, but all in all, there was no bloodshed."

Everyone laughed, and I found myself smiling.

Was that a sense of humor? Saraknyal quipped.

Oh, shut up, old man. I have a perfectly good sense of humor!

Oh, yes, and I have a perfectly good appreciation for gnomish architecture!

I snorted a quiet laugh.

"Something funny, Hashi?" Tori eyed me sidelong.

"Oh, nothing." I covered my lapse with another bite and a sip of brandy, and changed the subject. "So, Kevril, what do you plan to do if we *don't* meet up with a sufficient fleet to face the Toki armada?"

"Well, I don't intend to fight a losing battle. We're not martyrs.

If we have a few allied ships, we might harass the smaller vessels, maybe take one of the middle sized ones, man it with islanders and a competent commander, then slip away without losing too much, I'd count ourselves lucky."

"And leave the islanders of Twin Capes to fend for themselves?" Tori asked.

"The chiefs aren't fools." Kevril reached for the bottle of wine Preel and Tori were sharing and topped up their glasses. "They may have already retreated into the jungle, for all I know, and I couldn't blame them."

"Another possible question for my talent," Preel said.

"But if the Toki take the city..." I looked from face to face.

"They'll find themselves beset on one side by islanders and our rag-tag fleet on the other. Twin Capes has no deep draft approach to shore, which means they'd have to invade by boat, which would be costly. It's not as valuable a port as Hyko, and, of course, they can't resupply by land."

"The god-emperor's military advisors aren't fools, certainly," Tori said with a nod. "Taking Hyko was the logical and tactically sound first step. Next they must neutralize naval opposition."

"And General Koto told me exactly that. He seemed confident; two thousand soldiers and a hundred komei aboard fifteen ships. That's certainly enough to take any of the island city states, and probably Haven, or at least blockade them. Sariff, on the other hand, would be a harder nut to crack."

"If they try to invade Sariff, the jaguar warriors will eat them alive," I said. "They're consummate jungle warriors, and fearless."

"Sounds like you're speaking from first-hand knowledge," Kevril said.

I nodded. "I was forced to flee Sariff, and the king sent a team of jaguar warriors after me. They tracked me in the dark, and very nearly killed me."

"How many?" Tori asked.

"Six. Two survived." I took up my snifter, sipped, and choked when I took too much. "Sorry."

"Don't be," Kevril said. "We've all done things we're not proud of in the interest of survival."

"There are no pacifists in nature," Tori added, raising his glass. "Here's to survival."

"Here, here!" Kevril and Preel raised their glasses, and I complied, though my heart wasn't in it.

"I have a question for you, Hashi, but I must phrase it carefully." The admiral smiled at his wife. "That trick you do where you dissolve metal or wood. I assume it won't work on enchanted weapons. That's why you're concerned about komei."

And Tori's elf blade, Saraknyal reminded me.

"Yes, it doesn't work on anything enchanted, or metals that resist decay, gold or silver, for instance." I didn't mention stone, since there wasn't a lot aboard ship.

"And size is no object. You destroyed that ship's mainmast with a touch."

"Well, I don't think I could destroy an entire ship, if that's what you're asking, but..."

Only if you want to drown.

"Interesting..." Kevril swirled his tumbler and pursed his lips.

"What are you thinking, Kevril?" Preel asked.

"Oh, just tactics, love." He flashed her a smile then tilted his glass to me. "Aside from dismasting, there are several points of a ship that are critical to holding the hull together. The keel timber, for instance. Destroy that, and the ship will open up like a mussel in a stew."

"The trick would be getting out alive with the ship coming apart around me." I swirled my brandy and realized that my plate was empty. I wasn't truly hungry anymore, but that fish had been delicious. I resisted taking a second helping.

"Yes, you *can* drown, I suppose," Tori said.

"I suppose I can, though I've never tried." I smiled at him, then nodded to our host. "So, I'm not invulnerable, no, but if a Toki warship comes up alongside, I can...dissuade them."

"Okay, good to know." Kevril sipped his drink and patted his middle. "Well, that was delicious, but if nobody wants another round, I'll have Hemp clear."

"No, thank you." I dabbed my mouth with my napkin and set it aside.

"I'm saving myself for tartberry crumble," Preel said with a smile.

"And I," Tori declared. "Delicious fare indeed, Admiral. I hate to see it go to waste."

"Oh, it won't. It'll be chowder for the crew by morning watch, I'm sure. Hemp!"

The steward appeared before the echo died. "Ready to clear, sir?"

"Yes, and some port with dessert, please. That was delicious, Hemp."

"Glad you liked it, sir." Hemp took the platter, handed it to a sailor, then cleared our plates with an economy of brisk movements. For such a raggedy fellow, he knew his way around the table, and obviously took pride in his work.

"You command a great deal of loyalty from your people, Admiral," I commented. "They seem utterly devoted to you."

"Necessary aboard ship," he said. "And they're devoted to me because I'm devoted to them. Tyranny afloat is a recipe for disaster."

"Tyranny of any sort is a recipe for rebellion," Tori added with a respectful nod.

I remembered Miras' betrayal and said, "Not only tyranny, I've found."

"Oh?" Kevril looked shocked. "I wouldn't think a necromancer had to worry about mutiny."

"Anyone who wields power has to worry about betrayal, Admiral. Even necromancers."

"Sea captains aren't immune to that, certainly." He glanced to Preel, and reached out to take her hand. "We've all experienced it, one way or another. I find the only solution is to remove the threat swiftly and permanently."

"Well, that's one advantage of necromancy," I said with a wry smile. "The person who tried to stab me in the gut is now one of my minions. Showing everyone her fate cut down on future instances of betrayal."

"Kevril also made an example of the man who betrayed us." Preel squeezed her husband's hand hard. "In *spectacular* fashion."

"Well, I wouldn't call it spectacular, but it did set a precedent."

He smiled ruefully.

"Elves are also quite experienced with betrayal, which is why we tend to keep ourselves separate from other cultures." Tori raised his wineglass to us. "Or, in my case, disguised."

"So, if I might ask," Preel began, "if you're not really a dishonored duelist escaping the Fengotherond Court, why are you here?"

"Investigating the region at the behest of the Elvin Council." Tori grinned. "And, of course, in search of wine, women, and song."

"You'd get along famously with Miko, then!" Kevril laughed. "She's made a career of all three."

"Including enjoying Illian's intimate company, yes, I know." Tori grinned and looked at me sidelong. "We all have something to fight for, to risk our lives for, don't we, Hashi?"

"Yes, I suppose we do." I gave him a tight smile. "Mine is to be left alone."

He opened his mouth to reply, but Hemp returned with a tray and a stack of small plates. "Tartberry crumble!"

"Saved by dessert," I said. "Your timing is perfect, Hemp."

"Oh, I lurk with my ear against the door for just the right moment!" He cackled a laugh as he placed the bubbling dish and plates.

"Which is why we have a lock on our door," Kevril retorted.

"Yes, they say there are no secrets aboard ship." Tori nodded as Hemp placed tiny crystal glasses and offered port. "That must be challenging for you, a loving couple with so little privacy."

"Not so much," Preel smiled and nodded to Hemp. "We're blessed with such a devoted crew."

"Well earned, from what I've seen," I added, trading my empty snifter for a glass of port. "I spoke briefly with Kivan. She fairly idolizes you, Admiral."

"Well, she's turned into an amazing young officer, and I'm quite proud of her. Boxley, too, for that matter." He sighed as Hemp served out the dessert. "The attrition rate among young pirates, however, is sometimes difficult to handle."

"The first rule of war is that people die." Tori sampled his dessert and arched an eyebrow. "Dealing with loss is a life-long career. Elves live a very long time."

Maybe that's why they're such insufferable snobs, Saraknyal quipped.

"Here's to living for today, free and beholden to none!" Kevril raised his glass and we all followed.

"Indeed, Admiral, I'll drink to that." I sipped and sampled the crumble, tart and sweet at the same time. "In fact, I think that would make a good motto for the entire Blood Sea Protectorate, if it ever comes together. Each member free, yet part of a greater whole, independent, but unified."

"Agreed!" The admiral beamed. "If Haven's Council ever quits squabbling amongst themselves, no slight intended."

"None taken!" Tori chuckled. "Governments are messy things, especially when they're young."

"Says the elf older than any government in the world," I said.

Tori barked a laugh, but Kevril and Preel stared slack-jawed.

"Um..." Kevril cleared his throat. "Well, *that's* something."

"Everything is something, and nothing is nothing! Ha!" Tori raised his glass. "Here's to years and fears and tears, none of them worth my pointy ears!"

I grimaced. "Oh, that was *dreadful*, Tori!"

"Oh, if you think *that* was dreadful, you haven't heard the one about a pirate, an elf, a necromancer, and a truthsayer who walk into a bar!"

We all laughed, but he wasn't finished.

"The bartender asked what they'd have, and the truthsayer said, 'Brandy, wine, whiskey, and a good night's sleep.' The bartender started to say they didn't rent rooms, but the truthsayer was already snoring!"

We all groaned and laughed, and Preel blushed, dabbing her eyes with her napkin.

When our mirth died down, Preel asked, "So, you've actually met other truthsayers?"

"Yes. Three others, but you're by far the prettiest." He raised his glass to her.

She blushed again, and I glared at Tori. "You'll have to forgive Lord Blackbriar. He's cursed with two thousand years of pent up libido."

"Alas, it's true," Tori admitted with a sigh. "And a surplus of charm and good looks."

"Yet not a whit of modesty," I countered.

"Modesty is highly overrated, my dear," he said.

"Said the man without a whit of modesty." I grinned and raised my glass to him. "We can do this all night, but I'd rather enjoy the admiral's hospitality. This port is wonderful, and the crumble..."

"I'm delighted that you're enjoying yourself, Hashi." Kevril glanced at Preel, then back to me. "We were afraid you wouldn't appreciate the overture. You made it clear when we met that you didn't want friendship."

"Yes, well, I don't generally socialize." I took a tiny bite of crumble and chased it with a sip of port, savoring the flavors.

"You're a most complicated woman, Hashi," Tori said.

"Not really. I'm just wrong occasionally."

More than occasionally, Saraknyal added.

"Wrong?" Preel looked perplexed. "About what?"

"About people." I gave her a smile and swallowed hard. "I've never had any luck with friendships, you see, so I...decided that I didn't need people. It's safer for me that way, or at least I thought so." I sighed and shook my head. "I've never...had such a wonderful evening; never had...friends. Anyone I felt comfortable being myself with. So, I'm very happy to be proven wrong."

"To friends." Admiral Longbright raised his glass.

"To friends," Tori echoed.

Preel raised her glass to me, smiling with a warmth that filled my heart.

"Yes," I agreed, raising my glass, "to friends." Then I thought, *And that includes you, old man.*

I'm...touched, Hashi. Thank you.

You're welcome.

Chapter Thirty Six
Beholden to One

From the diary of Kevril Longbright —
A friend in need is the most welcome friend of all, I've found.

We decided to hold off on employing Preel's talent. If the need arose, we could always ask an urgent question, but we agreed that we'd both prefer her to be awake for the coming conflict.

The morning dawned to low clouds threatening squalls, but clear air. The isle of Twin Capes loomed high to the southeast, and the cape effect winds on the northern point forced us to reef sails. Our pursuers spilled wind rather than reefing, their lug-sails more easily managed, and gained a bit. The Toki fleet sailed in a precise formation barely two miles astern, the flagship in the center, lesser vessels arrayed in a staggered double V, poised to break any direction to envelop their prey.

That prey was us.

"Admiral Miaku's no fool," Tori said.

"No, he's not." I scanned the palm-lined shore all the way down to the southern point. "I'm wondering if *we* are. I see no sign of any ships or islanders."

Preel touched my arm, showing me the page of her notebook. "Should we ask about allies?"

"Not quite yet, love. We'll see what happens." The howling wind eased, and I ordered the reefs shaken free of the sails. Short-handed, it took longer than it should have, and we lost some of our lead.

We sailed on, about half a mile from the shore, just far enough that the winds weren't too fluky. All the ships lost headway in the lighter air. I scanned the shore again. Nothing.

Hemp arrived on the quarterdeck with a pot of blackbrew and

another of tea. I took a cup, but everyone else declined. Hashi stood at the taffrail, silent and grim with her wraith komei at her side, glaring at the Toki armada as if she could destroy them with her gaze alone.

"Deck there! They're putting out sweeps!"

"Bugger!" I raised my spyglass and saw that the three smaller warships had indeed put out long sweeps. That wouldn't help their speed much, sailing as we were, but it would add to their maneuverability and allow them to make way to windward, cutting off one avenue of evasion to us.

"Sail off the cape!" called out the foretop lookout, and I wheeled around to scan the sea to the south.

I saw nothing but the occasional white crest of a wave. "Where away?"

"She's a small craft, sir! Maybe a fishing smack!"

"Boxley?" I wondered aloud, then raised my voice. "Can you tell me if it's the *Gull*?"

"No, sir! She's hull down."

"I might be able to give you more information aloft, Admiral," Tori offered. "Sharp eyes, and all that."

I gave him the nod. "Take a glass from the locker."

He delved the locker, tucked a spyglass through his belt, and dashed forward. I watched him scramble up the ratlines like a spider, flip up to the crow's nest, then climb up to the topgallant yard as if he'd been doing it all his life. He settled in beside my lookout, one arm and one leg around the flagstaff, and brought the spyglass to his eye.

I waited, chewing a nail to the quick. Preel gripped my arm and gave me a questioning look. "We'll know soon, love."

She nodded, and I could see her nervousness. Busashi and his nokitu had taken up duties as common seamen, a welcome addition, but if it came to a fight, I'd prefer they protect Preel. We'd argued about that, and she'd won. If we were going to maneuver *Scourge* in battle, we needed sailors.

"Admiral!" Tori called from the foremast. "The smack's flying one black jib! I can't be certain, but I think it's—"

A haunting song from windward cut him off, drawing every eye on the ship. A single soaring note, at first, then joined by others, then a chorus, varying in tone, rising on the wind from the depths of the jungle.

"Conch horns," I realized. The multi-tonal song rose and spread like fire to the north and south, dozens, scores, then hundreds, all howling out their unnerving tones. "Gods and devils deliver us, I think..."

They came from the jungle in a wave, painted and tattooed, feathered and masked, some bearing shields, others shouldering great outrigger war canoes, all of them howling ululating cries of war. They hit the low surf as one, plunging forth, clambering aboard their narrow-hulled crafts and taking up broad-bladed paddles. A few larger vessels sporting twin hulls bound together with timbers, raised masts and deployed woven frond sails, rowers thrashing the sea to propel them away from shore into the wind.

Hundreds of islanders, easily, perhaps a thousand, strove forth. Warriors stood in the bows, shields raised, blowing into their conch horns and shaking spears at the Toki armada.

"Landward warships breaking formation!" the mizzen lookout called.

Two of the larger ships broke away from the rest, angling to intercept the fleet of islanders, but it was like trying to swat a swarm of gnats with a sword. The fleet of war canoes covered an area more than a mile long, but instead of evading the larger ships, those nearest converged.

"Canoes and spears against warships..." My heart rose in my throat. I wanted to do something, to turn and attack, but with a complement of only forty souls aboard, what could we do?

"Admiral, what's that?"

I turned at Hashi's question. She pointed northwest at a nameless scrap of rocky island...and a triangle of red sails. "Lookout! Ship to the northwest!" Then, as I raised my spyglass, another sail, then another, and another, these all black, edged from behind the rocky isle. "Four ships!"

"*Blood Raven* in the van, sir! The others... *White Lady, Rogue,* and *First Light!* Sailing close hauled, east sou-east, right up their arses!"

"Well, that's four." I grinned to Preel. "And the Toki don't seem to have spotted them yet."

She nodded, but still looked worried. I couldn't blame her. We both knew what would happen to her if she was captured.

"The islanders are engaging!" the lookout called down, and I raised my spyglass.

War canoes raced forth, shields bristling with arrows as they closed in, some islanders falling or slumping, obviously injured or dead. On the rowers struggled, and spears flew. I couldn't see the windward side of the nearer warship where the bulk of the islanders struck, but I saw that some of them gained the deck. How many, I couldn't tell.

Fire blossomed on the deck of the second ship; probably flaming oil thrown from the islanders. Thrashing figures trailed in the wakes of both ships, and I ground my teeth. People were dying, and I was fleeing.

"Admiral!" Kivan called out from forward. I whirled to see her pointing off our port bow. "There, sir! The bigger craft! It's Master Rauley!"

"Rauley?" I raised my glass, and saw a mass of Haven sailors aboard the vessel with perhaps thirty more islanders. They were angling toward us, and a figure on the bow of the nearer hull waved. "Sonofabitch! Helmsman, a point to port! Boarding nets over the port side, Wix!"

Preel tugged on my arm and pointed. One of the inshore warship's sails blossomed into flames, and the deck of the other swarmed with dark-skinned islanders. Blood ran in rivulets from the scuppers. More war canoes were angling south to intercept the rest of the armada, while the three corsairs to the northwest beat hard to windward, cracking on with all sail in the higher offshore winds, closing fast.

"An hour," I estimated. "We'll never hold on that long."

"Turn and fight." Hashi left the rail to face us. "Take your people aboard, then engage them."

"Even with help, we'll be outnumbered two to one," I told her.

She grinned at me without humor. "Not for long, Admiral. Just get me aboard. I'll even the odds for you."

I thought for a moment, then nodded. "One of the smaller

ships. If we can take one intact, Kivan can take command with Rauley and the islanders. We'll have another ship."

"Exactly."

Preel tugged my arm again and held out her notebook. "Both ships will be undermanned."

"Initially, yes, but more islanders will join us." They were already closing on the other ships, but about a third of their entire force was either occupied aboard the two Toki warships closer to shore, or dead. "Better to fight them from a ship than a canoe!"

"Islander vessel comin' alongside!" Wix bellowed.

Whoever conned that craft knew their business. They swerved at the last possible moment to parallel our course on the windward side. Islanders and Scourges clambered aboard, easily forty in all, a skeleton crew staying aboard the strange craft to veer away. Rauley and Kivan embraced, and he handed her a bundle of blue cloth. She shrugged into her lieutenant's jacket and slipped her komei katana through her belt, her face beaming.

"Master Rauley to the quarterdeck, if you please!" I shouted, and my grinning sailing master sprinted for the stairs.

"Sir!" He mounted the stairs and snapped a salute. "Reporting for duty, sir!"

"Excellent! Take the helm and tell me what in the names of all Nine Hells is going on."

"Aye, sir! Red Moll filled us in yesterday." Rauley took the wheel in his hands as he spoke. "Don't know exactly what happened in Valaka. They sent Lady Severn's smugglers there to talk to the dragonlords. Sariff says they're considering the proposal. The Council sent two of Balshi's ships with emissaries to show they're serious. Ton Chi, Black Point, and Twin Capes are on board with the Protectorate. They supplied warriors to bolster our shipboard forces."

"More than four ships, I hope."

"Yes, sir!" He pointed to the south. "They should be showing themselves any... There!"

"Ships rounding the cape!" Tori cried from the foretop at that very moment.

I strode to the windward rail and raised my spyglass. Four ships rounded the southern cape in tight formation.

"*Golden Harlot*, *Tiger Lily*, *Temoin*, and *Sea Drake*, sir, and they're manned to the gills. *Sea Drake*'s got near a *thousand* aboard!"

I estimated the distance, about five miles, then turned to focus my glass on *Blood Raven* and the other two pirates closing in from the northwest. "Forty minutes if they crack on." I turned to Hashi. "Lady Severn, I can't wait that long. If we sail on, they may double back and attack the four corsairs. We need to cause enough trouble to keep the Toki armada busy for forty minutes."

Her teeth flashed very white. "Get me aboard those ships, Admiral Longbright, and there won't *be* a Toki armada in forty minutes."

"Very well! Master Rauley, prepare to wear ship. Master Wix, we're going to raise some hell! Kivan, man the forward ballista! If you see komei, kill them!"

They all replied affirmative, Wix more colorfully than the others.

I turned to Preel. "Things are going to get dicey, love. You'd best go below."

Preel shook her head emphatically. We'd fought about this, too, but I didn't intend to lose this argument.

"Preel, we're going to take fire. Archers and ballistae. One arrow..."

She gripped my arm and glared at me, scrawling in her notebook, "I will NOT hide below while everyone I love risks their lives!"

"Preel, I—"

"Admiral, please, can I suggest a solution." Hashi stepped up to us. "I can assign my wraith and some shades to protect you both. They're all but invulnerable to injury barring dismemberment. They'll see neither of you is harmed, and she can stay here with you." She grinned. "Besides, she's not as helpless as you presume."

Preel nodded and looked up to me pleadingly.

I glared all around, but I had to admit, the komei wraith and ten shades would be a formidable defense. "Fine! Do it!"

"Wraith, you will see to Preel's safety above all other concerns."

"Yes, mistress." The armored wraith took a stance beside my wife, hand on his sword, black eyes unflinching behind his komei mask.

Hashi called up her shades and stationed them around the quarterdeck with orders to defend it.

"All right, then! Wix, prepare to wear ship!"

"Ready, sir!"

"Rauley, port your helm!"

"Aye, sir." Rauley steered hard over, and we came about in a sweet curve, the mizzen booming over our heads as it jibed.

"Right at 'em, Rauley! The western smaller warship! Put us alongside!"

"Aye, sir!" We settled on our new heading as if Odea's own hand guided our course.

"Scourges!" I stepped to the forward rail and surveyed my motley crew. "And honored islander guests, I'm taking us into battle! Our aim is to take one of the smaller warships, and with Lady Severn's aid, I believe we can!" They cheered, but I raised a hand. "But we're outnumbered two to one, and they will *not* sell their lives cheaply! We must create enough confusion among the Toki armada to hold until the rest of our ships arrive! That means staying alive!"

They cheered again.

"You are all the finest I've ever had the honor to command! You are my family, and my soul." I choked down a lump in my throat, for many of the faces looking up at me, I knew, would be cold and lifeless in a matter of minutes. "Now, show these imperial lubbers what *real* pirates can do!"

The cheers shivered the sails overhead, and my heart swelled in my chest.

A hand on my arm, and I turned to find Preel beside me, tapping her silken gag. I untied it to reveal a beaming smile.

"I love you, Kevril Longbright!" She lunged up grasping me around the neck and kissed me.

The crew cheered again, the wind howled overhead, and the Toki armada bore down on us, but I didn't notice any of it.

Chapter Thirty Seven
Bloodwalker

From the journal of Hashi Severn —

I regret so much in my life. Most of all, I regret my own fear. I only ever had myself to worry about. Seeing what others have sacrificed, I'm ashamed. I am through with being selfish.

You ready for this, old man? I thought, as we roared on toward the nearest warship.

No. I think this is insane, but I don't see any other option.

Neither do I. I freed Soul Drinker from its forearm sheath and felt the power humming within. *I want to save as many as I can, old man, but we have to keep enough in reserve to face whatever they throw at us, komei, enchanted blades... For all I know, they have a wizard aboard one of these ships.*

The flagship, probably. I'll tell you when I need energy.

Good, then. I took a steadying breath and watched the smaller ship nearing, the deck teeming with soldiers.

Tori's coming over. Saraknyal showed me through his mind's eye view, and I noted an unusual lack of swagger in the elf's gait.

"Hello, Tori," I said without looking at him.

"Well met, Lady Severn." He stopped with our shoulders barely an inch apart and looked at me sidelong, his features incongruously serious. "Might I have the pleasure of this dance?"

"Dance?" I looked at him nonplussed. "Are you joking?"

"Far from it." He drew his elf blade and examined the flawless gleaming metal. "This is the dance we both know best, dear Hashi. The dance of death."

I stared at him for a long moment, expecting some joke, but his utter lack of mirth took me aback. "Very well, Lord Blackbriar, let's dance." I twirled Soul Drinker in my palm.

"Thank you." His almond-shaped eyes locked with mine. "My true name is Silar Tae-Cyrillion, by the way. You can continue to call me Tori, if you wish."

I nodded. "Silar, then." I glanced at the onrushing warship, now only a hundred yards or so away. "You don't have to do this, you know."

"Oh, I wouldn't miss it for the *world*, dear Hashi." That old humor flashed, and he raised his sword again. "I do believe they're shooting at us."

"Arrows!" Longbright bellowed from the quarterdeck as a storm of feathered shafts arched toward *Scourge*.

Sailors and Islanders ducked for cover but I just took a step to shield Tori from the deadly hail. *Dust to dust.* Arrows pierced my clothing and puffed into a cloud of splinters and rust borne away quickly by the wind.

You need to lay in more clothes if you're going to make a practice of this nonsense, Saraknyal quipped.

I barked a laugh and brushed the dust from my riddled shirt.

"Something funny," Tori dusted his shoulders and tossed his hair with a flick.

"Saraknyal says I'm hard on clothes. It's a long-standing joke between us."

"Well, I can't help you there." He eyed me and arched an eyebrow. "But I *do* rather enjoy your alterations."

Unrelenting, isn't he?

I've come to expect nothing less. I looked at Tori and smirked. "I thought you might."

Our forward ballistae cracked, but I didn't see where the bolt went. Both ships veered, barely yards away, beam to beam, and I staggered. Tori's hand steadied me.

"Grapples!" Longbright commanded, and sailors heaved iron hooks over the rail.

Another hail of arrows, and four ballistae fired from the warship's deck, their bolts lancing out high, trailing flames. I laughed terror, and the flames died. Unfortunately the accompanying wave of fear staggered as many friends as foes. Only Tori, myself, and my undead stood unaffected, the latter standing like arrow-riddled statues, shielding Preel and Kevril from the deadly shafts. The ballista bolts holed sails above us, but didn't catch them ablaze.

"Let fly sheets!" Longbright bellowed as the grappling ropes came taut with a twang. Both ships staggered, drawn together by their opposed momentum, like two massive dancers pirouetting on stage.

"Ready to dance, Silar?"

"Quite ready, milady." Tori flourished his sword with a grin.

"Go!"

The two of us sprinted across the deck and vaulted from the rail to leap high across the dwindling gap between the ships.

I screamed winter down at the shocked Toki soldiers, petrifying several where they stood, and sending others reeling, blinded by frost. We bowled the frozen soldiers over as we landed, and I skidded into the midst of those still stunned. Soul Drinker drew a line of carnage through their ranks, and Tori's elf blade sang at my back.

More rushed us, attempting to overwhelm us with sheer numbers, but I petrified those in the fore, and Tori's sword flicked like a silver bolt of lightning, deflecting blades and felling foes before they could touch him.

With a roar, pirates filled the space we'd made, Wix at the fore, daggers in each hand, bellowing curses like a maniac. We waded forth through the soldiers, swords, pikes, and arrows puffing to dust around me.

"The quarterdeck, Hashi!" Tori barked. "If we take the captain, the rest will surrender!"

"You *hope*!" A desperate officer lunged at me, her face a rictus of terror. I destroyed her sword with an open hand and snatched her wrist. *Death's chill.* She froze, petrified with fear, her eyes wide. I thought to transform her into a shade, but couldn't make myself do it. In that instant of indecision, an arrow from the quarterdeck aimed at me struck her in the neck, the forked head slicing through, sending an astonishing spray of blood across me.

Cursing, I flung her aside and charged for the stairs.

That was a komei arrow, Hashi. Have a care!

I ignored him, slashing through soldiers like paper when they were foolish enough to oppose me. I leapt up the steps three at a time, and just as Saraknyal had warned me, a komei stood at the top, sword drawn, ready to cut me down.

I froze him solid with a scream, and bowled the petrified corpse over.

"Kill her!" a man in an officer's coat commanded, pointing at me with a sword.

I need energy, Hashi!

I laughed terror as soldiers and another komei charged. The soldiers faltered, but the komei didn't. I dodged aside into the terrified soldiers to avoid the enchanted blade, taking two more souls with a single slash. But as I whirled to face the greater threat, Saraknyal gave me an instant of warning.

Hashi!

As I drew breath to scream, the komei's silvery katana slashed. I tried to parry with Soul Drinker, and the obsidian blade clashed against the enchanted steel. The force of the stroke twisted the dagger in my grasp, the serrated obsidian edge grating sparks from the komei's weapon. The sword struck me in the side, slicing through flesh and bone. I felt the injury like a static shock, jolting to the core, and grasped the man's wrist.

Death's chill!

He stiffened, and I thrust Soul Drinker into his armored chest. The corpse collapsed, leaving the katana deep in my chest. The deck came up and hit my knees.

Hashi, you're hurt!

No shit. I looked down, and wished I hadn't. The blade stood out from just beneath my left breast, bright red blood running in a torrent down my side. I sat back on my heels, and tried to take a breath. A froth of pink bloody foam surged up my throat.

Pain arrived, but staggering weakness struck harder. I felt myself falling, the entire world darkening at the edges.

"Hashi!" Hands closed on my shoulders, a gleaming elf blade clattering to the deck beside me. Tori knelt, his face ashen. "I've got you. Just hang on!"

No fingers... I thought, remembering telling Saraknyal to hang on what seemed ages ago. I coughed blood all over Tori's beautiful white shirt. "S...sorry."

Don't apologize, you fool! Just breathe!

"Just one moment!" Tori fished something from a pocket, a tiny vial, and thumbed the silver stopper from the neck. "This will save you, but I've got to remove the sword."

I blinked and nodded once.

"Ready?"

"Stu...pid ques...tion."

"Right!" He slipped two feet of steel from between my cloven ribs.

I screamed, I think, the world going dark, but a warmth flooded my gaping mouth, then my throat, then my chest, and the pain and weakness, vanished. The world cleared to needle sharpness, Tori's face only inches away as my every nerve burned like fire. The tingling warmth invaded my limbs, my heart pounding with renewed strength.

"Better?" Tori asked, his hands still on my shoulders, holding me upright.

The restorative, Saraknyal surmised.

I nodded and swallowed blood. "Thank you."

He grinned. "Always happy to help a lady in—"

Tori jerked, his hands flexing on my shoulders, his eyes widening. I felt something prick my chest, and looked down in time to see the komei arrow that had passed through Tori dissolve into dust. Blood jetted from the hole in his chest, and his body sagged.

"Tori!" I grasped him as he collapsed, his weight dragging me down with him. Our faces ended up so close that our noses touched. His illusory disguise melted, and I found myself staring into the multi-hued eyes of Silar Tae-Cyrillion.

"Oh...my..." His mouth gaped. "Hashi... I think..."

I watched the light leave his luminous eyes. A wail unlike anything I'd ever heard escaped my throat. Two thousand years, and he died saving my life. My soul shattered in my breast.

Hashi! Look out!

I looked up to find the komei who had killed my friend charging me, sword raised.

I pressed a hand to the deck, and thought, *Dust to dust.*

The boards beneath my assailant's feet vanished. Not the entire deck, thanks to Saraknyal's careful application of the spell, but enough to send the komei sprawling forward. The deck caught him in the chest, but he kept hold of his sword. The eyes behind his mask showed more surprise than fear as I lurched up to my feet. He struggled to clamber up, but I pinned his weapon to the deck with my foot.

"Two thousand years," I growled between clenched bloody teeth. The komei released his sword and reached for my ankle. I pinned his hand to the deck with Soul Drinker. "Destroy him, Saraknyal."

With pleasure. Saraknyal consumed him in one wrenching jolt, and the man's grip on the edge of the deck went limp. He fell into the cabin below, landing in a lifeless, soulless heap.

I stood. Though the battle still raged across the deck, I barely noticed. I knelt beside Silar Tae-Cyrillion and closed his eyes. The breeze felt icy on my face, and I realized that tears streamed down my cheeks. I brushed my fingers down his angular features, mourning my loss, wondering what happened to the souls of elves when they died.

Hashi, you've got to get up. People are dying.

"Yes." I picked up Tori's elf blade were it had fallen, feeling the peculiar magic within it warring with the darker, colder, yet familiar thrill of Soul Drinker.

You shouldn't handle that thing, Hashi. It interferes with my magic.

Deal with it, old man. I flexed my hand on the sword's hilt, light and amazingly well balanced.

The captain and a throng of soldiers stood at the stern, swords drawn, clearly terrified of me. I stalked toward them, the two magical blades in my hands, their conflicting energies humming through my bones.

"Surrender!" I screamed at them. "Or I will destroy you utterly, each and every one of you, body and soul!"

"Drop weapons!" The captain screeched, his voice cracking. "Do it now!"

The soldiers let their weapons fall to the deck and backed away.

Evidently, a bloodied necromancer who'd recently arisen from being nearly cut in half, capable of dissolving the very ship beneath their feet, posed a significant inducement.

I slipped Tori's elf blade through my belt and stepped up to the trembling captain. "Come with me and end this!" I gripped the collar of his coat and hauled him forward to the rail overlooking the embattled deck of his ship. "Now! Tell them!"

"Surrender the ship!" He screamed. "Lay down arms! This is your captain! Follow my orders at once! Disarm and stand down!"

His screeching plea got the attention of the entire deck, and the Toki soldiers and sailors complied immediately. Steel clattered to the deck, and Scourges and islanders cheered in victory.

I didn't feel much like cheering.

I shoved the cowering captain away and returned to Tori. Kneeling again, pressing a hand to his bloodstained shirt, his flesh still warm beneath my palm, I wept.

"Lady Severn!"

I looked up to find Kivan standing there, a throng of pirates and islanders with her. The sword in her hand was bloody.

"What?"

"Admiral Longbright needs you." She gestured, and I saw that the battle was far from over. The Toki armada was in disarray, harassed by islanders, but the massive flagship still sailed free, and they were regrouping.

"Fine." I stood and gestured down to Tori's body. "Please see he's taken care of, Kivan. He was..." I didn't know what to say, then I did, "...my friend."

"I will, lady. I promise!" She wiped and sheathed her sword, waving several sailors forward.

I turned away and strode down to the deck, dismayed at the carnage. I crossed to *Scourge*, and climbed to the quarterdeck. The admiral had an arrow wound in his left arm, bound with a strip of black cloth from Preel's shirt. My wraith and shades stood riddled with arrows, but steady.

"Tori's dead," I said, my voice utterly flat, as lifeless as my friend.

You should give him the elf blade, Hashi. It's interfering with my magic.

Fine. I resisted the urge to keep it as a remembrance of him, and slipped it from my belt. "Here. It was Tori's. It's an elf blade. He'd want you to have it, and I can't keep it."

"I... I'm sorry, Hashi." Kevril took the blade.

Preel crossed the deck to me and took me in her arms, a silent sob wracking her shoulders. I don't know why, but that simple gesture bolstered me more than anything else could have. I clutched her close for a moment, then released her, sniffing away tears.

"Kivan said you needed me, Admiral."

"Yes. We've taken two ships, and set one ablaze, but the armada's regrouping." He pointed north, then south where our additional eight ships were closing fast. "They know they're pinned, and now outnumbered, but I don't know what Admiral Miaku's going to do."

Even as he spoke, sailors cast off lines between *Scourge* and the Toki warship, and more islanders clambered aboard the two vessels from the fleet of canoes. I looked over the arrayed ships, but none of it made much sense to me.

I heaved a breath and let it out slowly. "Tell me what you need, Kevril."

"I need to convince them to withdraw, and I'd like to do it without losing half our ships and about a thousand more lives." He pointed to the massive flagship, now about half a mile off and surrounded by a tight cordon of lesser warships. "Admiral Miaku is the only one capable of giving the order to withdraw, and he's aboard their flagship. We've given them a serious bloody nose, but Toki honor may not allow him to disengage. They don't deem us a legitimate navy, but pirates, and their orders were to eliminate piracy from the Blood Sea."

"So, you need to convince him of our *legitimacy?*" It seemed inane with what we'd lost, what I'd lost, but I nodded. "If we're really a navy, that'll allow him to withdraw and save face."

"Yes."

Or we could simply destroy them, Saraknyal suggested.

I flexed my hand on Soul Drinker's hilt and slipped the blade into its sheath. "Well, since I'm now the only member of Haven's

Council of Lords present, I suppose I should have a talk with Admiral Miaku."

"I'm not suggesting you go alone, but..." He shrugged. "If you can convince him, it would save a lot of lives on both sides."

I nodded. "How can you get me aboard?"

"One of the islander craft under a flag of parlay." He pointed to one of the strange two-hulled vessels now lying beside *Scourge*, all but a few already aboard the larger ship. "I hope they'll honor it. If they don't..."

"If they don't, they'll shoot us like fish in a barrel."

"Yes."

Bad idea, Hashi. Admiral Miaku undoubtedly has a komei honor guard, and may even have a wizard.

And I've got you, I thought, remembering the light fading from Tori's eyes as I held him. I nodded to Admiral Longbright. "All right; let's do this."

With the Toki armada of five ships now sailing close formation slowly southward between four corsairs to the west, and seven more Protectorate ships to the east, we sailed across the intervening sea. The strange two-hulled vessel felt like a flighty horse under me, flatter than the smack, *Gull*, but jerky, every wave jostling us.

"No worry, lady!" The captain of the craft, an islander woman named Wakimo, grinned at me, her tattooed face alive with grim mirth. "They shoot us, they lose face! Toki got more honor than sense." She pointed up to the large white flag flying from our mast. "They respec that, even if they don't respec us."

I nodded. "Just get us close enough to hail the flagship. They'll listen."

Or perish, Saraknyal grumbled. Strangely, he seemed to have taken Tori's death as hard as I.

"Aye, lady!" Wakimo barked orders to her crew of four, and they adjusted the woven frond sail.

We cut between the tight cordon of ships, archers and ballistae following us every foot of the way. When we veered to parallel the towering flagship, barely thirty feet from her sheer side, one of the larger warships maneuvered to bracket us from the other side. We sailed along in a potentially devastating crossfire that could rip our fragile vessel apart.

A Toki officer stood at the rail some fifteen feet over our heads and sneered down at us. "What do you want?"

"I'm Lady Hashi Severn of the Haven Council of Lords! I want to speak to Admiral Miaku on behalf of the Blood Sea Protectorate."

The man frowned. "We don't negotiate with criminals and pirates!"

"Good! Since I'm neither, and the ships arrayed against you are duly appointed privateers of the Blood Sea Protectorate, we should have a productive discussion that can allow us to reach a mutually beneficial outcome."

Mutually beneficial, meaning they die and we don't, right.

If it comes to that, yes.

"And if we refuse?"

Quote Quen Lau Ush, Saraknyal suggested. *The one about a man who refuses to negotiate.*

"Sir, may I remind you of the words of your own philosopher, Quen Lau Ush: 'The man who refuses to negotiate in the face of a superior force is not only a fool, but doomed to ignominy.'"

The officer's frown deepened. "I'll relay your request to the admiral."

"Thank you!" I leaned back against the mast and tried to settle my tumultuous stomach.

"This Quen Lau Ush fellow, who that?" Wakimo asked.

"A Toki philosopher."

"Sound like a Chen name."

"His father was from Chen, an exiled holy man. He lived some centuries ago."

"Ah, dead philosophers is the best ones! They can't argue no more!" She barked a laugh.

I didn't feel like laughing, but I appreciated her attempt. I wondered if I'd ever feel like laughing again. We sailed along in the vast ship's wake for minutes, enduring the glares of archers and ballistae crews. I tried to look unconcerned.

Eventually, the same officer appeared at the rail. "You will speak with the admiral! You alone!"

"Of course!" I turned to Wakimo. "Closer, please."

"Aye, lady!" As the Toki sailors opened a boarding hatch and lowered a ladder, Wakimo maneuvered her vessel closer, her crew manipulating the looming sail to increase our speed to match the position of the ladder. "You wait for the down roll, lady, or you take a bath!"

"Right."

I lurched to the side of the vessel and gripped one of the shrouds. The ladder dipped and rose as the much larger ship rolled, and we also rose and fell on the swells. I waited until the ladder dipped and we rose, and grabbed a rung. The ship rolled, and the smaller vessel's deck vanished from beneath my feet. I scrambled for a foothold and hurried up. No one helped me through the hatch.

A squad of twenty soldiers and two komei, as well as the officer, encircled me. The officer bowed. "This way, Lady Severn."

He addressed you properly! You must have made an impression.

I followed, Saraknyal's nervousness humming along my bones.

As we climbed two decks to the flagship's lofty command deck, I marveled at the strange configuration of masts and sails. The five masts were offset from the centerline of the ship, and staggered to catch the most wind. The ship must have massed fifteen times what *Scourge* did, and the deck felt as solid as stone beneath my feet. By the time we reached the command deck, my stomach began to feel normal again.

There, Admiral Miaku stood among an honor guard of soldiers and six more komei. His hair was gray, and he looked stern, but not belligerent.

He took a step forward and bowed. "Lady Severn."

"Admiral Miaku." I returned the gesture. "Forgive my appearance. I've been in a battle today."

"We observed." He frowned. "Is Captain Yokiri alive?"

"Yes. Prisoner aboard his ship."

He looked me up and down. "You are injured?"

"I was, but..." I couldn't speak of Tori's final selfless act. "...no longer. Thank you for agreeing to speak with me. I learned from Admiral Longbright that General Koto was unwilling to accept the existence of the Blood Sea Protectorate. I'm glad you're wiser than he."

"I'm willing to *listen*." He glanced around, at what I had no way to know. "And to entertain the *possibility* that the city states of the Blood Sea have allied against the Toki Empire."

"We don't seek war, Admiral, only to be left alone and treated as equals. As with all new alliances, things...currently a little disorganized, but we're united in our purpose."

"And that purpose is conquest, from what I'm told. An ambassador from Mati said he was ensorcelled by one of your Council."

"Jhavika Keshmir, yes, that *was* true, but Keshmir is dead. That plot was hers, not the Council's. She attempted a coup against the Council, and lost." I shrugged. "We do *not* seek conquest, only sovereignty and recognition as an allied protectorate."

"And has the nation of Sariff joined this protectorate?"

Tell him yes.

"They're considering joining, but I believe they will. It's to everyone's best interest."

"Not ours."

I shrugged. "That is another discussion. What I'm offering you is withdrawal from this engagement with your honor intact. We *are* a legitimate allied protectorate. Unconventional, but united in defense of the Blood Sea. We are *not*, as you may have heard, pirates and criminals."

"And if I refuse to withdraw?" he asked, and I could see the calculation in his eyes.

I shrugged as if I didn't care. "Then you will meet the inevitability of defeat." I gestured to the deck beneath my feet. "Beginning with the destruction of your flagship."

His face flushed red. "Impossible!"

You're bluffing, right?

Not in the slightest.

Crazy woman, you'll be the death of...well...yourself.

I smiled without showing my teeth. "You may have spoken with the survivors of one of your lesser warships which met with...my capabilities two days ago. Believe me when I tell you, Admiral Miaku, that I can destroy this ship beneath our feet before you can stop me. I don't want to do that. Do *not* force me."

He looked stunned. "You would betray the sanctity of the flag of truce?"

"No, Admiral, but if you refute the sovereignty of the Blood Sea Protectorate, you may choose to try to take me prisoner." I smiled again, this time showing teeth. "That would be unwise."

His prodigious frown returned, but he said nothing. Again, he looked around.

What's he looking at, Saraknyal? I asked.

The other ships, I suppose. I wasn't paying attention, but there seem to be some sails on the horizon.

Show me! He did, and from the high vantage of the lofty command deck, I spotted several triangles of white far to the southwest. *Saraknyal, bless you!*

Why thank you, but for what?

For saving thousands of lives. I cleared my throat. "Admiral, if you're concerned about those ships to the southwest, you should be. Unless I miss my guess, that's the Sariff Navy come to join the fun."

He glared at me. "You're very sure of yourself."

"As sure as death itself, Admiral."

Still, he looked defiant. "There are quotes from Quen Lau Ush concerning arrogance, too, Lady Severn."

"Yes, there are, but this isn't arrogance, its *certainty*." I waved to the ships inshore, then those offshore. "I have friends aboard those ships, Admiral. A dear friend of mine died today saving my life, and I'm willing to do the same to save theirs. If that means sending us all to our watery graves, so be it. It's your decision."

He glared at me, obviously bristling with anger and ashamed of his own fear. As he opened his mouth to speak, however, a cry from high on the poop deck above us cut him off.

"Admiral! Look! It's... It's impossible, but..."

"What are you yammering about, Lieutenant?" Miaku turned, and the white-faced officer pointed to the southeast at the lofty peaks of Twin Capes.

"There, sir!"

The laughter of a necromancer rattled through my mind, deeper and more mirthful than I'd ever heard from him, before.

Saraknyal?

Look for yourself.

The scene leapt to crystal clarity in my mind, a vast winged shape diving low from the heights to skim over the water at terrific speed. Leathery wings the size of the flagship's lofty sails banked as the massive creature turned to circle the ships, and upon it's back sat a figure in blue flowing robes.

"And *that*, Admiral Miaku, is Valaka's dragonlord representative." I shrugged, proud that I'd suppressed a scream of triumph. "No one will think less of you for withdrawing from such a unified force. There is no dishonor in survival, sir. Take our best regards to your god-emperor, and tell him the Blood Sea Protectorate stands unified against Toki imperial expansion, but that we have no intent in conquest."

He glared at me again, but I saw defeat in his eyes. He bowed shortly to me then. "Very well, Lady Severn, we will withdraw this day, but I cannot promise that my emperor will not relieve me of my head for my cowardice and send a much larger fleet."

"I hope he doesn't, Admiral." I breathed deep and bowed to him. "We *both* need cool heads in command."

"So I hope as well." He gestured to my escort. "Show the lady off the ship. Hoist the white pennant and signal the armada. We are withdrawing."

"Thank you, Admiral." I turned and left the ship, both sorrowful for our losses and pleased that I'd been able to avert more.

Tori would have been proud of you, my dear, Saraknyal said, as I scrambled down the ladder to my waiting vessel.

Yes, I like to think he would have been. Thank you, Saraknyal.

You're welcome. Now, can we please find some dry land?

The small craft's deck lurched beneath my feet as I released the ladder, and I fell flat on my ass. I winced and endured the laughter of the captain and crew. *Not too soon, old man.*

Chapter Thirty Eight
Endings and Beginnings

From the journal of Hashi Severn —

I'm so changed, I hardly know myself. The grim recluse is broken, shattered into a million shards. I don't know if that is the result of one night among friends, or the loss of one of them. At least now, I know what I'm fighting for.

I stepped out of my carriage upon the highest promontory of Haven's unforgiving eastern shore, and took in the amassed crowd.

Well, at least you're not the only one wearing all black.

Hush, old man. I hid a smile, for he was right. Here, at my last farewell to Tori Blackbriar, my attire would blend right in.

The size of the crowd surprised me, but shouldn't have. If anyone in Haven had a surfeit of friends, Tori had. Most were women, of course, clad in mourning black and already crying their eyes out. I'd already shed all the tears I could for him, or so I thought.

I recognized a number of faces. The entire Council was there, of course, along with emissaries from Sariff and several of the islands, all of whom I'd met at the first Council of the Blood Sea Protectorate. The emissary from Valaka, Yoloff Volcuut, the very dragonlord who had made such a timely appearance at Twin Capes, had flown in astride his charge, Malceferex. The dragon sat perched on the cliffs to the south barely half a mile away. The dragonlord seemed amiable enough, rare among his ilk, though he professed to be a recluse. Dragonlords, like necromancers, made people nervous.

"Hashi."

I turned to find Kevril and Preel strolling toward me, both resplendent, he in a full dress admiral's uniform, and she in a mourning sari. Beside them strode Longbright's former first mate, now Captain Miko, and her companion, Illian, one of the few not clad in black. She wore an ivory gown the exact hue of her luminous skin, her flaxen hair waving in the sea breeze.

The two of you would make good models for opposing chess queens, Saraknyal commented.

True enough. "Kevril, Preel." I shook his hand warmly, and, of course, Preel embraced me without reservation. "Miko, good to see you again." I shook her hand, too. "Illian, I had the honor of seeing you at the Folly. Tori recommended I go, and I'll never forget your performance."

"You're very gracious, Lady Severn. Tori and I were distant cousins."

"Ah, I see." Her angular features didn't remind me of him, but then, the Tori I'd known had been an illusion. Her eyes, however, recalled to my mind the moment I'd seen the life leave his. Her hand felt very cool in mine. "Then you knew why he was here in Haven."

"Vaguely." Her mouth quirked into a sad smile. "He didn't know I was here, and seeing me rather startled him. I promised him I wouldn't ruin his disguise."

"Shall we?" Kevril gestured to the crowd and held out an arm to me. Preel clutched his other, and a memory of Tori's bawdy humor popped into my head unbidden.

"Why, Admiral, are you suggesting we *share* you?" I took his arm and smiled to Preel, enjoying the look of startlement on Kevril's face.

"Oh, well *played*, Lady Severn." Illian beamed and took Miko's arm. "That's *exactly* what Tori would have said."

By the gods, you do have a sense of humor!

I laughed and squeezed the admiral's arm. "It just came to me. I must be channeling his spirt or something."

Kevril cleared his throat. "Well, I must admit, you had me there for a moment."

Preel's eyes smiled above her veil, and we strode toward the crowd surrounding Tori's bier. The sea of black parted for us, and we stood facing east, the sun behind the mountains behind us casting us in shadow and painting the sky crimson.

After a long, quiet moment, Malchi stepped forward. "Thank

you all for coming. We're gathered here to pay our respects to Lord Tori Blackbriar. Tori and I didn't always see eye to eye, but I respected him greatly, and mourn his loss. I remember the day he arrived in Haven..."

Insufferable ass, Saraknyal mumbled.

I couldn't disagree, and as the speech continued, my temper simmered. I didn't like Malchi much, but I wasn't about to interrupt Tori's eulogy, even if it was a crock of self-aggrandizing crap. The sun descended farther, the shadow of the mountains edging out to sea, vibrant blue fading to black.

Like Tori's eyes, I thought, watching the light fade to duller hues.

*I admit that I'm going to miss *that* insufferable ass,* Saraknyal admitted. *If for no other reason than watching him torment you with his relentless come-ons.*

That I won't miss, I thought with a sad smile.

Malchi finally wore down and stepped aside.

You should say something.

I don't want to.

Life's full of doing things you don't want to do. So is death, as a matter of fact. Say something, Hashi.

Oh, all right. I sighed, and left my friends to stand where Malchi had, Tori's bier at my back. I scanned the faces, many familiar, many not, and spoke.

"I don't have many friends." I cleared my throat of the lump and struggled to continue. "But Tori Blackbriar, Silar Tae-Cyrillion, *was* one of them."

Several nodded, and many dabbed their eyes with kerchiefs.

"He taught me many things, the most cherished of which was to allow myself to care for someone. We were never...very close, really, but he showed me what was missing within myself. Tori showed me that friendship need not be onerous, that one need not always fear how things might go wrong. He showed me that true friendship is worth the risk."

The crowd shifted and people wept openly. I didn't.

"Tori lived well, loved with abandon, and cherished his friends. He cherished *me*, so much, in fact that his last act upon this world was to save my life." I swallowed hard, recalling the light leaving his eyes as I held him. "So, do not mourn Tori's passing, but live well, love with abandon, and remember him as I do. As a friend. He'd like that."

I stepped down, and to my shock, Illian stepped forth and embraced me, her white gown against my black one, light against darkness, her breath warm in my ear.

"Thank you, Hashi. He would have liked that."

I nodded to her, unsure what to say.

She stepped past me then, and as I resumed my place, Illian began to sing.

She sang in elvish, one language that Saraknyal couldn't translate for me, but he didn't need to for the deep emotion to ring clearly through me. We all listened, even more of us weeping openly at the wrenching sorrow of her amazing voice. The sea breeze chilled my dampened cheeks, and I didn't care.

When Illian fell silent and flowed back down to her place beside Miko, we all stood in silence for a very long time, everyone there, for good or ill, remembering Tori for themselves.

Then, the dragonlord Volcuut stepped up and faced us. He had chiseled dark features and hair as white as snow, his face lined with time. He had no speech, but simply raised his arms and called his charge forth to send Tori on his way to wherever elf souls go.

"Malceferex!"

The dragon answered a bellowing cry and took to the air, wings the size of a ship's sails clapping like thunder as they filled. The massive beast dipped low, beneath the cliff, then rose right behind Tori's bier, the great wings flapping as it stalled, motionless for a moment. A maw that could have swallowed my coach opened, and flame shot forth to envelop Tori's bier.

The dragon fell away, soaring in a wide arc to return to its perch, but the flames remained, rising into the darkening sky like a beacon.

We stood there for a very long time while some guests departed, trickling away from the crowd. A hand rested on my shoulder, and I turned to Kevril.

"You're welcome to come home with us, Hashi. Just for a drink and conversation."

"Thank you, but I'll stay for a while. Perhaps another time."

He nodded, and Preel embraced me again. Illian took my hands in hers and thanked me again for my words, and I thanked her for her song. They turned to go, and I strode up toward the pyre of my friend until the heat stopped me.

I stared into the flames for a long time, mesmerized by the play of colors. Thankfully, the fire hid the crumbling corpse of my friend within. The sky grew dark, and the first stars shone. The flames soared into the infinite sky.

There's someone behind you, Hashi, Saraknyal said, but there was no warning in his tone.

I turned to find a woman standing a few steps away. She wore black, but her gown plunged low, her face alight in the firelight behind a gauzy veil. I recognized her.

"Bea?" I'd only met the woman once at Tori's estate, but she was hard to forget.

"I'm delighted that you remember me, Lady Severn." She lifted her veil and joined me, her eyes on the fire. "I'd like to thank you for your words. They meant a lot, especially coming from you."

"You're welcome." I wasn't sure what she meant by that last bit, but I wasn't going to take it as an insult. "Tori meant a lot to me. He was...*relentlessly* friendly."

She laughed musically. "He was that, and so much more."

We stared at the fire for a time, then she broke the silence, her voice low, barely above a whisper.

"I'd like to speak with you if you'd allow it, Lady Severn. Not necessarily now, but at your earliest convenience."

I glanced at her sidelong. "About...?"

"About my services. Tori asked me to contact you, you see, if anything went amiss. He seemed to think you could...put my particular skills to good use."

Is she asking you if you'd like to—

Shut up, old man. I cleared my throat. "No offense, Bea, but I don't need the services of a courtesan, even if Tori thought I did."

She looked at me and smiled prettily. "Not *those* services, dear."

I opened my mouth to speak, then faltered. "Then...what?"

Her voice lowered even more, barely audible above the crackling flames. "You remember Tori told you that I supply him with information, yes?"

I nodded.

"Well, I must confess, I'm a bit more than a courtesan with a cocked ear." She smiled again, showing perfect teeth, and lowered her voice to a sultry whisper. "Before I came to Haven, I was Royal Spymaster for the Crown Prince of Fornice. I was forced to flee when the poor prince...lost his head, but I've retained my skills, *and* my network."

"I see." I couldn't imagine why I needed a spy, but kept my voice a whisper, simply because she did. "And why would Tori think that I needed your services? And please, call me Hashi."

She nodded and smiled. "Thank you, Hashi, and *that's* why I think we should talk." She glanced around us, but we were well and truly alone. Even so, she kept her voice low. "War is coming to the Blood Sea. I have operatives placed strategically in every city from Chen to Mati. If the god-emperor takes a piss, I know about it before the chamber pot is emptied. Trust me, you *need* my services."

I gaped at her, speechless.

Well, fuuuuuk me, Saraknyal quipped, jolting me out of my shock.

"All right, we should talk." I swallowed hard, my mind still spinning. "How do we do that discreetly?"

"By making our association look like something else entirely. You visited a trollop named Lola Marie Tonce a while ago, and spent the better part of an hour in her company." She grinned lasciviously and reached up to brush my cheek with her fingertips. "I'm *sure* we can arrange a convincing dalliance."

"I'm... sorry, but..." My brain stumbled, and her touch felt like static on my skin. I didn't know how to tell her that her simply standing so close made me uncomfortable, and not in a bad way.

It's not like you have a reputation to protect, my dear. And she's right, war is all about deception and information. You need her.

Bea put her hand on my arm and leaned in. "Don't worry, Hashi. I won't tarnish your good name."

I cleared my throat. "I...don't really have a good name."

"Then let's *talk*." She leaned in further, pressing her impressive decolletage against me. "If we're going to win this war, we've got to be *bad*." Then she kissed me, not chaste in the slightest, her tongue dancing expertly with mine, and I felt my knees go weak.

Oh...my... Saraknyal whispered.

She broke the kiss and beamed up at me. "We're being watched."

My boiling blood went suddenly cold. *Saraknyal? Where...*

*Sorry, I was distracted. Um... Oh, yes, there's someone out there in the dark. I can barely see them. She's *good*!*

Gods, I hope so... I took Bea's hand and said, "Come with me."

"Oh, I'm sure I will." She gave me that lascivious smile again, and we strolled to my carriage.

There's an old adage about business and pleasure, isn't there?

I opened my carriage door and helped Bea in. *Shut up, old man.*

About the Author

Born and raised in Oregon, Chris meet his wife and soulmate, Anne, while attending graduate school in Texas. Since then they have been nigh inseparable: gaming together since 1985, sailing together since 1988, married since 1989, and writing together off and on throughout their relationship. Most astonishingly, they have not killed each other during the creation or editing of any of their stories…although it was close a few times. Since 2009, the couple has been sailing and writing full-time aboard their beloved sailboat, *Mr Mac*. They return to the US every summer for conventions, always happy to sign copies of their books and talk with fans.

Preview Chris' books and get updates on upcoming events at jaxbooks.com. Follow Chris and Anne's cruising adventures at www.sailmrmac.blogspot.com.

Novels by Chris A. Jackson

From Jaxbooks
A Soul for Tsing
Deathmask

Blood Sea Tales
The Pirate's Scourge
The Pirate's Truth
The Pirate's Bane
Ash Walker
Blood Walker
Death Walker (2023)

Weapon of Flesh Series
Weapon of Flesh
Weapon of Blood
Weapon of Vengeance
Weapon of Fear *
Weapon of Pain *
Weapon of Mercy *
(* with Anne L. McMillen-Jackson)

The Cornerstones Trilogy
(with Anne L. McMillen-Jackson)
Zellohar
Nekdukarr
Jundag

The Cheese Runners Trilogy
(novellas – also on Audible)
Cheese Runners
Cheese Rustlers
Cheese Lords

From Shadow Alley Press
Pacifica
Stratos

From Dragon Moon Press

From Falstaff Books

From Paizo Publishing

From Privateer Press

From Fantasy Flight Games

From Catalyst Game Labs

Check out these and more at

JAXBOOKS.COM

Want to get an email about my next book release?
Sign up at http://eepurl.com/xnrUL